OCTAVIUS
and the
Perfect
Governess

PRYOR COUSINS #1

EMILY
LARKIN

www.emilylarkin.com

Octavius and the Perfect Governess / Emily Larkin. – 1st ed.

ISBN 978-0-9951366-8-7

Cover Design: JD Smith Design

Novel

It is a truth universally acknowledged,
that Faerie godmothers do not exist.

CHAPTER 1

Octavius Pryor should have won the race. It wasn't difficult. The empty ballroom at his grandfather-the-duke's house was eighty yards long, he'd lined one hundred and twenty chairs up in a row across the polished wooden floorboards, and making his way from one side of the room to the other without touching the floor was easy. His cousin Nonus Pryor—Ned—also had one hundred and twenty chairs to scramble over, but Ned was as clumsy as an ox and Octavius knew he could make it across the ballroom first, which was exactly what he was doing—until his foot went right through the seat of one of the delicate giltwood chairs. He was going too fast to catch his balance. Both he and the chair crashed to the floor. And that was him out of the race.

His cousin Dex—Decimus Pryor—hooted loudly.

Octavius ignored the hooting and sat up. The good news was that he didn't appear to have broken anything except the chair. The bad news was that Ned, who'd been at least twenty chairs behind him, was now almost guaranteed to win.

Ned slowed to a swagger—as best as a man could swagger while clambering along a row of giltwood chairs.

Octavius gritted his teeth and watched his cousin navigate the last few dozen chairs. Ned glanced back at Octavius, smirked, and then slowly reached out and touched the wall with one fingertip.

Dex hooted again.

Octavius bent his attention to extracting his leg from the chair. Fortunately, he hadn't ruined his stockings. He climbed to his feet and watched warily as Ned stepped down from the final chair and sauntered towards him.

"Well?" Dex said. "What's Otto's forfeit to be?"

Ned's smirk widened. "His forfeit is that he goes to Vauxhall Gardens tomorrow night . . . as a woman."

There was a moment's silence. The game they had of creating embarrassing forfeits for each other was long-established, but this forfeit was unprecedented.

Dex gave a loud whoop. "Excellent!" he said, his face alight with glee. "I can't *wait* to see this."

When Ned said that Octavius was going to Vauxhall Gardens as a woman, he meant it quite literally. Not as a man dressed in woman's clothing, but as a woman dressed in woman's clothing. Because Octavius could change his shape. That was the gift he'd chosen when his Faerie godmother had visited him on his twenty-fifth birthday.

Ned had chosen invisibility when it was his turn, which was the stupidest use of a wish that Octavius could think of. Ned was the loudest, clumsiest brute in all England. He walked with the stealth of a rampaging elephant. He was terrible at being invisible. So terrible, in fact, that their grandfather-the-duke had placed strict conditions on Ned's use of his gift.

Ned had grumbled, but he'd obeyed. He might be a blockhead, but he wasn't such a blockhead as to risk revealing the family secret. No one wanted to find out what would happen if it became common knowledge that one of England's most aristocratic families actually had a Faerie godmother.

Octavius, who could walk stealthily when he wanted to, hadn't chosen invisibility; he'd chosen metamorphosis, which meant that he could become any creature he wished. In the two years he'd had this ability, he'd been pretty much every animal he could think of. He'd even taken the shape of another person a few times. Once, he'd pretended to be his cousin, Dex. There he'd sat, drinking brandy and discussing horseflesh with his brother and his cousins, all of them thinking he was Dex—and then Dex had walked into the room. The expressions on everyone's faces had been priceless. Lord, the expression on *Dex*'s face . . .

Octavius had laughed so hard that he'd cried.

But one shape he'd never been tempted to try was that of a woman.

Why would he want to?

He was a man. And not just any man, but a good-looking, wealthy, and extremely well-born man. Why, when he had all those advantages, would he want to see what it was like to be a woman?

But that was the forfeit Ned had chosen and so here Octavius was, in his bedchamber, eyeing a pile of women's clothing, while far too many people clustered around him—not just Ned and Dex, but his own brother, Quintus, and Ned's brother, Sextus.

Quintus and Sextus usually held themselves distant from high jinks and tomfoolery, Quintus because he was an earl and he took his responsibilities extremely seriously and Sextus because he was an aloof sort of fellow—and yet here they both were in Octavius's bedchamber.

Octavius didn't mind making a fool of himself in front of a muttonhead like Ned and a rattle like Dex, but in front of his oh-so-sober brother and his stand-offish older cousin? He felt more self-conscious than he had in years, even a little embarrassed.

"Whose clothes are they?" he asked.

"Lydia's," Ned said.

Octavius tried to look as if it didn't bother him that he was going to be wearing Ned's mistress's clothes, but it did. Lydia was extremely buxom, which meant that *he* was going to have to be extremely buxom or the gown would fall right off him.

He almost balked, but he'd never backed down from a forfeit before, so he gritted his teeth and unwound his neckcloth.

Octavius stripped to his drawers, made them all turn their backs, then removed the drawers, too. He pictured what he wanted to look like: Lydia's figure, but not Lydia's face—brown ringlets instead of blonde, and brown eyes, too—and with a silent *God damn it,* he changed shape. Magic tickled across his skin and itched inside his bones. He gave an involuntary shiver—and then it was done. He was a woman.

Octavius didn't examine his new body. He hastily dragged on the chemise, keeping his gaze averted from the mirror. "All right," he said, in a voice that was light and feminine and sounded utterly wrong coming from his mouth. "You can turn around."

His brother and cousins turned around and stared at him. It was oddly unsettling to be standing in front of them in the shape of a woman, wearing only a thin chemise. In fact, it was almost intimidating. Octavius crossed his arms defensively over his ample bosom, then uncrossed them and put his hands on his hips, another defensive stance, made himself stop doing that, too, and gestured at the pile of women's clothing on the bed. "Well, who's going to help me with the stays?"

No one volunteered. No one cracked any jokes, either. It appeared that he wasn't the only one who was unsettled. His brother, Quintus, had a particularly stuffed expression on his face, Sextus looked faintly pained, and Ned and Dex, both of whom he expected to be smirking, weren't.

"The stays," Octavius said again. "Come on, you clods. Help me to dress." And then, because he was damned if he was going to let them see how uncomfortable he felt, he fluttered his eyelashes coquettishly.

Quintus winced, and turned his back. "Curse it, Otto, don't do that."

Octavius laughed. The feeling of being almost intimidated disappeared. In its place was the realization that if he played this right, he could make them all so uncomfortable that none of them would ever repeat this forfeit. He picked up the stays and dangled the garment in front of Ned. "You chose this forfeit; *you* help me dress."

It took quite a while to dress, because Ned was the world's worst lady's maid. He wrestled with the stays for almost a quarter of an hour, then put the petticoat on back to front. The gown consisted of a long sarcenet slip with a shorter lace robe on top of that. Ned flatly refused to arrange the decorative ribbons at Octavius's bosom or to help him fasten the silk stockings above his knees. Octavius hid his amusement. Oh, yes, Ned was *never* going to repeat this forfeit.

Lydia had provided several pretty ribbons, but after Ned had failed three times to thread them through Octavius's ringlets, Dex stepped forward. His attempt at styling hair wasn't sophisticated, but it was passable.

Finally, Octavius was fully dressed—and the oddest thing was that he actually felt *un*dressed. His throat was bare. He had no high shirt-points, no snug, starched neckcloth. His upper chest was bare, too, as were his upper arms. But worst of all, he was wearing no drawers, and that made him feel uncomfortably naked. True, most women didn't wear drawers and he was a woman tonight, but if his own drawers had fitted him he would have insisted on wearing them.

Octavius smoothed the gloves over his wrists and stared at himself in the mirror. He didn't like what he saw. It didn't just feel a little bit wrong, it felt a *lot* wrong. He wasn't a woman. This wasn't him. He didn't have those soft, pouting lips or those rounded hips and that slender waist, and he most definitely did *not* have those full, ripe breasts.

Octavius smoothed the gloves again, trying not to let the others see how uncomfortable he was.

Ned nudged his older brother, Sextus. "He's even prettier than you, Narcissus."

Everybody laughed, and Sextus gave that reserved, coolly amused smile that he always gave when his brother called him Narcissus.

Octavius looked at them in the mirror, himself and Sextus, and it *was* true: he was prettier than Sextus.

Funny, Sextus's smile no longer looked coolly amused. In fact, his expression, seen in the mirror, was the exact opposite of amused.

"Here." Dex draped a silk shawl around Octavius's shoulders. "And a fan. Ready?"

Octavius looked at himself in the mirror and felt the wrongness of the shape he was inhabiting. He took a deep breath and said, "Yes."

They went to Vauxhall by carriage rather than crossing the Thames in a scull, to Octavius's relief. He wasn't sure he would have been able to get into and out of a boat wearing a gown. As it was, even climbing into the carriage was a challenge. He nearly tripped on his hem.

The drive across town, over Westminster Bridge and down Kennington Lane, gave him ample time to torment his brother and cousins. If there was one lesson he wanted them to learn tonight—even Quintus and Sextus, who rarely played the forfeit game—it was to never choose this forfeit for him again.

Although, to tell the truth, he was rather enjoying himself now. It was wonderful to watch Ned squirm whenever Octavius fluttered his eyelashes and flirted at him with the pretty brisé fan. Even more wonderful was that when he uttered a coquettish laugh and said, "Oh, Nonny, you are so *droll*," Ned didn't thump him, as he ordinarily would have done, but instead went red and glowered at him.

It had been years since Octavius had dared to call Nonus anything other than Ned, so he basked in the triumph of the moment and resolved to call his cousin "Nonny" as many times as he possibly could that evening.

Next, he turned his attention to his brother, simpering and saying, "Quinnie, darling, you look so *handsome* tonight."

It wasn't often one saw an earl cringe.

Dex, prick that he was, didn't squirm or cringe or go red when Octavius tried the same trick on him; he just cackled with laughter.

Octavius gave up on Dex for the time being and turned his attention to Sextus. He wasn't squirming or cringing, but neither was he cackling. He lounged in the far corner of the carriage, an expression of mild amusement on his face. When Octavius fluttered the fan at him and cooed, "You look so *delicious,* darling. I could swoon from just looking at you," Sextus merely raised his eyebrows fractionally and gave Octavius a look that told him he knew exactly what Octavius was trying to do. But Sextus had always been the smartest of them all.

They reached Vauxhall, and Octavius managed to descend from the carriage without tripping over his dress. "Who's going to pay my three shillings and sixpence?" he asked, with a flutter of both the fan and his eyelashes. His heart was beating rather fast now that they'd arrived and his hands were sweating inside the evening gloves. It was one thing to play this game with his brother and cousins, another thing entirely to act the lady in public. Especially when he wasn't wearing drawers.

But he wouldn't let them see his nervousness. He turned to his brother and simpered up at him. "Quinnie, darling, you'll pay for li'l old me, won't you?"

Quintus cringed with his whole body again. "God damn it, Otto, *stop* that," he hissed under his breath.

"No?" Octavius pouted, and turned his gaze to Ned. "Say you'll be my beau tonight, Nonny."

Ned looked daggers at him for that "Nonny" so Octavius blew him a kiss—then nearly laughed aloud at Ned's expression of appalled revulsion.

Dex did laugh out loud. "Your idea, Ned; you pay," he said, grinning.

Ned paid for them all, and they entered the famous pleasure gardens. Octavius took Dex's arm once they were through the gate, because Dex was enjoying this far too much and if Octavius couldn't find a way to make his cousin squirm then he might find himself repeating this forfeit in the future— and heaven forbid that *that* should ever happen.

Octavius had been to Vauxhall Gardens more times than he could remember. Nothing had changed—the pavilion, the musicians, the supper boxes, the groves of trees and the walkways—and yet it *had* changed, because visiting Vauxhall Gardens as a woman was a vastly different experience from visiting Vauxhall Gardens as a man. The gown undoubtedly had something to do with it. It was no demure débutante's gown; Lydia was a courtesan—a very expensive courtesan—and the gown was cut to display her charms to best advantage. Octavius was uncomfortably aware of men ogling him—looking at his mouth, his breasts, his hips, and imagining him naked in their beds. That was bad enough, but what made it worse was that he knew some of those men. They were his friends—and now they were undressing him with their eyes.

Octavius simpered and fluttered his fan and tried to hide his discomfit, while Ned went to see about procuring a box and supper. Quintus paused to speak with a friend, and two minutes later so did Sextus. Dex and Octavius were alone—or rather, as alone as one could be in such a public setting as Vauxhall.

Octavius nudged Dex away from the busy walkway, towards a quieter path. Vauxhall Gardens sprawled over several acres, and for every wide and well-lit path there was a shadowy one with windings and turnings and secluded nooks.

A trio of drunken young bucks swaggered past, clearly on the prowl for amatory adventures. One of them gave a low whistle of appreciation and pinched Octavius on his derrière.

Octavius swiped at him with the fan.

The man laughed. So did his companions. So did Dex.

"He *pinched* me," Octavius said, indignantly.

Dex, son of a bitch that he was, laughed again and made no move to reprimand the buck; he merely kept strolling.

Octavius, perforce, kept strolling, too. Outrage seethed in his bosom. "You wouldn't laugh if someone pinched Phoebe," he said tartly. "You'd knock him down."

"You're not my sister," Dex said. "And besides, if you're going to wear a gown like that one, you should expect to be pinched."

Octavius almost hit Dex with the fan. He gritted his teeth and resolved to make his cousin *regret* making that comment before the night was over. He racked his brain as they turned down an even more shadowy path, the lamps casting golden pools of light in the gloom. When was the last time he'd seen Dex embarrassed? Not faintly embarrassed, but truly, deeply embarrassed.

A memory stirred in the recesses of his brain and he remembered, with a little jolt of recollection, that Dex had a middle name—Stallyon—and he also remembered what had happened when the other boys at school had found out.

Dex Stallyon had become . . . Sex Stallion.

It had taken Dex a week to shut that nickname down—Pryors were built large and they never lost a schoolyard battle—but what Octavius most remembered about that week wasn't the fighting, it was Dex's red-faced mortification and fuming rage.

Of course, Dex *was* a sex stallion now, so maybe the nickname wouldn't bother him?

They turned onto a slightly more populated path. Octavius waited for a suitable audience to approach, which it soon did: Misters Feltham and Wardell, both of whom had been to school with Dex.

"You're my favorite of all my beaus," Octavius confided loudly as they passed. "Dex Stallyon, my *sex stallion*. You let me ride you all night long." He uttered a beatific sigh, and watched with satisfaction as Dex flushed bright red.

Feltham and Wardell laughed. Dex laughed, too, uncomfortably, and hustled Octavius away, and then pinched him hard on his plump, dimpled arm.

"Ouch," Octavius said, rubbing his arm. "That hurt."

"Serves you bloody right," Dex hissed. "I can't believe you said I let you ride me!"

Now that was interesting: it was the reference to being ridden that Dex objected to, not the nickname.

Octavius resolved to make good use of that little fact.

He talked loudly about riding Dex when they passed Lord Belchamber and his cronies, and again when they encountered the Hogarth brothers.

Both times, Dex dished out more of those sharp, admonitory pinches, but Octavius was undeterred; he was enjoying himself again. It was fun ribbing Dex within earshot of men they both knew and watching his cousin go red at the gills.

He held his silence as two courting couples strolled past, and then swallowed a grin when he spied a trio of fellows sauntering towards them. All three of them were members of the same gentleman's club that Dex frequented.

Dex spied them, too, and changed direction abruptly, hauling Octavius into a dimly lit walkway to avoid them.

Octavius tried to turn his laugh into a cough, and failed.

"You're a damned swine," Dex said. It sounded as if he was gritting his teeth.

"I think you mean bitch," Octavius said.

Dex made a noise remarkably like a growl. He set off at a fast pace, his hand clamped around Octavius's wrist.

Ordinarily, Octavius would have had no difficulty keeping up with Dex—he *was* an inch taller than his cousin—but right now he was a whole foot shorter, plus he was hampered by his dress. He couldn't stride unless he hiked the wretched thing up to his knees, which he wasn't going to do; he was already showing far too much of his person. "Slow down," he said. "I've got short legs."

Dex made the growling sound again, but he did slow down and ease his grip on Octavius's wrist.

Along came a gentleman whom Octavius didn't recognize, one of the nouveau riche judging from his brashly expensive garb. The man ogled Octavius overtly and even went so far as to blow him a kiss. Instead of ignoring that overture, Octavius fluttered his eyelashes and gave a little giggle. "Another time, dear sir. I have my favorite beau with me tonight." He patted Dex's arm. "I call him my sex stallion because he lets me ride him all night long."

Dex pinched him again, hard, and dragged him away from the admiring gentleman so fast that Octavius almost tripped over his hem.

"*Stop* telling everyone that you ride me!" Dex said, once they were out of earshot.

16

"Don't you like it?" Octavius asked ingenuously. "Why not? Does it not sound virile enough?"

Dex ignored those questions. He made the growling sound again. "I swear to God, Otto, if you say that one more time, I'm abandoning you."

Which meant that Octavius had won. He opened the brisé fan and hid a triumphant smile behind it.

Dex released his wrist. Octavius refrained from rubbing it; he didn't want to give Dex the satisfaction of knowing that it hurt. Instead, he walked in demure silence alongside his cousin, savoring his victory . . . and then lo, who should he see coming towards them but that old lecher, Baron Rumpole.

"I warn you, Otto," Dex said, as Rumpole approached. "Don't you *dare.*"

Rumpole all but stripped Octavius with his gaze, and then he had the vulgarity to say aloud to Dex, "I see someone's getting lucky tonight."

The opening was too perfect to resist. Warning or not, Octavius didn't hesitate. "That would be *me* getting lucky," he said, with a coy giggle. "He's my favorite beau because he lets me ride—"

"You want her? She's yours." Dex shoved Octavius at the baron and strode off.

Octavius almost laughed out loud—it wasn't often that he managed to get the better of Dex— but then Rumpole stepped towards him and the urge to laugh snuffed out.

He took a step back, away from the baron, but Rumpole crowded closer. He might be in his late fifties, but he was a bull-like man, thickset and bulky—and considerably larger and stronger than Octavius currently was.

Octavius tried to go around him to the left, but Rumpole blocked him.

He tried to go around him to the right. Rumpole blocked him again.

Dex was long gone, swallowed up by the shadows.

"Let me past," Octavius demanded.

"I will, for a kiss."

Octavius didn't deign to reply to this. He picked up his skirts and tried to push past Rumpole, but the man's hand shot out, catching his upper arm, and if he'd thought Dex's grip was punishingly tight, then the baron's was twice as bad. Octavius uttered a grunt of pain and tried to jerk free.

Rumpole's fingers dug in, almost to the bone. "No, you don't. I want my kiss first." He hauled Octavius towards him and bent his head.

Octavius punched him.

If he'd been in his own shape, the punch would have laid Rumpole out on the ground. As it was, the baron rocked slightly on his feet and released Octavius's arm.

Octavius shoved the man aside. He marched

down the path, his steps fast and angry. How *dare* Rumpole try to force a kiss on him!

Behind him, Rumpole uttered an oath. Footsteps crunched in the gravel. The baron was giving chase.

Octavius was tempted to stand his ground and fight, but common sense asserted itself. If he were a man right now he'd *crush* Rumpole, but he wasn't a man and Rumpole outweighed him by at least a hundred pounds. Retreat was called for.

Octavius picked up his skirts and ran, even though what he really wanted to do was pummel the baron to the ground. Fury gave his feet wings. He rounded a bend in the path. The shadows drew back and he saw a glowing lamp and two people.

The baron stopped running. Octavius didn't, not until he reached the lamp casting its safe, golden luminescence.

He'd lost his fan somewhere. He was panting. And while rage was his predominant emotion, underneath the rage was a prickle of uneasiness— and that made him even angrier. Was he, Octavius Pryor, *afraid* of Baron Rumpole?

"The devil I am," he muttered under his breath.

He glanced over his shoulder. Rumpole had halted a dozen yards back, glowering. He looked even more bull-like, head lowered and nostrils flaring.

The prickle of unease became a little stronger.

Discretion is the better part of valor, Octavius reminded himself. He picked up his skirts again and strode towards the people he'd spied, whose dark shapes resolved into two young sprigs with the nipped-in waists, padded shoulders, and high shirt-points of dandies. "Could you escort me to the pavilion, kind sirs? I'm afraid I've lost my way."

The sprigs looked him up and down, their gazes lingering on the lush expanse of his breasts.

Octavius gritted his teeth and smiled at them. "Please? I'm all alone and this darkness makes me a little nervous."

"Of course, darling," one of the sprigs said, and then he had the audacity to put his arm around Octavius's waist and give him a squeeze.

Octavius managed not to utter an indignant squawk. He ground his teeth together and submitted to that squeeze, because a squeeze from a sprig was a thousand times better than a kiss from Baron Rumpole. "The pavilion," he said again. "Please?"

The man released his waist. "Impatient little thing, aren't you?" he said with a laugh. He offered Octavius his arm and began walking in the direction of the pavilion. The second sprig stepped close on Octavius's other side, too close, but Octavius set his jaw and endured it. The pavilion was only five minutes' walk. He could suffer these men for five minutes. They were, after all, rescuing him.

Except that the first sprig was now turning left, drawing Octavius down one of the darker paths . . .

Octavius balked, but the second sprig had an arm around his waist and was urging him along that shadowy path. "I don't like the dark," Octavius protested.

Both men laughed. "We'll be with you, my dear," one of them said, and now, in addition to an arm around Octavius's waist, there was a sly hand sidling towards his breasts.

Octavius wrenched himself free. Outrage heated his face. His hands were clenched into fists. He wanted nothing more than to mill both men down, but he was outweighed and outnumbered and the chances of him winning this fight were slim. "I shall walk by myself," he declared haughtily, turning his back on the sprigs and heading for the lamplight.

Behind him, he heard the sprigs laughing.

Octavius gritted his teeth. A plague on all men!

He reached the slightly wider walkway, with its lamp, and glanced around. Fortunately, he didn't see Baron Rumpole. Unfortunately, he couldn't see *any*one. He wished he'd not steered Dex towards these out-of-the-way paths, wished they'd kept to the busier promenades, wished there were people around. He picked up his skirts and headed briskly for the pavilion, but the path didn't feel as safe as it once had. The lamplight didn't extend far and soon he was in shadows again. He heard the distant sound of music, and closer, the soft crunch of footsteps.

They weren't his footsteps.

He glanced around. Baron Rumpole was following him.

Octavius began to walk more rapidly.

The footsteps crunched faster behind him.

Octavius abandoned any pretense of walking and began to run, but his skirts restricted his strides and the baron caught him within half a dozen paces, grabbing his arm and hauling him into the dark mouth of yet another pathway.

"Let go of me!" Octavius punched and kicked, but he was only five foot two and the blows had little effect.

"Think too highly of yourself, don't you?" Rumpole said, dragging Octavius deeper into the dark shrubbery. Rough fingers groped his breasts. There was a ripping sound as his bodice gave way. Octavius opened his mouth to shout, but the baron clapped a hand over it.

Octavius bit that hand, punched Rumpole on the nose as hard as he could, and tried to knee the man in the groin. He was only partly successful, but Rumpole gave a grunt and released him.

Octavius ran back the way he'd come. There were

wings on his feet again, but this time he wasn't fueled solely by rage, there was a sting of fear in the mix, and damn it, he *refused* to be afraid of Rumpole.

The path was still too dark—but it wasn't empty anymore. There, in the distance, was Sextus.

Sextus was frowning and looking about, as if searching for someone, then his head turned and he saw Octavius and came striding towards him.

Octavius headed for him, clutching the ripped bodice with one hand, holding up his skirts with the other. He heard fast, angry footsteps behind him and knew it was Rumpole.

The baron reached him first. He grabbed Octavius's arm and tried to pull him towards a dark and shadowy nook.

Octavius dug his heels in. "No."

"Stupid bitch," Rumpole snarled, but Octavius was no longer paying him any attention. He was watching Sextus approach.

His cousin's stride slowed to an arrogant, aristocratic stroll. His expression, as he covered the last few yards, was one that Sextus had perfected years ago: haughty, aloof, looking down his nose at the world. "Rumpole," he drawled.

The baron swung to face him, his grip tight on Octavius's arm. "Pryor."

Sextus glanced at Octavius. He saw the torn

bodice, but his expression didn't alter by so much as a flicker of a muscle. "I must ask you to unhand the lady."

Rumpole snorted. "She's no lady. She's a piece of mutton."

"Always so crass, Rumpole. You never disappoint." There was no heat in Sextus's voice, just boredom. His tone, his words, were so perfectly insulting that Octavius almost crowed with laughter.

Beneath that instinctive laughter was an equally instinctive sense of shock. Had Sextus actually said *that* to a baron?

Rumpole flushed brick red. "She's mine."

"No," Sextus corrected him coolly. "The lady is a guest of my brother tonight."

"Lady?" The baron gave an ugly laugh. "This thing? She has no breeding at all."

"Neither, it appears, do you." Again, Sextus's tone was perfect: the boredom, the hint of dismissive disdain.

Octavius's admiration for his cousin rose. Damn, but Sextus had balls.

Rumpole's flush deepened. He released Octavius. His hands clenched into fists.

"I believe that's Miss Smith's shawl you're holding," Sextus said, and indeed, Octavius's shawl was dangling from one meaty fist, trailing in the dirt.

Rumpole cast the shawl aside, a violent movement, and took a step towards Sextus.

Sextus was the shortest of the Pryors, but that didn't mean he was short. He stood six feet tall, eye to eye with Rumpole, but whereas the baron was beefy, Sextus was lean. He looked slender compared to Rumpole.

Octavius found himself holding his breath, but Sextus gave no hint of fear. He returned the baron's stare with all the slightly bored arrogance of a duke's grandson.

For a moment the threat of violence hung in the air, then the baron muttered something under his breath that sounded like "Fucking Pryor," turned on his heel, and stalked off.

Sextus picked up the shawl, shook it out, and put it around Octavius's shoulders. "You all right, Otto?"

Octavius wrapped the shawl more tightly around himself, hiding the ripped bodice. "You were just like grandfather, then. All you needed was a quizzing glass to wither him through."

Sextus ignored this comment. "Did he hurt you?"

Octavius shook his head, even though his arm ached as if a horse had kicked it. Damn Rumpole and his giant-like hands. "It's a shame you're not the heir. You'd make a damned good duke."

"Heaven forbid," Sextus said, which was exactly

how Octavius felt about his own ducal prospects: heaven forbid that *he* should ever become a duke. It was little wonder Quintus was so stuffy, with that multitude of responsibilities hanging over him.

"Come on," Sextus said. "Let's get you home." He took Octavius by the elbow, matching his stride to Octavius's shorter legs.

They were almost at the Kennington gate when someone called out: "Sextus!" It was Dex. He reached them, out of breath. "You found him! He all right?"

"Rumpole practically ripped his dress off," Sextus told him. "What the devil were you doing, leaving him like that?"

Dex looked shamefaced. "Sorry, I didn't think."

"That is patently clear," Sextus said, a bite in his voice. "Tell the others I'm taking him home."

Dex obeyed without argument, heading back towards the pavilion.

"It was my fault," Octavius confessed, once they were through the gate and out in Kennington Lane. "I pushed Dex too far."

Sextus glanced at him, but said nothing. He still looked angry, or rather, as angry as Sextus ever looked. He was damned good at hiding his emotions.

Several hackneys waited in the lane. Sextus

26

handed Octavius up into one and gave the jarvey instructions.

"It *was* my fault," Octavius said again, settling onto the squab seat.

"What? It's your fault that Rumpole almost raped you?" A shaft of lamplight entered the carriage, illuminating Sextus's face for an instant. Octavius was surprised by the anger he saw there.

"He didn't almost rape me," he said, as the carriage turned out of Kennington Lane and headed towards Westminster Bridge. "And honestly, it *was* as much my fault as Dex's. Neither of us thought Rumpole was dangerous. I didn't realize until too late just how puny I am." He remembered the baron forcing him into the dark shrubbery and gave an involuntary shiver. And then he remembered Sextus facing Rumpole down. "I can't believe you spoke to him like that. He'd have been within his rights to call you out."

Sextus just shrugged.

The carriage rattled over Westminster Bridge. When they reached the other side, Octavius said, "When I was fourteen, Father and Grandfather had a talk with me about sex. Did your father . . . ?"

"We all had that lecture," Sextus said.

Octavius was silent for several minutes, remembering that long-ago conversation. He'd given his word of honor to never force any woman into bestowing sexual favors, regardless of her station in life. "I'd wager Rumpole didn't have a talk like that with his father."

"No wager there," Sextus said dryly.

They sat in silence while the carriage trundled through the streets. Octavius had given his word all those years ago—and kept it. He'd never forced women into his bed, but he had ogled the ladybirds, snatched kisses, playfully pinched a time or two. It had seemed harmless, flirtatious fun.

Harmless to *him*. But perhaps those women had disliked it as much as he'd disliked it tonight?

Octavius chewed on that thought while the carriage rattled its way towards Mayfair.

CHAPTER 2

*O*ctavius and his brother and his cousins each had their own residences in London. Octavius had a neat set of rooms in Albemarle Street, Dex was in Clarges Street, Sextus in Halfmoon Street, and Ned had taken a set at the Albany. But Quintus, as heir to the Linwood dukedom, had not just rooms but an entire house in Curzon Street.

Curzon Street was where they tended to congregate, and Octavius headed there on the afternoon after his misadventure in Vauxhall Gardens.

Quintus might be an old sobersides, but none of them stood on formality in his house. Octavius let himself in the door without plying the knocker, cast his hat and gloves alongside the others on the pier table in the entrance hall, and made for the sitting room and the low rumble of masculine voices.

Everyone was there, the full set of Pryors, drinking

claret and discussing horseflesh. Ned had his feet up on the rosewood sofa table, philistine that he was.

Conversation halted as Octavius stepped into the open doorway.

"Otto," his brother said, lowering his glass. "How are you?"

"Prime twig," Octavius said, although it wasn't exactly the truth. He'd been feeling out of curl all day, restless and bored. He crossed to the decanters, poured himself some claret, then leaned against the sideboard and looked at his brother and cousins, lounging in various armchairs and sofas.

His restlessness and his boredom merged into something close to anger. Not at Ned for the forfeit, not at Dex for abandoning him last night, but anger that Rumpole was walking around, a threat to women, and none of them was doing anything about it.

But what could they do? What could anyone do?

Octavius drank a mouthful of claret and thanked God that he'd been born male. He hadn't realized, until last night, just how truly awful it was to be a woman.

"What about that roan of Weatherby's?" Quintus said. "Got good movement."

Dex shook his head. "Too short in the hock."

Octavius topped up his glass, crossed to a sturdy sofa, and flung himself down on it. "I want to do something about Baron Rumpole," he announced.

Conversation halted again. Everyone turned their heads to stare at him. He saw astonishment on all four faces.

"Define 'something,'" Sextus said in that cool, aloof way of his.

"I want to stop him preying on women."

"We can't," Quintus said reasonably. "Short of castrating the man, there's no way to stop him."

Octavius drank his claret, scowling at the glass, wishing he could castrate Rumpole and knowing that he couldn't. But if he couldn't castrate the man, perhaps he could scare him so thoroughly that he'd never touch another woman again?

The question was, how?

Imprisonment was a toothless threat against a man such as Rumpole. His pockets were too deep. Nothing less than hellfire would scare him.

Octavius sipped his claret, and eyed Dex thoughtfully.

After a moment, Dex noticed him watching. He put down his wine glass. "Look, Otto, I'm sorry about last night—"

Octavius waved the apology aside. "You could dangle him over a pit of flames."

"Uh . . . what?" Dex said.

"Rumpole," Octavius said. "You could dangle him over a pit of flames until he gives his word never to molest another woman."

"Lord, are you still on about Rumpole?" Ned said. He swung his feet down from the sofa table and stood. "I must be off. See you tomorrow."

Octavius glowered at his cousin as he left the room. Ned's heavy footsteps echoed in the hallway, then the front door opened and closed. Octavius turned his attention back to Dex, who was still looking at him with a bemused expression. "Rumpole," he said again. "You could do it, Dex."

"Where would I get the pit of flames from?" Dex asked. He didn't deny that he could do the dangling, because that was the gift Dex had chosen from their Faerie godmother: levitation. He could make any object—including himself—lift off the ground.

"You could dangle him over the Thames," Octavius suggested. "Drop him in it, even."

"What if he drowned?" Dex countered. "Can you imagine what Grandfather would say? Using my magic to kill someone?"

Octavius grimaced. He could well imagine what their grandfather would say. And even if ridding the world of Baron Rumpole wouldn't be a bad thing, murder *was*.

He heard a muffled footstep by the sitting room door. He glanced over, but the open doorway was empty.

A floorboard creaked, and then another one.

Octavius exchanged a glance with Dex.

Dex rolled his eyes. "We can hear you, Ned."

"Damn it." Ned became visible just inside the doorway. He scowled at them, turned, and left without a word of farewell. Once again the front door opened and closed.

Dex gave one of his loud cackles of laughter. Quintus laughed, too, and even Sextus cracked his aloof façade and smiled.

Octavius didn't laugh. He frowned, and turned his attention back to Baron Rumpole.

Men like Rumpole didn't have consciences—and nothing Octavius could do or say would make Rumpole grow one. Leopards couldn't change their spots, after all . . . but perhaps leopards could learn lessons? *If* the lesson was applied forcefully enough.

Could he teach Baron Rumpole a lesson so painful that the man changed his behavior?

Was that possible?

His ears caught a faint shuffling sound, followed by the groan of a floorboard. Octavius raised his voice: "We can still hear you, Ned."

A pungent oath came out of the air. Ned's

footsteps thudded back down the corridor. The front door opened and then closed with a slam.

Even Octavius laughed this time.

⎯⎯⎯⎯⎯⎯

Octavius left not long after Ned and headed for Brooks's, but he didn't feel like claret and conversation at his club any more than he'd felt like claret and conversation at his brother's house. Walking was good. It gave him time to think.

He did a circuit of St. James's Square, then headed back to Piccadilly and up Old Bond Street, past the Albany, where Ned had his rooms. He traversed Mayfair, and then his feet took him in the direction of Brook Street, where Baron Rumpole had his London residence. The house was nothing out of the ordinary, four stories of gleaming windows and marble pediments, just one more elegant townhouse in a street filled with similar properties. Octavius turned into the mews at the rear of those houses and slowed to a stroll, examining the Rumpole residence from the back: the servants' entrance, the coal cellar, the outhouse.

As he watched, a housemaid emerged from the servants' door. She set off along the mews at a brisk pace.

Octavius followed her, noting the details of her appearance: the mobcap and the starched apron, the dress, the cuffs and the collar, the shoes.

When the woman reached the corner, Octavius stopped following her; he'd seen enough.

ceⱷɔ

Octavius acquired all his clothing from a tailor, but he was aware that not everyone had that luxury. He knew that shops existed where garments were sold ready-made, and even shops where clothes were sold used, but he had no idea where to find them.

Fortunately, the jarvey he hailed knew of several such places. Twenty minutes later Octavius found himself outside an emporium in Holborn. This bustling establishment held all the items he required for his next encounter with Rumpole. He exited the emporium with a large parcel under his arm. The jarvey he'd hired was still waiting. Octavius gave directions to his grandfather's house on Hanover Square. "Wait here," he told the jarvey, when the hackney came to a halt outside that imposing edifice. "I shan't be more than a few minutes."

Octavius ran up the steps and let himself inside without knocking. His grandfather-the-duke was in his eighties and no longer ventured out of

Gloucestershire, but Octavius's father-the-marquis and mother-the-marchioness were in London, along with their retinue of servants. Two footmen were lighting the hundreds of candles in the great chandeliers in the vestibule, under the watchful eye of the butler.

They all looked around at his entrance. One of the footmen teetered slightly on his stepladder.

"Lord Octavius?" the butler said, in that stately manner that all butlers had. "Your parents are—"

Octavius waved this aside. "Didn't come to see m' parents, Titmus. Came to see you."

"Me, sir?"

"Yes. Tell me, Titmus, at what times of the day is one *least* likely to meet a servant on the servants' stairs?"

Titmus blinked. "The servants' stairs?"

"Yes."

His question answered, Octavius went back to his rooms in Albemarle Street, where he spent the rest of the evening plotting.

❧

He decided to draft Dex to his cause. Accordingly, he sent a message around to his cousin in the morning asking him to be at home in the early afternoon and to give his valet a few hours off. He didn't explain why.

Dex sent back a note. One sentence only: *I am your most obedient servant.* The words didn't look sarcastic, but Octavius knew that they were.

Octavius took a hackney to his cousin's rooms even though it was a mere ten minutes' walk to Clarges Street. He unwrapped the bulky parcel of servant's clothing in Dex's bedchamber.

"Lord," Dex said. "I see why you told me to give my man the afternoon off." He picked up the apron and the mobcap, examined them critically, then looked at Octavius. "You planning on wearing these?"

Octavius nodded. "I need you to help me dress."

"This about Rumpole?"

Octavius nodded again. "I'm going to teach him a lesson, and it'll be best coming from a woman."

Dex considered this for a moment and then said, "But a servant?"

"I'd wager he practices *droit de seigneur*," Octavius said.

"Masters' rights?" Dex grimaced. "I should think that he does." He unpacked the parcel, spread the clothing out on his bed, and said, "Right, let's get started."

Half an hour later, Octavius peeped from the

door of the house in which Dex had his rooms. He scuttled down the steps and out onto the flagway.

He'd walked through Mayfair thousands of times before, but walking these streets as a female was quite different from walking these streets as a male. Octavius felt disconcertingly self-conscious. He tried not to hunch his shoulders, tried not to dart nervous glances around. He was dressed as a servant; odds were that no one would notice him. After all, he never noticed servants.

It turned out that he'd been overly optimistic. He was noticed several times on his walk from Clarges Street to the Brook Street mews. A footman made an extremely lewd suggestion in Berkeley Square, someone surreptitiously pinched his bottom as he waited to cross Grosvenor Street, and one of the grooms in the Brook Street mews invited him into a horse box for a quick swive. Octavius was feeling mildly outraged by the time he reached Baron Rumpole's townhouse. Did female servants have to deal with such annoying attentions every single day?

He climbed the short, narrow flight of steps leading to the servants' entrance. His palms were sweaty. He wiped them on his apron, then took a deep breath, eased the door open, and crept into the house.

He was immediately presented with several choices: a short corridor terminating in a door, stairs leading up, and stairs leading down. Octavius chose the stairs leading up purely because they took him further from the servants' hall in the lower reaches of the house. He tiptoed up one flight of narrow, uncarpeted stairs and came to a landing with another door.

The stairs continued upward, but Octavius crossed to the door and poked his head out. He could tell at a glance that he'd reached family territory—the corridor was wide and carpeted, and an elegant Grecian dado decorated the walls.

He slipped through the door and closed it quietly behind him. His heartbeat picked up speed, a quick pitter-patter of anticipation. He hoped Baron Rumpole was at home.

Octavius smoothed his apron, patted his mobcap to make certain it was in place, and set out on the hunt for Rumpole.

The first thing he came to was the main staircase. At this time of day, if Rumpole were at home he'd most likely be in the library or his study, both of which were probably on the ground floor.

As a servant, Octavius shouldn't be on the main stairs. He tiptoed down them anyway and found himself in an even wider corridor. He saw several doors, some open, some closed. He wished he had a prop of some sort—a feather duster, a jar of beeswax, a polishing cloth.

He tried the open doors first, crossing swiftly to each one and peeking inside: a library, a drawing room, a dining room.

Footsteps echoed in the corridor above. Heavy footsteps. Masculine footsteps. They came down the staircase.

Octavius darted into the dining room and bent his attention to arranging the porcelain figurines on the mantelpiece. The footsteps went past the door. He glanced up and glimpsed Baron Rumpole.

Rumpole didn't see him.

The footsteps continued and turned into the library.

Octavius couldn't have asked for anything more perfect. He grinned triumphantly and met his own gaze in the mirror above the mantelpiece—and recoiled when he saw himself.

That's not me, his brain said instinctively. But it was him. The blonde hair, the blue eyes, the soft, feminine mouth—right now those were his hair and eyes and mouth.

Octavius shuddered. It felt wrong to be female. More wrong than any shape he'd ever taken.

He turned away from the mantelpiece and the

40

mirror. Best to get this over with quickly. Then he frowned. What possible reason would a maid have for entering the library at this time of day?

He thought for a moment, then tiptoed across to the decanters lined up on the sideboard. He picked one up. He really should carry it on a silver tray, but he didn't have one.

Octavius squared his shoulders and marched briskly into the library.

Rumpole was reading the *Gazette.*

In Vauxhall Gardens at night, Rumpole had been somewhat intimidating; in his library in daylight he wasn't intimidating at all, but he was repugnant. The man couldn't help his coloring—the florid cheeks and coarse, sandy hair—but he could help the perpetual sneer on his mouth and the scowl that permanently knotted his brow.

Octavius gave what he hoped was a realistic start. "Oh, I beg your pardon, sir," he said, in as close to an East London accent as he could manage. "I didn't realize anyone was here." He bobbed a timid curtsy, scurried over to the sideboard, put down the decanter—and realized that he'd never seen a maid with a decanter before. Decanters were the territory of footmen and butlers.

He cringed inwardly at this blunder. Damn. Would the baron notice?

He turned to face Rumpole, bracing himself to meet suspicion and accusations of imposture, but the baron was looking him up and down, a comprehensive glance that stripped Octavius of his clothes.

"You're new," the baron said.

Octavius bobbed another timid curtsy. "Yes, sir."

Rumpole's lips turned up in a smile. It wasn't a nice smile. "Come here."

"Me, sir?"

Rumpole threw aside the *Gazette* and stood. "Yes."

Octavius advanced, trying to look flustered and apprehensive, when what he really felt was exultant.

"You're a pretty one," Rumpole said.

Octavius knew he was. He'd deliberately given himself a shapely figure and a beautiful face. He tried to look bashful, fixing his gaze on the floor.

Rumpole reached out and caught his chin.

Octavius shrank back, but Rumpole dug his fingers in, and *ouch*, that damned well *hurt*.

Rumpole forced his chin up. "Give me a kiss."

Octavius couldn't prevent himself from recoiling—as much as he was able to recoil with someone holding his chin. "Please, sir, don't."

"Do you want to lose your position?"

Octavius shook his head as best he could with his chin still held fast. "No, sir," he whispered, pretending to be afraid.

"Then kiss me." Rumpole hauled him closer and put an arm around Octavius's waist. "Or I'll see that you're turned out into the street."

At Vauxhall, Octavius had been five foot two. Today, he'd given himself four more inches of height—and those extra inches made it much easier to slam his knee into Rumpole's groin.

The baron gave a strangled gasp, released him, and doubled over.

Octavius swung his fist and hit Rumpole's nose with a gratifying *crunch*. Blood spurted. He watched in satisfaction as Rumpole toppled to the floor.

"*That* will teach you," he said, his East London accent slipping slightly.

He turned on his heel and strode victoriously from the room, retracing his steps up the main staircase and along the corridor, buoyant with triumph. He'd done it! He had taught Rumpole a lesson the man wouldn't quickly forget.

Ahead of him, a door opened and a woman stepped out into the corridor. Octavius's buoyancy evaporated. He ducked his head and scuttled past, heading for the servants' door.

"Are you all right?" the woman asked.

The only person she could be speaking to was him. Octavius reluctantly halted. He turned towards her but didn't dare meet her eyes. "Who? Me?" And then he added, "Ma'am."

"There's blood on your apron."

Octavius looked down at himself. The woman was correct: a scarlet splash of blood decorated his apron. It looked quite lurid against the pristine whiteness of the fabric.

Octavius covered his nose with one hand. "Bloody nose, ma'am," he said in a muffled voice, and glanced up to meet her eyes.

Time stood still. His heart seemed to stop beating. He forgot to breathe.

Octavius had never given any thought as to what the ideal woman looked like, but now he knew. She had auburn hair and golden eyebrows and blue-gray eyes.

It wasn't one specific thing that signaled her perfection; it was many things. The alertness of her gaze. The stray tendrils of hair curling at her temples. The scattering of freckles across her nose. It was her earlobes and throat and chin, the line of her jaw. It was everything.

Who *was* she, this perfect female?

The woman appeared to be wondering who he was, too. "Are you new?" she asked, and even her voice was perfect, a low contralto.

Octavius bobbed a curtsy, still holding his nose. "Yes, ma'am."

"Miss," the woman corrected him, and that word

made his heart sing because it meant she was un-married. "I'm Miss Toogood. The new governess. And you are?"

Octavius's mind went blank. He gazed at her. Toogood. Even her name was perfect. "Lucy," he stammered at last. "Ma'am. I mean, miss."

"Do you need help tending to your nose, Lucy?" Miss Toogood asked.

"No, miss," Octavius said, and he fled to the servants' door, closed it behind him, and clattered down the narrow stairs.

He walked back to Clarges Street in a daze.

Toogood.

Miss Toogood.

Miss Toogood, the perfect governess.

CHAPTER 3

*O*ctavius told Dex what had happened with Rumpole, but he didn't tell him about Miss Toogood. Their meeting seemed too momentous, or perhaps too improbable. He didn't believe in love at first sight, but that's what it felt like: love at first sight.

Had he gone mad?

He pondered that question while Dex helped extricate him from the maidservant's clothes. "These things as uncomfortable as they look?" Dex asked, examining the stays dubiously.

"They're deuced unpleasant." But the worst thing about dressing as a woman wasn't the stays, it was the fact that women didn't wear drawers. He felt horribly exposed with air wafting around his genitals. "Turn your back," he told Dex, then stripped out of his chemise and wished himself into his own body. Magic crawled up and down his bones and prickled over his skin.

"What're you going to do with these things?" Dex asked, tossing the stays onto the pile of discarded garments. "Burn them?"

"Keep them," Octavius said. His voice was his own and his body was his own, and it was such a relief that he just stood there for a moment and gave thanks that he was himself again.

"Why?" Dex asked. "You going back to Rumpole's?"

"Maybe." Octavius rummaged through the clothes on the bed and found his linen drawers.

"You think he needs another lesson?"

"No." Octavius stepped into the drawers and gave thanks for them, too. Lord, but it felt good to have his nether regions covered.

"What, then?"

Octavius hesitated. Did he really want to discuss this with his cousin? But Dex was looking at him expectantly, so Octavius shrugged and said, "I met a governess."

"A governess?"

Octavius told him about his encounter with Miss Toogood. "I'd like to see her again." Because either he'd gone completely mad or he was in love, and he needed to find out which it was.

Dex gave a knowing smirk. "A prime article, is she?"

Octavius considered this for a moment, then shook his head. Miss Toogood wasn't pretty. She wasn't really even beautiful, not with that unfashionable hair. "She has a great deal of countenance."

Dex lost his smirk. "Countenance?"

Octavius fished his shirt out of the pile of clothes on Dex's bed. "She's interesting."

"Interesting?" Dex said, a scoffing note in his voice. "You don't know a single thing about her. You've exchanged all of a dozen words!"

Octavius might only have exchanged a dozen words with Miss Toogood, but he thought he had a fairly accurate estimation of her character. She was a governess; therefore she was intelligent. She hadn't fallen into the vapors when she'd seen the blood on his apron, so she was calm and cool-headed. She'd asked if he needed help, even though he was only a maidservant, so she was compassionate. But he didn't tell Dex that; he merely shrugged again and said, "That's why I want to meet her properly."

Dex picked up the chemise, folded it roughly, then stood and watched while Octavius shrugged into his shirt. "Are you certain about this, Otto? Just stop and think for a moment. She's only a governess and your father's a marquis—"

"Quintus has to marry well," Octavius said. "I don't. And anyway, she's well born. I could tell from her voice."

Octavius pulled on his stockings and breeches. Making Miss Toogood's acquaintance was going to be difficult. He didn't want to meet her as a maid-servant, he wanted to meet her as a man, but he had no reason to visit Baron Rumpole's house, let alone speak with a governess.

That problem occupied his brain while he finished dressing. Dex gave him a fresh neckcloth and helped him into his tailcoat and top boots, then he said, "If you're really going to pursue this, Newing-ham might be able to help."

"Newingham?" Octavius was unable to think how Viscount Newingham could possibly be of any assistance. "How?"

"His sister was Rumpole's second wife. The bar-on's daughters are his nieces."

"They are?"

"As their uncle, he can invite the girls and their governess out to Richmond Park for a picnic," Dex said.

And if Octavius were at Richmond Park at the same time, he could meet Miss Toogood as himself. "You're a genius," he told his cousin.

"I know," Dex said.

Octavius strode down Clarges Street, and as he strode an idea took shape in his mind. Why settle for a picnic in Richmond when there were other options? He'd ask Newingham to invite the girls and their governess to Newingham's estate in Wiltshire for a fortnight. And Octavius would invite himself along, too. He'd have fourteen days in Miss Toogood's company. Time enough to decide whether he was madly in love or just mad.

He ran up the steps to Newingham's door two at a time, bursting with energy, but suffered a setback when he found the viscount in his study. Newingham might have been at school with Octavius, he might be a good friend, a very good friend, but that didn't mean that he was willing to help.

"Why not?" Octavius demanded.

"Because I can't stand Rumpole and I make a point of having as little to do with him as I can."

"But—"

"I pay the girls a visit once every quarter," Newingham told him. "No more, no less."

"But—"

"And I've already paid this quarter's visit."

"But they're your nieces," Octavius said. "And I really must meet their governess again."

"That brown-haired dab? Why?"

"She's not brown-haired."

"They have a new one? Can't say I'm surprised. The governesses never seem to last long."

"Why not?"

Newingham shrugged. "Don't know. Don't care."

Octavius could think of a reason why governesses left Baron Rumpole's household so frequently and it alarmed him.

What if he hadn't taught the baron enough of a lesson?

"Come on, Bunny," he said. "Be a good sport."

"No," Newingham said. "And that's *Lord Newingham* to you."

Octavius left before he could lose his temper. Coming to cuffs with Newingham wouldn't further his ends, and anyway, he knew exactly what carrot to dangle in front of the viscount's disobliging nose.

If there was one thing Newingham loved it was horses. In particular, blood bays. But the best team of blood bays in London belonged to Francis Pruitt, from whom Newingham had once stolen a mistress. Octavius knew for a fact that Newingham had offered to buy the horses—had offered Pruitt twice what the man had paid for them—but Pruitt had refused, because he was almost as much of a prick as Baron Rumpole was and he enjoyed flaunting those bays in front of his rival.

But if there was bad blood between Newingham and Pruitt, there was no bad blood between Octavius and Pruitt, so he visited Francis Pruitt that evening as the lamplighters were doing their rounds and came away considerably lighter in the pocket but the possessor of the best team of blood bays in London. And then he had the pleasure of driving those same blood bays in Hyde Park the following morning and encountering Viscount Newingham.

Newingham's mouth literally dropped open. "Aren't those Pruitt's horses?"

"They're mine now," Octavius said, lifting the reins preparatory to driving onwards.

"Wait, Otto!"

"That would be *Lord Octavius* to you," Octavius said loftily, and flicked the reins and drove off.

An hour later, Newingham was on his doorstep. "How much do you want for them?"

"They're not for sale," Octavius informed him.

Two hours after that, Octavius strolled around to Newingham's.

"You've changed your mind?" the viscount said eagerly.

"No," Octavius said. "Unless . . . you've changed yours?"

Newingham eyed him for a long moment. He looked as if he wanted to gnash his teeth. "All right," he said with bad grace. "I'll invite the girls to my seat."

"As soon as possible. This month."

Newingham grumbled, but only halfheartedly. He sat down at his desk and scrawled a note and sent it around to Baron Rumpole with a footman. After that, Octavius took the viscount to the stables where he'd quartered the blood bays and let Newingham run his hands covetously over them. They *were* magnificent beasts.

Their return to Newingham's coincided with the return of the footman, bearing a missive from Baron Rumpole. "Aha!" Newingham said triumphantly, taking the note into his study and breaking the seal. His face fell as he read. "The Rumpoles are leaving town tomorrow," he said, handing the sheet of paper to Octavius.

Octavius read swiftly. Baron Rumpole thanked Newingham for his invitation, but said that his family would summer at his estate in Hampshire, as was their custom. He went on to point out that Newingham's household was a bachelor one and not suited for visits from schoolgirls.

"There's nothing to be done," Newingham said, crossing to the decanters arrayed on the sideboard.

Octavius read the note a second time. Was this an impasse? No. It might feel like an impasse, but he refused to let it be one.

"Brandy?" Newingham asked. "Madeira?"

Octavius didn't reply. He was thinking.

Newingham sprawled in a wingbacked leather armchair, glass in hand. "So, about those bays—"

"Write back and invite yourself to Hampshire," Octavius said.

"What?"

"Tell Rumpole that instead of the girls visiting you, you'll visit them in Hampshire. Tell him you're going into Wiltshire next week and you'll spend a few days at Rumpole Hall en route. And tell him you'll be bringing a friend with you."

"Dash it, Otto, I can't do that! It's damnably rude."

"Do you want those bays or not?"

Newingham did gnash his teeth, then. "All right," he said crossly. "I'll try. But he'll say no, I'm certain of it."

"Word it so that he can't refuse."

The viscount grumbled, but obeyed. It took half an hour and three glasses of brandy, but eventually he produced the perfect letter. In a stroke of genius, he even credited Rumpole with the idea of a visit to Hampshire and thanked the baron in advance for his hospitality. "Now, about those bays," he said, when the letter had been signed, sealed, and sent round to Brook Street.

"They're yours, once we're in Hampshire."

An hour later, Baron Rumpole's reply came. He said, grudgingly, that he would be pleased to offer hospitality to the viscount and his friend for a night.

Octavius laughed when he saw it. "A *week*," he said. 'We're staying a whole week, Bunny—or you don't get those bays."

Newingham curled his upper lip at him, but made no protest.

"And I think . . ." Octavius leaned back in his chair, sipped his brandy, and swung one foot to and fro. "I think . . . one of my cousins will come with us. Or perhaps my brother."

"What?" Newingham said. "Why?"

Because Octavius wanted to make certain that Rumpole had learned his lesson—and for that, he needed someone to help him dress in female clothes. He shrugged. "Because."

"Dash it, Otto! I can't be so rude as to bring *two* guests."

"You want those blood bays? In fact . . ." He glanced at the clock on the mantelpiece. "Would you like to drive them in Hyde Park right now? The Grand Strut's about to start."

Newingham stopped protesting. He climbed to his feet with alacrity.

That evening, Octavius headed for his brother's house in Curzon Street, where he found not only Quintus, but also Ned and Dex.

He expected a barrage of questions about his foray into Rumpole's house, but they didn't come. Ned was fully occupied ribbing Dex.

Octavius tried to follow Ned's jokes and Dex's increasingly prickly responses while he poured himself a glass of claret, but they made little sense. He sat down beside Ned on one of the sofas—the philistine had his boots on the rosewood sofa table again—and said, when his cousin paused to quaff a mouthful of wine, "What's happened?"

"Dex and his latest widow have parted ways," Ned informed him.

There was nothing unusual about that. Dex was a rake. He liked aristocratic young widows and they liked him. He bounced from bed to bed, a few weeks here, a few months there—an arrangement that left both Dex and the widows happy.

Except that Dex didn't look happy tonight. He was scowling into his wine.

"What of it?" Octavius said, and then: "Get your feet off the damned table."

Ned stayed exactly as he was, except that he grinned more widely. "Not your house, Otto. Not your table."

Octavius resisted the urge to cuff his cousin around the ears. "What of it?" he asked again.

Ned glanced at Dex and then leaned close. "The widow has put it about that Dex has vigor but no finesse."

Octavius uttered an astonished laugh.

Dex noticed. "It's not funny," he said, with a flare of temper.

Octavius held up a placatory hand. "Sorry."

He sipped his claret. Vigor but no finesse? The widow had said that about Dex, in *public*?

He winced. Ouch.

Octavius drank some more claret and spared Dex a moment's sympathy—then he set thought of his cousin aside, because Miss Toogood was more important than Dex right now. Not merely because he might be in love with her, but because she resided in Baron Rumpole's household and the baron was a danger to women.

Octavius put his glass down and leaned forward.

"I'm going into Hampshire shortly. I need one of you to come with me." And then he explained about Baron Rumpole and the risk he posed to governesses.

CHAPTER 4

Pip Toogood loved mornings—there was something about watching dawn steal across the sky that made her heart quietly sing—but for the past three weeks she'd been flinging back her bedcovers with even more than her usual enthusiasm.

There were two reasons for this, and their names were Edith and Frances Rumpole.

Pip had been a governess for seven years. In her previous positions, her time had been filled with spelling and arithmetic, geography and French. In Baron Rumpole's household those things still took up the greater part of her day, but the main lesson she was trying to teach the baron's daughters—the single most important thing—was belief in themselves.

It was a lesson she could impart regardless of what they were actually studying. French, arithmetic, geography—those subjects were merely vehicles for what she was really teaching the girls: that their thoughts were valued, their opinions were valued, that *they* were valued.

It was not something their father had taught them.

From what she could see, the only thing the baron had taught his daughters was that they were worthless. *Shut up and get out of my sight.*

She was undoing that damage, building their confidence—and by confidence she didn't mean the blustering, bullying arrogance their father had, but a quiet and steady self-worth that would hopefully last them a lifetime.

She'd been in the baron's household less than a month and already she could see a difference in the girls, a shy and tentative blossoming. What difference would a year make? Two years? Three?

Pip was eager to find out.

She scrambled out of bed, crossed to the window, and flung the curtains back. Early morning light streamed in. Pip leaned on the sill and gazed out over the gardens and the lawns towards the steep and thickly wooded hillside that lay beyond. Anticipation hummed beneath her breastbone.

She was looking forward to today.

Although it had to be said that she wasn't looking

forward to *every* single thing about today. Baron Rumpole was a trial. In fact, if she were entirely honest, she wished Rumpole would go to Jericho. Or if not Jericho, then at least back to London. She could think of nothing better than being left in Hampshire with the girls for the whole summer.

She imagined Edie and Fanny making kites and then flying them, running across those lawns, laughing with delight, happy children instead of timid little mice.

And then she imagined the baron's reaction if he came upon such a scene. Whatever he said would be at full volume, an ugly man spewing ugly words, and it would undo everything she'd achieved so far.

So, no kites.

But perhaps she could take the girls rambling in the woods?

Pip considered that idea while she readied herself for the day, washing her face, putting on her chemise, pinning up her hair.

Someone rapped on her bedroom door—a housemaid come to tie her stays and button her gown. "Good morning, Miss Toogood."

"Good morning, Jenny."

The maid worked briskly, tightening the laces, fastening the buttons, and then bustled out the door, in a hurry to get on with the rest of her chores—and there would be many extra chores today. Guests were arriving this afternoon. Specifically, guests for the girls. Which had displeased the baron greatly. Yesterday morning, when he'd discovered that Viscount Newingham was bringing not one but *two* friends with him, he'd flown into a red-faced, spluttering rage that had reminded Pip of nothing so much as a child's tantrum. She'd had to bite her lip not to laugh out loud.

By nightfall the baron had subsided to discontented grumbling, and while he might grumble in front of his daughters, Pip knew he wouldn't grumble to his guests' faces, because two of the three men outranked him. One was a viscount and one was a marquis's son, and even if the third man was a mere mister, he was a mister whose grandfather was a duke.

Pip ran the names over in her head while she pulled on her stockings.

Lord Robert Newingham.

Lord Octavius Pryor.

Mr. Decimus Pryor.

She hoped the viscount wasn't like Rumpole, that he'd have patience with Edie's and Fanny's shyness, that he'd talk *with* the girls, not *at* them.

But the very fact that Newingham was coming spoke in his favor. It told her that he had affection for Edie and Fanny. Why else would he be visiting?

Pip tied her garters and slipped on her shoes. She headed for the door, in almost as much of a hurry as the maid had been, but—hurry or not—she paused on the threshold and tapped the door jamb with her thumb: *tup, tup, tup.*

Three times for good luck—something her father had always done.

Three times as a blessing for the day.

Three times for the success of Lord Newingham's visit.

Some governesses demanded silence during breakfast; Pip saw breakfast as an opportunity to encourage Edith and Frances to speak. She turned the conversation towards Lord Newingham while they ate their toast and eggs.

"What will we say to him?" nine-year-old Fanny whispered anxiously, her gaze fixed on Pip's face.

"What do you usually say when you meet your uncle?" Pip asked.

Fanny bit her lip.

"Nothing?" Pip guessed.

A nod was her answer.

"Well, this time you'll bid him good day and tell

him that you're very pleased to see him. And if you wish, you may ask him a question about his journey."

"A question?" Eleven-year-old Edie shrank back in her chair, seemingly terrified by this idea.

Pip smiled at the girl. "Yes. He'll have just driven from London. What questions do you think you might ask him?"

By the time they'd finished their breakfast, the girls had thought of half a dozen questions they might ask their uncle—if they dared. Pip wasn't at all certain they would dare, so she set that as the first English exercise of the morning: writing out the questions they might ask the viscount. When that was done she asked the girls to write replies to questions their uncle might ask them.

"He might ask *us* questions?" Edie said, her eyes wide with alarm.

"Has he never asked you questions before?"

The girls exchanged a doubtful glance. After a moment, Edie said, "He says hello and gives us each a guinea and goes away again."

"Perhaps he's shy with little girls?" Pip said, although it sounded as if Lord Newingham was uninterested rather than shy. But if he was uninterested, then why was he visiting? "Now, what questions do you think he might ask you?"

Edie shook her head.

"He might ask you how old you are now. Or what your favorite subject is. Or what you've been doing today. Or how you plan to spend your summer. How would you reply to those questions?"

The girls glanced at each other, wide-eyed and apprehensive.

The rest of the morning was spent formulating answers.

After luncheon, the girls practiced their curtsies and their greetings. They both stumbled over the name Octavius.

"It's an unusual name, isn't it?" Pip said. "It's Latin. Do you know what it means?"

Both girls shook their heads.

"Eighth. And Decimus is Latin, too. It means tenth."

Fanny's brow creased. "Why are they called that?"

"It's probably a family tradition. Now, let's practice: Lord Oc-tav-i-us."

"Lord Oc-tav-i-us," the girls chorused.

They were in the middle of a lesson in geography when the sound of a carriage arriving rose to the schoolroom windows. Pip thought both girls stopped breathing for a moment.

"Shall we have a look?" she said.

They went to the windows and peered down at the courtyard three stories below.

It wasn't one carriage, but three. Two curricles, and a traveling chaise for the servants and the luggage. Pip looked down at the milling figures. "Would you like to practice your curtsies and greetings again?"

The summons came ten minutes later. The girls, who'd been jittery with anxious excitement, went quiet. They clung to Pip's hands as they made their way downstairs. She could feel them trembling with nervousness.

The three guests were in the drawing room with Baron Rumpole. The rumble of male voices drifted out into the corridor, pleasingly deep; at least two of them possessed baritones. Pip halted in the doorway and observed the newcomers for a moment. The blond man must be Lord Newingham, because the other two men were clearly related to each other. They had dark hair and dark eyes and their noses were remarkably similar. They were both tall and good-looking. Better looking than Lord Newingham. She tried to guess which was the marquis's son and decided he was the one who was ever so slightly shorter. He had a swagger that his cousin lacked, a cockiness. But his swagger wasn't like Baron Rumpole's swagger; it said *I know I'm handsome,* not *I am a bully.*

"There you are," Baron Rumpole said petulantly, as if they'd kept the men waiting for hours rather than minutes. "Well, come in, then."

Fanny and Edie cringed under their father's attention and shrank closer to Pip, as if wishing they could hide in her skirts. Pip gave each girl's hand an encouraging squeeze and led them into the room.

Rumpole introduced his daughters perfunctorily, not bothering to name the viscount's friends: "Edith and Frances, make your curtsies."

Pip winced internally. Had the man *no* manners?

Edie and Fanny obediently released Pip's hands, bobbed their curtsies, and greeted their uncle in almost inaudible voices, and then Edie said, with great courage, "It's very nice to see you again, sir." Pip wanted to hug the girl. She restrained herself. At this moment she was little more than furniture, and furniture didn't hug little girls.

"How do you do?" Newingham said cheerfully. He had a round, good-humored face. "May I present my friends? Lord Octavius Pryor and Mr. Decimus Pryor."

Pip blinked her surprise. The cocky one wasn't the marquis's son.

The girls curtsied again. "Good afternoon, Lord Octavius," they said, and, "Good afternoon, Mr. Pryor." Their voices were still barely audible, but at

least they'd found the courage to say the words—
and they hadn't stumbled over the lord's name.

As soon as they were back in the schoolroom Pip
was going to lavish them with praise.

The marquis's son was looking at her. So were his
cousin and Lord Newingham. "And this is . . . ?"
the viscount said.

"The girls' new governess," Rumpole said,
brusquely dismissive.

All three men continued looking at her. Newingham and Mr. Pryor appeared faintly bemused, as if
she wasn't at all what they expected a governess to
look like, while the marquis's son was staring with
oddly intent curiosity.

For some reason that intent gaze made the hairs
on the back of Pip's neck lift. It was almost a shiver,
but not one of fear. It was a shiver of awareness.

Pip looked hastily back at the viscount.

"Miss . . . ?" Newingham prompted.

"Toogood," Pip said, and made her own curtsy.

"I knew a Miss Toogood once," Mr. Pryor said.
"Jane, her name was. I don't suppose you're a Jane,
too?" It was said with an easy grin and a light, play-
ful tone.

Was he flirting with her?

No. Wealthy, well-born men with *I'm-so-handsome*
swaggers didn't flirt with governesses. Especially

redheaded governesses with freckles on their noses.

"No, I'm a Philippa," Pip said.

"Philippa," Mr. Pryor repeated, and cast a glance at his cousin.

Pip risked a glance at him, too.

The marquis's son was still staring at her.

There was an awkward moment of silence, and then Baron Rumpole, Lord Newingham, and Mr. Pryor all started talking at once. Fanny's hand crept back into hers. A second later, so did Edie's.

Lord Rumpole offered his guests refreshments in an offhand manner and suggested they entertain themselves with a game of billiards. It looked as if escape to the schoolroom was imminent—but then the marquis's son stopped staring at Pip and turned his attention to Lord Newingham, giving the man a look that was as strong as a nudge. Newingham immediately declined the baron's offer and instead proposed an afternoon stroll with the girls. "A little ramble in the countryside." He rubbed his hands together in an approximation of enthusiasm, but Pip had the impression that the viscount would rather drink brandy and play billiards than go for a walk. "That's what the countryside's for, ain't it? Rambling? And you must come, too, Miss Toogood."

Lord Octavius smiled.

Mr. Pryor smirked.

And Pip took the girls upstairs to change their shoes and fetch their bonnets.

CHAPTER 5

They made their way through the gardens Pip had looked down upon that morning, crossed the wide expanse of the lawns, and came into a little woodland area with paths, a pretty shrubbery, a stream, and some beech trees. On the far side of the trees was a narrow country lane.

Pip inhaled deeply, breathing in the scents of honeysuckle and freshly scythed grass. If the viscount and his friends hadn't been with them, she and the girls could have picked up their skirts and run down the lane. She imagined it: the three of them capering and laughing. But capering and laughing weren't things one did in the presence of a viscount and a marquis's son, or even a mere mister, so she walked sedately, as a respectable governess should.

Edie and Fanny stayed close to her, bashful in the

company of three men, but by the time they reached the end of the lane, the viscount had coaxed the girls to walk with him and Mr. Pryor.

Pip found herself strolling alongside the marquis's son. For a moment she felt almost shy and self-conscious. She, Pip Toogood, was walking down a country lane in the company of a marquis's son. And not just any marquis's son, but a marquis's son whose gaze made her heart beat a little faster.

Stop behaving like a goosecap! she scolded herself. *You're twenty-five years old. You're a mature and responsible adult. You don't blush. You don't become awkward or tongue-tied. You're perfectly capable of conversing sensibly with marquises' sons, however good-looking they are.*

To reinforce this message, she tapped her thumb and forefinger together: once, twice, thrice. Three times for good luck. Three times for calmness and composure.

The three little taps helped, as they always did.

What also helped was that Lord Octavius was remarkably easy to talk to. So easy to talk to that after five minutes Pip had entirely forgotten he was a marquis's son.

One lane led to another, and then another. The girls hunted for wildflowers along the verge, and the viscount and Mr. Pryor helped them. Pip and

Lord Octavius strolled unhurriedly, talking about books and music and the theater. He told her about seeing John Kemble and Mrs. Siddons perform at Drury Lane, and Pip told him about the time she'd been to the Theatre Royal, when one of the actors in the farce had run off the stage into the pit.

Lord Octavius laughed out loud at that, and Pip discovered that when he laughed he stopped being merely good-looking and instead became the most attractive man she'd ever met.

She looked away. *Don't you dare become smitten with him*, she told herself sternly. *He's a marquis's son and you're only one step up from a servant.*

And anyway, he was leaving tomorrow.

She felt a faint pang of disappointment at that thought, and resolutely ignored it. She was *not* such a fool as to pine over marquises' sons, however charming they might be and however attractive they were when they laughed. Lord Octavius's life had intersected with hers for an afternoon, but tomorrow their paths would diverge again, and that was how it was meant to be.

They strolled in companionable silence for several minutes. Pip heard the twitter of birdsong and the hum of bees and the soft crunch of dirt beneath their shoes. The viscount's voice drifted back to them on the breeze.

The lane curved right, and then left. A farm cart trundled past. Edie and Fanny picked daisies for their bonnets and then hunted for four-leafed clovers. The viscount and Mr. Pryor hunted for four-leafed clovers, too. Pip watched, and while she watched she found herself telling Lord Octavius about her plans for the girls this summer. "There's a book—perhaps you've read it—*The Natural History and Antiquities of Selborne,* by the late Reverend White?"

"Can't say that I have," Lord Octavius said. He bent and plucked a daisy the girls had missed. It had white and pink petals and a bright yellow heart.

"Reverend White lived not a mile from here and he wrote about all this." Pip's gesture encompassed the lane and the wildflowers, the trees and the paddocks, the hillside rising steeply. "I'd like to follow in his footsteps with the girls. I daresay it sounds boring to you, but—"

"Not at all. Sounds a dashed sight more enjoyable than sitting indoors with one's books." He held out the daisy in an oddly courtly manner. "For you, Miss Toogood."

"Oh," Pip said. "Thank you." And silently, to herself: *Don't you dare blush, Philippa Mary Toogood.*

Mercifully, her cheeks stayed cool while she took off her bonnet and tucked the daisy into the ribbon that circled the crown. She told herself that Lord Octavius was just being friendly and that she was not flustered *at all*. To prove this to both herself and to him, she continued calmly: "And reading Reverend White's book *is* study. They'll learn about plants and insects and animals."

Lord Octavius picked another daisy and presented it to her. "Did the reverend climb trees?"

"I don't know," Pip said, accepting this second offering. "If he did, he didn't write about it."

"You should teach them that, too," Lord Octavius said. "How to climb trees, how to paddle in creeks. Indispensable knowledge for a child, don't you think?" He bent and plucked two more daisies.

Pip did think so, but she doubted Baron Rumpole would. She bit her lip.

Lord Octavius cocked his head at her. "You disagree?"

"The baron—"

"I asked what *your* opinion was, Miss Toogood. Not the baron's."

"I think that all children should climb trees and paddle in creeks," Pip admitted.

Lord Octavius grinned at her. "I'm good at climbing trees," he said. "I offer my services as instructor. We can start tomorrow."

"You're leaving tomorrow," Pip reminded him.

Lord Octavius shook his head.

"You're not?" Pip glanced ahead to where Viscount Newingham, Mr. Pryor, and the girls were plundering a patch of honeysuckle. "The baron said you were only staying one night."

"Oh, we'll be here for a week," Lord Octavius said blithely.

"A week?"

"At the very least." Lord Octavius smiled at her as he said this, and there was such warmth in his dark brown eyes that Pip very nearly blushed.

I am twenty-five years old, Pip reminded herself sternly. *I am too old to blush.* "Oh," she said aloud. "That's . . . good."

"Yes," Lord Octavius said. "It is. Very good." He handed her the two daisies he'd picked.

Pip busied herself affixing them to her bonnet. Lord Octavius probably smiled at everyone like that, she told herself as she put the bonnet on again and retied the ribbons. She was not going to be a chucklehead and fancy herself in love with him. Even if she liked him and even if he was staying for a week.

Especially if he was staying for a week.

She tapped her thumb and forefinger together— once, twice, thrice—took a calm, steadying breath, and resumed strolling.

"Creeks and trees," Lord Octavius said, falling into step beside her. "What else, Miss Toogood? Any other adventures planned for the summer?"

"I'd love to make kites with the girls," Pip admitted.

"An excellent idea."

Pip shook her head.

His eyebrows quirked. "*Not* an excellent idea?"

"The baron wouldn't like it at all."

"Kites it is, then," Lord Octavius said cheerfully.

"Lord Octavius, I daren't—"

"But *I* dare," he said, a glint in his eyes. He raised his voice: "I say, Bunny! Dex! We're making kites tomorrow!"

Everyone turned to look at them. Pip saw astonishment on all four faces, and then the astonishment transformed into a variety of expressions. Edie and Fanny looked ready to burst with excitement, Viscount Newingham looked resigned, and Mr. Pryor looked as if he'd just heard a great joke. "Kites?" he said, directing a smirk at his cousin. "How simply delightful."

CHAPTER 6

Dinner was the most tedious meal Octavius had ever endured in his life. He hadn't liked Baron Rumpole before they sat down to dine, and he liked him even less afterwards.

Sextus had been spot on in his assessment of the man: he was crass. And not only was he crass, he was brash, boorish, and overflowing with belief in his own superiority. A completely unjustified belief, in Octavius's opinion; an hour and a half at the dinner table had confirmed that Rumpole possessed neither wit nor breeding. It had also confirmed that the baron's conversation had only two themes: either he was puffing himself up or he was putting someone else down.

Octavius had never been so glad to see the covers cleared from a table before.

Footmen placed the decanters within easy reach

and withdrew. Octavius poured himself some brandy. He leaned back in his chair. "Nice place you've got here, Rumpole."

The baron grunted his thanks.

"I've a fancy to stay longer. What do you say, chaps? Shall we stay for a week?"

Rumpole choked on his port.

"A week sounds good." Dex's smile looked more like a grimace.

"That's settled, then." Octavius nodded affably at Rumpole. "We're much obliged to you, baron. It's most hospitable of you."

The baron looked anything but hospitable. In fact, he looked as if he was about to turn the three of them out on their ears.

Octavius headed him off: "My grandfather, the duke, always says that you can tell a man's breeding by how hospitable he is."

The word "duke" hung in the air for a moment, reminding the baron that Octavius outranked him. Rumpole's cheeks puffed in and out several times, then he gave a stiff nod.

Octavius raised his glass to the man and directed a wide, sunny smile around the table. "A week in Hampshire. I can't think of anything better. Can you, chaps?"

Dex rolled his eyes, and swallowed the last of

his brandy in one long gulp. Newingham looked almost as dyspeptic as the baron.

Rumpole refilled his glass with port and drank it as if it were water. His color was higher than it usually was, his jowls almost puce against the white of his neckcloth.

The faintest of bruises marked the bridge of his fleshy nose and a smudge of discoloration lay under one eye.

Octavius wondered whether the lesson he'd tried to teach Rumpole in London had taken, or whether, like the bruises, it had faded.

There was only one way to find out.

"Anyone up for a game of billiards?" he asked, putting down his glass.

"Billiard room's past the library," the baron said, with a curt wave at the door.

"Billiards?" Newingham said. "Yes, let's have a game." He pushed his chair back.

The three of them trooped out into the corridor.

"Damn you, Otto," Newingham whispered. "A whole week?"

"Just think of those blood bays," Octavius whispered back.

Newingham muttered under his breath and turned toward the billiard room. Dex made as if to follow him, but Octavius caught his elbow. "I need a quick word with my cousin," he told the viscount. "You go ahead, Bunny. We'll join you shortly."

He waited until Newingham was out of ear-shot, then said, "Come upstairs with me. I need to change."

They climbed the stairs quickly. "Lord, did you see Rumpole's face?" Dex said, as they crossed the half landing. "I thought he was going to die of apoplexy!"

Octavius grinned unrepentantly.

"I don't think I can endure another dinner with him," Dex went on. "Do you think we can dine in the nursery for the rest of the week? Bunny *did* come to see those girls, after all."

"Worth a shot," Octavius said. And if it worked, it would put them in Miss Toogood's company.

Octavius's bedroom was empty, but the curtains had been drawn and the candles lit. He locked the door and began to undress.

Dex leaned against the mantelpiece. "I must say, your Miss Toogood isn't what I expected."

"She's not?" Octavius tossed his shirt on the bed. "I told you she had a great deal of countenance."

"You didn't tell me she had ginger hair."

"Auburn," Octavius corrected. He narrowed his eyes at his cousin. "What of it?"

Dex shrugged and said, "Nothing," and then he said, "So . . . you still like her?"

"Yes." He'd thought that an afternoon in Miss Toogood's company would cure him of the mad notion that he was in love with her. It hadn't. The certainty that they were meant for each other had only grown stronger.

Right now, he wanted to marry her, which was disconcerting and exhilarating and quite possibly crazy, but if he still felt the same way at the end of the week then he was going to propose, caution be damned.

But he didn't tell Dex that. Instead, he peeled off his breeches and stockings. "Where's that chemise?"

Tonight, Octavius chose to be brunette. He gave himself a heart-shaped face and large hazel eyes. When he was dressed, he examined himself in the mirror. His mobcap was straight, his collar was straight, his new apron was straight, his cuffs were straight. He looked as neat as wax.

"Right," he said in a brisk and disconcertingly high-pitched voice. "It's time to put temptation in Rumpole's way."

Dex pulled a face.

"What? You think it's wrong to tempt him? You think he's got the right to swive me if he thinks I'm pretty?"

"Of course not," Dex said. "It's just . . ." He shook his head. "Just be careful, Otto. He might be old, but he's twice your size. He could really hurt you."

"He won't." Octavius said. He headed for the door. "Give Bunny my apologies. Tell him I had a letter to write."

∽◌∾

Octavius lingered in the upstairs corridor until Dex was long gone, then he crept down the staircase. The female clothes were unpleasant to wear—the constriction of the stays, the nakedness of his loins. Damn it, he ought to have bought a pair of boy's drawers before leaving London. The airiness around his nether regions was extremely disconcerting. All someone had to do was flip up his skirts and he'd be exposed.

How could women bear to walk around like this?

The door to the billiard room was ajar. Octavius peeked in and saw Dex and Newingham.

He backed away and went in search of the baron. Rumpole was no longer in the dining room. He'd moved to the library, where he was pouring himself another glass of port.

Octavius watched from the doorway as Rumpole pushed away from the sideboard and staggered to the nearest armchair. He sat, belched loudly, then slurped from his glass.

Octavius's upper lip curled in disgust. He pressed

two fingers to his mouth, forcing his lip flat. He was a housemaid, and housemaids didn't sneer when their employers belched or slurped their port. They kept their gazes down and their faces expressionless.

Housemaids also didn't carry out tasks in the library after dinner, but Rumpole looked too drunk to notice such a detail.

Octavius sidled into the room, not making eye contact with the baron. He scuttled across to the sideboard. Rumpole hadn't bothered to replace the stopper in the port decanter, so Octavius did that, with a tiny *clink*, then he made certain that the bottles were perfectly aligned, a quarter of an inch between each one. His hands were busy, but his attention was on the man seated behind him, alert for the smallest sound—but the baron said nothing, not even when Octavius lingered, taking the time to arrange the decanters according to the color of their contents: the deep red of port, the amber of brandy, the pale gold of sherry.

He'd been in the library more than a minute and the baron still hadn't said anything. Was it possible the man *had* learned his lesson?

Octavius turned away from the sideboard, bobbed a curtsy, and said in as close to a Hampshire accent as he could manage, "Do you need anything, sir?"

His gaze was fixed on the carpet, a rather fine

Axminster, but he was aware of the baron seated not two yards away. If he'd had ears like a dog's they'd have been pricked at the man.

Rumpole didn't speak.

Octavius risked a glance at the baron. Rumpole was looking at him. The expression on his face was predatory.

Octavius's heartbeat sped up. He took a wholly unintentional step backwards.

The baron stared at him. Octavius forced himself to stand still. He held his breath and waited. It was going to happen. He knew it. The baron was going to open his mouth and say . . .

"You. Come here."

Octavius had grown up in houses filled with servants, but he'd never heard anyone speak to a housemaid like that, as if she was less than a person. Less, even, than a dog. He was so offended that for a moment he didn't obey.

"Come here," the baron said again.

Octavius gritted his teeth and trod closer, slowly and deliberately. He had to force himself not to clench his hands. *Don't look him in the eyes,* he told himself. *Not yet. Look at his feet.*

He halted in front of the baron, unlocked his jaw, and said, "Sir?" to the baron's shoes.

He was expecting the man to demand a kiss, as

he had in London, but instead Rumpole said, "Play my flute."

For several seconds Octavius literally couldn't breathe. It was as if every part of him froze—his brain, his heart, his lungs—all were paralyzed with outrage.

Play the baron's *flute*?

His head jerked up. He stared at the baron's smug, red, well-fed face.

Rumpole drained his glass. "Go on," he said. "Kneel for me and play my flute. Or I'll see that you're turned off."

Octavius felt a surge of rage so strong that he actually shook with it. His hands curled into fists. His lips drew back in a snarl.

Rumpole was too drunk and too complacent to notice. "Hurry up," he said.

Octavius was more furious than he'd ever been in his life. He was more furious than he'd thought humanly possible. His rage was so consuming that he was afraid that if he hit the baron once, he wouldn't be able to stop until he'd killed the man. So, instead of punching Rumpole so hard that his nose broke and his teeth fell out—which was what he wanted to do—he uncurled one fist. "How *dare* you!" he said, rage hissing in his voice, and since he couldn't risk punching the baron, he slapped him as hard as he could, once on each florid cheek, the sounds as sharp as pistol shots in the room.

The baron reared back in his seat. He gaped at Octavius, mouth open in shock, face even redder than it had been before.

"I may be a servant," Octavius said. "But I am *not* a whore!" He turned on his heel and stormed from the library before he could give in to his rage and rip the baron's head off his neck.

He ran past the dining room, where servants were clearing the table, ran past the drawing room, past the parlor, to the end of the corridor, where he ducked into a darkened room. His bosom was heaving like a heroine's in a gothic novel. His heart was thundering and his hands were balled into fists and he was so angry he couldn't think straight. He paced for several minutes, practically gnashing his teeth. He wanted to punch something—the walls, the furniture, a person. How dared Rumpole ask a maidservant to play his flute?

Play Rumpole's *flute.*

The thought was so repulsive that Octavius's dinner threatened to make a reappearance. He stopped pacing, squeezed his eyes shut, and concentrated on breathing shallowly and carefully. The nausea slowly retreated, and with it, some of his rage. But not all of it. He was still furious. His heart was still beating stupidly fast. Energy still coursed through him. Lord, but he wanted to punch someone.

But not Rumpole. Not tonight.

Octavius smoothed his apron and straightened his mobcap. He'd done enough for tonight. He'd tested the baron and found him wanting. Now, he needed to get out of these horribly uncomfortable clothes and back into his own body.

And then, he needed to think.

He wasn't going to leave Hampshire until he'd taught Rumpole a lesson that would stick—a lesson that was both forceful and indelible. There had to be a way—he *knew* there was—but he also knew he wouldn't find it while he was this angry. He needed to calm down and talk it over with Dex. Between them, they'd come up with something.

Octavius peered out into the corridor. He saw no one.

He walked quietly back past the now-dark dining room, pausing at the library to take a quick peek inside. The baron was no longer there.

Octavius continued along to the billiard room. He peeked in that door, too. Dex and Newingham were both there.

Dex glanced up and saw him. He gave a minuscule nod.

Octavius knew his cousin well enough to interpret that nod: Dex would come to undress him just as soon as he could.

⌘

He was in his room, struggling with the dress, when someone knocked on the door. He froze. Was it his valet? Or was it Dex?

He didn't dare ask; his voice was still female.

"Otto?" someone asked. "You in there?"

Octavius crossed swiftly to the door and unlocked it.

Dex slipped inside. "Well? Did Rumpole like your looks?"

Octavius locked the door again. "He did."

"And?"

"He told me to play his flute."

"He *what*?"

"You heard me." Octavius was growing angry again, just thinking about it. He reached behind himself, trying to undo the gown.

Dex took over, freeing the buttons from the holes. "What did you do?"

Octavius discovered that he'd clenched his hands into fists. He shook them out. "I slapped him."

"*Slapped* him?" Dex echoed, disbelief in his voice. "Lord, I'd've knocked his damned block off!"

"I wanted to," Octavius said, pulling the gown over his head. "But I was so angry I was afraid I'd kill him."

Dex was silent while he undid the stays. Once the laces were undone, he met Octavius's eyes in the mirror. "Rumpole is . . ." He shook his head, apparently unable to find a word that sufficiently described the baron's depravity.

The door handle rattled as someone tried the door. "Lord Octavius?" It was his valet.

Shit, he was still in female form—complete with a female voice. Octavius stripped out of the chemise and hastily changed shape. "I shan't need you tonight, Staig," he called out.

"Very good, sir."

They waited for the sound of the man's footsteps to die away, then Dex turned to him. "So, what are you going to do?"

Octavius tossed the chemise on the bed and hunted for his nightshirt. Where had Staig put the damned thing? Ah, there it was. He pulled it over his head. "I'm going to teach Rumpole a lesson he'll never forget."

"How?"

"I have no idea," Octavius admitted.

CHAPTER 7

In the morning Pip was even more eager to climb out of bed than she'd been the day before. She crossed to the window and threw back the curtains. Daylight spilled into her bedchamber. The sun had just risen and everything was tipped with gold.

She leaned against the windowsill and drank in her fill of the view. The day brimmed with things to look forward to—making kites, flying them with the girls, exploring Selborne. But if she was honest with herself, she was also looking forward to time spent in Lord Octavius's company, and that was foolish. Dangerously foolish.

Pip turned away from the window and went to wash her face in cold water from the ewer. Lord Octavius was charming and amusing and one of those people with whom one felt instantly at ease. Yesterday he'd made her feel as if there was nothing he'd rather do than talk with her, but the truth of the matter was that there must be hundreds of people he would rather have spent an hour talking to. He was a marquis's son with good manners, and that's all yesterday had been: a nobleman being polite to a governess. Pip dried her face and looked at herself in the mirror, seeing red hair and gray eyes and a scattering of freckles. She leveled a stern finger at her reflection. "*Don't* be flattered by his attention; he's like that with everyone. *Don't* imagine that he's interested in you, because he's most definitely not. And above all, *do not* fancy yourself in love with him." She waited a beat, and then said, "Do you hear me, Philippa Mary?"

Yes, she did hear herself.

After breakfast, Pip resumed the geography lesson that had been interrupted yesterday. Half an hour passed. Then a whole hour. Her anticipation dwindled, and faded, and finally withered into nothing.

It ought not to surprise her that the men had reneged on their promise. There were undoubtedly a great many things they'd rather do than fly kites with little girls. Even so, her pang of disappointment was sharper than it ought to have been.

"Open your French grammar books," Pip said, as cheerfully as she was able.

They were conjugating the verb *devoir* when she heard male voices in the corridor. Newingham poked his head into the schoolroom. "I say, are we in the right place?"

Pip's heart gave a foolish little leap. "Indeed you are, Lord Newingham."

The viscount stepped into the room. Behind him were Lord Octavius and Mr. Pryor.

"Good morning," Lord Octavius said, and the smile in his dark eyes seemed to be just for her.

Pip's heart gave a much larger and even more foolish leap. "Good morning," she said, and then silently, to herself, *He smiles at everyone like that. Don't let it go to your head, Philippa Mary.*

Newingham laid a handful of sticks on the worktable by the window and Lord Octavius placed a ball of string alongside it—and that, Pip realized, was why they were so delayed: they'd been gathering supplies.

"You have paper and scissors and paste?" Newingham asked.

Pip did, and she hurried to set them out on the table.

In theory, kites were simple to make; in practice, they took quite some time to construct. The girls watched with rapt attention as Newingham showed them how to bind the sticks together and notch them for the string, how to measure the paper and glue it down. Their shyness dissolved beneath the viscount's easy cheerfulness and Mr. Pryor's jokes and Lord Octavius's good-natured patience. They asked questions timidly at first, then less timidly, and finally, without any timidity at all.

Pip, who had some experience with kites made of paper and paste—in particular with the way in which they tended to disintegrate in mid-air—made a kite from an old apron, cutting off the strings and stitching cross-channels to hold the sticks in place.

She sat on the opposite side of the worktable from the girls, so she could give approval and encouragement whenever they looked at her, which was often. She tried to confine her attention to those two things only—her sewing, and the girls—but it kept straying.

In the hour that it took the girls to make their kites, Pip discovered that Lord Octavius's hands were large and well-shaped, that his fingers were strong and lean and deft, that his voice was probably the most pleasant baritone she'd ever heard in her life, that one lock of his wavy black hair had a tendency to fall forward over his brow when he bent his head, and that his eyelashes were quite absurdly long.

She also discovered that he smiled whenever their eyes met.

Each time their gazes caught, her heart would give a little leap, and after her heart had leapt Pip would look back at her sewing and remind herself that Lord Octavius smiled at everyone like that. *Don't be flattered by it,* she told herself sternly, and, *Don't you dare become smitten with him*—and then she'd look up and it would happen all over again: smile, leap of heart, silent scolding.

It was rather annoying.

Pip tied off the last seam, set aside her needle, and reached for the two sticks she'd chosen. "May I be of assistance, Miss Toogood?" Lord Octavius asked.

Her heart gave another of its foolish little leaps, even though she knew his offer was nothing more than courtesy. "If you wish."

Lord Octavius moved to sit alongside her. He helped her feed the sticks into the channels she'd sewn. Their fingers brushed more than once. Pip's heart stopped making little leaps and instead began beating altogether too fast. *I'm twenty-five years old,* she reminded herself. *I am past the age of blushing.* To reinforce this message, she surreptitiously tapped the table. Three times for cool cheeks. Three times for being too old to blush.

The three taps helped, as they always did.

At last the sticks were in place and the string was tied. Lord Octavius examined the kite's construction. "Perfect," he announced. "But I'd expect nothing less from a Toogood."

I'm twenty-five and I do not blush, Pip told herself, but it was too late; her cheeks were warm. Not because of Lord Octavius's words, but because of the way he was smiling at her, not just with his mouth, but with his eyes as well.

That wasn't the sort of smile he gave just anyone, was it?

It didn't feel as if it was. It felt as if his smile was especially for her, warm and teasing and friendly.

Which was a very foolish thing to think.

"I'm hardly perfect," Pip said, and busied herself with clearing away the scraps of cloth and thread.

"I refuse to believe it," Lord Octavius said cheerfully, and then he moved around the table to help Edie finish her kite.

They went for a walk while they waited for the paste to dry. Pip took the Reverend Gilbert White's book with her. "'A vast hill of chalk, rising three hundred feet above the village; divided into a sheep-down, a high wood, and a long hanging wood called a hanger,'" she read aloud. "'The down is a pleasing parklike spot, commanding a very engaging view, being an assemblage of hill, dale, woodlands, heath, and water.'" She looked up from the book. "Shall we fly our kites up on the sheep-down when the paste has dried?"

Both girls looked to the viscount for this decision, but he declared that he couldn't possibly decide without seeing the sheep-down first.

So they climbed the hill, all three hundred feet of it. Pip was out of breath by the time they reached the top. She was relieved to see that the men were, too. In fact, Newingham put on quite a show for the girls, huffing and puffing, making them giggle.

Pip watched while she caught her own breath.

Lord Octavius came to stand beside her. "A penny for your thoughts, Miss Toogood."

Pip hesitated. There were a dozen replies she could have made, but she decided to tell him the truth: "I think that today is probably one of the happiest days of the girls' lives."

Lord Octavius looked at Edie and Fanny. "You think so?"

"Yes." She'd never seen the girls in such spirits, their faces flushed with exertion and laughter and the simple joy of being alive. "I'm glad Lord Newingham came to visit. I hope he'll do so again. Usually they're so wary of men. Frightened, almost. I've never seen them laugh like this."

Lord Octavius said nothing. A frown gathered on his brow while he watched the girls.

"They're not frightened of you," Pip said hastily.

He transferred his frown to her. "Are they frightened of their father?"

Pip hesitated again, because the girls *were* afraid of the baron's anger, his brusque impatience, his disparagements and his criticisms. "Of course not," she said, but she heard an uncertain note in her voice, and if she heard it then Lord Octavius most likely heard it, too. "The baron has little patience for children," she hastened to explain. "Which is . . . understandable. Many fathers are the same."

Lord Octavius continued to frown at her. Did he think she was criticizing her employer?

"I mean no disparagement of the baron!" she said, even more hastily.

Lord Octavius's frown deepened. He glanced at the girls, and then back at her. He lowered his voice and said, "Miss Toogood, may I speak privately with you for a moment?"

Pip's heart sank. He was going to reprimand her. Which was no less than she deserved. "Of course," she said woodenly.

They retreated a dozen paces, still within sight of Newingham and Mr. Pryor and the girls, but out of earshot.

Pip's chest was tight and the rapidity of her heartbeat had nothing to do with the hill they'd just climbed; it was entirely due to dread. She composed her face into an expression of polite attention and braced herself to accept Lord Octavius's censure with humility, but the emotion she felt wasn't humility; it was mortification. Mortification that a man she was attracted to was going to scold her as if she were an errant servant—and that was her pride talking, because she *was* only one step up from a servant, and while it was a large step to anyone employed in a household, it was a very small step to someone such as Lord Octavius, looking down at her from all the lofty height of his pedigree.

In his eyes, she undoubtedly was no better than a servant.

Lord Octavius didn't immediately speak. He frowned out over the sheep-down, clearly selecting just the right words to highlight her failings. Then he looked back at her. This time, when their eyes met, her heart didn't give that foolish leap; it contracted slightly.

"I know this is an impertinent question, Miss Toogood, but I must ask whether the baron has behaved inappropriately towards you."

Pip's dread transformed into astonishment. "I beg your pardon?"

"Have you ever felt threatened by him?"

Pip shook her head, not in answer to his question but as an expression of her surprise.

Lord Octavius took her headshake for a *no*. His eyebrows lowered and he searched her face intently. "Are you certain? He's never made you feel the slightest bit uneasy?"

Pip hesitated, and then admitted, "A few times. But I don't know why. He's never said or done anything to warrant it. It's just my imagination."

He shook his head. "It's not your imagination."

It was her turn to frown. "What do you mean?"

He glanced at Newingham and Mr. Pryor and the girls, and then back at her. He lowered his voice: "He practices *droit de seigneur*."

The statement was so shocking that it took a moment for Pip to process it. Her mind stumbled over the words, translated them, and then rejected their meaning.

Lord Octavius flushed. "It means, uh, . . ."

"Master's rights," Pip said, and then she flushed, too.

They both looked away, as if the sheep-down demanded all their attention, but Pip's attention wasn't on the pastures spread before her, it was on the words Lord Octavius had uttered.

Droit de seigneur.

It sounded pretty enough in French, but the meaning was ugly: rape.

"I beg your pardon, Miss Toogood," Lord Octavius said, still staring out over the sheep-down. "I know this is improper of me—I'm little more than a stranger—but I need to . . . to *warn* you, and to make certain that you're safe."

"What makes you think that I'm not?"

He glanced at her then, and her heart gave that familiar, foolish little leap when their eyes met. "Have you sensed nothing among the servants? Have there been no incidents that have given you cause for concern?"

Pip worried at her lower lip with her teeth for several seconds. "There was something in London," she admitted. "A maidservant with a bloody nose. I never saw her again and . . . the baron had a bruised face."

He nodded, as if this wasn't a surprise. "Is that all? There's been nothing else?"

Pip thought some more. "When I first arrived here, the housekeeper told me to stay away from the corridor where the baron has his rooms. I thought nothing of it, because of course I wouldn't go there, but . . . perhaps she was warning me away from him?"

"Perhaps," Lord Octavius said. "What about the maids? Have they said anything?"

Pip shook her head. "I have very little to do with the servants. My only contact with them is when—" She stopped speaking. Her lips parted in a silent *Oh* of realization.

"What is it?" Lord Octavius asked.

"Every evening one of the maids comes to help me with my buttons. When she leaves, she tells me to lock my door for the night. I thought she just had a nervous disposition, but perhaps . . ."

"She's been warning you," Lord Octavius said, sounding quite certain. "Have you been locking your door?"

Pip shook her head.

"From now on you must."

"Of course," Pip said, in automatic response to the authoritative note in his voice, and then, "But are you *certain*? Because there are many reasons for bloody noses, and no one's actually said that the baron—"

"I'm certain," Lord Octavius said grimly. "When I say Rumpole practices *droit de seigneur*, I'm not guessing; I *know* he does."

102

Pip wanted to ask how he knew, but that conversational pathway belonged to the "here be dragons" category. Or, more accurately, the "here be subjects too inappropriate to discuss with a man who is practically a stranger" category. "Do you think I'm in danger?" she asked instead.

"I don't know. But Newingham says the girls' governesses rarely stay more than a few months, and that worries me."

Pip looked across at the viscount. He was gesturing as he talked—at the sky, at the sheep-down, at the valley beyond. Edie and Fanny were hanging on to his words. "What about the girls? Are they safe?"

"I don't know," Lord Octavius said again. "But I *do* know that I don't want you in this household, and I think it would be better if the girls weren't in it, either. Baron Rumpole is . . ." His lip curled contemptuously. "Not a pleasant man."

"No, he's not." It was an admission Pip shouldn't have made about her employer, not to anyone.

Lord Octavius glanced sideways at her. "How does he treat you?"

Pip grimaced briefly. "As if I'm the lowliest creature alive, but he does that to everyone in his employ. He's very proud of his breeding."

Lord Octavius snorted. "Breeding? He hasn't any."

Pip almost laughed out loud. Fortunately, she managed to smother the sound. She looked out across the sheep-down, rather than at Lord Octavius. "There have been a few times when he's made me feel . . . I don't know how to describe it, but sometimes he looks at me in a way that makes me feel quite uncomfortable." She gave a helpless shrug. "I'm sorry, I can't explain it, and it probably *is* just my imagination."

"It's not your imagination," Lord Octavius said, his tone grim again. "You must be careful, Miss Toogood. Good God, if he should try—" His face twisted. "It doesn't bear thinking of. You must leave immediately. Today!"

"Today?" Pip shook her head. "I can't do that."

He took a step towards her. There was urgency in his gaze. He looked as if he wanted to grip her shoulders and shake her. "You must."

"It's impossible," Pip told him. "Even if I wished to leave—and I don't know that I do—I'd need to secure a new position first, and that would take weeks."

Lord Octavius frowned prodigiously at this.

"While you're here, I'm safe," Pip pointed out. "Rumpole wouldn't dare do anything when there are guests in the house. It would be the height of rashness."

Lord Octavius's prodigious frown didn't abate. "Will you at least allow me to teach you how to defend yourself?"

Pip's eyebrows rose, and so did her voice: "Defend myself? You mean . . . physically?"

He nodded. "A few moves that you might use to protect yourself, if you have need to." It was an exceedingly irregular offer, and Lord Octavius knew it. His cheeks colored faintly, but his gaze didn't drop. "Please, Miss Toogood?"

Pip took several seconds to think about his suggestion—but really, why was she even pausing to consider it? Irregular or not, she was going to say yes. Not merely because she wanted to learn how to protect herself, but because she wanted to learn from *him*, to spend time with *him*. "Thank you," she said. "That would be very kind of you."

The color in his cheeks mounted, as if it embarrassed him to be called kind.

Pip looked across to where the girls stood. If Lord Octavius taught her how to protect herself, there would be no need to find another position. She could stay—and aside from foolish daydreams of falling in love with marquises' sons, that was what she most wanted: to stay with Edie and Fanny. They didn't need another governess; they needed *her*.

The next governess might not foster their tentative confidence. She might not listen to them and encourage them and teach them that they were valued. She might not love them. And the next governess might fall prey to Baron Rumpole—and *that* was another reason to stay. How could she leave, knowing what she knew? How could she let some other woman walk into that?

Resolve grew in her. Yes, she would learn Lord Octavius's method of fighting off unwanted advances, but she wouldn't leave; she'd stay.

Lord Octavius was watching the girls, too. "What kind of father is the baron?"

"The kind who belittles and bullies and browbeats. The girls *are* afraid of him. I wish . . ."

"You wish what?"

She wished a great many things, most of which were too foolish to voice out loud. "I wish I could give them a home where they're loved," she said. "Everyone deserves that."

Silence fell between them for a moment. High above, a skylark sang. "Did you have such a home?" Lord Octavius asked.

As questions went, it was startlingly personal—and wholly inappropriate for a conversation between two people who barely knew each other.

"Yes," Pip said. "Did you?" Which was even more inappropriate, given that his status was so much higher than her own.

"Yes. I'm fortunate in my family." Lord Octavius gazed out across the sheep-down, his expression almost meditative. "Extremely fortunate. I could as easily have been born the son of a shepherd as the son of a marquis, and while I don't doubt that shepherds are good fathers, they can't give their children what my father was able to give me."

Pip stared at him. What an extraordinary statement for a nobleman to utter.

Lord Octavius glanced at her. His eyebrows lifted. "What?"

Pip thought she'd just heard him admit—in a roundabout way—that while his station in life might be higher than most men, it wasn't because he was better than them, merely that he was luckier.

That was what he'd said, wasn't it?

"That's not a sentiment many of your peers would agree with," Pip said. In fact, she doubted that any of them would agree with it. In her experience, aristocrats believed themselves superior by virtue of their breeding, not their luck.

Lord Octavius lifted one shoulder in a shrug. "Wait until you meet my grandfather. He holds very strong views on the dangers of hubris."

"Your grandfather? You mean . . . the duke?"

He nodded.

Pip couldn't think of anything to say in response

to that. She was too disconcerted, but she wasn't certain what disconcerted her the most—that a duke could think hubris was a bad thing, or that Lord Octavius thought she might actually meet his grandfather.

What she *did* know was that this was the strangest conversation she'd ever had in her life.

"Luncheon?" Lord Newingham called out. He and Mr. Pryor approached at something close to a gallop, the girls running at the viscount's coat tails like lambs after their mother.

Pip took a second look. No, the girls were literally hanging on to Newingham's coat tails—and the viscount didn't appear to mind at all. In fact, he was laughing.

"We've decided we're as ravenous as wild beasts," Mr. Pryor informed them as he bounded past. "Race you to the bottom!"

CHAPTER 8

In the afternoon, they walked back to the sheep-down with the kites. Newingham demonstrated how to launch them into the air and the girls watched with earnest attention. It hurt Pip's heart to see how eager they were and yet how cautious, how afraid of making mistakes and bringing criticism down upon their heads.

Mistakes were made and the kites did fall from the sky, but Newingham only laughed and offered cheerful encouragement—and then the magic happened: the kites stayed aloft and the girls ran back and forth across the sheep-down, shrieking with laughter. Pip's heart no longer hurt; it expanded with joy.

She flew her kite, too, and it swooped high in the air, an apron given freedom on the end of a piece of string. She found herself thinking that if aprons could be joyful, this one was.

Finally she stopped, breathless and laughing. Someone clapped loudly. "Bravo!"

It was Lord Octavius.

Her heart did its foolish little leap. Heat rose in her cheeks.

"May I?" he asked.

Pip handed over her kite and hoped that he attributed the blush to exertion.

She watched him while he flew the kite. It was impossible not to notice how fine he looked. Not fine in terms of his attire, although everything he wore was of the best quality, but fine in a corporeal sense, in terms of flesh and bone. The buckskins had molded themselves to his muscular thighs, the cream, gold, and green waistcoat was snug across his torso, and the tailcoat had clearly been designed to showcase the breadth of his shoulders. He shone with health and vigor, a strong and energetic male animal.

Pip's gaze wanted to linger on him. She forced herself to look elsewhere—at the sheep-down, at the girls and Lord Newingham, at the apron-kite tugging joyfully on the end of its string, and from the kite she looked higher and further, turning on her heel as she took in the view. How vast the sky seemed, how empty, when really it was filled with so many things: wisps of cloud laid out like ripples in water, the distant specks of hawks, skylarks riding the currents while they sang, sparrows and starlings and swallows, bees darting and humming, butterflies flitting. And now kites.

The paper-and-paste kites eventually disintegrated, but Pip's kite didn't. She let the girls run with it, back and forth across the sheep-down.

"The perfect governess has made the perfect kite," Lord Octavius observed.

To her annoyance, Pip felt herself blush again. "I'm hardly perfect."

"No?" He glanced at her, a sideways smiling glance that prompted her heart to do another of its foolish little leaps.

"I have red hair," Pip pointed out. "That's surely proof that I'm not perfect."

His eyebrows lifted. "You think red hair a flaw?"

"Of course. Most people do."

"But not everyone," he said, with another of those smiling glances.

Pip felt her cheeks flame with heat. She fastened her attention on the girls. *He is not flirting with me,* she told herself. *He's a marquis's son, and marquises' sons don't flirt with governesses.*

But it felt a little as if he *was* flirting.

She watched Edie and Fanny run across the meadow. After a minute, Lord Octavius said, "My

111

grandmother, the Duchess of Linwood, had red hair when she was younger."

Pip didn't know how to respond to that remark, but it did explain why he didn't think red hair was a flaw. *See,* she told herself. *He wasn't flirting.* The girls chose that moment to return to her, panting and exhausted. "Can we make more kites tomorrow?" Edie asked, and Fanny slipped her hand into Pip's and beseeched with her eyes. "Please, Miss Toogood?"

Pip smiled down at them both. "Of course we can."

"Kites like yours?" Edie begged. "With stitching, not paste."

"If you wish."

Both girls nodded eagerly.

"I shall make one, too," Newingham declared.

Everyone looked at him in surprise. "Can you sew, Uncle Robert?" Edie asked.

"After a fashion."

"That means no," Mr. Pryor said. "And neither can I, but I'm willing to learn. I'm sure my cousin is, too. Aren't you, Otto?" He elbowed Lord Octavius vigorously in the ribs.

Lord Octavius winced, and rubbed his side. "Certainly. If you care to teach us, Miss Toogood?"

Teach a viscount and two duke's grandsons how

to sew? "I can if you wish me to," Pip said, feeling faintly nonplussed.

"You're too good, Miss Toogood," Mr. Pryor said, with a smirk.

"Ha!" Newingham said. "You're too good, Miss Toogood! Did you hear that, Otto?" He dug an elbow into Lord Octavius's ribs.

"Ouch," Lord Octavius said, and tried to elbow him back—and the afternoon degenerated into a laughing, shrieking game of tag across the sheep-down.

Pip ate her meals with the girls in the nursery. That evening, to her surprise, the table was set for six. Not only were there three extra place settings, but those settings had crystal glasses and silver tableware and snowy-white napkins. As an accessory to the finery on the table, was a footman.

"What's all this for?" Pip asked.

"The viscount and his guests are dining here tonight," the footman said. His tone told her that he considered waiting on the nursery table to be beneath his dignity.

Pip had eaten hundreds of dinners during her years as a governess, all of them adequate, many of them good, but this dinner was unquestionably the best. Not because of the food—although the food *was* better than she was used to—but because of the company. She couldn't reprimand the girls for talking across the table, nor for laughing out loud at dinner, because Newingham did both of those things. They all did, and Pip thought that if today had been the happiest day of the girls' lives, then this dinner was probably the happiest meal of their lives.

"What happens now?" Newingham asked, after the footman had finished clearing the table.

"Now we usually play cards or jackstraws," Pip said.

"Jackstraws?" Newingham's face lit up. "Lord, I haven't played that in forever! What do you say, Otto? Dex? Shall we stay for a game of jackstraws?"

They stayed for three games. Lord Newingham made a performance of playing, rubbing his hands together and declaring he was going to thrash everyone soundly, screwing his face up when he made each move, cackling fiendishly if he succeeded, groaning piteously when he didn't.

The girls loved it.

But the viscount's performance didn't win him any games, because Fanny was a demon at jackstraws.

"She beat me again!" Newingham said indignantly.

"A nine-year-old *beat me again*. By Jove, that's not on!"

Fanny looked delighted enough to burst.

When the viscount challenged his nieces to another match, Lord Octavius glanced at Pip. "Cards?" he suggested.

She nodded.

The two packs of cards in the nursery had been shuffled together. They began the task of sorting them apart. "When the girls go to bed, I'd like to give you that lesson we talked about," Lord Octavius said quietly, as he separated the cards into two piles. "Would that be all right with you?"

Pip hesitated.

Lord Octavius glanced up from the cards. "You're worried about the impropriety of it?"

Pip nodded.

"Newingham and my cousin will stay, too. No one could think it improper, then."

Pip laughed at that statement. "Improper? You're going to teach me how to fight. Of course it's improper!"

"But no one will know that's what we're doing," he said reasonably. "They'll think we're talking about the girls. Newingham's their uncle, you're their governess." He shrugged, as if to say *What of it?*

Pip hesitated. He was correct. He was also correct

115

that there was propriety in numbers. A governess and a gentleman alone together had the appearance of a tryst, but a governess and three gentlemen? Especially if one of those gentlemen was Lord Newingham? No tryst at all, but a discussion about the girls' education, with a couple of bystanders for good measure. Nothing that could compromise anyone.

"All right," she said.

The two packs of cards were now separated. Lord Octavius laid one aside. "What would you like to play?"

Behind them, Newingham gave such a loud crow of triumph that Pip jumped.

"I say, keep it down, Bunny," Lord Octavius called out. "You're scaring the ladies." And then he winked at her.

For some reason that wink didn't just prompt Pip's heart into a little leap; it made her heart lurch like a carriage about to tip over.

She looked hastily down at the table. *Do not fall in love with this man, Philippa Mary. Do you hear me? Don't you dare be so foolish.* After a moment, she risked a glance at Lord Octavius. He was briskly shuffling the cards. "Why do you call him Bunny?" she asked.

"Robert, rabbit, bunny," Lord Octavius said.

Pip considered this for a moment. "It has a certain logic."

He grinned at her. "Of course it does."

"I assume there's logic to your names, too? You and your cousin, I mean."

"Logic? Yes." He pulled a face.

"You don't like your name?"

"In town we're known as the Numbers."

She didn't say *And you don't like that?* because it was obvious he didn't. Instead, she said, "How many of you are there?"

"Ten. Well, not really, but . . . wait a moment . . . it'll be easiest to explain it like this . . ." Lord Octavius quickly sorted through the pack and extracted all the spades. He laid the king and queen on the table. "My grandparents, the Duke and Duchess of Linwood."

Beneath those two cards he laid the ace, the two, the three, and the four, side by side. "My father, Primus, and my uncles Secundus, Tertius, and Quartus."

Pip nodded to show she understood.

Lord Octavius turned the queen and the four of spades over, so that their backs showed. "Dead," he said. "Scarlet fever, when Quartus was a baby." He shuffled through the cards, selected the queen of hearts, and placed it on the other side of the king of spades. "My grandfather's second wife." He glanced at her and smiled. "The redhead."

Pip felt herself blush, although she had absolutely no reason to.

Lord Octavius examined the rest of the spades thoughtfully, then pulled out the knight and added it to the row of sons. "My uncle, Mercury. He's illegitimate. Grandfather didn't know he existed for years."

Pip wasn't sure what surprised her most: that Lord Octavius had an illegitimate uncle, or that he was telling her. "Your family acknowledges him?"

"Absolutely. Uncle Mercury's part of the family. Grandfather is very definite on that score."

"Oh," Pip said, for lack of anything better to say.

Lord Octavius glanced at her and then at the jack-straw players behind them, hesitated for a moment, then said in a very low voice, "His life was fairly brutal before he found us. I think Grandfather still feels guilty about it."

"Oh," Pip said again, taken aback. Was Lord Octavius this open with everyone? Or was it just her?

He picked up the rest of the spades and laid them out on the table. The five and eight went below the ace. "My brother, Quintus, and me." The seven and ten went below the two. "My cousins Septimus and Decimus." He turned the seven of spades face down.

"Septimus was stillborn." Lastly, he placed the six and nine below the three. "My cousins Sextus and Nonus."

But Lord Octavius wasn't finished yet. He shuffled through the pack and finally fished out the ace of hearts. This card he lay alongside the ten. "Dex's sister, Phoebe. The only girl among us." He gave a flourish of his hand. "And there you have it: the Pryor family, in all our numerical glory."

"I take it you don't intend to continue the tradition?"

"Heaven forbid! My children will *not* be numbers." Lord Octavius picked up the remaining cards and held them out to her. "Your turn, Miss Toogood."

"Mine?" Pip took the pack and sorted through it thoughtfully. She pulled out the nine of diamonds and laid it on the table. "My father, Llewellyn Toogood." Nine for the number of letters in his name, but also because nine was a number her father had loved, a magical number that contained three sets of three.

She flicked through the cards, found the four of diamonds, and placed it alongside the nine. "My mother, Mary." Beneath that pair of cards she laid the three of diamonds, for herself—Pip—and then she turned over the four of diamonds and said, "My mother died not long after I was born."

She glanced at Lord Octavius and saw sympathy on his face, but he said nothing.

Pip looked down at the cards again and turned the nine of diamonds over, too. "My father died when I was twelve." This time, she didn't glance at Lord Octavius. She didn't want to see if his expression had become pitying.

She shuffled through the cards instead and pulled out the five of diamonds. "My aunt, Sarah," Pip said, placing the card on the table. "She took me in. She was very good to me.

Her family looked very sparse compared to his. And then she remembered, and reached out and turned her aunt's card face down.

Her family looked even sparser now. Pip's throat tightened and her eyes stung for a second. She blinked, and said brightly, "I come from ecclesiastical stock. Both my grandfathers were vicars, as was my father. If I marry, it will doubtless be to a vicar."

A flurry of noise arose among the jackstraw players. Mr. Pryor whooped loudly and the girls were in fits of giggles.

"By Jove!" Lord Newingham said indignantly. "That's just not fair! It was *my* turn to win."

Pip glanced at the clock and realized that it was past the girls' bedtime. She clapped her hands briskly. "Time for bed, girls."

CHAPTER 9

*W*hen Octavius had told Dex and Newingham that he intended to teach Miss Toogood some techniques with which to defend herself, Dex hadn't turned a hair. Newingham, however, had been shocked. Shocked about the *droit de seigneur.* Shocked that Octavius intended to give Miss Toogood a lesson in self-defense. Shocked, period.

But Newingham was a pretty easygoing fellow, and after he'd stopped squawking and spluttering he'd agreed to assist with the lesson.

Now that the girls had gone to bed, that time had come.

"The schoolroom?" Octavius suggested.

Miss Toogood lit the candles in the schoolroom, then blew out the taper and turned to face him. She looked a little self-conscious, a little awkward, and he couldn't blame her. What they were about to do was highly irregular. Scandalous, even. But despite being irregular and scandalous, it was also necessary and important, and he wasn't going to go to bed until he'd armed Miss Toogood with the skills she needed.

The question was: where to start?

He thought back to Vauxhall Gardens and what he'd done to free himself. "Right, let's begin."

"Are you going to teach me how to box?" Miss Toogood asked dubiously.

Octavius shook his head. "I'm going to teach you how to hurt someone enough to make them let you go."

She looked even more dubious. "Hurt someone?"

"Yes," Octavius said, the memory of Baron Rumpole trying to drag him into the shrubbery vivid in his mind. "If you're subject to an advance that's physical and forceful, then you'll need to be physical and forceful to escape it."

She chewed on her lower lip for a moment.

"He probably won't expect you to fight back," Octavius said, to reassure her. "The surprise of that alone will give you an advantage. Chances are you won't need to hurt him much at all."

Miss Toogood looked somewhat relieved by this statement.

Octavius glanced at the others. Dex was leaning

against the closed door, his arms folded, idly interested. Newingham had taken up position by the worktable. He also had his arms folded. He didn't look idly interested, though. He was frowning, as if he thought that Octavius was being a great deal too blunt.

Octavius ignored him. Bluntness would keep Miss Toogood safer than ambiguity and polite roundaboutation.

"There are three places you should aim for," he told Miss Toogood. "The eyes, the nose, and the groin."

Newingham's frown intensified at the word "groin."

Octavius took no notice. "Let's start with the nose. Punch it, if you can, but you might not be able to, in which case you can use your hand like a hammer." He showed her what he meant, closing his hand in a fist and wielding it like a hammer. "You can use your elbow or the heel of your hand, or even your forehead." He beckoned to his cousin. "Dex."

Dex peeled himself away from the door and sauntered into the middle of the schoolroom.

Octavius demonstrated breaking Dex's nose with a punch, a hammer blow, an elbow, the heel of his hand, and a headbutt. Miss Toogood watched closely. "If you're going to do it, commit to it," Octavius told her. "Don't hesitate. Do it hard. Put all your strength into it."

She nodded.

"Now, with the eyes, you can punch or use your elbow, but you can also scratch and gouge and try to poke them out."

Miss Toogood pulled a face, but she nodded again.

"As for the groin . . . men are very easily hurt here. It's our Achilles heel, if you will. Hit a man hard enough in the groin and you'll bring him to the ground."

Her eyebrows lifted at this. "Truly?"

Octavius nodded. So did Dex. Newingham, who was clearly struggling with his sense of propriety, just looked like a stuffed fish.

"It's the most effective way to disable a man," Octavius told her. He grabbed Dex's shoulder for balance and then aimed his knee at his cousin's groin, halting only a few inches away.

Dex winced and tensed, but stood strong. It was Newingham who recoiled and said, "By Jove, Otto. Is this really necessary?"

"Yes," Octavius said, and demonstrated the move again. He didn't give a damn how inappropriate it was. "As you can see, your skirts may get in the way if you have to do this."

Miss Toogood nodded thoughtfully.

Octavius released his cousin's shoulder and stepped back. "You can kick a man there, too, or use your elbow if you get the chance, or even punch, but whatever you do, do it as hard as you can."

Miss Toogood nodded again.

"And if you can't do anything I've shown you, if you can't punch or kick, use your teeth. Bite him somewhere. Bite *hard*. Sink your teeth into his hand until you hit bone. Bite his ear off if you have to. Bite his *nose* off. Make a noise, be as loud as you can. Grab his head and scream into his ear. Deafen him. Make him *want* to get away from you."

His voice had risen as he spoke. His final words echoed loudly in the room. There was a slightly shocked silence. Everyone was staring at him.

Octavius refused to feel embarrassed. This was important, damn it.

"Are you right-handed?" he asked Miss Toogood. She nodded.

"Let's suppose he grabs your right wrist." Octavius did just that, reaching out and gripping her tightly. Miss Toogood's wrist was slender, much more finely boned than his, and it struck him how vulnerable she was—how vulnerable all women were—and just how important it was that she learned to defend herself. "Can you get away?"

Miss Toogood tugged and twisted but couldn't pull free, and he knew exactly how that felt, thanks to Baron Rumpole.

"If I have your right wrist it doesn't mean you're helpless. You can use your left hand and elbow. You can use your feet and your knees. You can bite my hand and scratch my face and kick and scream." He smiled at her. "Go on, try it."

"Try screaming?" she said doubtfully.

He laughed. "No. Try using your left hand. What can you do with it?"

After a moment, Miss Toogood mimed scratching his eyes out.

"Good," he said. "And what else?"

"Hit him on the nose," Dex suggested helpfully.

After Miss Toogood had metaphorically bloodied Octavius's nose by a variety of methods, he swapped wrists and had her practice some more. Then he took hold of both of her wrists, one in each hand. "Now, what can you do?"

"Scream," she said. "And bite. And kick you in the, ah, the groin."

"And the knee," Dex said abruptly. "Kick him hard enough in the knee and he'll fall right over."

"True," Octavius said, and wondered why he'd not thought of kicking Rumpole's knee at Vauxhall Gardens.

The answer was that he'd felt too threatened, that he'd been too panicked.

"You can break a man's knee that way," Dex said helpfully. "Give it a try, Miss Toogood. Don't use your toe; use your heel. As if you're stamping on something. Put your whole weight behind it."

Dex demonstrated the movement on Octavius's left knee, and it was his turn to wince instinctively. Miss Toogood mimicked Dex. The hem of her dress rose as she did so. Octavius noted that she had very fine ankles. In fact, based on that glimpse, he'd go so far as to call them the finest ankles he'd ever seen.

After Miss Toogood had practiced several times, Octavius released her wrists and stepped back, glad that his knees were still intact. "Do you think you could do any of that for real, if you had to?"

Miss Toogood considered this question seriously and then nodded. "If I had to, yes."

"Good," he said. "Let's practice again tomorrow night."

"Is that necessary?" Newingham, the voice of propriety, asked from his position by the worktable.

"Yes," Octavius said. "It is." He met Miss Toogood's eyes and spoke quietly, trying to convince her without scaring her: "If you should ever be attacked, it won't be like this. You'll be afraid and you won't have time to think things through. The more you

127

practice now, the more likely it is that you'll be able to fight back." He almost added, *Trust me, I know,* to the end of that statement, but managed to stop himself in time; he couldn't refer to Vauxhall Gardens, however obliquely, without inviting questions he couldn't answer. "So, another lesson tomorrow?"

Miss Toogood barely hesitated. "Yes."

"Good." He was relieved enough to grin. "You did very well, Miss Toogood. Perfectly, in fact."

He wondered if she heard what he'd come to think of as their private joke in that "perfectly." He thought she might have. Her mouth tucked in at the corners as if she was suppressing a smile. "Thank you," she said, and then she looked past him to Newingham and said, "Lord Newingham, I know it's not my place to thank you for coming to see Edith and Frances, but your attention and your kindness mean the world to them. I hope you won't take it amiss if I thank you on their behalf?"

Newingham went bright pink with embarrassment, because the only reason he was in Hampshire was that team of blood bays. "Not at all," he said. "It's been my pleasure. They're, uh, they're good girls."

"Yes, they are," Miss Toogood said. "Very good-hearted. But they're also extremely shy, and you've been so kind to them and so patient. I've never seen them as happy as they've been today."

Newingham went even pinker. "My pleasure," he said again, and then, "By Jove! Is that the time? We'd best be going."

Octavius would have gladly lingered in the schoolroom with Miss Toogood, but Newingham was heading for the door with great determination. "Come along, Otto, Dex! Miss Toogood, it's been a pleasure. Good night."

"Good night," Octavius said to Miss Toogood. He wanted to take her hand and kiss it, but it wouldn't have been at all appropriate, so he merely nodded to her and followed Dex from the schoolroom.

Newingham hustled them along the corridor and down one flight of stairs, then halted on the landing. "You *do* remember that we're the baron's guests, don't you, Otto? We're meant to be spending our evenings with him, not with governesses."

"We're unwanted guests," Octavius reminded him.

Newingham inhaled in a manner that could only be called pompous. "Courtesy demands that—"

"The devil with courtesy," Octavius said. "You came here to see your nieces—ostensibly. They're still in the schoolroom, too young to dine downstairs, so why shouldn't you dine upstairs with them? Rumpole's not going to complain. In case you haven't noticed, he likes you about as much as you like him."

Newingham impersonated a fish for several seconds, opening and closing his mouth, then said, "But it's the height of rudeness."

"No," Dex said. "Merely middling rudeness. But if it bothers you so much, old fellow, you can dine with your brother-in-law. Otto and I will be up in the nursery having dinner with your nieces."

Newingham gritted his teeth and then said, "I don't *want* to dine with Rumpole."

"Then don't," Octavius said.

Newingham scowled at them both. "You've got no manners, the pair of you."

"No manners at all," Dex said cheerfully. "But we're very good-looking, so that makes up for it."

Octavius snorted at this nonsense. So did Newingham.

They descended another flight of stairs and halted on the next landing.

"Billiards?" Newingham said, with no real enthusiasm.

Octavius shook his head. "I think I'll turn in. That hill knocked the stuffing out of me." He sent Dex a significant glance.

"Me, too," Dex said.

"What a pair of old fograms you are," Newingham said, and then smothered a yawn. He bade them good-night and headed off down the corridor.

Octavius glanced at Dex.

"You're not really tired, are you?" his cousin asked.

"No." He rubbed his hands together. "I want to go hunting."

CHAPTER 10

*O*ctavius decided to have blonde hair tonight. He gave himself rosy cheeks and a full bosom. Dressing went swiftly; Dex was getting much faster at lacing the stays. "How long do you think you'll be?" Dex asked once Octavius had pinned up his hair and settled the mobcap into place.

"Shouldn't take long." Either he'd find the baron downstairs, or he wouldn't. "Ten minutes?"

Dex flung himself down in the armchair by the fireplace. "I'll wait here, then." He yawned widely, then gestured at the door. "Hurry up. You might not be tired, but *I* am."

Octavius made his way swiftly and silently downstairs. He peeked into the library. The candles were lit, but the room was empty. He tiptoed further. The billiard room was empty, too.

Damn, he'd hoped Rumpole would still be up.

He turned away from the door, disgruntled, and headed back towards the staircase, and as he passed the dining room he saw that the candles hadn't been snuffed.

He backtracked and peered inside, and discovered that the reason the candles were still burning was that the baron was there, sprawled in his seat, his legs extended beneath the table, drinking port.

As he watched, Rumpole drained the glass and pushed back his chair. He yawned, tugged at his neckcloth, and stood.

Octavius's heart leapt with a huntsman's glee. He stepped hastily back from the doorway and tried to anticipate what Rumpole would do next. Where would the man go? To the library? Or to his bedroom?

The baron yawned again, loudly. He sounded like a man ready for his bed.

Octavius picked up his skirts and ran on tiptoe for the stairs. He climbed the first flight swiftly and whisked along the corridor in the direction that he thought Rumpole's room lay, then halted in the shadows to wait.

A minute passed. Then a second minute.

Curse it, he'd made the wrong choice.

Octavius headed for the staircase—and paused

when he saw movement on the half landing. Was that the baron?

Yes, it was.

He took several hasty steps sideways until he stood directly beneath a wall sconce with two glowing candles, so the baron might see him more clearly.

Octavius's grandfather didn't require his housemaids to pretend to be invisible. Neither did his father. But Rumpole did. Octavius had noticed it today, so he turned to face the wall, trying to make himself as invisible as was possible for a person standing directly beneath two bright candles.

He stared at the wall and listened to the baron's footsteps. The wallpaper was maroon red, with vertical black stripes.

Rumpole's footsteps drew closer. The skin on the back of Octavius's neck tightened. His heartbeat sped up. He stared at the wallpaper without seeing it. All his attention was focused on the baron. Were Rumpole's steps slowing? Was he looking at Octavius? Was he thinking unspeakable thoughts?

The baron halted directly behind him.

Octavius held his breath. The hairs on his scalp felt as if they were standing on end beneath the mobcap.

"You," the baron said.

Octavius bobbed a curtsy, still facing the wall. His nose almost bumped the maroon wallpaper. He felt ridiculous. "Me, sir?" he squeaked.

"My room," Rumpole said. "Now."

Octavius held absolutely still while the words sank in.

Rumpole hadn't learned his lesson.

A fierce, warlike emotion leapt in his chest. He wanted to turn around and punch the baron; instead he said, "But, sir . . ."

Rumpole grabbed Octavius by the arm, a grip that was both familiar and painful. He marched Octavius along the corridor, flung open a door, and hauled him inside.

There was someone else in the room. A valet.

"Out," Rumpole said.

The valet glanced at Octavius, his gaze resting for a moment on the tight grip Rumpole had on his arm. He didn't look shocked; instead, he smirked faintly.

The smirk outraged Octavius. He almost wrenched free and launched himself at the man. With effort, he forced himself to stand still.

The valet departed. Rumpole still didn't release him. Octavius thought of the techniques he'd shown Miss Toogood only half an hour earlier. It was tempting to try them now, to scream and bite and kick, but he had something else in mind for the baron tonight, something no female would ordinarily be able to do, so he waited.

Rumpole shoved him towards the bed. "Lift your skirts."

Octavius cowered. "I don't want to, sir! I'm a good girl, I am."

Rumpole ignored this protest and shoved him again. Octavius stopped cowering. He grabbed the baron's wrist, pulled and twisted, and flung the man to the ground in a perfect cross-buttock throw, then he stamped his foot in front of Rumpole's gaping, astonished mouth and said loudly, "No!"

As punctuation to this statement, he picked up the ewer of water the valet had left on the wash-stand and upended it over the baron's face. Then he stormed out of the room.

Two minutes later he tiptoed into his own bed-chamber and found Dex waiting there, yawning and bored.

Octavius closed the door and locked it. His grin felt slightly maniacal.

Dex looked him up and down. His eyebrows lifted. "What did you do?"

Octavius's grin became even more maniacal. "Cross-buttock throw, and then I dumped a ewer full of water on his head."

Dex laughed. "Well done!" He climbed to his feet and said, "Let's get you out of those clothes," and then, "Wait a moment. What have we here?" He took Octavius by the shoulder and lifted his arm, and Octavius discovered that he'd ripped open quite a few seams.

It appeared that maidservants' clothes weren't suitable for performing cross-buttock throws.

"Damn it," Octavius said, inspecting the torn seams.

"Just as well Miss Toogood's teaching us to sew tomorrow, eh?"

It only took a few minutes to extricate himself from the clothes, and while he undressed, he thought. The baron hadn't learned his lesson in London, and he hadn't learned it last night, and Octavius doubted he'd have learned it tonight, either. The man's lechery was ingrained too deeply, his soul too corrupt. "How the devil are we going to stop Rumpole?" he demanded of Dex.

"Dashed if I know," Dex said. "But I'm not sure violence is the answer. I think . . . honestly, Otto, I think we need to put the fear of God into him."

"How?"

Dex shrugged. "No idea."

Octavius lay awake for several hours that night, thinking about the fear of God and about the various magical abilities that he and his cousins possessed. He still didn't have a plan when he finally fell asleep.

CHAPTER 11

*Y*esterday had been an excellent day, but today was turning out to be even better. Pip wasn't a giggler, but she found herself suppressing giggles that morning. In fact, whenever she looked around the worktable and saw Lord Newingham, Lord Octavius, and Mr. Pryor bent over their sewing, mirth bubbled up in her chest. She stifled it successfully a dozen times, but it rose up again, buoyant and effervescent, while she watched Lord Newingham sew quite the crookedest seam she had ever seen anyone sew. He looked up and must have read her expression correctly, for he gave her a lopsided, rueful grin—and Pip couldn't help herself. She giggled.

Newingham didn't appear to mind. His grin widened and he gave a laugh, and then Mr. Pryor looked at the viscount's sewing and he laughed, too, and Lord Octavius joined in, and suddenly all four of them were cackling away, while Edie and Fanny stared at them in bewilderment.

"What's so funny?" Fanny asked.

"Me," Lord Newingham wheezed through his laughter. "My sewing. I'm undoubtedly the worst seamstress in England." He displayed his crooked stitches to his nieces.

There was no denying it; sewing was a skill that Newingham did *not* possess. Lord Octavius's seams were much straighter, but surprisingly it was the cocksure I'm-so-handsome Mr. Pryor who was the best of the three. Pip watched him for a moment, approving of his neat, deft stitches, before allowing her gaze to stray to Lord Octavius, whose stitches were misshapen rather than neat and dogged rather than deft. He frowned as he sewed, eyes narrowed in concentration, lips pursed, but despite the frown there was still something very appealing about his face.

Pip studied him, trying to determine what made his face so attractive. Was it the symmetry of his features? The strength of his nose and jaw and cheekbones?

But Mr. Pryor had similar symmetry and strong features, and he wasn't nearly as attractive as his cousin.

Pip surreptitiously examined the two men, trying to puzzle out why her eyes preferred one to the other. They both had good bone structure, both had dark eyes that sparkled with humor, both had mouths that naturally quirked upwards—and yet one face pleased her much more than the other.

It was character, Pip decided, after ten minutes of covert scrutiny. Or rather, the stamp that character made on a person's face.

Mr. Pryor tied a knot in the thread, snipped off the excess, then looked at his cousin and smirked. "I finished first!" And *that* was the difference between them: where Lord Octavius grinned, Mr. Pryor smirked.

Which was why she liked Lord Octavius's face better.

"It's not a race," Newingham chided, hunching over his kite and sewing even faster and more sloppily.

Fifteen minutes later all seams were sewn, all sticks inserted, and all strings tied. They carried the kites up to the top of the hanger and flew them on the sheep-down, running backwards and forwards, shouting and laughing.

It was, without doubt, one of the best mornings that Pip could remember.

After luncheon, they took the Reverend Gilbert

White's book and explored the nearby woods. The reverend had been a great observer of nature. In his opinion, the beeches that cloaked the Selborne hanger were "the most lovely of all forest trees." He had much to say about their "smooth rind" and "glossy foliage" and "graceful pendulous boughs."

After several minutes admiring those things, Lord Octavius said, "It's my belief that people can't fully appreciate trees until they've climbed one." So they spent the next half hour looking for the perfect tree to climb, and when they found it, it *was* perfect, with branches that looked as if they'd grown for no other purpose than to be climbed upon, so broad and well-spaced they were.

Newingham went first, clambering upwards as easily as if he were a monkey. Mr. Pryor helped Edie and Fanny onto the lowest branches, then all four of them climbed higher. Pip gazed up at them. The emotion she felt as she watched the girls scramble upwards wasn't anxiety; it was envy.

"Well?" Lord Octavius said. "Aren't you going to climb, too?"

She glanced sideways, and found him watching her. "I can't."

"Of course you can."

Pip shook her head. "I'm not ten years old anymore."

He grinned. "I had noticed."

Lord Octavius had a very attractive grin. A *too* attractive grin. The sort of grin that made young ladies fall in love when they ought to know better. Pip made herself ignore it. "And neither am I a man. I can't climb in this dress."

The grin faded. Lord Octavius studied her for a moment and she had the disconcerting impression that her reply had disappointed him. "Age has nothing to do with it," he said, finally. "And you *can* climb in that dress. I wager it."

She narrowed her eyes at him. "Oh, you do, do you?"

"I do." He looked at the tree-climbers, high above them. "Don't you want to?"

Pip hesitated. Yes, she did. Very much.

Lord Octavius correctly interpreted her hesitation. "I'll go first." He scrambled up onto the lowest bough, then crouched and reached a hand down to her. "Come on."

The dress did make it difficult; she had to tuck it up several times, but Lord Octavius averted his eyes with scrupulous politeness and he held her hand whenever it was necessary—in fact, he held her hand even when it wasn't necessary, but Pip decided not to point that out, because she rather liked it.

And that was how Pip found herself halfway up a tree, perched on what the Reverend Gilbert White would have described as a smooth and pendulous bough, sitting alongside a marquis's son, while a viscount who was perched two boughs above read aloud from the reverend's book.

It was perhaps the most unusual half hour of Pip's life, and also one of the best, and when it came time to climb down she was quite disappointed. Her descent was tricky and awkward and unladylike, and she managed to tear six inches of her hem, but when they were back on solid ground and Lord Octavius asked, "Well? Was it worth it?" she said, "Yes," quite emphatically.

He grinned at her, then—that dangerously attractive grin—and her heart lurched and teetered on the brink of falling in love, but fortunately didn't make that fatal plunge.

Remember who you are, Pip scolded herself, turning away to watch the girls descend. *Remember who he is. Who his father is.* But it was perilously easy to forget the gulf in rank between them when they flew kites and climbed trees. Lord Octavius treated her as an equal, a friend, and that was even more beguiling than his too-attractive grin.

His father is a marquis, she told herself sternly, and then she repeated that last word three times—*marquis, marquis, marquis*—as if it were a spell and had the power to stop her falling in love with Lord Octavius.

"You lost the wager," he informed her later, as they made their way back to Rumpole Hall, all six of them disheveled and rosy-cheeked and in high spirits.

"What wager?"

"That you *could* climb a tree in that dress."

"Oh." Pip had forgotten there'd been a wager. "We didn't set a stake, so it doesn't count."

"It counts."

"What's the stake, then?"

"I'll let you know," Lord Octavius said, and then he smiled and looked away and whistled a few bars of a tune that Pip didn't recognize.

Marquis, marquis, marquis, she told herself, and she tapped her thumb and forefinger together three times for good measure.

It didn't help much.

The men dined with them again that evening, and then they all played jackstraws until it was time for the girls to go to bed. Newingham continued his losing streak, much to his chagrin.

"Cheer up, Bunny," Mr. Pryor said, as they made their way to the schoolroom for Pip's lesson in defensive techniques. "It's only a children's game."

That observation didn't improve Newingham's mood. He grumbled while Pip lit the candles, grumbled while Mr. Pryor moved the schoolroom furniture back against the walls, and grumbled while Lord Octavius peeled out of his tailcoat and turned up his shirt sleeves, but he stopped grumbling and watched intently when Pip went through the moves she'd learned last night. Newingham's advice was surprisingly constructive. "Don't punch with your hand; punch with your whole shoulder," he said, and, "Try gouging his eyes out with your thumbs; they're stronger than your fingers."

The moves came more easily than they had yesterday, as if they'd settled into her brain overnight. When Lord Octavius took her by one wrist and she couldn't pull free, Pip didn't feel helpless; she scratched his face and bloodied his nose with the heel of her other hand, and when he took her by both wrists, she broke his kneecap. Or perhaps she merely bruised it. It was all metaphorical, of course.

Part of her wished that she really *could* punch and kick as he'd taught her, just to see if it really did work—and part of her hoped that she would never need to find out whether it worked or not.

"What else could you do?" Newingham said, in his self-appointed rôle as examiner.

"Scream like a banshee," Pip said. "Kick his groin. Bite off his ear."

Lord Octavius grimaced expressively, and released her.

"Well done, Miss Toogood," Mr. Pryor said. He pushed away from the wall he'd been leaning against. "Let's have a go, Bunny. You be Miss Toogood and I'll be the villain."

"Why do I have to be Miss Toogood?" Newingham asked, as he obligingly peeled out of his tailcoat.

"You're shorter." Mr. Pryor swaggered out into the center of the schoolroom and stood akimbo, leering villainously at the viscount.

Newingham tossed aside his tailcoat, then approached Mr. Pryor with small and mincing steps, his gaze demurely lowered. When he came close, Mr. Pryor reached out and seized his arm.

The viscount gave a high-pitched squawk.

Pip watched open-mouthed as the fight played out, torn between laughter and horror. It was a game—they weren't *really* trying to maim each other—but the altercation was faster and more brutal than anything she'd practiced with Lord Octavius. She gasped when the viscount threw a punch that would have undoubtedly broken Mr. Pryor's nose if he hadn't pulled it at the last moment, gasped again as he swung his elbow like a scythe, barely avoiding breaking Mr. Pryor's nose a second time.

Mr. Pryor yelped, although the elbow hadn't actually connected, and reeled back theatrically, his hands clapped to his nose, then dropped to his knees. Newingham didn't turn and run, which is what Pip would have done at that point; he closed in on Mr. Pryor and aimed a kick at his groin.

Mr. Pryor flinched, and so did Lord Octavius, alongside her, but the kick didn't land.

The viscount mimed a second kick and then bent and pretended to bite Mr. Pryor's ear off.

"Ow!" Mr. Pryor said loudly. "Get off me, you brute!"

The viscount straightened and strutted victoriously around the room, his arms upraised. "I win!"

"You bit my ear," Mr. Pryor said, climbing to his feet. "You actually *bit* my *ear*. I can't believe you did that, Bunny!"

Newingham lowered his arms. "I can't believe I did it, either." He scrubbed at his lips with one lacy cuff. "Excuse me, Miss Toogood, I need to wash my mouth out." He snatched up his tailcoat and departed, wearing a slightly nauseated expression.

Pip realized that she was still gaping like a yokel. She hastily closed her mouth.

"Did he really bite you?" Lord Octavius asked, sounding as astonished as she was.

"Yes, he really did," Mr. Pryor said. "Which is disconcerting, to say the least. Usually it's women who bite my ears." He grinned at Pip and winked.

Beside her, Lord Octavius bristled. "For God's sake, Dex, she's not one of your widows."

Mr. Pryor laughed. "I know that. Keep your hair on." He fingered his ear, and grimaced. "Excuse me. I need to wash Bunny's spit off me."

And then he, too, was gone.

"I apologize for my cousin," Lord Octavius said, once the door had closed behind Mr. Pryor. "He can be a little coarse."

"It's perfectly all right." Pip assured him, while wondering what on earth Mr. Pryor had meant by his remark about women biting his ears.

Was the biting of ears something that women did to their lovers?

Was it something that men *expected* them to do?

That they *liked*?

Pip thought it sounded rather unpleasant for both parties.

"Do you think you could do that if you had to?" Lord Octavius asked.

The cogs of Pip's brain jammed and for a few dreadful seconds she wasn't certain what it was he was asking her—and then he gestured to the space in the middle of the schoolroom where Newingham and Mr. Pryor had been locked in mock combat. "Could you fight like that?"

Pip put aside her puzzlement over the biting of ears and focused on Lord Octavius's question. His very serious question.

Could she fight as Newingham and Mr. Pryor had fought? Could she strike someone that swiftly? That brutally?

"I don't know," Pip said. "I'm not as fast as Lord Newingham, nor as strong." It stung to admit that, but it was the truth.

"Newingham's been fighting for years and you've only been doing this for two days." Lord Octavius smiled at her, a friendly smile that made his eyes crease at the corners. "And remember: you don't have to be as fast or as strong as Newingham; you just have to be fast enough and strong enough to get away from the baron."

He took a step closer and reached out and took one of her hands in both of his, curling her fingers into a fist. He guided it in a punch to his nose. "Surprise him, hurt him enough to make him let you go, don't panic, and you'll be all right."

Pip's heartbeat sped up. Her throat was too tight for words, almost too tight for breath. She nodded, aware of his hands cradling her fist, warm and strong.

"*Should* be all right," Lord Octavius amended soberly. "But I can't promise you will be." He frowned and let her hand go. "You should leave this household, Miss Toogood. As soon as possible."

Pip didn't want to leave the baron's household, and perhaps it was foolish but she no longer felt there was any reason to. She wasn't afraid of Rumpole. Not after these lessons. The baron wasn't young and strong and fast, like Lord Octavius. He was overweight and nearly sixty, and if she had to she would fight him off. But she didn't think she'd have to, because the baron was no longer a threat. Not because he'd changed, but because *she'd* changed.

Baron Rumpole might be a braggart and a bully, but he wasn't a complete fool. She knew how to hurt him, and he would recognize that in her and wouldn't touch her. She *knew* it. She *felt* it.

"Miss Toogood?" Lord Octavius said, still frowning at her. "You will leave, won't you?"

"I'll think about it," Pip said.

This answer didn't please him. His frown deepened, furrows proliferating across his forehead.

Pip turned away and began to put the chairs back in their proper places—and as she did, she realized she was alone in the schoolroom with him.

Newingham had gone. Mr. Pryor had gone. The only two people left were herself and Lord Octavius.

On the heels of that sudden realization came a flood of unfamiliar feelings. She felt flustered and self-conscious and awkward and a little too warm, but more than all of those things, she felt aware of Lord Octavius. Aware of his presence in the room. Aware of the creak of the floorboards as he moved the desks back into place. Aware of his breathing. *Aware.*

She wasn't looking at him, and yet all her attention was on him. She could feel him behind her, hear each step that he took, and she knew that he was still frowning, just as she knew that Baron Rumpole was no longer a threat.

When there was no more furniture to rearrange, she turned to face him and saw that she'd been right: Lord Octavius was still frowning. "You're locking your door at night, aren't you?" he said, rolling down his shirt sleeves.

"Yes."

"Good." His frown lessened. He shrugged into his tailcoat.

A new emotion found its way into the mix: anxiety. If anyone discovered her here with Lord Octavius they'd think it a tryst.

Pip crossed swiftly to the door. "We're alone," she

said. "If one of the servants should find us and tell Lord Rumpole, I'll lose my position."

He glanced up, and she saw him make the same realization she had. Surprise wiped the last of the frown from his brow—and then she saw the awareness strike him too, saw the exact second when he became as conscious of her as she was of him, alive to their aloneness and its possibilities.

Her own awareness of him doubled. Tripled. It seemed to vibrate in the air between them, a hum too faint to be heard but not too faint to be felt. It shivered over her skin and made her breathless. It felt like fear, except that it wasn't fear at all. It was the exact opposite of fear. It was expectancy. Hope that something would happen between them. That perhaps he would kiss her.

But Pip wasn't stupid. She had no intention of ruining her reputation and therefore her life, so she held the door open. "Good night, Lord Octavius," she said briskly.

Lord Octavius wasn't stupid, either. Nor was he a villain. Mr. Pryor, had he felt that awareness, might have lingered to steal a kiss, but Lord Octavius was a gentleman. He crossed the schoolroom and stepped through the doorway—and then he hesitated. "About that wager . . ."

"What about it?"

"I've decided what the stake was." He smiled at her, and it wasn't the smile of a gentleman. It was a smile that held a little mischief, a little wickedness.

Pip felt the shiver and the breathlessness again, only this time it *was* partly fear, a paralyzing mix of anticipation and nervousness.

Lord Octavius reached out and tilted her chin up with one fingertip.

"What are you doing?" Pip asked, her voice barely more than a whisper.

"Claiming my prize."

She should have stepped back, but she didn't, and so Lord Octavius dipped his head and kissed her.

It was a brief kiss. A light kiss. His lips brushed against hers for a fleeting second, while her heart thundered in her ears, then he lifted his head. "Good night," he said, and he was gone, striding down the corridor.

Pip stood in the doorway long after Lord Octavius's footsteps had faded into silence. The impression of his kiss lingered on her lips—warm and tingling and unexpected.

Her first kiss.

Her first kiss ever, and it had been from the son of a marquis.

Lord Octavius had *kissed* her. He'd kissed *her*, Pip Toogood. He'd kissed her, and it was startling and marvelous and altogether wonderful. She felt as if she was floating two feet off the floor.

Then uncertainty crept in.

Why had Lord Octavius kissed her? Was he angling after a dalliance?

It was a horrible thought, and it quenched the tingling delight most effectively. Pip no longer felt as if she was floating. In fact, she felt rather ill.

A dalliance. An affair, after which she'd be discarded, and not just discarded but ruined.

But no, she wouldn't believe that of Lord Octavius. She *couldn't* believe that of him.

Mr. Pryor, with his swagger and his smirk and his mention of women biting his ears, was the type for dalliances—she could believe he'd ruined a woman or two in his time—but Lord Octavius was altogether too honorable.

Although he *had* kissed her, and that hadn't been honorable at all. It had been reckless and reprehensible—kissing her where anyone might see them.

Pip laid her fingers on the doorframe and tapped: once, twice, thrice. The familiarity of it steadied her. She heard her father's voice in her ear: *Thrice for luck, Pippa-mine.*

She tapped again, firmly and deliberately: one, two, three.

Three times for good luck. Three times to ensure

that her world kept spinning on its axis and that nothing went awry.

"It was just a wager," she said aloud, to herself and to her father, whose memory hovered nearby.

Just a wager. Just a moment of foolishness. Nothing that would topple her world, because she wouldn't allow it to.

Pip tapped a third time, three little pecks of sound—*tup, tup, tup*—just to make certain.

CHAPTER 12

Octavius met his cousin on the stairs. "Do you need me tonight?" Dex asked.

"Need?" Octavius repeated blankly, his mind still caught up in kissing Miss Toogood—the surprise on her face, the softness of her lips.

"To help you dress."

"Uh . . ." All Octavius wanted to do was to retire to his bedroom and think about that kiss. Had it been a mistake? Had he ruined his chances with Miss Toogood? "Uh, yes." Because it was important that the baron learned his lesson. No, it was more than important; it was crucial. Because if Miss Toogood decided not to marry him, he needed to make certain she was safe in this household.

Dex came with him to his bedroom. Octavius changed shape and dressed in maid's clothing. They were getting good at this, he and Dex.

He made his way swiftly and silently down the main staircase. The dining room was dark. So was the library. It appeared that the baron had retired for the night.

Damn.

Octavius stood for a moment in the shadowy corridor, scowling, and then his thoughts slid sideways to that brief, sweet kiss.

He hoped it hadn't been a horrible mistake. He hadn't intended to kiss Miss Toogood tonight, but the moment had presented itself: the empty schoolroom, the empty corridor, the shadows and the warm glow of candlelight, the two of them alone together . . . It had been a moment of unsurpassed opportunity—a golden opportunity—the sort of opportunity that usually never presented itself, and he'd simply *had* to take it. To take the chance. To take the risk.

It had been stupid and spontaneous, and he hoped it hadn't been a colossal mistake.

It didn't feel like a colossal mistake. It felt like the beginning of something significant and life-changing.

He hoped it felt the same way to Miss Toogood.

Octavius slowly retraced his steps, along the corridor and up the main staircase. In taking his chance with Miss Toogood, he'd missed his chance with the baron. But it had been worth it. Everything that had happened since his arrival in Hampshire, every interaction with Miss Toogood, only strengthened his conviction that they were meant for each other.

He remembered the softness of her lips, the way her eyes had widened in surprise.

She hadn't stepped back, hadn't slapped him, hadn't called him a scoundrel or a knave or a lecher. She would have been within her rights to do any or all of those things, because it *had* been knavish of him to spend two evenings teaching her how to fend off unwanted advances and then to kiss her himself.

But she hadn't slapped him or called him names, so he was going to assume that while his kiss had been unexpected, it hadn't been unwanted.

Octavius grinned and hiked up his skirts and climbed the stairs two at a time. Unexpected, but not unwanted. Yes, that was how he was going to interpret—

Someone caught him around the waist when he reached the landing.

Octavius struck out instinctively, but his assailant was larger than him, stronger than him. He was lifted off his feet and shoved against the wall so hard that his head struck the paneling and he saw stars. "Ow!" he cried, and that high-pitched female voice shocked him for a moment, because it wasn't his. "Stop! Let me go!" He kicked out, just as he'd shown Miss Toogood, but his skirts were in the way and his attacker was crowding him. There was no space for a kick, let alone a punch, so he jabbed with his elbows and struck with his head and gathered his breath for a shout—

And then someone else was there, ripping him from his attacker's grasp, pushing him away.

Octavius stumbled and fell to hands and knees on the landing. Two shadowy figures faced off in the candlelight. *Dex!* he thought, but someone said, "Back off, Donald," in a low, fierce voice that was nothing like Dex's drawl.

Octavius blinked and shook his head to clear it. The shadowy figures resolved themselves into two men.

One was the baron's valet, the man who'd smirked last night and left him to his fate in Rumpole's bedroom.

The other was a footman. "Back off," he said again. His face was narrow and angular and as fierce as his voice.

Octavius climbed carefully to his feet, while the valet balled his hands into fists and raised them pugnaciously.

The footman did the same, and while he was

significantly thinner than the valet, he was taller and every bit as pugnacious.

For a moment it looked as if there'd be a fight— then the valet sneered and lowered his hands and stalked off down the corridor.

The footman waited until he was out of sight, then turned to Octavius. "You shouldn't be on these stairs."

"I'm sorry," Octavius said. "I got lost." He ventured a smile. "Thank you."

The footman didn't smile back; he frowned. "Did Mrs. Clark not warn you about Mr. Donald?"

Octavius had no idea who Mrs. Clark was, so he shook his head.

The footman looked him up and down. His frown deepened. "She doesn't usually hire girls like you."

Octavius glanced down at himself. His apron was askew, but he didn't appear to have ripped open any more seams. "Like me?"

"You're too pretty," the footman said. "You need to take care. If Donald catches you alone, he'll try again."

Octavius nodded soberly.

"Us footmen will help if we can, and Mr. Daley, the butler, but don't look to the baron for help. He's as like to tup you himself."

Octavius nodded a second time, even more soberly.

The footman looked Octavius up and down again. His mouth pinched tightly. "If you'll take my advice you'll leave this house first thing tomorrow morning. It's no place for someone like you."

Octavius had already come to that conclusion.

"The servants' staircase is that way." The footman pointed. "Stay away from the baron—and stay as far as you can from Mr. Donald!"

"I will," Octavius said. He gave the man a respectful curtsy. "Thank you."

The footman nodded curtly back.

Octavius walked in the direction of the servants' stairs, and then past them. He waited five minutes, then tiptoed in the opposite direction. He let himself into his bedchamber, frowning thoughtfully.

Dex was slouched in the armchair, looking bored, but he sat up as soon as he saw Octavius's face. "What happened?"

"I had a run-in with the baron's valet," Octavius said. "And I found myself a protector." He sounded as surprised as he felt.

"You found what?"

"A protector," Octavius repeated, locking the door behind him. "A footman."

"A footman?"

"He came to my aid when Rumpole's valet attacked me." Octavius took off his mobcap and apron and tossed them on the bed. "Apparently the housekeeper doesn't hire pretty housemaids. Have you noticed?"

"Can't say I have. Don't usually look at the maids." Dex leaned back in the armchair and smirked. "Pretty widows are more my thing."

Octavius snorted at that particular truth, then crossed to the mirror and twisted to see over his shoulder. "I didn't rip another seam, did I?"

Dex stood. "I bloody hope not. Mending your seams is not what I came to Hampshire for."

But another seam *had* been ripped.

"Damn you, Otto," Dex said, exasperated. "I told you not to try any more cross-buttock throws."

"I didn't. Rumpole's valet did this."

Dex's eyebrows came together sharply. "He what?"

"He was quite rough," Octavius said, and then revised this statement: "Very rough. And very fast. Very strong. In fact, I think . . ."

"You think what?" Dex said, as he began to un-button the dress.

"I don't think we've taught Miss Toogood enough."

CHAPTER 13

*P*ip watched the sun rise that morning, the sky filling with colors—a dozen different shades of orange and pink—and as she watched she felt uneasy.

Because of Lord Octavius.

Because of that kiss.

Had it been a joke? Or had it been the first step in an attempt to seduce her?

A joke, she told herself. *Definitely a joke.* Lord Octavius wasn't the sort of man to seduce governesses . . . was he?

She thought he wasn't, but she didn't *know* he wasn't, and so she watched sunlight spill across the parkland, tinting everything golden, and worried.

Lord Octavius's kiss had most likely been a joke—but it was imperative that she proceed as if it hadn't been, because if she was wrong, if he *was* attempting to seduce her, she could find herself in trouble. The sort of trouble that resulted in positions being lost and lives being ruined.

"I shall be courteous, professional, and distant," she told herself, and tapped the windowsill three times. The three taps made it feel like an oath, a vow she'd made to herself, something binding and unbreakable.

No more climbing trees. No more lessons in defensive techniques. And definitely no more wagers. Not if she wished to keep both her reputation and her position.

Courteous.

Professional.

Distant.

Strung together, the three words sounded like a protective spell. Pip ran them over in her head while she ate breakfast with the girls. If she could be those three things, then everything would be all right.

Even so, unease still lingered in her belly.

Lord Newingham and his friends appeared at the schoolroom door not long after nine o'clock. Pip's stomach tried to tie itself in a knot. She laid her hand on her desk and surreptitiously tapped three times with a fingertip, and the knot loosened slightly.

"What adventures do you have planned for us

today, Miss Toogood?" Newingham asked cheerfully.

"Rambling," Pip said. She smiled impartially at all three men, avoiding Lord Octavius's eyes.

"Rambling!" Newingham repeated. "Doesn't that sound just *too good*?" He winked at the girls, and they giggled at this pun on her name.

Edie and Fanny put away their books and they all trooped out of the schoolroom. For the briefest of moments, Pip and Lord Octavius stood exactly where they'd stood when he'd kissed her and she found herself wondering again why he'd done it—joke, or evil intent?—and then they were on the stairs, Newingham talking loudly with the girls, and Pip realized that it didn't matter what Lord Octavius's intention had been. All that mattered was that it never happened again.

Yesterday they'd explored trees; today they explored creeks. The girls took off their footwear and paddled, and the men did, too, but Pip couldn't bring herself to remove her half boots and peel off her stockings and hold up her skirts. She would have if Lord Octavius hadn't kissed her last night, but now she was afraid it might be interpreted as an invitation.

"Do come in, Miss Toogood," Newingham urged. "The water's just *too good*."

"Perfect, in fact," Lord Octavius said, with a hopeful smile, but Pip merely shook her head.

She saw disappointment on the girls' faces, and on Lord Octavius's face, too, as if he wanted her to paddle in creeks quite as much as he'd wanted her to climb trees yesterday, and that brought a flash of memory—holding his hand while climbing the perfect tree—and she knew she'd made the right decision.

No paddling. No climbing trees. No wagers. And definitely no kisses.

So she sat and watched while two children, a viscount, and two duke's grandsons explored a creek, turning over rocks and combing through reeds, looking for tadpoles and mayfly nymphs.

It was an unusual occurrence to see men without stockings. Pip tried very hard not to look at their legs, but it was almost impossible not to, given that they were all splashing around in a rather small creek. She pinned her attention on the girls and endeavored not to notice how muscular the men's naked calves were or how much hairier their skin was than hers.

"*Please* come in, Miss Toogood," Edie begged for the fifth time.

Pip shook her head. She would come paddling here with the girls once Newingham and his friends had gone, but today she didn't dare, because she didn't want to give a certain gentleman the wrong idea.

It wasn't safe for governesses to give gentlemen the wrong ideas.

After the creek, they rambled in the lanes and meadows. Three times Lord Octavius attempted to walk alone with her, and three times Pip moved closer to the girls.

They came to a stile. The men exchanged a glance, the significance of which eluded Pip until she found herself on one side of the stile with Lord Octavius, while everyone else was on the other side, scattering through an apple orchard, the girls shrieking with laughter as Newingham and Mr. Pryor chased them.

She set her foot hurriedly on the lowest step to follow, but it was too late: Lord Octavius blocked her path. "Miss Toogood, I apologize for last night." His voice was low and urgent. "It wasn't my intention to offend you or make you afraid of me. You must believe that!"

His expression was as earnest as his voice, his eyes were dark and intense, and he was so unmistakably contrite that any words Pip might have spoken dried on her tongue.

His brow creased at her silence. "Miss Toogood?" he said, and he looked even more earnest and even more contrite, as if he, a marquis's son, was afraid of what she, a mere governess, might have to say.

It scrambled her wits to have him look at her like that. Pip wrenched her gaze away and looked instead at the bottom step of the stile, at the gnarled wooden plank and the grass growing up around it, the daisies and the dandelions. "I'm not afraid of you," she told him.

"But you're not comfortable in my company, are you? It's why you didn't paddle with us."

Her gaze returned to his face. After a moment, she nodded.

His lips moved, forming neither a smile nor a scowl, but something sad and regretful. "I'm sorry. I shouldn't have kissed you. It was an impulse of the moment. You see . . . I've been wanting to kiss you since the moment I first saw you."

It took a few seconds for the words to sink in, and when they did Pip felt her cheeks go scarlet. "Me?"

Lord Octavius nodded. He gave her a smile that was wry and lopsided, but also slightly hopeful.

"Me?" Pip said again. "But . . . but *why?*"

"Because I like you."

Pip's heart was beating rapidly. "Thank you," she

said, in a stifled voice. "But I cannot . . . A dalliance isn't something I could ever contemplate."

Lord Octavius's eyebrows drew sharply together. "I should hope not."

"But . . . is that not what you mean?"

He looked quite affronted. "Of course not! My intentions towards you are wholly honorable."

"Oh," Pip said faintly. She stared at him for a long moment, while bees hummed and birds sang and the girls laughed in the orchard. "But you're a marquis's son."

His eyebrows twitched slightly upwards. "Yes?"

"Marquises' sons don't have honorable intentions towards governesses," Pip told him—and then she flushed scarlet again, because it sounded as if she thought that all marquises' sons were depraved seducers of governesses. "I beg your pardon. That came out wrongly. I mean . . . I mean that marquises' sons must marry within their own class, of course, and that governesses aren't suitable. That's all I meant. It wasn't a slur upon marquises' sons."

His lips twitched as if he was trying not to laugh. "Quite a few marquises' sons marry gentlemen's daughters," he assured her.

"They don't marry vicars' daughters."

"Sometimes they do."

"Not vicars' daughters who have to work for a living. Not governesses!"

He smiled at her, warmth in his eyes. "Only perfect governesses."

Pip found it impossible to look at him, not when he was gazing at her like that. She stared at the ground, at the grass and the dandelions. "I'm not perfect," she told him.

"No?"

She shook her head fiercely.

His tone became serious: "In case I haven't made myself clear, I admire you greatly, Miss Toogood."

"But you *can't*! You've only known me for three days."

"Three minutes was enough."

The words drew her eyes to him. Lord Octavius's face was as serious as his voice, all traces of amusement gone, his gaze steady and earnest.

Extraordinary as his statement had been—unbelievable as it was—it appeared that he truly meant what he'd said.

"But . . . I'm a governess, and I have red hair and freckles!"

"So?" He smiled at her and held out his hand. Pip took it without thinking. She climbed the stile before she even realized she'd done it.

They made their way through the orchard, following the sound of voices. Bees staggered in the air, seemingly drunk on pollen. Pip felt a little intoxicated herself.

Lord Octavius liked her?

He had honorable intentions towards her?

He'd admired her after knowing her for only *three minutes?*

She realized with a sense of shock that he was still holding her hand. It felt deliciously dangerous. Heat tingled up her fingers, up her arm, making her heartbeat flutter, and how could something that felt so exhilarating be so wrong?

Very easily, a little voice said in her head.

Pip carefully removed her hand from his.

Think, she told herself. *Think hard. Don't get swept up in a Faerie tale, because Faerie tales aren't real. If you make a mistake now, you'll have to live with it for the rest of your life.*

But she wasn't certain which would be the mistake: encouraging Lord Octavius's attentions, or spurning them. She didn't know him well enough to make such a decision. How could she? Three days wasn't long enough to form an opinion of a person's character. That took weeks. Months. *Years.*

But sometimes it only took three minutes.

They came upon Newingham, Mr. Pryor, and the girls. Edie was explaining something to the viscount. Her expression was animated; his was perplexed. He looked up at their approach. "Miss Toogood, can you please explain to me what the crawls are?"

"Crawls?" Pip said.

"It's something to do with a dole," Newingham said. "I think?"

"You mean the Tichborne Crawls?"

"Yes!" Edie said triumphantly. "You see, Uncle Robert, it's true!"

"What is?" the viscount said, still looking perplexed.

"Several centuries ago, Lady Tichborne crawled around an area of land," Pip told him. "Every year after that, the grain from that land went to the poor. It's called the Tichborne Dole."

"Twenty-three acres!" Edie said. "And she *crawled* it."

"How big is twenty-three acres, Uncle Robert?" Fanny asked.

"Um . . ." Newingham glanced around the orchard, and then at Pip, a look of hopeful entreaty on his face.

"One acre is ten square chains," Pip said.

"Yes," Newingham said. "One acre is ten square chains, which means that twenty-three acres is . . . um."

Pip came to his rescue again: "It will be easier to calculate if we can write it down. We'll do it at luncheon. We can work it out in yards, and then come out here and see exactly how big twenty-three acres is."

That was what they did, and the calculation occupied Pip's mind quite effectively. It was difficult to think about the honorable intentions of marquises' sons while one was wrestling with feet and yards, furlongs and acres.

Twenty-three acres turned out to be rather larger than she'd thought. More than one hundred thousand square yards. They paced it out up on the sheep-down and Pip tried to imagine crawling that far, but couldn't.

Neither, apparently, could the viscount. "Why on earth would someone crawl twenty-three acres?" He turned on his heel, surveying the area they'd paced out, and scratched his head. "It makes no sense."

"She was dying," Edie said. "She couldn't walk."

"Then it makes even *less* sense."

"It was so there'd be food for the poor," Fanny told him.

"Yes, I understand that," Newingham said. "But what I don't understand is why she had to crawl. Why not just put the land aside?"

"Her husband was a miser," Pip explained. "He didn't want to give anything to the poor. He said he'd only put land aside for a dole if she crawled it."

"He didn't think she could do it, but she *did*," Edie said. "I think it was very brave of her!"

"She was undoubtedly a heroine," Newingham said, smiling down at the girl.

"And as for her husband, I can think of several names for him," Mr. Pryor said, *sotto voce.* "Alas, none of them are suitable for present company."

Pip glanced in his direction, then her gaze slid past him and fastened on his cousin. Who was looking at her with warm admiration in his eyes.

She lost the ability to think, to speak, to move. Blood rushed in her ears and thrummed in her veins.

"Father says she wasn't a heroine. He says she was a fool. And he says her husband was a fool, too, and that he shouldn't have put the land aside. He says *he* wouldn't have put land aside even if Mother *had* crawled it."

Pip jerked her attention back to Edie, appalled.

"But she didn't crawl," Fanny said. "We asked."

"You asked your father?" Pip said, astonished. She'd thought the girls too afraid of the baron to ask questions of him.

"We asked Archie, and he said Mother wanted to leave a dole for the poor and that she *would* have crawled if she'd been able to, but she couldn't even get out of bed, and when Archie said he'd crawl for her, Father hit him."

Shocked silence met this statement.

"How . . . illuminating," Mr. Pryor said. For once, there was no humor in his voice. "Who exactly is Archie?"

"Our brother," Edie said. "But he's only *half* our brother, because we have different mothers. He's very old. Nearly twenty!"

"Is he now?" Mr. Pryor said. "And how old was he when your father hit him?"

"Father's hit him lots of times," Edie said.

"Yes, but this particular time—"

"Ten," Newingham, said in a constricted voice. "Archibald would have been ten."

"He'll be a baron one day," Fanny piped up. "And a bishop, too!"

Mr. Pryor looked down at her. "Will he?"

"Yes. He's studying to take his orders. He's going to be a curate first, and then a vicar, and then a bishop!"

"When he's a bishop Father won't hit him anymore," Edie said. "Will he, Uncle Robert?"

"No," Newingham said, in that same constricted voice. He didn't look happy. In fact, he looked like a man who'd just been confronted by an extremely unpalatable truth.

"One would hope your father wouldn't hit a bishop," Mr. Pryor agreed. "Where is your brother now?"

"Oxford," Fanny said. "He's very clever! He reads *lots* of books. Father doesn't like it. He says only namby-pambies read so many books, and then he hits him, so Archie doesn't come home much anymore."

"I see." Mr. Pryor looked as if he was clenching his jaw beneath his smile.

"What's a namby-pamby, Mr. Pryor?"

"A namby-pamby is a very clever sort of fellow," Mr. Pryor said. "The very *cleverest* of fellows."

Lord Octavius made a quiet sound under his breath. Pip glanced at him. His lips were pressed tightly together.

Newingham's lips were pressed tightly together, too. He looked out across the sheep-down, then gave a little nod and turned back and said, "I'm going to set aside twenty-three acres in Amelia's name."

Edie inhaled sharply. Her eyes grew big. "You are? Truly?"

"Yes," Newingham said.

Fanny clapped her hands and gave a little skip of delight.

"Do you want us to crawl it?" Edie asked, very seriously.

Newingham laughed, and reached out and tweaked the brim of her bonnet. "No, I won't require you to crawl it, but you may walk it with me if you wish. And your brother, too."

"I want to walk it!" Edie and Fanny both said at

the same time. Fanny clapped her hands again and gave another skip of delight. Excitement shone in her eyes and flushed her cheeks.

"Then we shall all walk it together," Newingham promised. "Let's practice."

They headed back across the sheep-down. The viscount took huge, comically long strides, and the girls laughed and ran to keep up.

Pip followed more slowly. Her gaze was on the viscount, but her thoughts were still caught up in the scene Edie had painted: Amelia Rumpole on her deathbed, the baron hitting his ten-year-old son.

"Well," Mr. Pryor said. "That was . . ." His voice trailed off.

"Rumpole is a despicable person and an appalling father," Lord Octavius said flatly.

"No argument there," his cousin said.

Pip didn't say anything. She couldn't. She was too horrified by the thought of a ten-year-old boy wanting to do something charitable for his dying stepmother—and being *hit* for it.

It appalled her. It enraged her. She wanted to storm down to Rumpole Hall and hit the baron herself.

"I wish I'd been there," Lord Octavius said. "I'd have punched the bastard. I'm tempted to do it now."

Pip glanced at him, startled by how closely his sentiments mirrored her own. It was as if he'd spoken her own thoughts aloud.

Lord Octavius caught her look and his expression changed abruptly. His cheeks went pink. "I beg your pardon, Miss Toogood. I spoke without thinking. My language—"

"Please don't apologize," Pip said. "The baron is exactly what you said. It wouldn't distress me in the slightest if you hit him."

Lord Octavius blinked at her, his mouth half open in surprise.

Mr. Pryor laughed. "Bravo, Miss Toogood."

Lord Octavius didn't say anything, but he did close his mouth. And then he smiled at her. It wasn't one of those charming, too-attractive grins; it was a small, wry smile, a smile that made her feel an odd sense of connection with him, as if they knew each other's innermost thoughts.

Lord Octavius's smile slowly faded, but he didn't stop looking at her, and even though he was no longer smiling, the sense of connection between them grew stronger. Pip's heart began to beat faster. She found it difficult to breathe.

"Hurry up!" a distant voice cried.

The moment of connection was broken. Pip felt a little lightheaded, as if her lungs needed air. She looked away, and found that the viscount and the girls had halted and were looking back at them.

She inhaled a shaky breath and set off across the sheep-down towards them, and somehow, as she walked, she fell into step with Lord Octavius. It wasn't something she did on purpose, it happened quite naturally, and even though he wasn't smiling at her or even looking at her, that odd sense of connection grew up around them again, the feeling that she and Lord Octavius were attuned to each other, not on a conscious level, but on an instinctive level, the sort of level that made people think the same thoughts at the same time and walk in step with one another.

CHAPTER 14

*T*he men dined with them again and afterwards they played card games. The disconcerting sense of connection that Pip had felt on the sheep-down persisted, sometimes strongly, sometimes barely noticeable, but always there. It was as if a thread had been tied between herself and Lord Octavius, invisible to the eye and yet *there,* a persistent tug on her awareness, so that even when she wasn't looking at him she knew exactly where he was and what he was doing.

She wondered whether he felt it, too.

The girls went to bed, and it was time for Pip's lesson in defensive techniques. The four of them went to the schoolroom. The men pushed the desks back, took off their tailcoats, rolled up their shirt sleeves, and took turns pretending to attack her.

Pip practiced jabbing their eyes and kicking

their knees and punching their noses, and while she jabbed and kicked and punched, the sense of connection between herself and Lord Octavius transformed into something different. Something physical. Every time they touched, her skin tingled. When she tapped his nose with her fist, it felt as if her hand had caught a fever. When he grabbed one of her wrists, his fingerprints burned so hotly she expected to see red marks bloom there.

It didn't happen when Newingham and Mr. Pryor touched her.

They practiced for an hour. The movements came much more naturally. Pip didn't have to concentrate so hard, which was good, because her awareness of Lord Octavius was distracting. She pretended to hammer Mr. Pryor's nose and then scream in his ear, but her eyes strayed towards the marquis's son leaning against the wall with his arms crossed. She mimed elbowing Newingham in the throat and gouging his eyes out with her thumbs, but her gaze strayed again and she thought how attractive Lord Octavius was when he stood like that, his shirt sleeves rolled up to show muscular forearms.

She wondered whether Newingham and Mr. Pryor would leave them alone tonight.

She wondered whether Lord Octavius would kiss her, if they did.

She wondered whether she would kiss him back.

She didn't wonder whether she *should* kiss him back. The answer to that was obvious.

Mr. Pryor seized her by both wrists. "Got you," he said, with a mock snarl.

Pip pretended to bite his hand, stamp on his knee, and kick him in the groin—and then she wondered whether the next time Lord Octavius kissed her he'd ask her to marry him.

That *was* what he'd meant when he'd said his intentions were honorable, wasn't it? Marriage?

"I'm crippled for life!" Mr. Pryor exclaimed dramatically, and tottered away to slump in a chair.

Pip's gaze skipped to Lord Octavius again, leaning against the wall, laughing at his cousin.

Did she want to marry him?

It was a simple question that required a simple answer—yes or no—and yet it wasn't simple at all. It was complicated and confusing.

Did she want to marry Lord Octavius Pryor? Did she know him well enough to make that decision?

Newingham stepped away from the wall, flexed his hands, and came at her, grinning.

Think about this very carefully, Philippa Mary, Pip cautioned herself, and then mimed punching the viscount.

Tonight, she wanted Lord Octavius. She wanted

his company and his smiles, his conversation, his laughter—and yes, his kisses. But would she want those things in five years' time? Ten years' time? Would she want them *forever*? Because that's what marriage was: two people together forever.

Newingham snatched her wrist. Pip didn't try to break that hold; instead she clubbed his nose with her free hand.

Newingham didn't release her wrist. He pulled her towards him and growled at her.

"Bite him!" Lord Octavius said.

Pip pretended to do just that, then she scratched the viscount's eyes with her free hand.

"You're getting good at that," Newingham said, and released her.

"Thank you," Pip said, but her gaze skipped to Lord Octavius again. It was his praise she wanted. No, if she were honest she didn't just want his praise, she wanted everything he could give her—his attention, his jokes and his teasing, his quiet confidences, his hopes and his dreams.

But wanting Lord Octavius wasn't the same as loving him, and even if she *were* in love with him, which she wasn't quite yet, that wouldn't necessarily mean that she should marry him. In fact, it would probably be better for them both if she didn't.

Newingham came at her again. This time he grabbed both her wrists.

Pip pretended to headbutt him.

Newingham released her instantly. "By Jove," he said approvingly. "You've become a dashed Amazon, Miss Toogood."

"Thank you," Pip said again. One of her hairpins had come loose. She anchored it firmly back in place and glanced at Lord Octavius.

When he proposed—*if* he proposed—she needed to make a sensible choice. A mature and considered decision. The best choice not just for herself but for them *both*.

She and Lord Octavius might walk in step without meaning to and they might occasionally think the same thing, but the truth of it was that they had very little in common. He would do better to marry someone whose background matched his own and she would do better to marry a clergyman.

Pip felt a pang of loss at that thought, because although she didn't love Lord Octavius yet, she *almost* loved him. A few more hours in his company and it would undoubtedly happen. He'd grin that too-attractive grin and she'd fall in love with him.

Newingham advanced on her again. Pip made a fist and punched.

"No," Lord Octavius said. He pushed off the wall and came across the room. "Not like that."

"Like what?" Pip said. It had been an accurate

punch. It would have struck the viscount's nose if she hadn't pulled back at the final instant.

"Look at your fist."

Pip did, and discovered that she'd tucked her thumb inside her fingers. She hastily rectified this error.

Lord Octavius shook his head and tutted reprovingly. "After everything we've taught you, Miss Toogood. It really is *too bad* of you." He frowned at her, but his eyes were laughing—and that was when it happened.

Pip's heart plummeted over a metaphorical cliff and it was done. The irrevocable fall. Love.

It swept through her in a wash of heat and an inability to breathe. She was *in love* with Lord Octavius. Not because of a too-attractive grin, but because of a frown and a pun and a pair of laughing brown eyes.

The sense of connection flared between them, blazingly strong. Lord Octavius's frown faded. The gleam of laughter in his eyes changed into something else. Something primal and intense. Dimly, Pip heard Mr. Pryor clear his throat and say, "Well, I think that's enough for tonight, don't you, Bunny?"

"Er, yes," Newingham said.

Lord Octavius said nothing. He simply stared at her with that strange, fierce intentness.

Mr. Pryor nudged him. "Otto, old chap, you're standing right where this desk goes."

Lord Octavius blinked and took a step back. "Uh, the desks, of course." Color rose in his cheeks. He turned and crossed to where the chairs stood against the wall.

With the furniture back in place, Pip had no reason to stay. She ought to bid the men good-night and leave; instead, she waited while they rolled down their shirt sleeves and donned their tailcoats because she knew that when Mr. Pryor and Newingham left, Lord Octavius would stay.

And he would kiss her.

And this time, she'd kiss him back.

Pip pretended to arrange the books on her desk. Her fingers were trembling and her cheeks were hot. Her heart felt as if it was beating faster than it had ever beaten in her life.

Someone knocked on the schoolroom door.

Pip's heartbeat went from gallop to standstill in an instant. She froze where she stood. Had Lord Rumpole come in search of his guests?

But it wasn't Lord Rumpole, it was a housemaid. "Miss Toogood? Are you ready?"

"Ready for what?" Mr. Pryor asked.

Ready to undo Pip's stays, but that was something Pip couldn't tell them, so instead she said, "Oh, is it so late? I beg your pardon, Jenny." She cast a brief glance at the men, not letting her gaze become snared by Lord Octavius. "Gentlemen, I must bid you good night."

All three men hesitated, and then Lord Octavius nodded and said, "Good night, Miss Toogood," and headed for the door.

" Good night," Mr. Pryor said. He sent Pip a faint grimace, as if to say, *Sorry*.

"Good night," Newingham said, too, and then, "That was, um, a useful discussion about, um, the girls' curriculum. Thank you, Miss Toogood." He gave an awkward nod and followed his friends out the door.

CHAPTER 15

*O*ctavius halted when he reached the stairs. Dex halted, too. So did Newingham.

"Close call," Newingham said.

"Unfortunate," Dex said.

Octavius just grunted.

Together they descended the stairs. Frustration growled in Octavius's chest. Damn it, he and Miss Toogood had been so close to a moment alone. Perhaps close to *the* moment.

"Billiards?" Newingham said. "Or bed?"

"Bed," Octavius said, directing a meaningful glance at Dex.

"Bed for me, too," Dex said.

Newingham sighed. "You really are a pair of old fograms." He shook his head at them, bade them good-night, and headed down the corridor to his bedchamber.

They watched him out of sight, then Dex nudged Octavius none too gently in the ribs. "You owe him more than a team of horses."

"I know."

"You owe *me*, too."

"I'll knit you a coin purse."

Dex snorted, and then paused. "Actually, I *do* need a new coin purse. Thank you, Otto. I would *love* you to knit one for me. And I'll watch while you do it."

Octavius elbowed him in the ribs, none too gently.

Dex winced, and rubbed his side. "I take it you want to go hunting?"

"I do."

Octavius's manservant was waiting for him in his bedchamber. Octavius sent him away with a "Shan't need you tonight, Staig," and locked the door after him. Then he stripped, changed shape, and dressed in the maid's clothing. Dex was correct: Octavius did owe him for his help. Not a team of horses, and not a coin purse, but definitely something.

He left Dex lounging in the armchair and headed downstairs, but Rumpole wasn't in the dining room or the library or even the billiard room.

"Damn it," Octavius said. The sound of a female

voice coming out of his mouth was so disconcerting that he actually twitched.

He made another pass of the ground floor, but Rumpole still wasn't anywhere.

"Damn it," Octavius muttered again.

He lingered on the main staircase for ten minutes, hoping Rumpole's valet would accost him, but no one came.

"Damn." He let out a frustrated huff of breath, trudged up the stairs, and headed for his bedchamber. Before he reached it, a door opened. Dex's valet looked out. "You, girl, empty this," he said, and thrust something at Octavius.

Octavius took the object instinctively—and discovered it was a chamber pot.

"Be quick about it," the valet said, and stepped back into Dex's room and shut the door.

Octavius stood in the corridor, frozen with horror.

He was holding someone else's chamber pot.

Someone else's *full* chamber pot.

He risked a glance beneath the lid. There was only piss inside, thank God.

He walked two doors further down, to his own room, gingerly holding the chamber pot at arms' length. Very carefully, he opened the door. Dex was sprawled in the armchair by the fire, looking bored. He glanced up at Octavius's entrance. His eyebrows lifted. "What are you doing with a chamber pot?"

"Your valet gave it to me," Octavius told him, disbelief and indignation mingling in his voice. "He told me to empty it."

Dex laughed. He didn't get up from the armchair. He waved one hand carelessly and said, "Well, empty it, then."

Octavius almost did, all over his cousin. The only thing that stopped him was the fact that they were in his own bedroom and the mess would have been on *his* armchair and *his* floor. He thrust the pot at Dex, making the piss inside slosh. "You empty it."

"Me?" Dex slouched even more indolently in the armchair. "I'm not a housemaid."

Octavius hissed at him through his teeth.

Dex laughed again.

"It's not funny!" Octavius said. "He's waiting for me to bring it back. Empty!"

"So, empty it."

"I don't know where housemaids empty chamber pots!"

Dex shrugged. "Swap it with a pot from an empty bedroom."

The idea was both simple and brilliant, and one that he ought to have thought of himself. Octavius headed for the door, and then halted. "I can't. One of the maids will get blamed for it."

"Honestly, Otto, your conscience—"

"I'm not going to leave a full chamber pot some-where that will get a maid into trouble," Octavius said. He crossed the room and shoved the chamber pot at Dex. "It's your piss; you get rid of it."

Dex smirked and made no move to take the pot.

Octavius placed it on his cousin's lap, a precarious perch, and released it.

"Oi!" Dex said, grabbing the chamber pot before it tipped over. "What are you doing, you idiot?"

Octavius ignored him. He crossed to his bedside cabinet, fished out his own empty chamber pot, and headed for the door. He stomped down the corridor to Dex's room, knocked on the door, and waited for the valet to answer. And waited. And waited.

He knocked again, more loudly, and opened the door.

The valet wasn't in the room.

Octavius put the chamber pot in the cabinet and marched back to his own room. He didn't bother to knock, just stalked inside, almost slamming the door behind him. If Dex was still sitting there, smirking—

Dex wasn't sitting, he was standing. He *was* smirking, though.

Octavius narrowed his eyes at him. "What did you do?"

"Emptied it out the window."

"You what?" Octavius crossed the room quickly and opened the window. The wall below was cloaked in ivy, from which the faint scent of urine wafted up. He slammed the window shut. "God damn it, Dex. They'll think I pissed out the window!"

Dex shrugged, unconcerned. "Don't tell me it's something you've never done."

Octavius couldn't tell him that, so he scowled at his cousin.

"What?" Dex said, lifting his eyebrows and spreading his hands. "No gratitude? I'd have thought you'd be pleased. I even dried it for you."

"What with?" Octavius asked suspiciously. "I swear to God, Dex, if you used my towel I'll strangle you with it."

"I used your dirty neckcloth." Dex gestured at the fireplace. A neckcloth lay smoldering amid the coals.

Octavius tried to feel outraged that one of his neckcloths had been sacrificed, but all he could feel was relief that the problem had been dealt with. He remembered that he hadn't locked the bedroom door and hastily rectified that error, then turned back to his cousin. "Thank you," he said grudgingly. "That was a good idea."

"Well, I am the smartest of us all," Dex said.

Octavius snorted, and unpinned the mobcap. "No, Sextus is."

Dex ignored him. "*And* the best-looking."

"That's Sextus, too," Octavius said, unfastening his apron. "But you're the most degenerate of us, I'll give you that."

Dex wasn't offended; he smiled smugly, and then he helped Octavius out of his dress. "Did you find Rumpole?"

"No." Octavius stripped off the chemise and changed shape. Magic flowed like pins-and-needles through his bones and over his skin. "Bastard must have gone to bed early. Damn it. I really felt like teaching him a lesson tonight."

"I've been thinking about that," Dex said, tossing him his nightshirt. "I think we're going to have to use magic."

"I have been using magic," Octavius said, hauling the nightshirt over his head. "What do you think this has all been about?" He gestured at the pile of maid's clothing.

"I think it's going to take both of us."

"How?"

"Fear of God," Dex said, and gave a little wiggle of his fingers.

Octavius's feet lifted off the floor. He grabbed at the air in a vain attempt to stop himself rising. "Dex!" he hissed. "Put me down!"

Dex ignored him.

Octavius rose higher, drifting upwards as if he were weightless. He warded himself off from the ceiling with his hands. "Put me down!" he whisper-shouted at his cousin.

Dex ignored him. He picked up the maid's dress and folded it, whistling a jaunty tune under his breath.

Octavius growled at him.

Dex continued to ignore him. He folded the maid's petticoat, and then the maid's chemise, still whistling.

Octavius tried to swim to the window so that he could pull himself down using the curtains, but he couldn't move from where he was—couldn't descend to the floor, couldn't make his way to the door or the window or the four-poster bed, couldn't do anything but bob there helplessly. "Damn it, Dex, put me down. I'm not in the mood for this."

Dex rolled up the maid's stockings. "How does it make you feel?"

"It makes me want to rip your head off your shoulders," Octavius snarled.

"Only because you know it's me doing it. If you didn't know that, how would you feel?"

Octavius stopped trying to fight Dex's magic. How *would* he feel if he didn't know his cousin was doing this?

"Terrified," he admitted. "Panic-stricken."

"Fear of God," Dex said, and placed the rolled-up stockings alongside the neat pile of clothes.

Octavius floated, his hair brushing the ceiling. "So . . . you're saying you're willing to hold Rumpole over a pit of flames?"

"No pits of flames," Dex said, firmly. "And no bodies of water, either. Even if you're not afraid of Grandfather, *I* am."

Octavius wasn't afraid of his grandfather, but he didn't want to disappoint the old man, or worse, incur his wrath.

"We can scare the innards out of Rumpole without pits of fire." Dex settled himself in the armchair again, crossed his legs, and gazed up at Octavius. "Doesn't matter where he is; if I do this, he'll be frightened."

"But it's not going to stop him from preying on women."

"No, it's not. That part's up to you."

Octavius crossed his arms and frowned down at him. "How?"

"That's the question, isn't it? It's a damned shame you can't take the shape of a mythological creature. If you could be Medusa and tell the baron you'll turn his balls to stone if he so much as looks at a woman again—now *that* would scare him."

Octavius chewed on this thought for a moment. "I could be someone really big, like the giants one sees at fairs, or . . ." He frowned. "But it would be better if I were female. More fitting."

Dex shrugged.

"Joan of Arc?" Octavius said doubtfully. "Boadicea?"

"There are lots of females you could be." Dex swung one foot idly. "Question is, are any of them sufficiently frightening? Would they scare Rumpole enough?"

A gorgon would scare the baron enough. So would a gryphon. But he couldn't become creatures that didn't actually exist in the real world—that had been the rule laid down by his Faerie godmother.

"I need to think about it," Octavius said. "Put me down."

Dex cocked an eyebrow at him.

Octavius gritted his teeth and then said, "Please put me down."

Dex gave that irritating smirk of his and lowered Octavius to the floor.

"Thank you," Octavius said, grudgingly.

Dex stood and stretched and strolled across to the door. "Night, Otto."

Octavius didn't reply. He was thinking. What female would scare Rumpole *enough*?

CHAPTER 16

*P*ip woke even earlier than she normally did. She stood at her window and watched as a hundred shades of gray gave way to the creeping colors of dawn. Sunlight tiptoed across the broad lawns, gilding the grass tips, and as the colors grew brighter so did her eagerness, until she was more eager for this particular day than she'd ever been for any other day in her life—eager to see Lord Octavius again, eager to hear his voice, to exchange smiles with him, walk with him, talk with him.

Today was a Sunday, a day for quietness and contemplation. Definitely not a day for kissing people one wasn't married to, but it might be a day for proposals, so Pip paid extra attention to her appearance, braiding her hair before pinning it up in an intricate knot, and choosing to wear not her second-best gown, but her very best.

St. Mary's Church, with its short Norman tower, was the church where the Reverend Gilbert White had once been curate. Pip didn't know what kind of preacher White had been, but she suspected he'd been an enthusiastic one. The present incumbent was not. Last week, she'd been disappointed, and worse, bored. She'd struggled not to yawn, struggled to appear alert and interested and to set a good example to the girls.

The baron hadn't bothered to set a good example; he'd simply fallen asleep, his chin pillowed in the stiff folds of his neckcloth. Even in sleep he'd looked dour and dissatisfied. Gravity hadn't been kind to his face, accentuating the petulant set of his mouth.

Today's sermon was as long-winded and hackneyed as last week's had been, but Pip couldn't find it in herself to be disappointed. Happiness hummed in her veins. The curate's voice was a dry, dusty monotone, the baron had gone to sleep, the congregation was bored and restless, but Lord Octavius was seated at the other end of the pew, and that was all that mattered. She couldn't see him unless she turned her head, but she knew he was there.

Lord Octavius Pryor, with his smiling eyes and his too-attractive grin and his honorable intentions.

Sunlight filtered through the stained-glass

windows, bathing the church in jewel-like colors—ruby and sapphire and emerald. Dust motes spun in the air like tiny flecks of gold, and it seemed to Pip that the little church was basking in a glow of sunshine and joy. The curate droned on, Baron Rumpole snored, the congregation fidgeted, and Pip's heart had never beaten so joyfully. She tapped her hymn book three times with a fingertip, not for good luck, but because she was so happy that it was impossible not to. *Once—twice—thrice, all is well in the world.*

After church, the baron returned to Rumpole Hall by carriage. Everyone else elected to walk the mile and a half. Pip's steps fell in time with Lord Octavius's without any conscious effort on her part. It happened quite naturally, as it had up on the sheep-down yesterday, and she wondered if it had been that way from the moment they'd first met and she just hadn't noticed.

Newingham and Mr. Pryor were engaged in a lively debate about the merits of a three-horse unicorn hitch, but she and Lord Octavius didn't talk. There was no need to. It was enough to simply walk side by side, exchanging smiling glances, while the girls gathered wildflowers and Newingham and Pryor argued about horse teams. The things she wanted to say to Lord Octavius—the things she wanted him to say to her—were too personal, too private, for a busy country lane.

When they reached the gates to Rumpole Hall, Lord Octavius paused and said, "I'd very much like to speak with you alone this afternoon. Will that be possible?"

Pip's heart felt as if it had grown tiny wings and was performing pirouettes in her chest. *Yes,* she wanted to say. *Yes, yes, absolutely yes!*

"Probably not," she admitted reluctantly. "The girls spend Sunday afternoons in the schoolroom."

His eyebrows quirked. "They do?"

"They write to their brother and work on the gifts they're making for his birthday. I could tell them we're doing something else, but . . ."

"But after what they told us yesterday, you'd rather they spent the time on their brother, because he deserves it."

"Yes," Pip said, relieved that he understood. "That's it, exactly."

Lord Octavius eyed her for a moment, and then smiled. "I was right. You *are* the perfect governess."

Pip felt herself flush. "Truly, I'm not."

"I beg to differ."

The warmth in his gaze—the approbation—brought even more heat to Pip's cheeks. She ducked her head and resumed walking, but an absurd little smile tugged at her mouth.

Lord Octavius fell into step beside her, past the carved stone gateposts and along the driveway. The girls had abandoned their flower-gathering, but Newingham and Mr. Pryor were still discussing horse teams.

Pip felt as if she was floating rather than walking, her feet not quite touching the ground, but her feet clearly *were* touching the ground because she heard the sound of gravel beneath her shoes.

The heat in her cheeks faded, but warmth lingered in her chest. The little smile lingered, too, plucking at her lips.

Lord Octavius wanted to speak with her privately.

He couldn't this afternoon, but somehow that didn't matter. What mattered was that he wanted to, and that, at some time in the future—perhaps tonight, perhaps tomorrow—he would speak to her alone.

And when he did, she knew he was going to ask her to marry him.

After luncheon, Pip set out writing paper and ink in the schoolroom and helped the girls to trim their quills. The room seemed ridiculously empty without the three men in it. How could someone's absence resonate so profoundly in a room? Particularly someone who'd been a stranger only a few days ago?

But it wasn't merely Lord Octavius whom she missed, it was Mr. Pryor, with his swagger and his smirk, and Lord Newingham with his unfailing cheerfulness.

If the girls missed their uncle, they didn't mention it. They were arguing about their letters.

"I'm going to tell Archie about the dole," Edie announced.

"But *I* want to—"

"You may both tell him about it," Pip said firmly. "But why don't you tell him about your uncle's visit first? Start with—"

"The kites!"

"Yes, the kites. And the tree-climbing and the creek, and then the dole."

Both girls settled down to write.

Pip decided to write a letter, too, to herself, as a way of ordering her thoughts and making sense of this strange upheaval in her life, this wholly unexpected act of falling in love. She laid out a sheet of paper, dipped her quill in ink, and wrote a burst of sentences. *I'm in love,* was the first one, at the very top of the page, and then, underneath that: *He's not at all the sort of man I thought I'd fall in love with. The exact opposite, in fact. But it feels so right that I can't doubt it.*

Underneath that: *He's asked to speak alone with me, and I know that when he does he's going to make an offer of marriage, because he told me his intentions are honorable.*

And under that: *I'm going to accept.*

I can't even begin to imagine how completely my life will change. I'll no longer be a governess; I'll be a—

Pip stopped writing. She looked across at Edie and Fanny, their heads bent over their letters, their fingertips already inky, eager and earnest and desperately in need of encouragement and love.

Pip looked down at what she'd written. *I'll no longer be a governess.*

She'd no longer be Edie and Fanny's governess.

She wouldn't be able to teach them confidence in themselves, or shelter them from their father's disapproval, or show them that they were worth something, that their thoughts and opinions were valued, that they were loved.

Slowly, she wrote: *I can't leave them. Not yet. Can I?*

Pip stared at those words until the ink dried on her quill, then she dipped it in the inkpot again and wrote: *I need to find someone who will care for them as much as I do. Someone who will be safe in this household.*

A stout, homely, middle-aged governess would be just the person. A governess who would mother the girls and whom Rumpole wouldn't look twice at. Although heaven only knew how Pip would find such a person, or how long it would take. Could she ask Lord Octavius for assistance? Would he be willing to help, or annoyed at her for laying such a task at his feet?

If I ask him to wait until I've found a suitable governess for the girls, will he be angry with me? Pip wrote.

I think that will be the test. The test of everything.

Because if Lord Octavius lost his temper, if he refused to wait, if he placed his own well-being ahead of Edie's and Fanny's, then he wasn't the man she wanted to marry.

But I think he'll wait, Pip wrote. *I hope he will. He wasn't angry this afternoon when I couldn't speak privately with—*

A light knock sounded on the schoolroom door. "May I come in?" Viscount Newingham asked.

"Of course," Pip said. She folded her sheet of paper and slid it into the top drawer of her desk.

Newingham advanced into the room, smiling. "Lord Octavius told me the girls are writing to their brother. I thought I'd join them. Write my own letter. Tell him about starting a dole in my sister's name, ask him to walk the land with us."

"Oh, yes, do!" Edie cried eagerly. "Sit between us, Uncle Robert!" She hurried to pull up another chair.

Pip found a quill and more paper and gave them to the viscount. He settled himself between the two girls and glanced at her. "My friends went for a walk in the rose garden. Perhaps you'd like to join them, Miss Toogood?"

Pip hesitated. "I shouldn't."

"I'll stay with the girls until you return," Newingham said. "Take your time. There's no hurry. I'm terribly slow at writing letters. It'll be an hour at least before I'm done." And then he winked at her.

Pip was so startled by that wink that for a moment she could only stare. Was the viscount assisting in an assignation between herself and Lord Octavius?

It appeared that he was, because he winked again, and said, "Run along, Miss Toogood."

It was almost an order, and Pip decided to take it as such. She left the schoolroom and headed for the stairs.

The rose garden, Lord Newingham had said.

Very well, she'd find the viscount's friends in

the rose garden, and no doubt Mr. Pryor would smirk and swagger off, leaving her alone with Lord Octavius.

And they would talk, and she would tell him that she couldn't leave the girls yet . . . and he would either be angry or he wouldn't.

Pip paused at the bottom of the stairs and tapped the banister three times for good luck. Then she took a deep breath and set out for the rose garden.

CHAPTER 17

*O*ctavius strolled in the shrubbery with Dex, waiting for Miss Toogood to join them. The stream burbled and the beech trees rustled their leaves and gravel crunched quietly beneath his feet. Ten minutes passed, then twenty.

"I don't think she's coming," Octavius said finally, kicking a lump of gravel into the bushes.

"Doesn't look like it. Sorry, old chap."

Octavius shrugged as if it didn't matter, but it did. He'd hoped Miss Toogood would join them but, obviously, perfect governesses didn't leave their charges, even when those charges were in the company of an uncle.

He suppressed a sigh.

Dex didn't tease him, which Octavius appreciated. In fact, there was a lot about his cousin that he'd come to appreciate in the past few days. Dex could be damned annoying, but he was also a good ally.

Octavius kicked another piece of gravel into the shrubbery. He owed Dex more than a coin purse for his help. Perhaps a pair of pistols by Manton?

But he'd give Dex a coin purse, too, just to see him laugh. Something pink. With tassels.

"Shall we try for Rumpole tonight?" Dex asked.

Octavius redirected his thoughts with effort. "We don't have a plan yet."

"So, let's make one."

He didn't want to think about Rumpole now. Not when he was waiting for an opportunity to propose to Miss Toogood.

But he was doing this *for* her, wasn't he? And not just for her, but for every female employed in Baron Rumpole's household.

He needed to think of a plan and then execute it. The sooner, the better. Tonight, if possible.

"It's a shame you can't be a harpy," Dex said. "Can you imagine that? An avenging harpy would scare Rumpole witless."

Octavius kicked another piece of gravel—and then halted. "I could be a lion first and then a person." He swung to face Dex. "That's how we'll do it: I'll be a lion first, to scare him, and then I'll change into a woman to deliver the message. And not just any woman; I'll be Justice!"

"What about your clothes?" Dex asked reasonably. "If you go from a lion to a person, you'll be naked."

Octavius deflated. "Damn." A lion would have been perfect. Then he had a thought. "What if you do the speaking? You'll need to be hidden nearby anyway, to lift him in the air. You can hide in a cupboard, and I'll be a lion and snarl and lash my tail, and *you* can tell him he'll go to Hades if he molests another woman." He paused. "Could you speak and hold him off the ground at the same time?"

"Yes, but I'm not going to."

"But—"

"He'll recognize my voice."

"You could make it deeper, or—"

"No, I couldn't. I'm not an actor. I'll hold him up for you, but you need to do the talking."

Octavius tried not to feel annoyed, but it was difficult not to.

They strolled for several minutes in silence, along paths dappled with sunlight and shade, then Dex said, "Are we going to punish him out of the blue, or wait until he tries to swive you?"

"Wait," Octavius said, without hesitation. "The punishment will be a direct consequence of his actions."

Dex nodded. "When, then? Daytime? Night-time?"

"Doesn't matter," Octavius said. He halted, then

211

ticked the points off on his fingers: "Rumpole needs to be alone—doesn't matter where or when, just that he's alone. I approach him as a housemaid. He accosts me. You lift him off the floor and hold him there. I turn into Justice and deliver the message."

"How will he know you're Justice?"

Damn. Dex was right. He needed to be someone the baron would instantly recognize.

An idea leapt into being. He considered it for a moment, and decided it might work. He imagined a man in his mind's eye—a man with his body and someone else's head and neck and vocal cords—and wished for it. Magic prickled over his cheeks and jaw, over his scalp and down his throat. His neck-cloth was suddenly too tight. "How about this?"

Dex recoiled violently, flinging up his hands as if warding off an attack.

Octavius laughed. It wasn't his laugh; it was Baron Rumpole's.

Dex lowered his hands and glared at him. "Dash it, Otto. Warn a fellow before you do that!"

"Scary?" Octavius asked, in the baron's voice.

"Horrifying," Dex said, averting his gaze. "Change back, for God's sake."

Octavius did. "You think that would frighten him enough? If an invisible force picked him up and he was then confronted by himself?"

"Yes," Dex said. "But remember, you'll be dressed as a housemaid."

"We don't have to start with me being a housemaid."

"Then he's not going to want to swive you, is he?"

Octavius scowled. Dex could be dashed annoying sometimes.

He kicked a piece of gravel, and then another, and thought.

Female.

Recognizable.

Scary.

Boadicea was no good, and neither was Joan of Arc, because he'd have to tell the baron who he was. He needed to be someone Rumpole would recognize immediately.

"How about a hag?" Dex suggested.

"A hag?"

"You know, an old crone. Withered and toothless."

"Which crone?"

"Any crone."

"Why would I want to be a crone?" Octavius asked, exasperated.

"Because you'd be female and scary."

Octavius frowned.

"If you change from a young woman into an old crone in front of the baron, that'll scare him. And then if I lift him off the ground and you tell him his testicles will fall off if he ever forces himself on a woman again . . ."

"It could work," Octavius said grudgingly. He envisaged the head he wanted: an old crone's, with wispy hair and skin pleated into a thousand wrinkles, sunken cheeks, a toothless mouth, deep-set and hooded eyes.

The magic failed to come—as happened whenever he overstepped the bounds of his gift, because of course a crone's head on the body of the man wasn't natural.

Octavius tried again, picturing not just an ancient face but a scrawny body, too. Magic crawled across his skin and through his bones. He was suddenly a great deal shorter and his clothes were voluminously large.

Dex recoiled even more violently than he had before. His hands came up in an instinctive *stay-away-from-me* gesture.

Octavius pointed an accusing finger at his cousin. "If you force yourself on another woman, your testicles will shrivel and turn to dust," he said in a fierce, quavering, old woman's voice.

Dex winced and took a step back, his hands still held up defensively. "That's scary, Otto. Trust me." And then he looked past Octavius and said, "Uh, oh."

Octavius turned his head. There, on the path behind him, stood Miss Toogood. Her eyes were wide with horror. He had an instant's flash of how he must look: a gnarled old crone wearing a man's clothing.

He changed back into himself.

Miss Toogood recoiled even more violently than Dex had done. She turned and fled.

CHAPTER 18

"Miss Toogood," Octavius cried, running after her. "Wait! I can explain!"

Miss Toogood didn't stop. She darted down one of the paths, heading for the house.

"Miss Toogood!" he cried, skidding wildly in the gravel, almost crashing into a camellia bush. "Wait!"

Dex shoved past him.

Octavius lost his balance and fell into the camellia's embrace. Branches scratched and poked at him. He fought his way free and launched himself after Miss Toogood—and almost bowled his cousin over.

Dex stood quite still in the middle of the path. Half a dozen yards distant, Miss Toogood also stood quite still—no, she wasn't standing, she was floating, a foot off the ground, her arms outstretched for balance, her hands clutching futilely at the air, her hem swirling gently around her ankles.

"Dex, what the devil?"

Dex rotated Miss Toogood until she faced them.

Her eyes were very wide. Her chest rose and fell in fast, shallow breaths. Her throat worked, as if she was holding back a scream.

"Put her down!" Octavius said.

"But—"

"*Put her down!*"

Dex set Miss Toogood on the ground.

"Miss Toogood," Octavius said urgently. "I can explain it all! Please don't run."

She took a wary step back, and he knew she was going to flee again. She'd just seen an old woman turn into a man. She'd been lifted off her feet and held prisoner in the air. And even though neither of those things was happening right now, she was still confronted by two men who were larger and stronger than she was.

Of course she was going to run.

Octavius awkwardly lowered himself to kneel on the path. He held his hands down by his side, palm-out, trying to look as harmless as possible. "Miss Toogood," he said quietly, but no less urgently. "Please, don't run. Let us explain. It's not what you think."

She took another step back. "You're demons," she said in a choked voice. He saw fear in her eyes, saw fear on her face.

"We're not," he said, even more urgently. "I promise you we're not! We're just men. Ordinary men—who have a Faerie godmother."

She shook her head, and took another wary, backwards step, gravel crunching softly beneath her shoes.

"It's true," Octavius said desperately. "We have a Faerie godmother and she gave us each a wish. I can change my shape and Dex can levitate anything. That's all. Nothing else. Nothing evil. We're not demons. I swear it."

Miss Toogood took two more cautious steps back. She was preparing to turn and run again.

"It was me!" he said. "In London! The housemaid with the blood on her apron. That was me."

Miss Toogood halted.

"I told you my name was Lucy, and you asked if I needed help. Remember?"

Miss Toogood eyed him, still fearful, still tense, but she didn't take another step back.

"It started at Vauxhall Gardens," Octavius told her. "I lost a race to my cousin, Ned, and the forfeit was that I had to go to Vauxhall as a female, and Baron Rumpole was there, and he tried to force me to have relations with him, and I wanted to teach him a lesson, so I went to his house and pretended to be a housemaid and he did it again, and I hit him and then I ran upstairs and met you."

He was speaking fast, almost babbling, desperate to make her understand.

"And you saw the blood on my apron and asked if I needed help, and you told me your name was Miss Toogood and I said mine was Lucy. Remember?"

He held his breath. After a moment, Miss Toogood nodded, a small, stiff, wary movement.

Octavius released the breath he was holding. "I came here for you," he told her. "To Hampshire. I came to keep you safe, because the baron's dangerous and someone has to stop him and I think we can do it—Dex and I. I think we can put the fear of God in him. That's what we were practicing: how to scare him enough to make him stop. I promise you we're not evil. We're not demons. We're just trying to find a way to stop Rumpole preying on women."

He was aware of gravel digging painfully into his knees, aware of Dex standing silently alongside him.

"Please, Miss Toogood, don't run. Stay. Stay and talk with us. Let us explain."

She shook her head, doubt and suspicion on her face, but she didn't take another step back.

"We won't touch you," Octavius promised. "And Dex won't levitate you again, will you, Dex?"

"You have my word that I won't, Miss Toogood," Dex said.

"We'll stay where we are and you can stay where you are and we'll just talk. You must have questions. You must want to know why we have a Faerie godmother and how it works and . . . everything."

He held his breath again, and waited.

Miss Toogood didn't look quite as frightened as she had before. Still wary, still mistrustful, but not completely and utterly terrified. She wasn't panicking as she stared at them; she was thinking.

"How do I know you're not evil?" she said finally. "How do I know you're not demons?"

"I give you my word of honor we're not," Octavius said. "We'll swear it on the Bible."

Miss Toogood looked unimpressed by these reassurances, as well she might, because they were just words, words anyone could utter whether they meant them or not.

Octavius looked at his cousin, helplessly.

Dex shrugged.

"We're not evil," Octavius said again. "We might be able to do things no one else can do, but we're not evil, I swear. I hope you can trust us enough to believe that."

Miss Toogood frowned faintly, but she didn't run.

"Grandfather made us give our words of honor that we'd never harm anyone with our magic, and he can hear lies, so he knows we told the truth." He paused, and then said hopefully, "Would you like to meet him? Grandfather?"

Her eyes widened slightly.

"Do you remember I told you he has strong opinions on hubris? Well, he also has strong views on how we use our magic, because his mother was more than a little mad and she wanted him to use his magic to rule England, and he refused, and he made our fathers promise that they'd never harm anyone with their magic, or aggrandize themselves, and he made us promise, too, so you see, we couldn't be evil even if we wanted to—which we don't—because we promised Grandfather and he can hear lies and he'd *know*."

Octavius paused, aware that he was babbling again, and also that he wasn't presenting his case very well. He took a deep breath, looked Miss Toogood in the eye, and said, very firmly, "We're not evil, any more than you're evil. But I can't prove it to you, except by telling you that the housemaid you met in London was me, and that I hit Rumpole because he wanted master's rights, and we came here to Hampshire to protect you—you and every female in his household—and to teach him that he doesn't have the right to force himself on his housemaids. Or on any other women."

He paused again, and waited for Miss Toogood

to speak, but she didn't. She was still frowning, but she looked thoughtful, not angry.

"Would you like to meet Grandfather?" he said again. "He'd like to meet you, I'm sure of it, and I'd like you to meet him."

She eyed him skeptically. "Why?"

"Because I want to marry you," Octavius said, and felt himself blush a little.

Miss Toogood stopped looking at him and directed her gaze at the toes of her shoes, instead.

"If you can bring yourself to marry a man who has a Faerie godmother," Octavius said.

She glanced at him, but said nothing.

"And I do think that talking with Grandfather would help, regardless of whether you accept my offer or not. He's very moral. He holds strong views on what's right and wrong. If you talked to him you'd see that even though we can do magic, it doesn't make us evil."

She studied him for a long moment, but still said nothing.

"Let's sit down," Dex suggested. "There's a bench over there, and I'm sure you have more questions, Miss Toogood. This all must seem rather peculiar to you."

Miss Toogood looked at Dex and then, after a beat, said, "Peculiar?"

Octavius could tell from her voice that she thought it a great deal more than merely peculiar. "Extraordinary?" he suggested. "Fantastical?"

"All of those things," Miss Toogood said, and his ears delighted in the dryness of her tone. *See?* he wanted to say to Dex. *She has a sense of humor even when she's afraid. Isn't she amazing?*

"It's more implausible than a gothic novel," Octavius said, relieved that she was speaking instead of running. "Isn't it?"

"Or a Faerie tale," Dex said, not to be outdone.

"It is a Faerie tale," Octavius said. "*Our* Faerie tale. And we should tell it to Miss Toogood before she makes up her mind about us."

Miss Toogood's eyes narrowed for a thoughtful moment. Her lips pursed slightly, then she nodded. "Very well."

CHAPTER 19

Octavius expelled a huge sigh of relief. He climbed to his feet and brushed the gravel from his breeches.

Dex walked to the bench and sat at one end. Octavius sat next to him, so close that their shoulders touched, leaving as much space for Miss Toogood as he possibly could.

After a moment, she followed them and perched at the opposite end of the bench. Three feet separated them.

Octavius kneaded his hands together nervously, realized he was doing it, and made himself stop. "What would you like to know?"

Miss Toogood eyed him, and then said, "How is it that you have a Faerie godmother? How are Faeries even *real*?"

"Truthfully? We don't know."

Miss Toogood frowned at this answer.

"But I'll tell you what we do know," Octavius said hastily. "We don't know how or why we got a Faerie godmother, or even when, but it happened centuries ago. She comes on our twenty-fifth birthdays and grants us one wish." He shivered in memory. "She's not nice. In fact, she's quite terrifying."

Miss Toogood's eyebrows lifted. "Terrifying?"

Octavius nodded. So did Dex.

"There are restrictions on what we can wish for. Grandfather sets boundaries, but Baletongue does, too—that's what we call her: Baletongue. No one knows her real name."

"I don't think humans are meant to know that Faeries exist," Dex said. "Let alone know their names."

Octavius continued: "Baletongue sets limits on our gifts. For example, I can only change into creatures that exist in real life. I can't become a gryphon or a hydra or a dragon. And Baletongue can't grant wishes that are too big, either. Our Uncle Tertius wished for an end to warfare, but Baletongue said it was beyond the extent of her powers. So he wished for no more famines, and she said that was beyond her powers, too. Then he wished for an end to slavery and she said she couldn't do that, either."

Miss Toogood frowned thoughtfully, and nodded.

"Grandfather's restrictions are different. He makes us swear not to choose wishes that harm anyone or raise us above other people, and that's because of his mother. Her wish went wrong and four people died, and Grandfather won't let anything like that happen again."

"How did it go wrong?"

He pulled a face. "She made a wish that Baletongue didn't like, and Baletongue punished her—and that's another thing you need to know about Faeries: they hate humans and if they can harm us, they will. One of our ancestors was deaf in one ear and she wished not to be, but she phrased it wrong. Instead of saying 'I want to be able to hear with both ears,' she said, 'I don't want to be deaf in one ear,' and Baletongue made her deaf in *both* ears."

Miss Toogood's eyebrows rose.

"It's true," Octavius said. "At least, we think it is. My great-grandmother had a journal that's been passed down through the family, and it's written in that. But Grandfather says we can't trust that everything in it's true. He can hear lies when they're spoken, but he can't see them when they're written."

Miss Toogood nodded thoughtfully.

"Our great-grandmother chose a wish that Baletongue didn't like, and the punishment was that Grandfather became Duke of Linwood that very day. But he was fifth in line, so four people died. Two of them were children."

"My goodness." Miss Toogood raised one hand to her throat. "Your great-grandmother must have felt dreadful."

Octavius exchanged a glance with Dex. "Actually, she was quite pleased to have that wish granted."

"Pleased?"

"She wasn't a very nice person. Grandfather says she had no conscience at all. But he does have a conscience, and so do we. All of us."

Miss Toogood lowered her hand.

"We know that how things are isn't how they're meant to be." Octavius gestured at himself and his cousin. "We shouldn't have what we have. Grandfather shouldn't be a duke. Dex and I should have to work for a living, go into the army or the church, but we don't because we've been lucky—at the expense of other people's lives. Children's lives."

Miss Toogood nodded soberly.

"Grandfather says we must never forget what happened and that it's our responsibility, as a family, to make certain nothing similar happens again. And we *will* make certain of it. All of us. And we'll make certain that our children do, too. And their children."

"Amen," Dex said, under his breath.

"Your grandfather sounds . . . admirable."

"He is," Octavius said. "He has more integrity than anyone I've ever met." He paused, and then added, "He is a little intimidating, though."

Dex huffed a laugh. "That he is."

Octavius looked at Miss Toogood hopefully. "Is there anything else you'd like to know?"

She pursed her lips thoughtfully. "So, everyone in your family has a magic gift?"

Octavius shook his head. "The wishes used to go to the female line only—for centuries it was only the women who received them—but Great-grandmother decided to transfer it to the male line. That was the wish that made Baletongue angry. She doesn't like humans and she particularly doesn't like men, so she punished Great-grandmother and killed four people. Except that Great-grandmother didn't think it a punishment."

Miss Toogood stared at him, a faintly bemused expression on her face. "Tell me if I've understood this correctly: it used to be only the women who got wishes and now it's only the men?"

"Yes." He waited a beat, and then said, "Is there anything else you'd like to know?"

Miss Toogood thought for a moment. "How many people know about this?"

"No one outside the immediate family."

Miss Toogood's head tilted slightly to one side. "How many is that, though? You're a large family."

"Our family's large now, but it didn't use to be. One daughter per generation."

"Uncle Tertius went back through Great-grand-mother's family tree and he couldn't find any other branches," Dex said. "To the best of our knowledge, it's just us."

Octavius nodded. "Our mothers know, of course, and Grandmother and Dex's sister, but that's it." He risked a faint, hopeful smile at her. "And now you."

"I find it hard to believe that no one else is aware of your abilities, given that you're so indiscreet about using them," Miss Toogood said, a little tartly.

Octavius felt his face flush. It *had* been extremely indiscreet of him to change his shape in the shrubbery. Grandfather would flay him alive if he ever found out. "We're usually very careful," he assured Miss Toogood. "Grandfather makes us promise to take every possible precaution."

He hadn't taken precautions today, though. He'd been rash and irresponsible.

"We thought you weren't coming," he offered as both an explanation and an apology. Or perhaps it was an excuse.

"Lord Newingham told me you were in the rose garden," Miss Toogood said.

Octavius shook his head. "Shrubbery." Curse Bunny and his sieve of a brain. This mess was all his fault.

Except that it wasn't Newingham's fault at all. It was his own stupid fault for changing shape in the shrubbery, where anyone might see him.

"What were you doing?" Miss Toogood asked. "Why did you look like . . . like *that*?"

"Because we want to scare the baron. I can't be Medusa or a harpy, so Dex thought maybe I could be a crone."

Miss Toogood's forehead creased slightly.

"We want to put the fear of God in him," Octavius explained. "I'll be a housemaid, and when Rumpole accosts me Dex will lift him off the ground and hold him there. I'll change into someone frightening and threaten him with a dreadful fate. Rumpole will think it's the hand and voice of God, and with any luck he'll be so scared he'll never do it again."

Miss Toogood nodded thoughtfully.

"We're having difficulty deciding who I should turn into. I need to be human, so I can speak, and female, because I'll be wearing maid's clothes, and scary, because we want to terrify him. A crone's the best we've come up with." He shrugged.

Miss Toogood thought for several seconds, and then said, "What about one of his dead wives? Or his mother?"

Octavius stared at her for a long moment, speechless, and then turned to Dex. "*That's* who I'll be. His wife or his mother. It'll scare the daylights out of him."

Dex grinned. It was a particularly wolfish expression. "I like it."

"There are portraits of both his wives in the gallery here," Miss Toogood said. "And his mother."

Octavius turned back to her. "You're the most clever woman in all England," he declared.

Miss Toogood turned ever so faintly pink.

"Are there any suits of armor here?" Dex asked. "Because I think we need a sword, too. To give our threat teeth."

Miss Toogood shook her head. "Not that I've seen, but there might be one somewhere."

"Doesn't matter if there isn't one," Octavius said buoyantly. "We'll scare the stuffing out of Rumpole."

"Rumpole, certainly," Dex said. "But what about the valet? We don't know what his mother looked like, or even if she's dead."

"Valet?" Miss Toogood said.

"Rumpole's valet attacked me the other night," Octavius told her. "Well, not *me* me, but the housemaid he thought I was."

Her eyebrows rose. "He attacked you?"

"Attacked," Octavius repeated, rubbing the lump

he'd acquired on his head when the man had thrown him against the wall. "He was more violent than Rumpole. In fact, of the two of them, I think the valet's the most dangerous."

"You do?" Dex said dubiously.

Octavius rubbed the lump again, remembering the speed and viciousness of the valet's attack. "Yes. Rumpole manhandled me at Vauxhall, but he thought I was a lightskirt. With the maids, he's used threats of dismissal rather than violence. But the valet grabbed me without warning and hit me hard enough to make me see stars. If I truly *had* been a female, I'd have been hard-pushed to fight him off."

There was a long moment of silence. Octavius heard bees humming in the shrubbery, heard leaves rustle in the breeze, heard the burble of the creek. "They're predators," he said. "Both of them, Rumpole and his valet, but one of them's a fat, old fool and the other one isn't. The valet's more dangerous."

"Then we should use a sword for the valet," Dex said. "Even if we don't use one for Rumpole."

"*Use* a sword?" Miss Toogood said.

"Only as a threat," Octavius hastened to clarify. "We won't hurt him. You have my word." Although the valet would undoubtedly be the better for a little castration.

"And my word," Dex said. "Grandfather would have our guts for garters if we used magic to harm anyone."

Miss Toogood studied Octavius's face for a moment, and then Dex's, and what she saw must have satisfied her, for she nodded. Octavius took a few seconds to study her, too. She didn't look wary or mistrustful any longer. She looked alert and curious. Interested.

Some of the tension in his chest eased. Interested was good, wasn't it? Interested meant Miss Toogood didn't think that he and his magic were evil.

Interested meant he still had a chance, that if he asked for her hand in marriage she might—possibly—consider it.

But he wasn't going to ask her today.

He might have been stupid enough to change shape where Miss Toogood could see him, but he wasn't stupid enough to ask her to marry him immediately afterwards. Not when he'd frightened her so badly that she'd run from him.

He rubbed his hands over his knees and said cautiously "So, are we good, Miss Toogood?" He didn't know precisely what he meant by "good," but Miss Toogood seemed to understand, for she nodded. Not a tentative nod, but a firm nod, the nod of someone who didn't think that he and Dex were evil.

More of the tension in his chest eased. "Would you mind showing us the portrait gallery?"

CHAPTER 20

$\mathcal{P}$ip looked in at the schoolroom, where she found the girls showing Lord Newingham the gift they were making for their half brother's birthday—a pair of embroidered slippers, the left slipper being embroidered by Fanny and the right by Edie. "By Jove!" Newingham was saying. "They're capital. Absolutely capital!" Then he caught sight of the three of them in the doorway. "Oh, hello. What are you lot doing up here?"

"We're going to look at the family portraits," Pip said. "Would you like to come?"

The viscount and the girls did indeed wish to come, so the six of them trooped down one flight of stairs to the gallery, a long, gloomy room hung with a great many portraits of a great many people.

"Here's Mother!" Edie cried, running ahead and pointing to a painting.

Pip had seen the painting when she'd first come to Hampshire, but she examined it again. There was the baron, with his scowling eyebrows and sulky mouth, stout and red-faced and unattractive, and there was his second wife, and there was his son.

"Lord, but she looks young," Mr. Pryor said. "How old was she when she married Rumpole?"

"Seventeen," Newingham said. His voice was grim. When Pip glanced at him she saw that his jaw was grim, too. "And twenty-one when she died."

She looked back at the painting. Amelia Rumpole's face was round and pale, her eyes hazel, her hair dark blonde. "Is this a good likeness?" she asked.

"Of Amelia? No."

Pip was aware of the Pryor cousins exchanging a glance. "Are there any other paintings of her?" Lord Octavius asked.

There were two others: one of Amelia Rumpole sitting at a writing table, looking insipid, and one of her holding an infant.

"That's me," Edie said proudly.

"I was there, too," Fanny said. "Inside her."

Mr. Pryor smothered a laugh.

"Which is the best likeness?" Lord Octavius asked.

"Not that one," Newingham said, with a gesture at the painting with the writing table. "Doesn't look like Amelia at all." He turned to the other portrait. "This one does, though." There was a note in his voice that Pip's ears identified as sadness. She glanced at him. He was staring at the portrait of his sister, the set of his mouth regretful. *He misses her,* Pip realized.

"Were you close in age?" she asked.

"She was four years older than me, but it seemed like more." Newingham hesitated, and then said, "My mother died when I was a boy. Amelia helped to raise me. She was more my mother than my sister."

"Archie says she was *his* mother, too!" Fanny piped up. "Even though she really wasn't. But she used to sing to him and tell him stories and cuddle him and kiss him good-night."

Newingham smiled down at the girl. "Your mother loved children, and she had the kindest heart of anyone I've ever known."

Pip examined the portrait. Amelia Rumpole hadn't been beautiful, any more than Newingham was handsome—their faces were too round, their noses too short—but they both had good hearts, and the girls had inherited those three things: round faces, short noses, good hearts.

She walked back to the portrait of Amelia Rumpole with her husband and stepson. Archibald

Rumpole had his father's sandy hair, but that appeared to be all he'd inherited from the man. He looked slender and timid.

He has a good heart, too, Pip thought, looking at the boy's pale face. Archibald Rumpole was going to be a clergyman, not a bully, and he wanted to help people, not harm them—and those things could probably be attributed to Amelia, because she'd been his mother for four years, and she'd loved him and shaped his character and taught him how to be compassionate, not cruel.

Someone came to stand next to her. She glanced sideways, expecting to see Lord Octavius, but it was Newingham.

"My father gambled away his fortune," he said, staring at the painting. "And then recouped it all by selling Amelia to the highest bidder."

Pip listened to the bitter note in his voice, and returned her gaze to the portrait. "When did your father die?"

"Six months after she married Rumpole." Newingham's voice was even more bitter.

Pip looked at the girl in the painting. "I'm sorry."

"Amelia's loss, my gain," Newingham said flatly. "I inherited a lot of money."

Pip considered that statement, then shook her head. "Archibald's gain, too. He deserved to have a loving mother, even if only for a few years."

Newingham was silent for a moment, then he said, "Yes, he did." He glanced at her and smiled faintly. "You're very wise, Miss Toogood."

Pip shook her head again.

Newingham looked past her, to where the others stood. He frowned. "The girls . . ."

Pip waited a moment. When he didn't speak, she prompted: "The girls?"

Newingham's frown deepened. "I wish . . ."

Pip never found out what the viscount wished, because Edie called out gleefully, "We're going to look for suits of armor!"

᥈᥈

They found two suits of armor, both carrying battle-axes. The axes were great unwieldy things with spikes for stabbing and huge, curved blades. Mr. Pryor prized one from the gauntlet that gripped it. "Oof," he said. "Heavy." He swung it in a short, wobbly arc, then exchanged a glance with his cousin and shook his head.

Edie and Fanny clamored to wield the battle-ax, too.

Pip opened her mouth to turn down this request—but Newingham beat her to it. "You have to be eighteen before you can swing a battle-ax," he said, loudly and cheerfully. "Law of the land." He winked at Pip. "But come and feel how heavy it is before we put it back."

Pip watched Newingham supervise the girls, letting them hold the great, blackened handle while the vicious spike rested on the floor. She hoped the ax had never been used in battle, hoped that no one had been spitted by that spike or hacked open by that blade.

"Do you wish to try, Miss Toogood?" Newingham asked.

Pip picked the ax up briefly—it *was* heavy—then gave it to Lord Octavius. He hefted it in one hand. "Nothing subtle about this, is there?"

Pip shook her head. No, there was nothing subtle about the ax. It was a tool forged purely to maim and to kill.

Lord Octavius wedged the ax back into the gauntlet's grip.

"What shall we do next?" Mr. Pryor asked. "I know! Let's explore the attics."

⬦

They spent an hour in the vast, dusty expanse of the Rumpole attics. There were no more suits of armor and no swords. When the last corner had been investigated and the last trunk prized open, the girls went back to the schoolroom to embroider slippers and the men went downstairs to read newspapers or play billiards or whatever it was that young noblemen did on Sunday afternoons. Pip sat at her desk and tried to marshal her thoughts into some kind of order. They felt as tangled as a briar patch, and it wasn't just her thoughts that were tangled; her emotions were, too. This new knowledge was simply too huge and too shocking to make sense of.

Magic was real? Faerie godmothers actually existed?

Impossible, said a voice in her head. But it wasn't impossible because she'd seen it with her own eyes. She'd experienced it. Mr. Pryor had picked her up without touching her and held her in the air.

Pip sat at her desk, while her thoughts spun in a chaotic whirl. Slowly the different strands began to unsnarl themselves. The events in the shrubbery— the shock of seeing Lord Octavius change shape, the terror she'd felt when Mr. Pryor had caught her with his magic—those things were one strand. A jagged and rather unsettling strand.

The revelations about the Pryor family legacy was another strand.

They had a Faerie godmother? And a great-grandmother who'd wanted them to rule England?

That was a strand she wanted to know more about. She wanted to read the journal they'd spoken of and she wanted to talk with Lord Octavius further, perhaps even speak with the grandfather he was so in awe of, because it was all so inconceivable and so fascinating and she had a thousand questions she wanted to ask.

Pip almost reached for paper and a quill and began listing her questions, but if she started she'd never stop, and there were other strands she needed to untangle first.

The revelation about Lord Octavius's run-ins with Lord Rumpole was one of those strands, and his encounter with the valet was another. Lord Octavius had called that encounter an *attack*. A violent attack.

Those strands felt thick and prickly and un-comfortable in her head. That such things had happened! That she lived in a household with two such unspeakable men! But uncomfortable or not, those strands were easily tidied away, because Lord Octavius and Mr. Pryor were going to take care of the baron and his valet.

That thought led her down another looping strand, one that quite canceled out the terror of seeing Lord Octavius change shape and the panic of being caught by Mr. Pryor.

Lord Octavius and Mr. Pryor were going to stop Rumpole and his valet *by using magic.*

That felt . . . not disturbing at all. On the contrary, it felt intriguing. A little exciting.

She wanted to know more about their plan—how exactly were they going to scare Rumpole and his valet into good behavior?—but there was still one very important strand to unravel first: her feelings for Lord Octavius.

Pip looked across the schoolroom. Edie and Fanny sat side by side at the worktable, diligently sewing colored beads on their half brother's slippers.

She let her eyes rest on their bent heads for a moment, then gazed past them to the long bank of windows.

How had this afternoon changed her feelings for Lord Octavius?

Had it changed her feelings for him?

She felt as if it ought to have changed them. Lord Octavius wasn't the man she'd thought he was, except that . . . he *was.* Her knowledge of him might have changed, but he hadn't changed. He was exactly the same man he'd been yesterday. All that was different was that she knew his secret. His huge, shocking, unbelievable secret.

But even if his secret was huge and shocking, it didn't actually alter her opinion of him. He was still patient and kind and good-natured. He was still a man who didn't swagger or smirk, a man who taught little girls how to make kites and how to climb trees, a man who had honorable intentions towards governesses.

Pip considered this for several minutes, and decided that discovering Lord Octavius's secret *had* changed her opinion of him, because Lord Octavius had come to Hampshire to deal with Baron Rumpole. He'd come here for that express purpose.

Which made him more than a little heroic.

CHAPTER 21

The men dined with them in the nursery and then they all played jackstraws. Pip probably ought to have read from the Bible given that it was a Sunday, but her father had allowed gentle entertainments on Sundays, and anyway, what was the harm in jackstraws and laughter? It did the girls good. It did them *all* good.

After the girls had gone to bed, Newingham stirred the jackstraws on the table. He was frowning. Not the frown of mock outrage that he'd worn when Fanny had beaten him yet again, but a real frown. "I wish . . ." he said.

Mr. Pryor leaned back in his chair. "What?"

The frown on Newingham's face deepened, pulling his eyebrows together. He pursed his lips, then shook his head.

"Out with it, Bunny," Lord Octavius said.

"I wish the girls didn't live with Rumpole."

There was a moment of silence, and then Mr. Pryor said, "He's their father."

"I know." Newingham pushed aside the pile of jackstraws. "I know that. I just . . . He was vile to Amelia, and he's going to be vile to the girls, too, and I just . . . wish they didn't have to live with him."

No one said *He's their father* again, but Pip thought they were all thinking it. "Could you become their guardian?" she asked.

Newingham shook his head. "He wouldn't let them visit me because I'm a bachelor. He's sure as blazes not going to give me guardianship." He rubbed his brow. "What about a boarding school? Do you know of any good ones, Miss Toogood?"

"I've heard of some schools," she said, "but I can't speak as to how good they are. It's something that could certainly be looked into."

"You think Rumpole would pay to send his daughters to a good school?" Lord Octavius asked. He began to gather up the scattered jackstraws. "He'd probably ship them off to one of those York-shire schools and call it good riddance."

Pip had heard of Yorkshire schools. They were notoriously brutal. She repressed a shiver.

"*I* would pay for it," Newingham said. "I'd pick the school and I'd pay for it and I'd call it a gift, and Rumpole wouldn't have any say in the matter except to give permission, which he'd do . . . don't you think?" He looked at Pip, a hopeful expression on his face. "An education for his daughters that he doesn't have to pay for? He'd jump at it!" And then he said, more tentatively, "Don't you agree, Miss Toogood?"

"I can't imagine he'd refuse, unless he did so out of spite." Which was something she *could* see the baron doing. "But it would need to be a school where the girls would thrive. They've very shy. They need kindness and encouragement. The wrong school would crush them."

Too late, Pip realized that she should have phrased that as a suggestion. It had sounded as if she, a mere governess, was telling a viscount what to do.

But Newingham didn't appear to mind. "Will you help me select the school?"

Pip nodded. "I'll write some letters, ask for some recommendations."

Newingham beamed at her.

Once the jackstraws were put away, they repaired to the schoolroom for a lesson in defensive techniques. With Lord Octavius's description of the valet's attack in mind, Pip practiced diligently, and perhaps Lord Octavius had been thinking of the valet, too, for after she had broken Mr. Pryor's nose and gouged out his eyes, he said, "There's something else I'd like to show you."

"There is?"

"This is a choke hold." Lord Octavius stepped up behind his cousin and hooked one arm around his neck. "How do you think you'd get out of it?"

Pip examined the hold. Mr. Pryor couldn't bite his cousin when he was held like that, or kick or punch easily. "Elbow him in the stomach?" she suggested. "Stamp on his foot?"

"Those are both possibilities." Lord Octavius released his cousin and beckoned to her. "Come see what it feels like."

Pip cautiously stepped forward.

Lord Octavius had rolled up his shirt sleeves earlier. Now he unrolled them and came to stand behind her. He angled one arm around her neck, not as tightly as he'd done with his cousin, but still tightly enough that it made her feel trapped. All Pip's senses sprang to full alert. She felt a faint frisson of fear and a stronger frisson of awareness at how *close* Lord Octavius was. Close enough for her to smell clean linen and soap. Close enough to hear his breathing. Almost close enough to feel his heart beating. His arm was pressed against her throat, a strong and inexorable barrier, his linen sleeve warm and rumpled against her skin. Her back wasn't pressed to his chest, but it *almost* was, and that thought made her shiver.

"If someone ever does this to you, they'll hold you much more tightly." Lord Octavius flexed his arm. For a second Pip felt uncomfortable pressure on her throat. Her heartbeat accelerated, the frisson of fear blooming into something close to panic, and then the pressure eased.

"What's your first instinct when you're held like this?" Lord Octavius asked.

Pip was conscious of two conflicting instincts. A small and wholly inappropriate instinct urged her to press herself back against Lord Octavius's chest, to get closer to him. The second instinct—which was much stronger—demanded she do the exact opposite. It didn't like that arm around her throat, didn't like the sense of being trapped and helpless, of knowing her breath was dependent on someone else. That was the instinct Lord Octavius was talking about, so Pip tugged on his arm—which didn't move. Next, she tried to elbow him in the stomach, but Lord Octavius stepped to one side, pulling her with him, forcing her to take several backwards, off-balance steps. Pip tugged on his arm again and stamped, trying to find his foot, but again he moved aside.

"Our cousin Ned used to do this a lot," Lord Octavius said, his voice almost in her ear. "Wasn't a day went past when he didn't catch one or other of us like this."

Mr. Pryor snorted. "Most annoying six months of my life. Idiot didn't stop doing it until Sextus broke his arm."

"Ned broke Sextus's arm?" Newingham asked, his eyebrows lifting.

"No, Sextus broke Ned's arm."

Newingham's eyebrows climbed even higher. "He did?"

Mr. Pryor nodded. "And not about time. I was about ready to break Ned's damned *neck*." Which statement he followed with, "Begging your pardon, Miss Toogood."

The swearword didn't bother Pip, but Lord Octavius's arm did. She wanted it gone, wanted the freedom to move as she pleased, to breathe without that pressure on her throat. *Let me go!* she almost demanded, but she had just enough pride not to. "How does one get out of a choke hold?" she asked instead. Her pulse was agitated, but her voice was calm.

"Sextus did it by tipping them both down the stairs," Mr. Pryor said.

Newingham gave a huff of laughter. "Is that how Ned broke his arm?"

"It was," Mr. Pryor said, grinning. "Most effective, it was, too. Ned hasn't tried to put anyone in a choke hold since."

"A broken arm will do that to you," Lord Octavius said, dryly, and then he said, less dryly, "But I don't recommend trying to do that, Miss Toogood, if you're ever attacked on a staircase. It's too dangerous. You could kill yourself."

"How, then?" Pip asked, resisting the urge to tug uselessly on his arm again.

"A couple of ways," Lord Octavius said, at the same time that Mr. Pryor said, "Fingers."

Pip gave in to the urge to tug on Lord Octavius's arm again, feeling the power in the muscles, the sheer implacable strength. Then she sought out his fingers. They weren't easy to find, nor was it easy to get a grip on one.

"If you can get hold of a finger and yank hard enough, you'll dislocate it, perhaps even break it," Lord Octavius said. "He'll release you in a jiffy." He did just that: releasing Pip and stepping to one side. "Then you either run or fight—depending on what your attacker is doing."

Pip nodded and rubbed her throat, not because it hurt, but because being held like that had been deeply uncomfortable. "What's the other way?"

Lord Octavius beckoned to his cousin. "Put me in a choke hold, Dex."

Mr. Pryor obliged, pushing away from the wall and hooking his arm around his cousin's throat.

"Arm's too strong for me to break the hold." Lord Octavius demonstrated, tugging as futilely on Mr. Pryor's arm as Pip had tugged on his.

Pip nodded.

"It's my chin that stops me sliding out of the hold, can you see that? Gets hooked up on Dex's arm."

Pip nodded again.

"But if I turn my head to the side . . . Watch."

Pip watched in utter astonishment as Lord Octavius turned his head until his chin lined up with his shoulder, gave what looked like a little tug on his cousin's arm, bent his knees, and dropped out of the hold.

He rose to his full height, grinning. "Like that."

Pip stared at him, realized her mouth was open, and closed it.

"By Jove," Newingham said. "That's something, that is. May I try?"

Newingham had a go, and Pip did, too, and then Lord Octavius said, "You don't always need to turn your chin to get free. Let's show them, Dex."

The two cousins set themselves up again.

"Here, where the elbow is, there's a tiny bit of

space." Lord Octavius pointed to the crook of his cousin's elbow. "Tuck your chin down into it, pull on his arm, and sometimes you can squeeze out that way. An inch is all you need." He demonstrated—tucking his chin, tugging on Mr. Pryor's elbow, gaining that precious inch of space, and dropping out of the hold.

Pip and the viscount practiced that, too. When they'd both done it several times, Lord Octavius said, "Sometimes none of those things work, but the thing is, Miss Toogood, if someone has you in a choke hold they're going to expect you to do nothing more than kick and flail. As long as you don't panic, you've got a good chance of getting away."

Pip nodded.

"Right, one last hold. Dex, come here."

Mr. Pryor did.

Lord Octavius stepped up behind him and swiftly took him in another hold, hooking his arms under his cousin's armpits, then up and back until his hands were clasped behind his cousin's neck. Mr. Pryor's head was bent forward, his arms stuck out at an awkward angle, and he looked utterly helpless.

"How would you get out of this?" Lord Octavius asked.

Mr. Pryor definitely couldn't bite or punch or even scratch, not held like that. "Kick," Pip said, and beside her Viscount Newingham nodded.

Lord Octavius shook his head and grinned. "It's really quite simple. Show them, Dex."

Mr. Pryor raised his arms and bent his knees at the same time—and slid free. Pip blinked, unable to believe it had happened at all, let alone so swiftly and easily.

"Want to try?" Lord Octavius said.

Pip most definitely did.

"Stand with your back to me. I'll do it slowly . . . my arms go under yours . . . then I reach up and interlock my fingers behind your neck . . ."

Several of the seams around her shoulders protested loudly.

"Sorry," Lord Octavius said, loosening his grip. "Is that better?"

"Yes," Pip managed to get out in a choked voice. Her seams no longer felt quite so close to bursting, but even held loosely the hold was quite incapacitating. Her head was pushed forward, her arms flapped uselessly, and she felt quite immobilized.

"Drop down in a crouch and lift your arms up at the same time," Lord Octavius told her. "You'll slide right out."

It seemed impossible, but Pip bent her knees and let her body weight take her down while her arms went up . . . and an instant later she was free.

"Bravo, Miss Toogood!" the viscount said, clapping.

Pip felt her cheeks flush with a mixture of satisfaction, pleasure, and triumph.

She and Newingham took turns escaping the hold, and after she'd successfully freed herself for the third time, she asked, "Did your cousin do this to you, too?"

"For about a week," Mr. Pryor said. "Until we figured out how to get out of it. We done, Otto? Let's put the furniture back in place."

Pip helped move the chairs and the desks, but she couldn't stop thinking about the holds they'd just practiced and why Lord Octavius and Mr. Pryor knew how to get out of them.

"Why the frown?" Lord Octavius asked.

Pip hesitated, and then said, "Your cousin . . . the one who used to catch you in those holds . . . is he a bully?"

"Ned?" Lord Octavius laughed and shook his head. "No, he's just a big, clumsy oaf who likes to tease people. I say, Dex, would you call Ned a bully?"

"No, but he *is* an idiot."

Newingham snorted a laugh. "Do you remember that time he fell in the Serpentine?"

"Which time?" Lord Octavius said dryly. "He's done it twice." Then he smiled down at her and said, "Does that set your mind at rest?"

"Yes." Pip lost herself in his gaze for a moment,

until a laugh and a muffled grunt made her look around. Newingham and Mr. Pryor were rough-housing, grappling with each other.

"Don't break the furniture, you idiots," Lord Octavius told them. He shook his head. "I apologize for my cousin, Miss Toogood. He's—"

There came a loud thud. The floorboards shook beneath Pip's feet. She turned and saw Viscount Newingham sprawled on the floor.

"What the devil?" Lord Octavius said.

"Cross-buttock throw," Mr. Pryor said with a smirk.

"For God's sake, Dex, they probably felt that all the way down in the cellar." Lord Octavius held out his hand to the viscount. "You all right, Bunny?"

"Caught me unawares," Newingham said, climbing to his feet. "Wouldn't have thrown me otherwise." He brushed himself down, then said, "Rematch?"

"Not in here." Lord Octavius pointed at the door. "Out, the pair of you."

CHAPTER 22

"Could I do that?" Pip asked, once Mr. Pryor and Lord Newingham had departed, grumbling.

Lord Octavius shook his head. "Probably not. It's almost impossible for a woman to throw a man. You don't have the height or the weight." He glanced around, as if to check that the schoolroom was indeed empty, then lowered his voice and said, "I did throw the baron the other night, but it wasn't easy. Only managed it because I've been doing it for years."

"You did *that* to the baron?" Pip said, gesturing at the spot where Newingham had fallen.

Lord Octavius nodded. "Laid him out on the floor, then poured a ewer of water over him."

Pip opened her mouth, found herself speechless, and closed it again.

Lord Octavius grinned. "I'll show you how it's

done, shall I?" He took hold of her wrist. "You grab and pull, and as you pull you twist. Like this, see? And then you throw them over your hip." He didn't go so far as to throw her over his hip, but he did pull and twist—gently—and even done gently it tipped Pip off balance. She caught herself by placing her free hand on Lord Octavius's chest, then snatched it back, because placing one's hand on a man's chest wasn't at all proper, even if the man in question was going to ask one to marry him, then put it back because she *did* need it for balance.

She looked at her fingers resting on his silk damask waistcoat, then risked a glance at his face.

Lord Octavius was watching her. His gaze was intent. Unnervingly intent. Spine-tinglingly intent.

Heat flared in Pip's body, and alongside it, nervousness. It became impossible to swallow, almost impossible to breathe. Her heart began to beat exceedingly fast. She was intensely aware that they were almost embracing, intensely aware of his fingers around her wrist, the heat of skin against skin.

She ought to step back. It was what a respectable governess would do. But she didn't feel like a respectable governess right at this moment; she felt like a woman who wanted to be kissed by the man she was in love with.

Lord Octavius must have discerned this, for he

bent his head and skimmed his lips over hers. It was the lightest and briefest of kisses, and yet it made her heartbeat stutter.

He raised his head and looked at her, assessing her reaction.

Pip smiled shyly at him.

Lord Octavius smiled back, and kissed her again, a kiss that was still light, but not quite as brief. She felt his lips, soft and warm, felt his breath against her cheek, felt her pulse skip and jump with delight.

Lord Octavius was kissing her. Kissing her properly. And not merely one kiss but many, a full dozen of them laid in a delicious, tingling path from one corner of her mouth to the other, as if he was mapping its shape. Then his tongue touched her lower lip in a tiny and intimate caress. It felt startlingly good. Pip gave an involuntary shiver of pleasure and parted her lips.

Lord Octavius released her wrist and gathered her to him. His arms were around her, but this wasn't a hold Pip wanted to break. She clutched his waistcoat and pressed even closer. His tongue caressed her lower lip again and then dipped briefly into her mouth, an intimacy that was even more startlingly wonderful.

Pip's pulse thundered in her ears. She felt as if she was Sleeping Beauty being kissed awake by her prince, as if she'd been asleep her whole life and now, suddenly, she wasn't just awake, but *alive,* blood racing in her veins, heat spilling over her skin.

Lord Octavius didn't stop kissing her until they were both out of breath. Reluctantly, their lips parted. Reluctantly, they eased their embrace. Pip stared up at him. His cheeks looked as hot as hers felt. His eyes were hot, too. Hot and dark.

He hadn't quite released her and she hadn't quite released him. His hands rested lightly at her waist; her fingers still clutched his waistcoat. Pip knew she ought to step back, but she didn't want to. She wanted to stand here, toe to toe with Lord Octavius, face hot, lips tingling, forever.

"Will you marry me?" he asked—and then he winced and stepped back, releasing her. "I beg your pardon, Miss Toogood. It's too soon after what happened in the shrubbery. I know I shouldn't—"

"Yes," Pip said.

Lord Octavius stopped speaking, his mouth open, a word half formed on his lips, and then his eyebrows quirked, as if he couldn't quite believe his ears.

"Yes," Pip said again.

The expression of disbelief on his face transformed into something bright and hopeful. "Yes, you'll marry me?"

"Yes, I'll marry you," Pip confirmed.

Lord Octavius uttered a joyful laugh, then picked her up by the waist and swung her in an exuberant, dizzying circle.

Pip clung to his shoulders. He laughed again, and she laughed, too, giddy with happiness, giddy with love.

Lord Octavius swung her around one more time, then set her carefully on her feet. "You're quite certain?" he asked, his hands still at her waist.

"I'm quite certain."

He smiled down at her and Pip smiled back, and for a moment she almost felt lightheaded. How had something so extraordinary happened? A week ago she hadn't even known of his existence, and now she was going to marry him.

Someone knocked loudly on the schoolroom door. They sprang apart.

The door opened and Mr. Pryor poked his head into the room. "Thought I'd find you both still here," he said, with a smirk.

A hot rush of embarrassment flooded Pip's cheeks.

"What do you want?" Lord Octavius said.

"Are we going to teach Rumpole his lesson tonight?" Mr. Pryor asked. "Or had you forgotten about him?"

Lord Octavius's expression became rather sheepish. Clearly, he had forgotten.

"Baron Rumpole," Mr. Pryor said, in an annoyingly pedantic voice. "The villain of this piece, who needs to learn an almighty lesson. Remember him? Or has kissing Miss Toogood addled your brain?"

Lord Octavius stopped looking sheepish. "That's enough, Dex," he growled.

Mr. Pryor's smirk deepened. "So, are we doing it tonight?"

"Yes," Lord Octavius said, and then, "No, we're not ready." He rubbed his forehead. "I need to practice being Amelia, decide what I'm going to say."

"Let's do that now, then," Mr. Pryor said, throwing himself down in one of the chairs.

"Not here," Pip said, aware that a housemaid would come looking for her at any moment—a fact she'd completely forgotten while she and Lord Octavius were kissing.

She sent up a brief prayer of thanks that it hadn't been a maid who'd interrupted them.

Mr. Pryor climbed to his feet again. "Your room then, Otto."

Lord Octavius bent and kissed her cheek. "Good night," he whispered against her skin.

"Good night," she whispered back.

The men departed. "I still think we need a sword," Mr. Pryor said, as the door closed behind them.

Pip stayed where she was, listening to the silence and the slow thump of her heart. Her lips still tingled. She pressed her fingertips to them.

Lord Octavius had kissed her.

Lord Octavius had asked her to marry him.

Lord Octavius had asked her to marry him—and she'd said *yes*.

He'd called his family's magic fantastical that afternoon, but this was every bit as fantastical. She, a vicar's daughter, was going to marry Lord Octavius Pryor, grandson to a duke. It was astonishing and miraculous and almost unbelievable . . . and his family would not be pleased.

A tiny scrap of worry winkled its way into her brain.

What would Lord Octavius's parents think when they learned that their son was throwing himself away on a mere governess?

The door swung open. Lord Octavius came into the schoolroom in a rush. "I'm off to London," he said, crossing to her in three long strides and taking both of her hands in his. "First thing in the morning."

"London?" Pip said.

"I'll be back the next day. Word of honor!"

"London?" she said again. "Why?"

"To get a sword," Mr. Pryor said, from the doorway. "I told him he doesn't need to travel all the way to London to get one, but he wants to." He winked at her.

Pip stared at him, baffled. What on earth had that wink been for?

"Doctors' Commons," Mr. Pryor said.

Pip still had no idea what he was talking about.

"Special license," Mr. Pryor clarified.

Pip looked at Lord Octavius. He was grinning at her. "Special license," he agreed.

"But . . . do you think that's wise? Your family—"

"Oh, we'll have the wedding at Linwood Castle," Lord Octavius said cheerfully. "Everyone'll be there. Special license just means we can get married whenever and wherever we want."

Pip removed her hands from his. "Your parents may not wish to have a governess for a daughter-in-law."

He took her hands back. "You're worried about what they'll think? Don't be. They'll love you. Won't they, Dex?"

Mr. Pryor nodded.

Lord Octavius lifted one of her hands to his mouth and pressed a kiss to her palm. "I'm off to London tomorrow, I'll be back the next day, we'll deal with Rumpole and his valet, and then we'll start thinking about *us*."

"I can't leave the girls," Pip protested.

"We'll sort something out, I promise." Lord Octavius kissed her other palm. "What's your full name?"

"Philippa Mary Toogood," Pip said, feeling faintly discombobulated.

"Daughter of Llewellyn and Mary, correct?"

She nodded.

"Excellent." Lord Octavius bent and kissed her cheek, released her hands, and headed for the door. He sent her a smile bursting with happiness, and then he and his cousin were gone.

Pip pressed one hand to her cheek, where his last kiss had landed. She felt as if a whirlwind had picked her up, spun her around, and set her on her feet again. She also felt a tiny bit uncertain. This was all happening so fast.

CHAPTER 23

*O*ctavius left at daybreak, which was somewhat earlier than he'd have liked, but the sooner he left, the sooner he'd be back, the sooner they could deal with Rumpole and his valet, and the sooner he could carry Miss Toogood off to Linwood Castle. He dozed for the first twenty-five miles, then spent the next twenty-five planning. By the time they reached London's outskirts, he had a good idea what Amelia Rumpole's "ghost" was going to tell her husband. The threat was quite simple—castration—and the sword she'd be holding would reinforce it. Which was why the sword was important. It would work for Rumpole and it would work for the valet. Accordingly, as the carriage rattled over the bridge into London, he said to his manservant, Staig, who was seated across from him, "I need you to purchase two things for me this afternoon."

"Very good, sir," Staig said.

"The first thing is a sword. Not a foil or a rapier, but something like a cavalry officer's sword, or perhaps one of those swords the Romans used."

Staig looked as if he had no idea what a Roman sword had looked like.

"About this long and this wide," Octavius said, sketching a shape in the air with his hands.

"Very good, sir," Staig said again.

"There's a place on Piccadilly that sells swords, and another on Bond Street." He fished out his pocketbook and rifled through the banknotes. "Doesn't have to be fancy—plain is fine—just as long as it looks dangerous, the sort of thing you wouldn't want anyone waving near your face."

Or your balls, he refrained from adding.

"Very good, sir," Staig said again.

"The other thing I need you to buy is two kites. The best kites you've ever seen. Made out of silk, with long tails and bright colors. But sturdy, mind—something that will last more than five minutes." He paused, and thought for a moment, and then said, "Actually, make that *six* kites. Four run-of-the-mill ones, and two that are the best you can buy." He handed Staig several bank notes.

Staig pocketed the money. "Six kites and one sword," he said. If he thought his employer had gone mad, he concealed it well.

The carriage halted.

Octavius peered out and saw that they'd reached Doctors' Commons. "The carriage is yours for the rest of the afternoon," he told Staig.

⚬⚬⚬

Purchasing the special license took a matter of minutes, but waiting for the clerk to laboriously inscribe the names on the license took a great deal longer than Octavius thought necessary. He shifted his weight from foot to foot, checked his pocket watch, and managed, with great restraint, not to fidget with his cuffs. At last it was done—the names had been written, the ink was dry, the precious piece of paper was in his pocket, and he could move on to the next thing on his list. The next *very* important thing on his list.

Octavius took the stairs two at a time down to the street and hailed a hackney. Twenty minutes later, he was in Hanover Square. He stared up at the palatial residence his parents inhabited, took a deep breath, and climbed the stairs to the towering front door. "Are my parents home?" he asked Titmus, the butler, in the vast, echoing expanse of the entrance hall.

"His lordship is in his study and her ladyship is in the music room."

"Thanks, Titmus." He headed for his father's study, knocked once on the door, and opened it.

The Marquis of Stanaway looked up from his paperwork. "Otto? I thought you were in Hampshire."

"I was," Octavius said. "I'm going back tomorrow, but I need to talk to you. You and Mother both."

His father studied him for a moment, then laid down his quill. "Important, is it?"

"Yes, sir. Very."

The marquis pushed back his chair and stood. Together they climbed one flight of stairs, to the sunny music room where Octavius's mother spent a great deal of her time.

Lady Stanaway was tuning her violin when they entered. She lowered the instrument, alert enquiry on her face. "Otto, darling, what are you doing back in London so soon? Is something wrong?"

"Nothing's wrong, Mother. Quite the opposite." And then he told them about Miss Toogood.

⁂

Next on his list was Quintus, and after him, Sextus and Ned. Providentially, he found all three of them at his brother's house on Curzon Street. Ned had his boots up on the rosewood sofa table again.

They looked up at his entry. He saw surprise on

their faces. "Thought you were going to be away a whole week," Quintus said.

Octavius flung himself down on the sofa beside Ned and kicked his cousin's feet off the table. "Came back to buy a special license."

"What?" three voices said.

"I'm getting married."

They gaped at him in wide-eyed, opened-mouthed astonishment. Sextus found his voice first. "Not that governess you went to protect?"

Octavius nodded.

"Do Mother and Father know?" Quintus demanded.

"Just been to see them."

"And?"

"They want to meet her. They're closing the townhouse and heading to Gloucestershire later this week." He climbed to his feet, went over to the sideboard, and poured himself some claret. When he turned to face them, they were all frowning, even Ned. "We'll be married within the month," Octavius told them. "So you'd better come up to Gloucestershire if you want to be at the wedding."

"Seems rather fast," his brother said, in an extremely neutral voice. His expression was extremely neutral, too. He looked as if he was trying very hard not to frown.

"It is a little fast," Octavius admitted. "But we're well-matched."

Three pairs of eyes stared dubiously at him. There was a long beat of silence, and then Sextus said, "So who is she, this governess?"

"Her name's Miss Toogood. Her father was a vicar."

"What's she like?" Ned asked.

"She's a capital girl. Full of pluck. Devilish smart, too; it was her idea that I become Amelia Rumpole's ghost."

"Amelia Rumpole's ghost?" Sextus said, his brow wrinkling.

"And she can punch like a Trojan," Octavius said, warming to his theme. "And climb trees and fly kites. Got a damned good head on her shoulders. Didn't have hysterics when she found out about my magic."

"Can we go back to the ghost?" Sextus asked.

Octavius drank a mouthful of claret, leaned against the sideboard, and explained about his multiple attempts to teach Baron Rumpole a lesson and the plan that he, Dex, and Miss Toogood had finally come up with.

"It *is* a good plan," Quintus admitted, when he'd finished.

"It's a brilliant plan," Octavius said, pouring himself another glass of claret. "And Mother had a good idea, too. Amelia's ghost is going to make Rumpole give his daughters to Newingham."

This statement prompted a rather long moment of silence. "I take it that's a good thing?" Quintus said, finally.

"It is. Rumpole's not someone who should have charge of children."

"Is Newingham?" Ned asked, putting his boots on the rosewood sofa table again.

"He is," Octavius said. He went back to the sofa—and kicked Ned's feet off the table. "You should see him with the girls. He's quite paternal."

"Bunny? Paternal?" Ned said, putting his boots back on the table.

Octavius kicked them off again. "Paternal."

They eyed each other narrowly.

"So, this wedding . . ." Sextus said. "Within the month?"

"Within the month," Octavius confirmed.

"Then I guess we'd better head up to Gloucester-shire," Quintus said, in that very neutral tone again.

It was clear that his brother thought he was making a mistake, that they all thought he was making a mistake—but once they met Miss Too-good they'd realize that the mistake would be to *not* marry her. "Tell me what's new in London," Octavius said, to change the subject.

Ned shrugged. "Not a lot."

"Vigor," Sextus said cryptically.

Ned snorted a laugh, and Quintus grimaced.

"Vigor?" Octavius said, willing to be distracted by whatever oddity this was.

"It's what everyone's calling Dex," Sextus told him.

"They are? Why?"

"Vigor, but no finesse," Quintus said.

A vague memory stirred in the recesses of Octavius's brain. "His last widow said that about him?"

Quintus nodded. "You can imagine how everyone took it up. It's the latest *on-dit*."

"It's a good thing he's in Hampshire," Sextus said. "He wouldn't want to be in town right now."

"That bad, is it?"

"I wouldn't go so far as to say he's a laughing-stock," Quintus said. "But . . . it's close."

"Seventy-two," Ned said, then yawned loudly. "I counted yesterday. Seventy-two times I heard someone mention it."

Octavius pulled a face. Seventy-two? That was much worse than he'd thought. "Damned good thing he's in Hampshire, then." With any luck the *beaumonde* would be sharpening their tongues at some other poor sod's expense by the time Dex came back to London. He might be an annoying son of a bitch, but he was an excellent person to have at one's back. Together, he and Dex made a good team.

It suddenly occurred to him that all five of them would make an even better team.

Octavius let his gaze rest on his brother for a moment, on Sextus, and lastly on Ned. "Have you ever considered that the five of us, with our gifts, could . . . do things?"

"You mean, like paint the statues on top of Spencer House bright pink?" Ned asked. "I was thinking that just the other day. Dex could levitate me up there and—"

"No, you idiot. I mean help people. Use our magic to right wrongs. Like what Dex and I are doing in Hampshire."

All three of them gaped at him. Ned was the first to recover his voice. "You mean . . . you want us to be like the Knights of the Round Table? Dashing off on white chargers and rescuing maidens from villains? With our magic?"

Trust Ned to turn it into a joke. Octavius felt his face flush. "Why not?"

Ned gave a hearty guffaw. "He wants us to be heroes!" he crowed.

Octavius resisted the urge to box his cousin's ears. He looked at his brother instead. Quintus was wearing one of his frowns, the one that was both worried and dubious at the same time. He'd been practicing it as long as Octavius could remember, because dukes' heirs took life very seriously.

Sextus wasn't frowning. He was looking at Octavius, his expression partly surprised and partly something else that Octavius couldn't quite identify, but that he thought might possibly be approval.

"I say we should do it!" Ned declared loudly. "Quintus can scry for villains, Dex, Otto, and I can rescue the maidens from their clutches, and once they're safe, Narcissus can make their teeth whiter or their eyelashes longer or whatever gift it was that he chose."

Sextus didn't rise to the bait; he merely said, "Glossy hair," and smoothed one hand over his undeniably glossy hair.

Octavius had a very good idea what Sextus had wished for on his twenty-fifth birthday and it wasn't glossy hair, but if Ned hadn't figured it out yet, he wasn't going to tell him.

He watched the two brothers exchange barbed smiles and wished, not for the first time, that Ned wasn't such a blazing idiot and that Sextus wasn't quite so touchy.

"What shall we call ourselves?" Ned put his feet on the rosewood sofa table again. "How about The Heroic Pryors?"

Octavius didn't bother to respond to that suggestion. He merely kicked his cousin's feet off the table again.

"The Dashing Pryors!" Ned said, and then, "No, we should be knights, don't you think? And we need to have a table of our own." His gaze landed on the sofa table. "The Knights of the Sofa Table!" he cried, and then, "No, that doesn't sound right. How about . . . the Knights of the Oval Sofa Table? The Knights of the Mahogany Sofa Table?"

"It's rosewood, you idiot," Octavius told him.

"Even better! The Knights of the Rosewood Sofa Table!" Ned grinned hugely. "Has a nice ring to it, don't you think?"

The best strategy when Ned was prattling nonsense was to ignore him. Octavius turned his attention to his brother. "What else has happened in town?"

"Not a lot." Quintus shrugged. "Grantley got drunk and challenged Fasthugh to a duel, and Fasthugh chose feather dusters as the weapons."

Octavius uttered an astonished laugh. "He what? Why on earth is everyone talking about Dex when they should be talking about that?"

"Because the duel never took place. Grantley said Fasthugh was mocking him—which he was—and he flew into a pelter and went off to Brighton."

Octavius snorted into his wine. Grantley might be an earl, but he was also a short-tempered fool. "What else has happened?"

"There's a new opera dancer that everyone's talking about."

Octavius shook his head, uninterested in opera dancers. "Anything else?"

Quintus shrugged. "Southport swears his house is haunted. That's about it."

"Haunted?"

"He says he hears footsteps in empty rooms."

Octavius glanced at Ned, sitting sprawled on the sofa alongside him.

"What?" Ned said. "It's not me." Then he grinned. "Although it's not a bad idea."

"It's a terrible idea," Quintus said, aiming a frown at Ned. This one was his "the earl does not approve" frown.

"It's a *fantastic* idea. Let's be ghosts!" Ned leapt to his feet. "In fact—I know!—let's resurrect the Ghostly Cavalier of London."

"The Ghostly Cavalier of London?" Quintus repeated, looking pained.

"The ghost our fathers invented. Don't tell me you've forgotten!"

"I haven't forgotten," Quintus said. "Nor have I forgotten that Grandfather forbade it."

"He forbade *them;* he hasn't forbidden *us.*" Ned was practically bouncing with excitement.

"He would if he thought we had the least intention of—"

"Oh, come on, Quin, don't be such a stick in the mud!"

"Grandfather would not be pleased—" Quintus began pompously.

"I bet the costume's in the attics at Hanover Square. Do your thing and see if it's there!"

Quintus shook his head. "No."

Ned made a sound of disgust. "Aren't you in the *least* bit curious to see it?"

Octavius was a little curious. He wouldn't mind seeing the infamous costume, if it still existed.

"Let's just see if it's in the attics," Ned wheedled. "Come on, Quin. You know you can do that in two minutes."

"The costume will have been eaten by moths years ago," Quintus said.

"Maybe," Ned said. "Maybe not. Let's just find out. Pleeease."

"Not if you're going to put it on and sneak around London scaring people."

"I just want to see it," Ned said, bouncing on his toes, looking like a six-foot-six, two-hundred-and-thirty-pound child. "Come on, Quin! Don't tell me you don't want to see it?"

Quintus heaved a put-upon sigh, but he must have been a little bit curious about the costume because he went to the sideboard and fished out the silver bowl he used for descrying. He upended the decanter of claret into it, then gazed into the dark pool of liquid.

Ned waited, still bouncing on his toes.

After half a minute, Quintus said, "It's in the Hanover Square attics."

"I knew it!" Ned punched the air with one fist. "Where in the attics?"

Quintus sighed, and said, "South-west corner. In a trunk."

"Can you find the trunk?"

"Yes."

"Let's go then!"

Octavius saw the conflict in Quintus's face. Sometimes his brother didn't want to be a dutiful duke's heir. Sometimes he just wanted to have fun.

"No harm in looking at it," Octavius said mildly. "It's probably moth-eaten, after all."

Quintus glanced at Sextus, who could usually be counted on to side with him, but Sextus must have wanted to see the costume, too, because he shrugged and said, "Why not?"

CHAPTER 24

*T*he attics of the family castle in Gloucestershire were cavernous, the sort of attics one could get lost in for days. The attics of the townhouse in Hanover Square were much smaller and surprisingly bare. There were a number of trunks and hatboxes, two old mirrors, a couple of paintings under Holland covers, and a stack of chairs that were no longer fashionable. Quintus went unerringly to the trunk containing the costume. It was in the farthest corner, behind the chairs, the mirrors, and the paintings. "Looks as if someone was trying to hide it," Sextus observed.

Octavius thought so, too.

They unfastened the buckles and lifted the lid. A choking scent of camphor rose from the trunk. Ned gave a loud hoot of delight. "Not moth-eaten!"

The trunk was full to the brim. Octavius spied

velvet and lace and an ostrich feather before Ned started hauling out clothes. The first item was a blue velvet doublet trimmed with gold braid. The second was the bodice of a woman's dress.

"That's for you, Otto," Ned said, flinging the bodice at him. "You can be a lady ghost."

Octavius threw the bodice back, hitting Ned in the face. "No, thanks."

"Why not?"

"Because I loathe being female."

Ned shrugged and tossed the bodice on the floor, then went back to pawing through the trunk, but Sextus said, "Loathe? That's a strong word."

"Loathe," Octavius repeated. "Being female is simply awful. You've no idea."

"What's awful about it?"

"Everything."

Quintus sneezed, and looked up from examining a wide-brimmed cavalier's hat with a curling ostrich plume. "Everything?"

"I've been a female half a dozen times now, and there is not one single good thing about it."

"There must be," Sextus said, as Ned pulled a wig with long, flowing black ringlets from the trunk.

"There isn't."

"Breasts!" Ned said, putting the wig on his head. "That's a good thing, that is."

"For us it is," Octavius said, unearthing a cavalier's boot from the trunk. "Not for women."

"Why not?"

"Because men touch them all the time."

"There must be some benefits to being female," Sextus said, as tenacious as a terrier at a rabbit hole.

"Breasts," Ned said again, fussing with his ringlets.

Octavius decided to ignore him. He examined the boot. It had an elevated heel and large shiny buckle.

"Women don't go bald?" Quintus offered, and then sneezed again.

"And they don't have to shave every day," Sextus put in. He rummaged through the trunk and pulled out a pair of breeches made from the same blue velvet as the doublet.

"Ha! I've got one," Ned said. "They don't have to worry about getting erections in public." His smirk was very like Dex's. "That's a big advantage, that is." And then he added, "But I still think breasts are the best thing they have going for them."

Octavius threw the boot at his head and missed. He looked in the trunk for its mate, but instead found a petticoat. He tossed it on the floor and rummaged further, finding what was surely the cavalier's cape—but when he shook it out it was a woman's skirt. He folded it up again, and while he folded he thought about the times he'd been female, and he thought about Miss Toogood, and then he thought about his cousin, Phoebe, and about his mother and his aunts and his grandmother. "In all seriousness, though, do you think there are any advantages to being female? Because if there are, I can't think of 'em."

"In all seriousness?" Sextus asked.

"In all seriousness."

Sextus took off the cavalier's gauntlet he was trying on and frowned.

Octavius tried to articulate his thoughts. "Seems to me the biggest difference between us and them is that we were lucky enough to be born male and they were unlucky enough not to."

"Unlucky?" Quintus said, and sneezed for a third time.

"You don't think so? You think there's even *one* good thing about being born female?"

Quintus rubbed his nose.

"They're smarter than us," Ned said.

Everyone turned to look at him.

"What?" He emerged from the trunk, holding a wide lacy collar. "They are."

"Smarter than us?" Sextus said.

"Well, maybe not smarter than *you*, but most of 'em are a great deal smarter than me, and they're at least as clever as Quin and Otto here."

Everyone stared at him.

"If you went out and found the thousand most intelligent people in England, I bet at least half of 'em would be females, and the shame of it is that they can't go to university or vote or— And that's another thing! I wager that if it was the House of *Ladies*, not the House of Lords, there'd be fewer wars." Ned waved the lacy collar to emphasize his point. "Stands to reason, don't it? They're less bloodthirsty than we are. They'd rather talk than kill people."

There was a long moment of a bemused silence. At least, the silence was bemused on Octavius's part.

"What?" Ned said. "I might be stupid compared to Narcissus here, but I'm not *that* stupid. Females are clever. At least as clever as men, if not more so." He took off the wig and put on the lace collar instead. "They're more cunning than us, too."

"Cunning?" Octavius repeated, blankly.

"They have to be, don't they?" Ned said, arranging the collar at his throat. "If a female wants to get ahead, she's got to know what to say and how best to say it."

"Manipulative?" Quintus said, his brow creasing into a frown that could only be called bewildered. "Is that what you mean?"

"Cunning, manipulative, persuasive." Ned shrugged, and put the wig back on. "Doesn't matter what you call it, but women are better at it than we are. They have fewer opportunities to advance themselves, so they get what they want by words rather than by brute force."

There was a rather long moment of silence, which was broken by another of Quintus's sneezes.

Octavius looked at Ned in his wig and lacy collar and thought that his cousin might be an idiot, but he wasn't completely stupid.

"Women would make better spies than men," Ned stated, turning back to the trunk. "If I was England's spymaster, I'd be recruiting females for the job. There's only one boot in here."

"The other one's on the floor behind you," Quintus said.

Ned sat on the dusty floorboards and tried to take his own boots off. They were too well-fitted. "I say, Otto, give a fellow a hand."

Octavius crouched and tugged his cousin's boots off. "So . . . you think women are better with words than men?"

"Of course," Ned said, as if this was blindingly obvious.

Octavius looked at Sextus, who shrugged and said, "The wittiest people I know are women."

Octavius thought about this, and realized that the wittiest people he knew were women, too. "What else are women better at?"

"Well, they're more observant than us for a start. Notice all the little details." Ned climbed to his feet and paced up and down in front of the trunk. "Ha! These fit."

"They're more intuitive than us," Sextus put in, reaching into the trunk and pulling out a leather baldric.

"More compassionate," Quintus said, winding a wide satin sash around his waist. "Kinder."

"More practical and commonsensical," Ned said, placing the hat with its curling feather atop his wig. "And definitely more organized. *Far* more organized."

Octavius considered these suggestions, and nodded. "What else?"

"They're more patient than we are," Sextus said. "In general that is, and I think . . . they endure better."

"Endure?" Quintus said. He tied the sash in place, and sneezed loudly again.

"Remember when Dex and Phoebe got sick last year? Who complained more?"

"Dex," they all said.

Sextus shrugged, having made his point, and rummaged in the trunk. "I say, look at this." He pulled out a sheathed sword.

"Let me see that," Octavius said, appropriating the sword and wrenching it from its scabbard.

It was quite blunt, and also very badly rusted.

He handed both sheath and sword back to Sextus, disappointed. "Women might be more patient than us, and wittier and more organized and whatever else, but I still don't want to be one. The advantages are all ours."

"Of course they are," Sextus said, sliding the sword back into its sheath. "It's a man's world. We have the power. Women are treated little better than children."

"That's a bit harsh," Quintus objected.

"You think so? Look at Phoebe. She's what, twenty? Think about what Dex was allowed to do at that age and what Phoebe's allowed to do."

Octavius picked up the petticoat and folded it, and thought about Dex at twenty. He'd had no restrictions on his behavior. None of them had. They'd stayed out all night if they wanted. Caroused and got drunk. Driven their curricles to Bath and back on a whim.

Phoebe couldn't do any of that. Because she was female.

"But she's not treated like a child," Quintus said.

Sextus shrugged. "Can't say I'd want to have m' father manage my money and make my decisions for me."

"Uncle Deuce doesn't make *all* her decisions for her," Quintus protested, and then sneezed again.

"No, only the important ones." Sextus put the sword back in the trunk. "And her husband will do the same once she's married."

"She'll be allowed to choose who she marries," Quintus pointed out. "That's an important decision."

"Phoebe will get to choose, yes. But a lot of women don't."

Octavius thought about the painting hanging in Baron Rumpole's gallery—Amelia Rumpole with her husband and stepson. The baron would have controlled every aspect of Amelia's life. If he'd wanted to beat her, he could have. It was his right, by law. Just as he'd had the use of her body whenever he wished.

That was a terrible thought. One he'd never had before. He watched Ned strut around in his wig and plumed hat, watched Sextus unearth a wooden box from the very bottom of the trunk, watched Quintus sneeze yet again. "Women can't refuse their husbands entry to their beds, can they?"

"No, they can't." Sextus opened the box. "I say, look! A beard and mustache."

The beard was small and black and pointed and the mustache curled at both ends. Sextus held them up to his face.

"I think the mustache is meant to curl up, not down," Quintus said.

Octavius put the petticoat back in the trunk. How could it possibly be right that a husband could bully his way into his wife's bed and take what he wanted? The idea of someone having that kind of power over him was quite appalling.

It wasn't right, any more than it was right for an employer to demand sexual favors from his servants or for a valet to try to rape a housemaid.

He bent and picked up the bodice Ned had tossed aside. It was low cut, but not as low as the one he'd worn to Vauxhall Gardens—and that was another thing that wasn't right. It wasn't right for men to force themselves on members of the muslin company, because even prostitutes should be able to say no.

He opened his mouth to ask the others what they thought on that last point, and then closed it without speaking. Ned was mincing up and down in the wig, plumed hat, and high cavalier's boots, Sextus was peering at himself in one of the old mirrors while he held the mustache first one way, then the other, and Quintus was fastening a flowing cape over his shoulders. Grown men playing games, while women were subjected to their husbands' sexual demands and female servants were assaulted by their employers and whores were almost raped in Vauxhall Gardens.

Quite suddenly Octavius had had enough. "I'm off," he said, tossing the bodice back in the trunk.

CHAPTER 25

*O*ctavius walked for some time, crisscrossing London's streets and squares before turning his steps towards Albemarle Street and his set of rooms, where he sat down to the next task on his list: writing a letter to his grandparents.

After ten minutes spent contemplating a blank sheet of paper, he poured himself a glass of brandy. It didn't help. Or perhaps it did, because he decided to stop trying to be concise and unemotional and to just tell his grandparents everything, and perhaps his letter was a little messy and perhaps it was a little effusive, possibly even rhapsodic, but it also told them all they needed to know about Miss Toogood.

That task done, he examined the sword and kites Staig had procured, declared them perfect, and sent the manservant out to fetch them both a meal from the nearest tavern.

It occurred to Octavius while he ate beef collops and a raised pigeon pie that this could well be his last night in these rooms. If everything went as he hoped, he'd be married when he next came to London. He and Miss Toogood would stay in one of the guest suites at Hanover Square until they purchased a townhouse.

A house of their very own. One that they would choose together and live in together. He and Miss Toogood.

Octavius had a vague feeling that he ought to be nervous about acquiring a wife and a house and everything else that went with marriage, but he didn't feel apprehensive at all. He felt excited, brimming with anticipation and eagerness. His life was going to change—it was going to change a lot—and he couldn't wait for those changes to start, because whatever happened—the good things and the bad things—he wouldn't be facing them alone. Miss Toogood would be by his side. Yes, he had his parents, and yes, he had his brother and his cousins and his uncles and aunts and grandparents, but Miss Toogood would be his *partner*. She would share his life in a way that no one else could—and for some reason that thought made him choke up slightly.

Octavius pushed his wineglass to one side. He had a horrible feeling that if he drank any more than he already had, and if he continued thinking about Miss Toogood any more than he already had, he might just turn into a mawkish, dewy-eyed watering pot. But it was confoundedly difficult *not* to think about Miss Toogood. He couldn't wait to get back to Hampshire. Couldn't wait to see her again. Couldn't wait to talk with her and go rambling with her and climb trees and eat dinner and play jackstraws and kiss her.

Couldn't wait to start their life together.

And, damn it, there was his throat choking up again.

He went to bed early, all the better to leave London early the next morning, but as he slid between the sheets he realized that there was one other important task that he really ought do while in London—namely, to look for the governesses who'd worked for Baron Rumpole previously and ask them why they'd left his employment.

"Damn," Octavius said, and scrubbed his hands roughly through his hair. He didn't want to spend another day in London. He wanted to get back to Hampshire as quickly as possible and make certain that Miss Toogood was safe.

He climbed out of bed, rummaged through his drawers, found paper and a quill, and dashed off a note to his brother.

Quin, old fellow, would you mind scrying for the governesses who left Rumpole's employment? If any of them are in London, could you ask them whether he attacked them? I'd stay to interview them myself, but I need to return to Hampshire with all haste and ensure that Miss Toogood is safe.

Yours in gratitude,

Otto

He climbed back into bed, blew out his candle, and tried to go to sleep, but his thoughts were buzzing around in his head like bees at a hive.

The next time he came to London, he'd be married.

He and Miss Toogood would go to balls and soirees together. They'd look for a house together. They'd share a bed.

Now *that* was a thought that made him shiver with anticipation. But on the heels of that shiver came a twinge of nervousness.

What if he had vigor but no finesse? How would he know? Dex hadn't known, after all, and he'd spent a lot of time in women's beds.

In fact, if Dex had no finesse, then it was extremely likely that Octavius had even *less* finesse, because he'd spent much less time than Dex practicing the featherbed jig.

What if Miss Toogood didn't enjoy his lovemaking? What if she found his caresses annoying rather than titillating? All the females he'd ever bedded had been professionals. They could have been pretending to enjoy his touches. How was he to know? It wasn't as if he had breasts of his own.

Octavius's thoughts came to an abrupt halt.

He *could* have breasts if he wanted. He could have a quim, too. And he could experience exactly what it felt like when both of those things were touched—whether it was good or bad, titillating or tedious.

Octavius sat up and peeled out of his nightshirt. He thought for a moment, then modeled himself on a painting of Venus he'd once seen. Magic crawled over his skin and along his bones . . . and he was a woman. He brushed a hand over his torso and encountered a soft, hairless stomach and breasts.

It was the first time he'd deliberately touched his breasts. He experienced two conflicting emotions. One was curiosity. He *loved* breasts. Loved looking at them, loved touching them, loved kissing them. The other emotion was embarrassment, because these were *his* breasts. It felt very odd to be stroking them. Did women fondle their own breasts?

The curiosity easily prevailed over the embarrassment. Octavius lay back down and began exploring his breasts. He was relieved to discover that it felt quite pleasant. He experimented for several minutes, caressing, kneading, pinching, tickling, learning what felt good and what didn't, but even when it felt good, it didn't feel *great*. Not as great as stroking his cock would feel. Which was disappointing.

He slid his hand down his body, over that soft, smooth belly and found his quim.

His body gave a little shiver from head to toe. Not a good shiver; a *bad* one.

Octavius removed his hand and shivered a second time. He didn't know why he was shivering, except that not having a cock and balls felt profoundly wrong. Wrong in his bones. Wrong in his gut. So wrong that he almost changed back into his own body, then and there.

The only thing that stopped him was thought of Miss Toogood. How would he learn sexual finesse if he didn't explore his own quim? If he wanted her to enjoy sharing his bed, how could he *not* do this?

Octavius made himself touch his quim again. He felt the same sense of wrongness, the same little shiver that combined confusion and dismay and something close to horror. The emptiness beneath his hand made him feel as if part of himself had been amputated. An essential part. Which was ridiculous. He wasn't his cock and balls and their absence shouldn't make him feel this way.

Octavius set his jaw. Ten minutes. He'd explore

his quim for ten minutes, learn what felt good and what didn't, and then he'd change back into himself and get his balls and cock back.

Reluctantly, he began to acquaint himself with his quim. In a tiny corner of his brain he acknowledged that his reluctance was ridiculous. He loved quims. They were wonderful things, fascinating and tempting and sublimely feminine. He'd never had a chance to explore one so thoroughly before. He should be enjoying this opportunity.

He wasn't enjoying it, but he was damned if he was going to stop. He concentrated on his task, tracing the folds, investigating their topography and their texture—that was familiar, he'd done it with women before, but it was disconcerting to be on the receiving end and to discover that it didn't feel particularly pleasurable. If he'd spent two minutes touching his cock, he'd be rock hard, heat pulsing in his groin, but two minutes spent touching his quim resulted in . . . not a lot. A mildly pleasant sensation of warmth, that was all. Nothing close to arousal. In fact, if he was asked to describe how it felt—titillating or tedious—he'd have to say tedious.

Was this yet another disadvantage that women were born with? The inability to feel strong sexual pleasure? Because that was a deeply disturbing thought. He didn't want to have sex with Miss Toogood if he enjoyed it and she didn't.

Three minutes later Octavius's fingers found something that felt rather nice. Not as nice as touching his cock and balls would have felt, but still better than nothing.

He persisted at his task and a few minutes later found something else that also felt quite nice. It was a relief to discover that women could experience arousal, because he'd begun to fear that they couldn't, but that warm, tingling sensation was definitely arousal. He began to think that climax might be possible.

Diligently, he continued with his quest. The tingling grew stronger. Quite nice became very nice. A feeling of urgency and heat took hold of him. Suddenly, climax wasn't just possible, it was inevitable, his body straining towards it as single-mindedly as it did when he had a cock.

Finally, Octavius reached the prize he'd been seeking: sexual climax. The orgasm was different from the ones he was used to. No clenching balls, no spurting cock. He felt spasms of pleasure in his quim, but he also felt a delicious clenching and unclenching deep inside himself. The sensation was strange but extremely pleasant.

He lay bonelessly afterwards, catching his breath, drifting on a wave of sexual contentment. That feeling of warm, sleepy satisfaction was the same whether he was male or female.

It was nice not to have a mess to clean up. That was definitely an advantage to being a woman.

Octavius changed back into his own body. The first thing he did was reach for his genitals. The deep, visceral burst of relief when he cupped himself was embarrassing. He *wasn't* his cock and balls, but some atavistic part of his brain appeared to think that he was.

Octavius pulled on his nightshirt, rearranged the bedclothes, and lay back to contemplate what he'd learned.

One: that women could definitely feel sexual pleasure from being touched.

Two: that it took longer for a woman to come to climax than it did a man.

If he'd been touching his cock it would have taken a couple of minutes to reach orgasm, not nearly twenty—but perhaps that was because he'd been unfamiliar with his female body? Perhaps, with practice, he could learn how to touch a quim more adeptly?

And that was the most important lesson he'd learned tonight: that people experienced arousal differently. His female body liked different things from his male body, and it was entirely possible that Miss Toogood liked different things again. All men weren't the same, and neither were all women.

If he wanted Miss Toogood to enjoy the marriage bed, he needed to tailor his lovemaking to *her*. He needed to be guided by *her* responses. Fast or slow, gentle or rough—if he paid attention he'd know exactly how and where she liked to be touched.

Octavius felt for his balls to reassure himself they were still there, then curled up on his side and went to sleep, no longer worried about his wedding night.

CHAPTER 26

At Lord Newingham's suggestion, the girls had their French lesson outdoors. They played "I spy," first in the stables, then the kitchen garden, and lastly the shrubbery. The French lesson segued into a botany lesson, and then into a lesson on insects. Newingham, Mr. Pryor, and the girls enthusiastically turned over leaves, discovering worms and beetles and centipedes.

"By Jove!" the viscount exclaimed. "Have a look at this one. It's enormous."

The girls clustered close.

"Do you know what it's called, Miss Toogood?" Newingham asked.

Pip shook her head.

"We need to give it a name," the viscount declared. "What do you think, girls? The Monstrously Large Beetle-shaped Beetle?"

Edie and Fanny giggled.

"It's got horns," Mr. Pryor pointed out. "I think we should call it the Horned Behemoth."

"What's a behemoth?" Fanny asked.

"Something very large," Pip told her.

"Myrtle!" Lord Newingham said. "Myrtle, the Monstrously Large Beetle-shaped Beetle."

Mr. Pryor shook his head. "It's a Horned Behemoth."

"There are some books on insects in the school-room," Pip said. "I'll fetch them and we can find out its real name."

"Nothing will be as good as Myrtle the Monstrously Large Beetle-shaped Beetle," Newingham said as she headed for the house, and Pip privately agreed.

She let herself in through a side door and climbed the servants' stairs quickly. On the second flight, she met the baron's valet coming down.

He halted. "Miss Toogood."

Pip halted, too. "Mr. Donald."

Mr. Donald was an unremarkable-looking man. Not handsome, not plain, just ordinary. Before yesterday she'd not given him a second thought. Now that she knew what he was, Pip had to stop herself from recoiling.

It seemed scarcely credible that this ordinary-looking man was capable of attacking a female violently, but she didn't doubt that Lord Octavius had spoken the truth, so she gave Mr. Donald a polite nod and moved past him carefully. The valet nodded politely back and stepped to one side, but not quite far enough. His arm brushed hers. Before yesterday Pip would have dismissed that brief touch as accidental. Today, she was certain it had been deliberate.

The hairs on the nape of her neck all stood on end. She continued up the stairs, not looking back, not hurrying—although she wanted to do both.

When she reached the next landing, she glanced back. Mr. Donald hadn't moved. He stood exactly where he'd been, watching her.

A shiver prickled its way across Pip's scalp and down her spine, and even though Mr. Donald was unremarkable and ordinary, she knew in her bones that he was dangerous.

Predator, a voice whispered in her head.

She crossed the narrow landing and continued up the stairs, faster now, glancing over her shoulder. Mr. Donald didn't follow her, but even so, Pip felt a little afraid. At the schoolroom, she hesitated over whether to shut the door or not. A closed door felt simultaneously safe and *not* safe, as if it could be both a defensive barrier and a trap.

She tapped the jamb three times with her thumb.

Those three light taps made her feel calmer and safer. Pip decided to leave the door open, because one could flee through an open doorway.

She crossed to the bookcase and scanned the shelves, finding both Harris's *Natural History of English Insects* and Forster's *A Catalogue of British Insects*. A quick look through the latter told her that the beetle Newingham had found was named the Rhinoceros Beetle.

Two whole minutes had now passed since she'd met Mr. Donald, but Pip still felt tense. Her ears were pricked for the sound of footsteps. This must be how mice felt when they knew a cat was nearby.

Pip tapped the cover of *A Catalogue of British Insects* three times. It was absurd how comforting those taps were, how a barely audible *tup-tup-tup* could soothe her ears and her soul.

Absurd. Childish. Irrational. Foolish.

She really ought to stop doing it. If Lord Octavius noticed, he would think she'd taken leave of her senses.

Pip grimaced slightly and put *A Catalogue of British Insects* to one side. She perused the shelves further, hesitated over *Instructions for Collecting and Preserving Insects* by William Curtis, and then discovered that the bookcase contained a copy of John Coakley Lettsom's *The Naturalist's and Traveller's*

Companion. She paged through that latter book, marveling at the beautiful illustrations, and while she was paging through it someone slid his arms around her waist and kissed her on the ear.

Pip yelped and struck out with the book, connecting satisfyingly hard with her attacker's head.

He yelped, too, and released her.

Pip turned and hit him again, a mighty swipe across the face with *The Naturalist's and Traveller's Companion*—and then she realized that the person she was hitting wasn't Mr. Donald at all. It was Lord Octavius—and he was bleeding.

She dropped the book and pressed her hands to her mouth. "Oh, my goodness."

Lord Octavius pressed his hands to his mouth, too. His eyes were watering. "Ow," he said.

"I'm so sorry!" Pip said. "I thought you were Mr. Donald." She dug out her handkerchief with fingers that trembled stupidly. "Here."

Lord Octavius cautiously lowered his hands. His upper lip was swelling. Blood trickled from his nose.

"Did I break your nose?" Pip asked, her voice hushed with horror.

"No."

"It's bleeding."

Lord Octavius carefully fingered his nose, winced, and said, "It's not broken." He took her handkerchief and dabbed at the trickle of blood.

"I'm so sorry," Pip said again. She felt sick to the pit of her belly. She'd *hit* him. She'd *hurt* him.

"My fault," Lord Octavius said. "Shouldn't have tried to sneak up on you." He grinned. "Excellent job, by the way."

"Excellent?" Pip repeated dumbly.

"First rate, in fact. Rumpole would be in full flight."

"I met Mr. Donald on the stairs," Pip told him. "Only a few minutes ago."

Lord Octavius lost his grin. "You did?"

Pip nodded.

"What did he do?"

"He was perfectly polite, but he made certain his arm touched mine when I passed." Pip bent to pick up the book. "I thought you were him."

"Mr. Donald would be in retreat now, too," Lord Octavius said. He folded the handkerchief and dabbed at his nose again.

Pip clutched the book to her chest. "Do you think so?"

"I might have surprised you first, but you surprised me harder." He smiled at her. "Well done."

Pip didn't smile back. Part of her was aware that she'd acquitted herself well, but the rest of her was appalled that she'd actually hit someone. That she'd drawn blood.

Lord Octavius's lessons had been almost a game. This had been *real*. Real fear when his arms had come around her. Real blood when she'd hit him.

"Miss Toogood? Are you all right?"

"I've never hurt anyone before," Pip said, clutching *The Naturalist's and Traveller's Companion* tightly.

"This? It's nothing. Look, it's stopped bleeding already."

Pip looked, and saw that he was correct.

"You want this back? No?" Lord Octavius tucked the crumpled, bloodstained handkerchief into his pocket, then he took the book from her hands and put it to one side. His arms came around her. This time it wasn't shocking or frightening. It was comforting.

Pip let herself relax against his chest. "I'm sorry I hurt you," she whispered into one of his lapels.

"I'm sorry I scared you," he whispered back. "And I want you to know that I'm *very* proud of you." He pressed a light kiss to her hair. "I hope you're proud of yourself?"

Pip considered this question for a moment, and then said, "I'm relieved." Relieved that she hadn't frozen in fear, relieved that she'd known how to fight back, relieved that she'd practiced often enough that she could defend herself without hesitation. "Thank you for the lessons."

"I'm glad they worked . . . despite finding myself on the receiving end of your skills." He chuckled.

"I'm sorry—"

"No, the fault was mine. I shouldn't have sneaked up on you. It's the sort of child's trick my cousin Ned would play—except you'd have heard *him* coming. He sounds like a stampeding elephant." He paused, and then said, "I told him about you. I told them all about you."

Pip pulled back slightly and looked at his face. "Even your parents?"

He nodded.

Apprehensiveness tightened her chest. "What did they say?"

"My parents are very much looking forward to meeting you."

Pip eyed him dubiously. "Did you tell them I'm only a governess?"

"I did, but they don't give a fig about that. No one does."

Pip rather doubted the accuracy of that statement. His parents must have been horrified to learn that he intended to marry a governess. His brother would have been horrified, too, and his formidable grandfather, when he found out, would be appalled—

Lord Octavius gave her a gentle shake. "Whatever you're thinking, stop it."

Could he read her thoughts on her face?

Apparently he could, for he said, "You think you'll not be welcome in my family? That you'll cause a breach between my parents and me? Well, you're wrong. Everyone will love you." He smiled down at her. "I told my parents that the luckiest day of my life was the day I met you."

Pip didn't know how his parents had felt when they'd heard that, but she knew how *she* felt. Sudden tears stung her eyes.

"I can't wait for you to meet my grandparents," Lord Octavius continued cheerfully. "I think you and Grandfather will get along splendidly."

Pip managed to blink back the foolish tears. "You do? Why?"

"For a start, he's going to love your hair."

Pip opened her mouth to tell him that even if the duke's wife had once had red hair that was no reason for the duke to like *her*, when he continued: "But most of all he's going to like your character."

"My character?"

"Your character," Lord Octavius repeated.

The admiration in his voice and the warmth in his eyes brought a hot blush to Pip's cheeks. She hid her head against his chest.

He put his arms around her again. "Philippa . . . may I call you Philippa?"

"I prefer Pip," Pip said, into his lapel.

"Pip," he said. "I like it. It suits you. It sounds exactly like someone who climbs trees and flies kites and picks flowers in meadows."

The comment gave Pip a warm feeling in her chest.

"And you must call me Octavius, or Otto if you wish. Whichever you like best."

Pip rather thought she liked Octavius best. It had a quaint, archaic formality to it.

She closed her eyes. Lord Octavius smelled of linen and soap and warm wool and something else, something that was purely him, something masculine, a little bit woodsy, a little bit citrussy, and wholly delicious. "You're back earlier than I expected."

"I left London before dawn," Lord Octavius said, and then he said, "I have something to show you." He released her and dug in his pocket and handed her a piece of paper.

Pip had known that he'd intended to get a special license in London, but *knowing* it and *seeing* it were apparently two different things. All the air left her lungs. For a moment she couldn't breathe, couldn't speak—and then she forced herself to do both those things: "The girls . . . I can't leave until—"

"The license is valid for three months," Lord

310

Octavius said. "But I don't think we'll need that long. I have a cunning plan."

"You do?"

"It's my mother's cunning plan, actually, but I think it will work." He paused dramatically, and then said, "Rumpole's going to give Newingham guardianship of the girls."

Pip raised her eyebrows. "He is?"

Lord Octavius nodded. "Yes. Because Amelia Rumpole's ghost is going to insist upon it. Quite vehemently."

"You're right: that is cunning." She folded up the special license and handed it back.

"I have the whole speech worked out," Lord Octavius said. "She's going to call him a loathsome molester of women and a vile debaucher and the basest, most contemptible worm to ever crawl upon this earth. Would you like to hear it?"

"Very much," said Pip. "But not now. I must get back to the shrubbery. Everyone's waiting for me."

"Tonight, then," Lord Octavius said. "After dinner. I'll practice my performance." He picked up *The Naturalist's and Traveller's Companion.* "Do you need this?"

"And the *Catalogue of British Insects,*" Pip said.

Lord Octavius picked that up, too, and headed for the door—and halted on the threshold. "Have I blood on my face?"

Pip examined him. His upper lip was a little swollen, but that was the only sign that she'd struck him. "No blood," she confirmed.

"My neckcloth?" He gave himself a double chin trying to peer down at it.

Pip scrutinized the snowy folds. "No blood," she said again.

"Good." He grinned at her and leaned close to drop a light kiss on her lips, and Pip wished that four people weren't waiting in the shrubbery for her to return.

The girls spent half an hour identifying the insects they'd found. When their enthusiasm waned, Lord Octavius said, "I've been in a carriage for hours. I need to stretch my legs. Let's go for a ramble!"

And so, they rambled. Along lanes and over stiles, through orchards and across meadows. The girls hunted for flowers, scampering here and there, trying to find as many different colors as possible. Lord Newingham scampered with them. After a few minutes Mr. Pryor abandoned his saunter and joined the hunt. "I'm going to find more colors than anyone else," he announced in a top-lofty manner.

Newingham and the girls began to scamper even faster.

"Miss Toogood," Lord Octavius said, and Pip thought he was going to suggest they start looking for flowers, too, but instead he said, "Do you think there are any advantages to being born female?"

The question was so unexpected and so very odd that Pip halted.

Lord Octavius halted, too. "Or do you think that there are none?"

Pip opened her mouth, and then closed it again.

"Because I've been thinking about it, and I can't think of one single advantage to being born female, and that's . . . well, frankly, it bothers me."

He appeared to be telling the truth. There was a crease between his eyebrows and his lips were compressed.

"Are there meant to be advantages?" Pip asked.

"There ought to be, don't you think? I mean, there are a lot of advantages to being male, so there ought to be *some* advantages to being female. It's only fair."

Pip was startled into a laugh. "I don't think it's something that's fair; it simply *is*."

Lord Octavius didn't return her laugh. His frown deepened. "Are you happy being female? Would you not prefer to be a man?"

Pip blinked. And blinked again. "I can truthfully tell you that I've never considered it before."

Lord Octavius didn't say anything, he simply

continued looking at her, a frown on his face, and after a moment she realized that he was waiting for her to answer his question.

Would she prefer to be a man?

Pip glanced away from him. The girls were wading through ankle-high grass in their quest for flowers. Newingham was on hands and knees under a hedgerow, the tails of his coat flapping, and Mr. Pryor was battling his way through a bramble patch.

Was she happy being female?

Would she be happier if she were a man?

Pip pondered those questions for a long moment, and then said, "I'm happy to be who I am."

The crease between Lord Octavius's eyebrows deepened. "You are?"

"You think I shouldn't be?"

He hesitated, and then said, "I wouldn't, if I were a female."

"That's because you're thinking of the things you'd lose if that were to happen, not the things you'd gain."

His frown became slightly quizzical. "I'd gain something?"

"Of course."

Pip resumed strolling. Lord Octavius fell into step with her. "What would I gain?" he asked.

"The ability to have children, for one. As a man, you'll never feel a child growing inside you and that's . . ." She pursed her lips, trying to articulate how she felt. Was pity too strong a word? "I feel sorry for you," she said finally. "That you'll never experience it."

"Sorry for me?" Lord Octavius said, a faint note of surprise in his voice.

"Yes."

He said nothing to that. Pip glanced sideways and caught an expression on his face that was close to a grimace. "What?" she asked.

Lord Octavius shrugged awkwardly. "I'm not sure I'd want to be pregnant. It looks dashed uncomfortable."

Pip laughed at the frankness of his response. "I believe it is uncomfortable, and painful, and sometimes dangerous, but don't you think the end result is worth it?"

He shrugged again, with his face as well as his shoulders. "Maybe?"

"It is," Pip said with certainty. "And for that reason alone I'm glad to be female, but there are other reasons, too."

"Such as?"

Pip strolled in silence for almost half a minute, trying to find the words to verbalize something that was hazy and nebulous. "I think . . . the world I inhabit is a gentler and safer place than the one you inhabit. Women encounter less violence in their lives than men do. We're not expected to fight, we can't be press-ganged or sent off to war, and perhaps *you* like fighting, but I don't, so that's another reason I'm glad I'm a woman."

Lord Octavius considered this for a moment, his expression thoughtful, and then he nodded. "Men are more aggressive than women. In general."

"In general," Pip agreed.

"Perhaps that could be a benefit to being female," he said, but he didn't sound entirely convinced.

"There's no 'perhaps' about it," Pip said. "It *is* a benefit. A very large benefit. As is being able to have children."

He made a movement that was half shrug, half nod. "If you say so."

"I do."

They strolled in silence for several paces.

"So that's two," Lord Octavius said, and then clarified: "Benefits to being female. In your opinion."

"Yes."

"Are there any others?"

"Well, I think women are generally less competitive than men."

His eyebrows lifted. "You do?"

Pip nodded. "Yes. It seems to me that men are often striving to get ahead of one another, whereas women tend to help each other."

"Perhaps you're right," Lord Octavius said, looking rather nonplussed.

"And I think women see more beauty in the world. I think we *add* more beauty to it. And I like that. I like seeing the beauty and adding to it."

"You mean . . . like arranging flowers and such?"

Pip laughed. "Flowers, yes, but all sorts of other things. I think women's eyes are more open to beauty than men's are."

Lord Octavius looked even more nonplussed. "So . . . the world is a more beautiful place to you than it is to me?"

"Yes."

They strolled another dozen paces, then Lord Octavius said, "So, do you think those benefits outweigh all the drawbacks? Because there are a great many drawbacks, as far as I can see."

"Such as?" Pip asked, curious to know what he thought were the disadvantages of being female.

"Lack of freedom," Lord Octavius said. "Lack of independence. Lack of choices."

"What sort of choices?"

"Most choices! You can't go to university. You can't vote. Most professions are closed to you. Your

317

world might be a lot safer than mine, but it's a damned sight smaller."

"The majority of men in England can't vote," Pip pointed out.

Lord Octavius frowned, and then shrugged and said, "True. But women get to make fewer decisions about their lives than men do. First their fathers decide things for them, and then their husbands do. And that's another thing! Did you know that you'll become my property when you marry me?"

"I did," Pip said.

"Why should you become *my* property? It's not right!"

His indignation made her smile. "Perhaps it's not right, but it's the way things are and I'm not going to rant and rail over it. It wouldn't achieve anything, except to make me unhappy."

This reply appeared to disconcert Lord Octavius. He stopped looking indignant and instead looked taken aback.

"I'm a woman," Pip told him. "I can't change that, and I don't want to be upset about the things that I *don't* have; I want to live my life being glad for all the things that I *do* have. I want to be happy I'm me." She thought about that last sentence, and rephrased it: "I *am* happy I'm me."

Lord Octavius came to a halt in the lane.

Pip halted, too. Was he annoyed at her for voicing her opinion?

"Have I told you yet how madly in love with you I am?" Lord Octavius said.

Pip felt herself blush hotly. She shook her head and fastened her gaze on his waistcoat.

"Because I am. Madly." He reached out and took both her hands in his. "You are a very wise person, Pip Toogood."

Pip shook her head again. "I'm not wise. I'm just . . . pragmatic."

"I like pragmatic women," Lord Octavius said. There was a smile in his voice, and when Pip risked a glance at his face, she saw a smile there, too. "In fact, I *love* pragmatic women. Will you marry me?"

"I've already said yes," Pip reminded him.

"I know, but I wanted to ask you again, because I love you even more madly today than I did yesterday."

His words, the warmth in his gaze, the affection in his smile, gave Pip a funny feeling in her chest, as if her heart had expanded several sizes. She rather thought that she loved Lord Octavius more today, too. He had an interesting mind and an extremely unconventional way of looking at things. "You are a singular man," she told him.

"Me?" His eyebrows lifted. "I'm quite ordinary.

Well, except for . . ." He cast a cautious glance over his shoulder and lowered his voice: "The magic."

Pip had a small moment of epiphany. Lord Octavius's magic was what made him interesting and unconventional, but not in the way he imagined. Because of his magical ability he'd looked at the world through other people's eyes and touched it through other people's skin—and those experiences had altered him. They'd altered the way that he *thought*.

She wondered whether he was aware of it. Had he noticed that he didn't think like most other Englishmen? Had his parents noticed? His grandfather?

As if to underline that he wasn't like most men, Lord Octavius chose that moment to say, "I want you to know that when I'm your husband I won't make your decisions for you and I will *not* think of you as my property."

Pip hadn't supposed that he would, not after his indignation on behalf of wives, but she said, "Thank you."

"And, uh . . ." He blushed, and said, "I want you to know that I'll never force you to do anything you don't want. Ever. I promise."

"Anything" was a very vague word, but the tone of Lord Octavius's voice coupled with the color in his cheeks told her that he was talking about the marriage bed.

Pip felt a blush rise in her own cheeks. She went back to staring at his waistcoat. "Thank you," she said again.

Lord Octavius clasped her hands a little more tightly. "I want you to be happy in our marriage," he said in an earnest voice.

"I want you to be happy, too," Pip said. It seemed the sort of thing one should say to a man's face, not his waistcoat, so she looked up at him again, and once she'd looked she couldn't look away.

If a gaze could be full-hearted, Lord Octavius's was. If a gaze could be impassioned, his was.

Pip found herself unable to move, unable to speak. She could barely breathe. All she could do was stand and stare up at him.

When Lord Octavius bent his head to kiss her, Pip didn't hesitate. She kissed him back with everything in her, kissed him with fervor and zeal and vehemence and passion.

"Tut, tut, tut," a voice drawled alongside them.

Never had three words been uttered to such dreadful effect. It was as if a bathtub of icy water had been upended over Pip's head. She gave a violent start, wrenched her hands from Lord Octavius's grasp, and stumbled back in horrified haste.

"Tut, tut," their interrupter said again. It was Mr. Pryor. He stood alongside them, shaking his head, a particularly wide smirk on his face.

Pip groped for her bonnet and found it still on her head. She felt off balance and befuddled. She looked for the girls and saw them busily hunting for flowers amid the long grass. Newingham was still on hands and knees under the hedgerow.

"Shocking," Mr. Pryor said. "Simply shocking."

It *was* shocking. The most shocking thing Pip had ever done. More shocking than climbing trees or learning defensive techniques or kissing Lord Octavius in an empty schoolroom.

She'd *kissed* a man in a public lane.

She kissed a man in a public lane *within sight of Edie and Fanny.*

The girls hadn't noticed, and neither had Lord Newingham, but that didn't alter the fact that it had been an appalling lapse of judgment.

"Shocking," Mr. Pryor said again, shaking his head.

"Do be quiet, Dex," Lord Octavius said.

Pip was more discomfited than she'd ever been in her life. She couldn't understand how she'd come to kiss Lord Octavius in so public a place, with the girls and Lord Newingham less than fifty yards away. What had she been thinking?

"Quite scandalous, in fact," Mr. Pryor said, warming to his theme. "Such a display of ardor—"

"That's enough, Dex," Lord Octavius said. He

looked as mortified as Pip felt. He clearly hadn't meant to kiss her in public any more than she'd meant to kiss him.

Mr. Pryor paid no attention to his cousin's pronouncement. "One would hope that you purchased a special license in town, because such disgraceful behavior can only be rectified by—"

"I did," Lord Octavius said. "And I bought a sword, too, and if you don't shut up I'll use it to cut off your head."

Mr. Pryor laughed at this threat.

"It's a very *sharp* sword," Lord Octavius told him.

"Good," Mr. Pryor said, his demeanor switching abruptly from teasing to businesslike. "Let's go and practice, shall we?"

"What? Now?"

"We want to teach Rumpole his lesson as soon as possible, don't we?" Mr. Pryor asked.

"Well, yes, but—"

"Tonight, if possible."

"Yes, but—"

"Then we should practice."

Lord Octavius looked at Pip, and then at the girls, and then back at his cousin. "Now?"

Mr. Pryor uttered an exasperated sigh. "We can't stay here forever, Otto. It's been six days already, and you might not want to get on with the rest of your life, but Bunny and I *do*."

Lord Octavius grimaced. "Of course. I beg your pardon. We'll practice now." He looked at Pip, and hesitated, and then said, "Miss Toogood, I apologize for . . ." He made an awkward gesture that could have meant a hundred different things but that Pip knew was meant to signify their kiss.

She nodded to show she understood.

Mr. Pryor handed her the flowers he'd picked. "For you, Miss Toogood."

Pip accepted the posy automatically. It consisted mostly of buttercups and dandelions.

Mr. Pryor headed in the direction of Rumpole Hall with his signature swagger. Lord Octavius made no move to follow him. He stood in the middle of the lane, looking at Pip.

She clutched the flowers and stared back at him, still feeling off balance and discombobulated.

"If you can tear yourself away . . ." Mr. Pryor called back in a sing-song voice.

"We'll talk later," Lord Octavius promised Pip, and then he strode hastily after his cousin.

CHAPTER 27

They visited the Long Gallery, stared at the best portrait of Amelia Rumpole for several minutes, then retired to the privacy of Octavius's bedroom. Octavius stripped off his clothes, changed shape, and donned the maid's clothing, then he stood in front of the mirror and practiced Amelia Rumpole's face and hair while Dex levitated the sword around the room. "Hold your right hand up," Dex said.

Octavius did. The sword flew neatly into his grip, hilt-first, then the sheath swooped off like a bird taking flight. Suddenly, he was brandishing a naked sword.

"Impressive," he said.

Dex smirked. "I know."

They ran through that part of the performance—the sword flying into his hand, the sheath swooping off—twice more, then Dex hoisted the armchair into the air as a substitute for Rumpole. "All right, let's hear your speech."

"You vile and contemptible worm!" Octavius cried. He flourished the sword—and then squawked as his feet left the ground.

"You need to be in the air, too," Dex said. "More menacing if you loom over him, don't you think?"

Octavius did think so—but that didn't mean he enjoyed floating. He didn't like that there was nothing but emptiness beneath his feet, and he especially didn't like that he had a skirt wafting around his legs and he wasn't wearing drawers. An updraft would expose his private parts to all and sundry. And, damn it, that was something else he should have bought in London: a pair of boy's drawers.

He gripped the sword tightly and began his speech again. "You vile and contemptible worm—"

"Your hair needs to be loose," Dex said. "Let me see if I can . . ."

Octavius hung motionless while the mobcap levitated off his head. The hairpins slid free and were suddenly gone. Amelia Rumpole's long hair unwound itself from the precarious bun on his head and began to drift behind him, as if he stood in a strong breeze.

"That looks good," Dex said. "Very otherworldly."

Octavius pointed the sword menacingly at the

armchair again. "You vile and contemptible worm!" he cried, and then gave a yelp as his skirts began to move. "Don't lift up my dress!"

"I'm not going to, you idiot," Dex said, frowning with concentration.

Octavius caught sight of himself in the mirror. His heart gave a tiny leap, an instinctive recoil that was part shock and part fright. That person floating in the air wearing a maidservant's clothes and a dead woman's face, with her hair and her skirts billowing in a non-existent breeze, that was *him*.

Dex was right: he did look otherworldly. Ghostly.

Octavius shivered, even though he knew the person in the mirror was him. No, he shivered *because* that person was him. That dead woman with the flowing hair.

"All right," Dex said. "Go."

Octavius looked away from the mirror. He ran through his speech from start to finish, punctuating his points with threatening slashes of the sword.

"Bravo," Dex said, when he was done. "I reckon you'll scare him off women for life."

Octavius lowered the sword. He hoped Dex was right.

CHAPTER 28

*P*ip had almost regained her equilibrium by the time she, the girls, and Lord Newingham returned to the house. She still couldn't understand how she'd come to kiss Lord Octavius in a public lane, but her brain had resumed functioning and she was able to tell Edie that yes, both moths and butterflies spent time in cocoons, and to assure Newingham that yes, he'd be more than welcome to dine in the nursery that evening. Newingham parted ways with them in the entrance hall. Pip climbed the main staircase with the girls. The first two flights were carpeted, but the third flight, up to the nursery, wasn't and their footsteps were suddenly loud on the bare floorboards. Pip was so busy explaining caterpillars and cocoons to Edie that she almost didn't notice that someone was descending the stairs.

She glanced up, and stopped in mid-sentence.

What was Mr. Donald doing on this staircase?

The girls clattered past their father's valet without appearing to notice his existence. Pip moved swiftly past him, too, the words she'd been about to utter frozen on her tongue.

The main staircase was much wider than the servants' stairs but even so, as she passed the valet, their arms brushed.

A shiver ran up her spine.

How could something so innocuous, so seemingly casual and innocent, feel so threatening? How could it make every hair on her body stand on end?

Pip gathered her wits and found her voice. "Not all caterpillars become butterflies. Some become moths."

At the half landing, she glanced back. Mr. Donald was gone from sight, but that didn't stop her shivering again.

Why had he been on these stairs?

Had he been waiting for her?

Lord Octavius, Mr. Pryor, and Lord Newingham joined them for dinner again. The two cousins were in good spirits, but Newingham was uncharacteristically quiet. His jaw was tight, his lips were thin, and there was a sharp little crease between his eyebrows.

Pip wondered what had happened to put him out of temper.

Lord Octavius and Mr. Pryor didn't appear to notice Newingham's quietness. They kept up a cheerful stream of conversation, joking and teasing across the table, making the girls laugh. Pip braced herself for some sly digs from Mr. Pryor, but they didn't come. It would seem that he'd forgotten what had happened in the lane.

Pip wished she could forget it, too. She felt hot with mortification every time she thought of it.

Lord Octavius pushed his chair back as soon as the meal was finished. "I have some affairs I need to discuss to with my cousin. Family business. If you'll excuse us?"

If Newingham was curious as to what family business his two friends needed to discuss at Rumpole Hall, he didn't show it. He was lost in thought, the crease between his eyebrows even sharper than it had been before.

"You'll stay and play jackstraws with us, won't you, Uncle Robert?" Fanny asked pleadingly.

Newingham lost his frown. "Of course. There's nothing I'd like more."

Pip watched Lord Octavius and Mr. Pryor depart.

She wished she could go with them and observe, but she couldn't. All she could do was tap the table three times and wish them a silent *Good luck*.

It was difficult to concentrate on jackstraws that evening. Pip played abysmally. So did Lord Newingham. The Pryor cousins hadn't returned by the girls' bedtime. Pip wondered what that meant. Had they found Baron Rumpole? Had they carried out their plan? Had it worked? Or were they still waiting for an opportunity?

The girls said their good-nights. Pip began to tidy away the jackstraws. Newingham picked up several and crammed them into the wooden box they came from. His movements were jerky, almost angry.

"Forgive me for asking, Lord Newingham, but . . . is something wrong?"

Newingham's mouth tightened and it seemed for a moment that he wouldn't speak, then he gathered up some more jackstraws and shoved them into the box. "I spoke to Rumpole before dinner, about the girls, and he said . . ." He shook his head sharply. "I can't repeat what he said. It's too offensive."

Silently they collected the last of the jackstraws and placed them in the box. Newingham closed the lid with a snap. "He thinks of them as livestock," he burst out. "And once they're of marriageable age that's how he's going to get rid of them: like cows at a marketplace. Cows! He actually said that." His jaw clenched and his hands clenched and for a round-faced and cheerful young viscount he looked astonishingly savage.

"I'm certain it won't happen," Pip said, wishing she could tell him that he'd soon be the girls' guardian.

"It happened to Amelia," Newingham said bitterly. His knuckles whitened as if he wanted to punch something. "And after he said that about the cows, he said . . ." His knuckles grew whiter. "But I can't tell you that." Color flooded his cheeks. He unclenched his hands. "I beg your pardon. I shouldn't have said any of that. Forgive me."

"There's nothing to forgive," Pip said. "Your sentiments do you great justice. The girls are lucky to have you as their uncle."

Newingham flushed even redder. He made her a hasty bow and departed.

Pip didn't depart. She stayed in the empty nursery and let the viscount's words play over in her mind.

Livestock.

A marketplace.

Baron Rumpole intended to get rid of his daughters as if they were cows.

CHAPTER 29

*O*ctavius tiptoed down the main staircase in the guise of a very pretty housemaid. Dex followed a few steps behind, the sword held inconspicuously at his side. They scouted the ground floor. Rumpole was nowhere to be seen, but candles were lit in the dining room and the long table was set for one person. They narrowly missed being spotted by a footman who was clearly waiting for the baron to come down to dinner.

"He must be upstairs dressing," Octavius whispered.

"Must be," Dex whispered back.

They retreated to the library to wait. Dex hid the sword behind an armchair and sat down with a newspaper. Octavius concealed himself in a shadowy alcove, in case anyone should come.

Five minutes passed. Then ten. Octavius gave in

and sat on the floor—which wasn't easy wearing a dress. He couldn't sit cross-legged unless he pulled his skirts up to his knees.

Damn, but he missed his breeches.

Another ten minutes passed. Octavius grew bored. The footman waiting in the dining room must be bored, too.

Finally, he heard footsteps and a voice. The footsteps could have been anyone's but that petulant voice could only belong to one person.

Dex lowered the newspaper.

Together, they listened to Baron Rumpole enter his dining room.

Octavius left his alcove and went to stand at the half-open library door, to hear better. He thought he caught the sound of wine being poured from a decanter and the soft clink of silverware. Footmen came and went for several minutes, bringing the baron his dinner, enduring his sharply voiced complaints. Finally, the servants departed. The only sound that reached the library was the almost inaudible scrape of cutlery on a plate.

Octavius hoped the bastard would eat fast. "You hide in that alcove," he told Dex. "With any luck, Rumpole will come in here afterwards to drink."

"The things I do for you," Dex said, but he crossed to the alcove and lowered himself to sit. From where Octavius stood, Dex was invisible.

"Here." He rolled up the newspaper his cousin had been reading and tossed it at him.

Dex caught it one-handed. "Where are you going to hide?"

"Across the corridor." Octavius peeked out the library door, checking for servants, then slipped across to the empty breakfast parlor.

Fortunately, the baron took less time to eat his dinner than he had changing clothes. Octavius was almost unprepared for the sudden bustle of footmen removing the covers. He watched through a crack in the door as ashets, tureens, and platters were taken back to the kitchen.

Finally, the footmen stopped scurrying to and fro. The baron didn't emerge from the dining room. Was he going to do his drinking at the table tonight?

Octavius waited, peering through the crack.

Just when he'd decided that the baron was going to stay in the dining room, he heard the sound of a chair being pushed back. Rumpole appeared in the corridor, belched loudly, and headed for the library.

Octavius watched him enter. His heart, which had been doing a steady trot, began to canter.

It was time to do this mad, outrageous thing.

He picked up a vase of flowers from the mantelpiece, took a deep breath, and left the breakfast parlor.

He crossed the corridor, holding the vase in front of him. Another deep breath, another half dozen steps, and he reached the library door.

Rumpole was at the sideboard, pouring himself a glass of port. He didn't notice Octavius standing in the doorway.

Octavius gave him time to finish pouring and to choose an armchair—the very one Dex had been sitting in earlier—before he slipped into the room. The baron still didn't notice him. He leaned back in the armchair and gave vent to another loud belch.

Octavius closed the library door as quietly as he could and turned the key. The baron didn't notice the quiet *snick* of the door locking; he was too busy slurping his port.

Octavius advanced into the room, holding the vase of flowers. He glanced at the alcove and saw only shadows, but he knew Dex was there, just as he knew there was a sword behind the armchair Rumpole sat in.

"Good evening, sir," he said, in a soft, shy Hampshire voice. He bobbed a timid curtsy, crossed to the mantelpiece, and placed the vase there. He spent a minute rearranging the flowers, giving the baron time to notice the curves of his waist and hips and buttocks, then he turned around and let the man see how pretty his face was and how well his breasts filled the bodice of his gown. He curtsied again and said in a meek little voice, "Is there anything I can do for you, sir?"

The baron's gaze drifted to Octavius's breasts and then down to his waist. He smiled.

It wasn't a nice smile.

Octavius's pulse gave an exultant leap. He made himself cringe from the baron's gaze. "Sir?"

"Come here," the baron said.

Octavius went with slow, reluctant steps and a galloping heart. "Sir?" he said again, when he was standing in front of the baron.

"Closer," the baron said.

Octavius shuffled nearer, until his skirts brushed one of the baron's knees. "Sir?" he said, in a timorous whisper.

The baron reached out and fondled Octavius's hip.

Octavius couldn't stop himself recoiling. He moved without conscious thought, taking a step back.

The baron lost his smile. His eyebrows drew together in their familiar scowl. "Closer, I said."

Rage ignited in Octavius's chest. He bowed his head submissively and made himself step close enough for his skirts to brush the baron's knee again.

Rumpole laid a hand on Octavius's hip and

fondled that plump curve. Octavius gritted his teeth and stared at the floor, enduring the caress. He didn't say anything. He couldn't. Fury choked his throat, making speech impossible.

The baron slurped another mouthful of port and dug his fingers into the roundness of Octavius's hip. "Sit on my lap."

Octavius couldn't prevent another recoil. He managed not to step back this time. He also managed to find his voice. "Sir, I don't—"

"You want to work for me, then you'll do as I tell you." Rumpole squeezed his hip painfully.

Octavius raised his gaze and looked at the baron. He didn't think he'd ever despised anyone as much as he despised Rumpole. He wanted to pick the man up and fling him across the room, wanted to beat conscience and compassion and kindness into him.

But you couldn't beat those things into someone. People either had them, or they didn't. And Baron Rumpole didn't.

"Sit," the baron said, with another painful squeeze of Octavius's hip.

Octavius let his magic flow through him, giving him Amelia Rumpole's face and Amelia Rumpole's hair. "You vile and contemptible worm!" he cried. He raised his right hand and the sword flew into it.

This time it was Rumpole who recoiled. He released Octavius and flung himself back in the armchair. Port sprayed from his glass.

The mobcap levitated off Octavius's head. His hair uncoiled and began to stream behind him.

Rumpole uttered a horrified croak. He threw aside his glass and tried to scramble out of the armchair. The chair fell over backwards—Octavius wasn't sure whether that was Dex's doing or not, but he knew Dex was responsible for the way in which Rumpole rose off the floor.

Rumpole gave a terrified choked-off wail. His arms and legs windmilled frantically.

Octavius found himself rising in the air, too. For once, it didn't bother him. He was filled with a savage, exultant glee. "You vile and contemptible worm!" he cried again, flourishing the sword. "You filthy debaucher! You loathsome molester of women!"

Rumpole flailed desperately, trying to retreat, but he couldn't move from his position in the midair any more than Octavius could. Both of them were at Dex's mercy.

"The time has come for you to pay for your wickedness," Octavius informed the baron. He felt like an avenging angel, sword aloft, his hair and skirts flowing behind him.

Rumpole shook his head wildly. "No," he cried. "Please! Amelia!"

"I have chosen your punishment," Octavius said, in as booming and godlike a voice as his female throat was capable of.

Rumpole shook his head again. "Please, Amelia . . ."

"It is castration!"

Rumpole clawed futilely at the air, realized he was trapped, and burst into tears. "No, no, please, no . . ."

Octavius waved the sword in the direction of Rumpole's groin. Candlelight glinted off the blade.

The baron shielded his crotch with his hands. "Please," he begged, through his tears. "Please! I won't do it again! I promise!"

"Your promises are worth nothing," Octavius told him. "Your heart is vile and corrupt!"

Dex brought Rumpole a little closer to the sword. The baron's voice rose in a shriek: "I promise! Never again! I promise, I promise!" He was crying loudly and messily, so frightened he was almost incoherent.

Octavius stopped feeling exultant. All of a sudden he didn't feel like an avenging angel; he felt like a bully.

"Please!" the baron implored him, sniveling and sobbing. He was kneeling in midair now, abasing himself, groveling. "I'm sorry, I'm sorry. I won't do it again. I promise!"

Their plan had worked. They'd scared Rumpole into a change of heart. But Octavius's strongest emotion right now wasn't triumph; it was shame that he'd reduced a man to such a state of terror.

The smell of urine was suddenly pungent in the library. Rumpole had wet himself.

Octavius felt even more ashamed. *Hurry up and get this over with,* he told himself.

"There will be no second chance," he boomed. "Do you understand me? If you force your attentions on even one more woman, I will return and castrate you."

The baron cowered beneath his gaze. "I understand," he babbled. "I promise I won't. I promise, I promise, I promise!"

Octavius felt revulsion. Revulsion for the baron— and revulsion for himself. "You are the basest and most contemptible worm to ever crawl upon this earth," he told Rumpole coldly. "I won't have my children anywhere near you. You will give them to my brother to raise."

"He can have them," the baron cried. "I'll give them to him. I promise!"

"A legal document, signed and witnessed." Octavius extended his arm until the tip of the sword touched Rumpole's chest. "Tomorrow morning."

The baron cringed from that bright, sharp blade. "I will! I will! I promise! Tomorrow!"

"If you break either of your promises, I shall return."

"I won't break them," Rumpole said frantically. "I won't! I promise!"

Octavius hung there for a moment, his hair and skirts wafting behind him, the sword tip resting on Rumpole's chest, and then he glanced at the alcove and gave Dex a nod.

Dex nodded back, and as he nodded the baron began to float towards the furthest corner of the library. Rumpole turned in the air as he drifted. By the time he reached the corner, he was facing the wall. Dex lowered the baron to the floor.

"Kneel there," Octavius told the man sternly. "Kneel and pray for your soul."

Rumpole obediently stayed on his knees, snuffling and sobbing.

Dex set Octavius down on the floor. It was a relief to stand on solid ground again and even more of a relief that it was all over.

They tiptoed hastily to the door. Octavius turned the key. Dex slipped through first, the sword sheath in one hand and Octavius's mobcap in the other. Octavius cast a glance back at the library—at the tipped-over armchair and the port glass lying on

the floor and the baron kneeling in the far corner—
then he stepped out into the corridor and quietly
closed the door.

CHAPTER 30

"*T*hat was capital sport," Dex said, once they'd reached the safety of Octavius's room. "Capital!"

Octavius grunted, and tossed the sword on his bed.

"Rumpole's going to be a monk from now on," Dex said, flinging himself down in the armchair. "Mark my words. A monk!"

Octavius grunted again.

Dex cocked his head at him. "What's wrong with you?"

Octavius couldn't articulate how he felt because he didn't understand it himself. He settled for shaking his head.

"What?" Dex asked.

Octavius shrugged, and said the first thing that entered his head: "He wet himself."

Dex shrugged, too. "Serves him right."

Octavius frowned.

Dex frowned back at him. "What?" he said. "You don't think so? He tried to *rape* you at Vauxhall."

"I know," Octavius said. "I know." He sighed, and rubbed his forehead. His hair hung around his face. The wrong hair, the wrong face, the wrong body. "Get me out of these clothes, will you?"

He undressed in silence and changed back into himself. The relief was enormous. He took a moment to be grateful for it: his own ears, his own eyes, his own hands, his own voice.

"Here." Dex tossed him his nightshirt.

Octavius didn't feel like going to bed. What he most wanted to do was to go for a very long walk, to climb the hanger and wander for hours along the hilltops, to clear his head and his lungs and his conscience—if such a thing were possible.

But it was past ten o'clock. Too late for long, solitary country walks.

He pulled on the nightshirt.

"You going to tell me what's wrong?" Dex asked.

Octavius sighed, and rubbed his forehead again. This time it was his own face, his own hair. "It made me feel like a bully."

"A bully?" Dex gave an incredulous laugh. "You're not a bully, Otto."

"I stood over Rumpole and threatened him until

he wet his breeches. If that's not bullying, I don't know what is."

"It was *justice*," Dex said. "Justice for every female Rumpole has ever forced to swive him."

Yes, it had been justice. But Octavius had always thought that justice would feel right, not wrong.

"He'll keep doing it forever, if someone doesn't stop him."

"I know," Octavius said. "We had to do it, it's just . . . I don't like how it made me feel."

To beat a bully, he'd become a bully.

Dex eyed him for a long moment, then shook his head. "You're softer than I thought you were."

Was he soft? He didn't think so. He just hadn't liked scaring another person so badly that he wet himself.

"What about the valet?" Dex asked. "You going to just let him get away with it?"

Octavius thought about Lord Rumpole sobbing and pleading in the library, the smell of urine—and then he thought about the valet attacking him on the stairs, the suddenness of it, the violence. "No. We'll do him tomorrow."

*C*HAPTER 31

*L*ord Newingham usually knocked on the schoolroom door not long after breakfast. That morning he didn't make an appearance. Neither did Lord Octavius. Or Mr. Pryor. Pip tried not to worry, but it was impossible not to. Had something gone wrong last night?

An hour passed. Arithmetic gave way to French verbs, and still Lord Newingham didn't come. Edie and Fanny were restless and fidgety. "Where's Uncle Robert?" Fanny asked, a whining note in her voice, when Pip asked her to decline the verb *pouvoir.*

Pip didn't reprimand her. She felt like whining, too. Where *was* Lord Octavius?

Another hour passed. Pip heard the sound of rapid footsteps in the corridor. Lord Newingham burst into the schoolroom. His face was flushed, as if he'd run up the stairs. "Guess what?" he cried.

Fanny bounced up from her seat. "We're going to fly kites?"

Newingham shook his head and beamed at her. "You're coming home with me."

Edie sprang up from her seat, too. "For the summer?"

"For *ever*," Newingham said, brandishing a piece of paper. "Your father has given me guardianship of you. You're going to live with me from now on."

Fanny gave a little squeal of delight, then ran to her uncle and shyly hugged him.

Newingham hugged her back, lifting her off her feet, swinging her around, and then he hugged Edie, too. His grin was wide and exhilarated.

"What about Archie?" Edie asked, clinging to her uncle. "Can he come live with you, too?"

"Your brother can visit as often as he likes," the viscount said.

Movement in the doorway caught Pip's eye. Lord Octavius and his cousin stood there.

"We're leaving first thing tomorrow morning," the viscount said. "Which means your trunks need to be packed today. Come! Let's get started." He swept the girls out of the schoolroom.

Pip followed. Lord Octavius fell into step with her. He touched her hand, a fleeting brush of fingertips that said *Hello* and *Good morning* and *I'm happy to see you.*

Newingham disappeared down the corridor, the girls frisking around him like puppies. Their voices echoed back, bright with excitement.

"Last night was obviously a success," Pip said.

"It was." Lord Octavius's tone was oddly neutral.

Pip glanced at him, and discovered that his expression was neutral, too.

She didn't have time to enquire further. First, she had to stop Newingham from flinging the girls' clothing willy-nilly onto their beds, then she had to direct the footmen to bring down the trunks from the attic and instruct two housemaids to pack the girls' belongings. Newingham was as excited as the girls. He darted here and there. "Do you want to take this?" he cried, waving a bonnet, "Or these?" brandishing a pair of slippers.

After fifteen minutes, Pip sent him outside with the girls. "Come back in two hours," she told him firmly. "All of you, go, shoo."

"I bought some kites in London," Lord Octavius said to the girls. "Fancy ones with long tails. Would you like to fly them?"

Newingham gave a loud whoop and departed down the stairs at a run. The girls and Mr. Pryor bounded after him. Lord Octavius exchanged an amused glance with Pip, then followed them. He reappeared five minutes later, alone. "How can I help?" he asked.

"Aren't you going to fly kites?"

He shook his head. "You're leaving tomorrow, too. We all are."

"Oh," Pip said. Her stomach gave a little squirm of excitement. She was leaving. Tomorrow. With Lord Octavius.

"How can I help?" he said again. "What needs to be done?"

"My trunk needs to be brought down from the attic."

"I'll see to it."

Pip went back to the schoolroom and began going through drawers, cupboards, and shelves. She was barely two minutes into her task when a floorboard creaked behind her. "That was quick," she said, turning around.

But it wasn't Lord Octavius who stood there; it was Mr. Donald.

Pip jerked backwards a step. "Mr. Donald." She pressed her hand to her chest, where her heart thudded rapidly. "What are you doing here?"

"Lord Rumpole has informed me that his daughters are leaving tomorrow. He has offered my services."

"Oh," Pip said. "That's very kind of him, but—"

"I'll pack their trunks."

"Thank you, but Jenny and Agnes are doing that."

Mr. Donald gave a disparaging curl of his lip. "I'll supervise." He turned to leave, and then paused. "Are you departing tomorrow, Miss Toogood?"

"Yes," Pip said.

His eyelids dipped slightly and he smiled. Something about that smile made all the hairs on Pip's scalp stand on end. *Predator*, a little voice whispered in her ear.

Pip watched him leave the schoolroom. His footsteps retreated along the corridor and faded from earshot.

He was gone, but she found it impossible to turn her back to the door and resume her task. She was still standing in the center of the schoolroom with her hand pressed to her chest when Lord Octavius returned. He took one look at her and frowned sharply. "What is it?"

"Mr. Donald was just here."

Lord Octavius's frown didn't change markedly—a slight narrowing of his eyes, an infinitesimal flaring of his nostrils—but he suddenly looked dangerous. "Was he?" His voice was pitched lower than it usually was and somehow that was dangerous, too.

"He knows I'm leaving tomorrow. I think . . ." Pip shivered. "I think he's going to try something tonight."

"I have no doubt of it," Lord Octavius said grimly.

His eyes narrowed further, his frown changing yet again, becoming less angry and more thoughtful. "May I borrow one of your gowns? Tonight's lesson would be best coming from you."

"You'll pretend to be me when you put the fear of God into him?"

He nodded.

Pip rather liked the thought of that: the predator getting his comeuppance from a governess. "I'll fetch a gown," she said.

Lord Octavius refused to let her go alone, which brought foolish heat to Pip's cheeks. She and Lord Octavius were walking *to her bedroom* and even though the reason wasn't romantic—was in fact the exact opposite of romantic—she found herself feeling ridiculously self-conscious.

"How did it go last night?" she asked, to distract herself.

Lord Octavius hesitated before answering. Pip saw his lips twitch in a brief grimace. "It went very well."

Pip wondered what that grimace had been for. "But something went wrong?"

"Wrong? No. Nothing went wrong."

"But?"

Lord Octavius sighed, and halted in the corridor. He rubbed his forehead and glanced at her and then away. "Rumpole cried and he wet himself and I just . . ." He shook his head. "It was harder than I thought it would be."

Pip reached out and touched the back of his hand with her fingertips. "You found it hard because you're a good person."

He made a sound that was half laugh, half sigh. "I don't feel like a good person. Not after last night."

"You are," Pip said, with certainty. She took his hand and gave his fingers a squeeze. "A very good person. A hero, in fact."

Lord Octavius blushed an adorable shade of pink. "I'm not a hero."

"I think you are," Pip said. She released his hand. "The next room's mine."

Lord Octavius didn't try to come in with her; he waited in the corridor like a guard and Pip found that she didn't care what the servants might think. Mr. Donald scared her and Lord Octavius made her feel safe, and that was all that mattered.

She went through her wardrobe swiftly. She didn't have a great many gowns. She selected the plainest one, sniffed the armpits to make certain they smelled of nothing other than clean cotton, and folded it neatly. "Here," she said, stepping out into the corridor and giving it to Lord Octavius.

He tucked it under his arm. "Stay in your room 'til I get back."

"Do you really think that's necessary?"

"I don't think you should be in the schoolroom, not if Donald knows you're up here alone. It's too isolated."

Isolated? Yes, it was isolated. If she screamed, it was unlikely anyone would hear her.

Pip repressed a shiver. "All right."

"I won't be long," Lord Octavius said.

Pip watched him disappear down the corridor. Lord Octavius was intending to wear one of her gowns tonight, and that was . . . disconcerting, and also a little embarrassing. The gown hadn't smelled to her, but perhaps it would smell to him?

He'd barely vanished from sight when two footmen arrived, lugging her trunk between them. "Set it down there, please," Pip said, pointing to a spot by the dresser.

The footmen deposited the trunk on the floor and departed.

Pip opened the trunk. Her valise was inside, but her hatboxes weren't. It took her a moment to remember where she'd put them: in the cupboard across from her bedroom.

She went out into the corridor, found the hatboxes, and brought them back to her room. As she laid them on the bed, someone stepped up behind her. A hand clamped over her mouth and an arm wrapped around her waist, lifting her off her feet.

It happened so fast that Pip didn't have time to turn her head and see who it was. She didn't even have time to scream. One moment she was placing the hatboxes on the bed, the next she was caught up in a tight grasp, struggling to breathe.

Panic swept through her like a river bursting its banks. She clawed at the hand over her mouth.

"You've been watching me," a man's voice rasped in her ear. "I've seen you, you little slut." He didn't smell like Lord Octavius smelled, didn't breathe like he breathed. His grip was crushing, merciless, his muscles straining with a terrible, taut eagerness. "You're begging for it, aren't you? Like a bitch in heat. Giving me those looks, enticing me into your room."

Pip couldn't breathe, couldn't think. She clawed again at the hand covering her mouth.

The man shook her roughly, then released her, shoving her onto the bed, sending her sprawling. Pip inhaled a ragged, desperate breath. *Fight!* a voice cried in her head.

Pip rolled off the hatboxes and kicked at her attacker. It was Mr. Donald, but he didn't look unremarkable and ordinary anymore; he looked terrifying, more demon than man. His lips were pulled back from his teeth in a grin that was savage and gleeful, a grin that said he was going to hurt her—and that he was going to enjoy doing it.

Pip's heart punched in her chest. Terror froze her to the bed—and then the voice in her head cried *Fight!* again. It sounded like Lord Octavius and Mr. Pryor and Lord Newingham all yelling at once.

Mr. Donald reached for her. Pip kicked, catching his arm, but the blow was glancing and seemed only to amuse him. His grin became even more gleeful. "Feisty, aren't you?"

Fear had stolen the strength from her limbs. Pip scrambled off the far side of the bed, fell to the floor, and floundered to her feet. She grabbed the nearest object: the ewer in her washstand. She swung it at Mr. Donald as he came at her and tried to scream, but the scream was short and weak and breathless.

Mr. Donald caught the ewer in one hand, wrenched it from her grasp, and threw it aside.

Pip tried to dart around him. Her legs moved too slowly, as if she was running through water.

Mr. Donald grabbed her wrist. His fingers bit in deeply.

Voices were screaming in her head, a panic-stricken cacophony, but that grip on Pip's wrist was familiar. She knew what to do when a man held her like that. She'd practiced it.

She bent her head and bit Mr. Donald's hand as hard as she could. The taste of blood blossomed on her tongue.

Mr. Donald gave a yelp and released her, shoving her violently away. Pip stumbled and fell backwards, full-length on the floor, smacking her head. She tried to roll over, to scramble to her feet, but it was too late: Mr. Donald was looming over her, rage twisting his face. He grabbed at her with claw-like hands, catching the neckline of her gown, ripping the bodice open, exposing her chemise.

The voices in her head shrieked even more frantically than before. *Fight!*

Pip drew back her knees and kicked Mr. Donald in the nose with both feet.

This time panic didn't steal her strength. Her kick landed with a satisfying crunch.

Mr. Donald gave a howl of pain. He stumbled back, clutching his face. Blood spurted from between his fingers.

Pip rolled and scrambled to her feet. She flung the door open, tumbled out into the corridor, and ran, her feet pounding on the uncarpeted floor, past the schoolroom, around the corner—where she collided with someone so violently that they both fell over.

They landed on the floor in a tangle of arms and legs and even though she hadn't seen the person's face yet, Pip knew it was Lord Octavius. It wasn't just that his smell was familiar, the very *feel* of him was familiar.

Lord Octavius sat up. "Pip?" he said, and then more sharply, "What's wrong? What's happened?" He saw her ripped bodice. Alarm flashed across his face. "Are you all right?"

Pip sat up, too, and tried to pull the ruined bodice up with shaking fingers. Her arms were shaking, too. Her whole body was. She knew that if she tried to speak she'd burst into tears, so she answered with a nod.

Lord Octavius moved her hands aside, then pulled the bodice up and tucked it into her chemise. His fingers brushed her skin, but there was nothing sensual about it. He was gentle, careful. "Did Donald do this?"

Pip nodded again.

"Is he in your bedroom?"

She nodded again.

Lord Octavius stood and helped her to her feet. "Are you all right? Did he hurt you?"

Pip inhaled a trembling breath. "I'm fine," she managed to say without bursting into tears.

Lord Octavius cupped her face in his hands and brushed one thumb lightly over her lower lip. "You're bleeding."

"I bit him."

Lord Octavius lowered his hands and drew her into an embrace. Pip pressed her forehead into his shoulder and closed her eyes. His arms were warm and strong. They made her feel safe.

The panic and the terror began to recede. The shaking eased slightly. She could stand like this forever, being held by him, but even as she formed that thought, Lord Octavius released her and stepped back. "Wait here," he said. "I'll see to Mr. Donald." His gaze fell to her mouth again and his lips tightened. He pulled a handkerchief from his pocket and handed it to her.

Pip took it and dabbed at her mouth. The handkerchief came away smudged with blood.

"He'll never touch another woman again," Lord Octavius said grimly. "I promise you that."

He was gone before Pip had time to wipe her mouth properly, vanishing around the corner, his footsteps quite martial, an aggressive *slap-slap-slap* of well-shod feet on wooden floorboards.

Pip moistened the handkerchief with her tongue and tried to scrub away the blood. Mr. Donald's blood. Mr. Donald of the savage grin and the sudden, terrifying violence.

Abruptly, Pip found herself concerned for Lord Octavius's well-being. He was younger, taller, and stronger than Mr. Donald, but the valet was possessed of a terrible, demonic madness. What if he hurt Lord Octavius? What if he killed him?

She headed for her bedchamber, the handkerchief clutched in her hand, but before she was halfway there she heard a choked cry of pain and the smack of a fist striking flesh.

Pip dropped the handkerchief, caught up her skirts, and ran. She burst through the open door to her room and halted, horrified.

The men were on the floor, grappling with one another. Lord Octavius was ascendant, straddling the valet, one hand gripping the man's throat. As Pip watched he drew back his fist and struck Mr. Donald in the face.

Neither man noticed her. Mr. Donald was trying to fend Lord Octavius off, and Lord Octavius . . . Lord Octavius now had both hands wrapped around the valet's throat.

"Stop!" Pip cried.

The men paid her no attention. Mr. Donald was clawing at Lord Octavius's hands quite as desperately as Pip had clawed at his—and with similar lack of success. He didn't look demonic any longer; he looked frantic, his face growing purple beneath its mask of blood.

"Stop!" Pip cried more loudly.

Mr. Donald scrabbled urgently at Lord Octavius's hands—to no avail.

Pip tugged at Lord Octavius's shoulder. "Stop! You'll kill him!"

Lord Octavius didn't appear to hear her. His lips were pulled back in a snarl that was every bit as terrifying as Mr. Donald's grin had been.

Pip looked at his fierce, vengeful face and realized that she didn't know Lord Octavius at all. This wasn't the man who'd been courting her for the past week. The man who flew kites and told jokes and played with little girls. This was someone else entirely. A stranger. Someone bloodthirsty and violent.

She knelt and grabbed one of Lord Octavius's wrists and tried to pull him off the valet, but it was like tugging on an iron hawser.

Mr. Donald's struggles were growing weaker.

"If you kill him I won't marry you!" Pip cried.

Lord Octavius was too caught up in his rage and his vengeance to hear her.

Pip tugged futilely at the hands wrapped so strongly around Mr. Donald's throat—and then she remembered the defensive techniques she'd been taught. She grabbed one of Lord Octavius's fingers and yanked on it sharply.

"Ow!" He released his hold and reared back, shock on his face.

"I won't marry you if you kill him," Pip told him fiercely. "I won't marry you!"

He looked even more shocked. Some of the rage drained from his face. "But he *attacked* you."

"I won't marry a murderer."

Pip climbed to her feet. Lord Octavius scrambled to his feet, too. Mr. Donald lay between them, gasping and bloody-faced. "But Pip—"

"Please take him away."

"But—"

"Please, just take him away."

Lord Octavius closed his mouth. He looked at her for a long moment, then bent and hauled the valet to his feet.

Pip watched as he manhandled Mr. Donald to the door. The valet wheezed and stumbled and made no attempt to resist.

Lord Octavius halted in the doorway and looked back at her. Unlike Mr. Donald, his face was quite pale. "Pip . . ."

"Not now," Pip said. She was shaking violently and she had an urgent need to cry. She hugged her elbows tightly. "I need to be alone."

Lord Octavius pressed his lips together and nodded. He headed down the corridor, hauling Mr. Donald with him.

Pip watched him out of sight.

She had thought she'd known who he was, but she hadn't. She'd only known part of him. The whole man, the man she'd just glimpsed, wasn't someone she knew at all.

CHAPTER 32

Baron Rumpole was in his study. He didn't look as if he'd moved in the past hour, but he must have, for he'd poured himself another glass of wine. The agreement that Rumpole and Newingham had signed, and that Octavius and Dex had witnessed, lay on the desk.

The baron glanced up at their entrance. His brows beetled together in a frown, but it was a feeble frown, a mere shadow of his usual scowl.

Baron Rumpole was a much meeker man than he'd been yesterday.

"What's this?" Rumpole said, his gaze going from Octavius to the blood-stained valet and back again.

"Your man attacked Miss Toogood in her bed-chamber," Octavius said, shoving the valet forward.

"She invited me in," Mr. Donald said hoarsely, his bloody handkerchief pressed to his nose. "Begging for it, she was."

Octavius experienced an almost overwhelming compulsion to hit the man. His hands clenched into involuntary fists. "She broke his nose fighting him off."

The baron's gaze flicked between them several times and finally settled on the valet. "Don't do it again," he told the man.

"No, sir," Mr. Donald said, the handkerchief still pressed to his nose.

"You may go," Rumpole said, with a dismissive wave of his hand.

The valet sent Octavius a malevolent glare, and departed.

"That's it?" Octavius said indignantly, once the door had shut behind him. "He attacks a woman *in her bedchamber* and that's all you're going to do?"

The baron shrugged. "What else can I do?"

"Dismiss him!" Octavius said. "Prosecute him!"

The baron's unwillingness to pursue either path was clear to read on his face. "You heard him. He won't do it again." He picked up his wineglass and drank. It was a more polite dismissal than the one he'd given the valet, but it was a dismissal nonetheless.

Octavius stomped out of the study and only just managed not to slam the door behind him.

Miss Toogood's dismissal had been even plainer than the baron's, so although the one thing Octavius most wanted to do was go upstairs and speak with her, he didn't. He decided to climb the hanger instead. The events of the past half hour replayed themselves in his head as he strode down the lane. He saw himself burst into Miss Toogood's bedroom over and over, saw himself confront the valet, heard the man's words: *The slut was begging for it. Like a bitch in heat, she was.* And each time he heard those words, he felt the same surge of rage, the same fury.

Hitting Donald had been the right thing to do. Knocking him to the floor had been right. Even throttling him had been right. The valet had deserved to choke and wheeze and fear for his life. It wasn't as if Octavius had actually intended to kill the man—he would have stopped before that happened—but even if he *hadn't* stopped, even if rage had carried him past that point, it still wouldn't have been wrong. Donald was a rapist and the penalty for rape was death. Any jury in England would have acquitted Octavius. He'd just been protecting the woman he loved.

At the bottom of the hanger, Octavius knew he hadn't done anything wrong. By the time he'd labored his way to the top, his gut still insisted he'd done nothing wrong, but his brain was beginning to doubt it.

What if he *had* killed the valet?

He was fairly certain he would have stopped before the man had asphyxiated, but he wasn't completely certain.

Miss Toogood had been certain. She'd thought she was witnessing a murder. And perhaps she had been.

He reached the top of the hanger and stood for a moment, catching his breath. Kites flew high over-head, bright splashes of color, their tails streaming joyfully in the wind.

Octavius stared up at them and wondered how kites and almost-rape and almost-murder could exist in the same small patch of Hampshire at the same time. It seemed impossible that Miss Toogood had been attacked and that he had almost killed Mr. Donald, while these kites bobbed so gaily in the breeze.

He made his way through the grass and the wild-flowers to his cousin. Dex looked windswept and happy. He laughed when he saw Octavius. "These kites are first rate!" he said, and then he did a double take. "Is that blood on your neckcloth?"

"Probably." Octavius peered down at himself, but couldn't see any blood.

"You all right, old chap?"

Octavius grunted something that could be either *yes* or *no*. He unknotted his neckcloth. By the time he had the thing off and had discovered that there was indeed blood on it, Dex had reeled in his kite.

"What happened?" his cousin asked.

Octavius glanced over at Newingham and the girls. "Not here." He jerked his head at the trees.

They walked in silence. Octavius folded up his neckcloth and stuffed it in his pocket. "What happened?" Dex asked, once they reached the trees.

Octavius told him. When he finished, his cousin was wide-eyed. "You almost killed him? Well done, old chap!"

Octavius remembered the expression on Miss Toogood's face when she'd hauled him off the valet. He shook his head. "No, it wasn't well done. I should have restrained myself."

"What? Why?"

"Females don't like violence."

Dex gave a dismissive snort. "This isn't about female sensibilities, you corkbrain, it's about doing what's right."

Maybe he was a corkbrain, because he was beginning to think that the difference between right and wrong wasn't that clear-cut. Things that were right could also be wrong.

He wondered if it was possible to explain this to Dex.

"What if it had been Phoebe?" he asked his cousin.

A savage expression crossed Dex's face. "I'd've ripped the fucker's head off his shoulders."

"No, what I mean is, what if Phoebe were there? What if she told you to stop? What if she didn't want you to kill him?"

"I'd still rip his head off."

Octavius looked at his cousin, saw the belligerent jut of his jaw, and decided there was no point trying to explain it to Dex, not when he didn't properly understand it himself. He turned and headed back down the hanger, crushing grass beneath his boots.

"Where are you going?" Dex called out after him.

"Rumpole Hall." He needed to find Miss Toogood and tell her that he hadn't actually intended to kill the valet.

"Lunchtime!" Newingham bellowed. "Who's going to be first to the bottom of the hill?"

CHAPTER 33

$\mathcal{M}$iss Toogood made an appearance at the luncheon table. She seemed as calm and unflustered as ever—certainly Newingham and the girls saw nothing different about her—but to Octavius's eyes she looked pale and tired. Fragile.

After luncheon, he drew her aside. "Pip . . . Miss Toogood, are you all right?"

"Yes, thank you."

"Can we talk?"

"We do need to talk." Her expression was somber. "Will you meet me in the schoolroom in an hour?"

Octavius spent the next sixty minutes pacing the schoolroom. He didn't have particularly warm feelings towards schoolrooms in general; they'd been the scene of thousands of hours of tedious lessons, far too many quizzes, tests, and examinations, plus the occasional painful punishment, but until this moment Octavius had never felt actual dread in a schoolroom. This afternoon, he felt dread. Miss Toogood's expression had not been encouraging.

Please don't let her have changed her mind about marrying me, he prayed as he paced, but when she entered the schoolroom and closed the door behind her, exactly one hour after luncheon, he knew that she had. He didn't need to hear her say the words. He could see it clearly on her face and in the way that she stood—the set of her shoulders, her hands clasped so tightly in front of her.

"I'm very sorry," she said, "but I can't marry you."

Octavius took a desperate step towards her. "I wasn't going to kill him. On my word of honor, I wasn't!"

Miss Toogood shook her head. "That's not my only reason."

"Then why?"

"We're too different. Our backgrounds are too different, our values are too different. I should never have accepted your offer. I beg your pardon. The fault is mine entirely."

Octavius opened his mouth to tell her just how wrong she was, but Miss Toogood continued: "We think we know each other, but we don't. Not at all. We've seen each other's public faces, and that only briefly. I don't know who you truly are, and you don't know who I am."

"Then we'll wait a few months, get to know each other better—"

Miss Toogood shook her head again. "We're too different. A marriage between us would never work."

"I disagree."

"We're too different," Miss Toogood repeated. "I'm sorry, but I can't marry you." She opened the door and stepped out into the corridor.

CHAPTER 34

*L*ord Octavius didn't try to speak with Pip at dinnertime, nor did he attempt to talk to her afterwards, which was a relief, because she was still shaken from the day's events, and not only shaken but exhausted, and any discussion between them would undoubtedly end in tears on her part and anger on his and she didn't have the resilience to cope with either of those things, let alone both.

But even though Pip was relieved that Lord Octavius didn't attempt to speak with her, she was also a little surprised. She'd expected him to try to fight for his vision of their future.

That evening, when she was climbing into bed, someone knocked quietly on her door. Pip froze, residual terror clenching in her breast. *Go away,* she wanted to call out; instead, she cautiously said, "Who is it?"

"It's me, Octavius." The voice was unfamiliar, and female.

Pip hesitated, the blankets clutched in her hands. She didn't want to talk to Lord Octavius. Her emotions were disordered, her nerves were raw, she kept wanting to burst into tears, and somewhere deep inside herself she was still shaking.

"Miss Toogood?" that female voice said. "Please? I just want to speak with you for a few minutes. I promise I won't stay long."

Pip was tired and upset and she'd said everything to Lord Octavius that needed to be said, but he wasn't a bothersome barrow boy to be shouted at through a door; he was the man who'd asked her to marry him, and as such he deserved the courtesy of being spoken to face to face.

She climbed reluctantly out of bed, twitched the bedcovers back into place, donned her robe, tied the belt tightly, and went to the door.

That soft knock came again. "Miss Toogood? Pip? Please?"

Pip tapped her thumb and forefinger together— *once, twice, thrice*—to give herself the forbearance to listen to whatever it was that Lord Octavius felt he needed to say and the emotional strength to not burst into tears while he was saying it. Then she unlocked the door.

A woman stood in the corridor, illuminated by the chamberstick she held. She had dark hair and dark eyes.

Pip stared at her. At *him.*

Lord Octavius was dressed identically to Pip in a nightgown and robe, but the nightgown was surely a nightshirt and the robe had masculine lines and . . . and that was *Lord Octavius,* standing at her door, in the shape of a *woman.*

Lord Octavius as a woman looked a lot like Lord Octavius as a man—the same black hair, the same brown eyes—but he also looked vastly different. His jaw was narrower and his mouth smaller, his lips fuller and softer, his nose almost delicate. The angle of his cheekbones was familiar, though, as was the directness of his gaze. "Miss Toogood," he said again, in a voice that was light and feminine and yet somehow held his intonation. "Pip. Please may I speak with you? A few minutes only, I promise."

Pip had intended to send him on his way politely, but she couldn't stop herself from staring at him, this woman who was actually a man, and while she was staring at him, she found herself opening the door wider and stepping back.

Lord Octavius entered her bedchamber.

Pip closed the door and turned to keep him in sight, still staring. A woman's long hair, a woman's hips and breasts, a woman's small hands. A woman's face. Dear Lord, his *face*. So different, and yet so unnervingly familiar.

And then, belatedly, she realized that she'd invited Lord Octavius into her bedroom and that conversation was inevitable. Or rather, that argument was.

Her exhaustion came rushing back, accompanied by a sinking feeling of foreboding.

Lord Octavius glanced around the room, his gaze skipping over the bed and the washstand, the trunk and the valise, the hatboxes, before coming to rest on the only unoccupied section of floor: beneath the window.

He put the chamberstick down on her dresser, crossed to the window, and sat on the floor there, his movements not quite feminine and yet not quite masculine, either. "Five minutes," he said, in that familiar-yet-unfamiliar voice.

"Five minutes?"

He nodded. "Five minutes of rational discussion between us."

It was impossible to refuse when he was already in her room, sitting on her floor, looking up at her expectantly.

Pip hid a sigh. "All right," she said reluctantly.

Something infinitesimal altered in his face and in the set of his shoulders, a barely perceptible easing, and Pip realized that he'd been afraid she'd refuse to speak with him.

Lord Octavius gave her a tentative smile and nodded at the bed, clearly expecting her to sit upon it, but Pip didn't feel like sitting on her bed while a man was in her room, even if he was a man who looked like a woman. She'd rather pretend the bed wasn't there. She went to the window and sat on the floor, as far from him as she could—which wasn't far—and tucked her nightgown and robe carefully around her legs so that not one inch of bare skin showed.

"Rational discussion?" she said, for want of anything else to say.

"Yes," he said. "You were correct this morning—perhaps we haven't known each other long enough to understand one another's values. I'd like to rectify that with some rational discussion."

"Discussion of our values?"

"Yes. You first. What are yours?"

Pip hid another sigh. A discussion about their values wouldn't change the fact that they were too different for a marriage between them to ever work. Nor would it change the fact that Lord Octavius had almost killed a man that morning.

He waited silently for her to speak, his eyes fixed on her face.

"I dislike violence," Pip said bluntly. "I don't want to ever kill anyone, and I don't want to marry someone who could kill anyone, either."

Lord Octavius's eyebrows twitched faintly, and so did his lips. "This is one of the things I like most about you," he said. "You don't wiffle-waffle."

Pip didn't reply, she simply looked at him and waited for his response.

He returned her gaze. Long black hair hung over his shoulder, and he was strange and familiar at the same time—a woman she'd never met before, but also the man she'd been on the verge of marrying. "Would it surprise you if I said that I don't want to kill anyone either?" he said.

Pip frowned, and opened her mouth to remind him that whether or not he'd wanted to kill Mr. Donald, he'd been within moments of doing so, but he held up a hand.

She closed her mouth.

"I didn't intend to kill him," Lord Octavius said. "I honestly didn't. I don't know what happened. One moment I was confronting him and he was saying the vilest things about you, and the next . . ." He shook his head. "It just happened, and I'm glad you stopped me, because I don't want to be a murderer any more than you do."

Pip eyed him.

Lord Octavius sighed, and even though he had female lungs and a female throat, the sigh still sounded like him. "But however much I don't wish to be a murderer, it's clear that I'm capable of it." He looked down at his lap, at the brown and gold brocade of his robe, and then back at her. "I think all of us are capable of it."

Pip frowned again and inhaled prior to disagreeing, but he held up a hand again. "I want you to imagine something."

She regarded him for a moment, still frowning.

"Imagine that your father's still alive, and you live together in a cottage half a mile from Chipping Campden."

Pip felt her brow wrinkle in confusion. Chipping Campden?

"One day your father's tending his roses and you're hoeing the vegetable patch. A man comes along. A vagabond. He's crazed with drink, and he knocks your father to the ground and begins to give him a hard drubbing."

Pip's shoulders tightened.

"You have a choice. You can run for help—or you can fight the man off with your hoe. What would you do?"

"Fight him off," Pip admitted.

Lord Octavius nodded. "You hit him as hard

as you can, several times, and in the heat of the moment, with all the fear and anger you feel, it's possible you might even kill him. But you wouldn't *intend* to kill him. All you want is to protect your father."

Pip bit her lip, and gave an unwilling nod.

Lord Octavius sighed again, the sound so oddly *him* despite his female body. "That's what happened to me this morning. In the heat of the moment I lost control of myself. When I saw him in your bedroom, when he said those things about you . . ." His lips compressed tightly. He shook his head. "I lost control. I didn't mean to kill him, it wasn't my intention . . . if you can bring yourself to believe that."

Pip found that she could almost believe it.

Lord Octavius met her gaze squarely. "Not killing people *is* one of my values."

It was impossible to doubt him. She saw sincerity on his face, heard sincerity in his voice. He was speaking from his heart, or perhaps from his soul.

"This morning was a . . . an extreme occasion. My emotions overmastered me. But the thing is, Pip, I can't promise it will never happen again. If someone ever tries to harm you—or if they try to harm anyone in my family—then I'll do whatever it takes to stop them. That's instinct, not reason. But I think it's an instinct we all have. Perhaps it's stronger in me than in you, perhaps it's stronger in men than in women, but it's there in all of us. If someone hurts you, I'm going to protect you, even if that means I have to kill them. It's instinct. It's *my* instinct."

Pip bit her lip and considered his words, and decided that he was correct: it was instinct to protect those one loved. To the death, if necessary.

"I don't want to kill anyone. I truly don't. But I might one day . . . if circumstances require it."

And if circumstances required it, if something dreadful enough happened, Pip might kill someone, too. She nodded soberly, and then she tapped her thumb and forefinger together three times. *Please don't ever let that happen,* she thought. *To me or to him.*

Lord Octavius didn't notice those three little taps. He shifted his weight slightly, smoothed his robe over his knees, and said, "Do you remember when we were up on the hanger and the girls told us Rumpole had hit their brother?"

Pip nodded. The scene Edie had painted was burned into her memory: Amelia Rumpole on her deathbed, begging her husband to put land aside for a dole, ten-year-old Archibald offering to crawl the acres for her, the baron hitting him.

"Afterwards, when we were walking back, I said

I'd like to punch Rumpole." Lord Octavius paused. "Do you remember what you said?"

Pip did remember. She looked down at her lap and pinched a fold of fabric between her fingers. "I said that it wouldn't bother me in the slightest if you did," she admitted reluctantly.

Lord Octavius didn't say anything. It appeared that he was waiting for her to say even more.

Pip thought back to that afternoon on the hanger. "Occasionally violence feels as if it might be justifiable or . . . or even *beneficial*," she admitted, even more reluctantly. "Which isn't to say that it actually is, just that it feels as if it might be. But not very often. I believe it's always better to solve problems with words rather than violence . . . except that it's not always possible. Sometimes words are of no use."

Words were of no use when dealing with men like Lord Rumpole and Mr. Donald. Remonstrances, rebukes, entreaties, pleas, appeals to their better natures—none of those would make any impression on the Lord Rumpoles and Mr. Donalds of this world.

"Discourse is preferable to brute force," Lord Octavius said.

"Yes."

"Defensive violence is justifiable, but offensive violence generally isn't."

Pip thought that through. "Yes."

"I was right to hit Donald, but wrong to throttle him."

"Yes," Pip said again.

His face twisted for a moment, and then he burst out: "But it doesn't *feel* wrong. It still feels—here— as if it was *right*." He pressed his hand to his chest.

"Do you wish you'd killed him?" Pip asked.

Lord Octavius's brow creased. He thought for a long moment. Pip had the impression that he was weighing things in his mind. Right and wrong. Justice and vengeance.

Finally, he shook his head. "No."

She could hear the truth in that word. Lord Octavius must have heard it, too, for the frown on his brow smoothed away and he smiled wryly. "I was right to hit him, but wrong to almost kill him."

"Yes."

"We agree on that score, too, then."

"Yes."

His smile faded. He looked at her, his gaze resting on her face, his expression serious. "What other values would you like to discuss?"

Pip plucked at the fold of fabric, twisting it between her fingers while she thought about values such as kindness and honesty and integrity. "Our values are probably very similar," she admitted finally. "But our backgrounds and our circumstances aren't. We're too different. We might *think* that we'll suit, but we don't know each other well enough to be certain."

Lord Octavius nodded, as if he found her statement reasonable. "Very well, what would you like to know about me?"

CHAPTER 35

"What? Now?" Pip said.

Lord Octavius nodded. "What would you like to know?"

Pip looked down at her lap. She twisted the fold of fabric she was holding into a tight little corkscrew. What *did* she want to know about him? And was now really the best time for such a discussion?

Yes, her heart told her. *Now is the time.*

Pip undid the corkscrew of fabric and smoothed her robe over her knees. She looked at Lord Octavius, this woman-man seated beside her. He was watching her. She saw hope in his eyes and nervousness in the way his hands were clasped together. He hoped she would talk with him, but feared that she wouldn't.

"Do you gamble?" she asked.

His posture didn't change, but the way he held

himself did. She almost visibly saw him relax. "Card parties sometimes, but gambling dens, no."

"Do you live within your income?"

"Yes."

"*Just* within your income, or—"

"I live well within my income," he said. "I'm not a wastrel, if that's what you're asking."

It was what she was asking, so Pip nodded and said, "What are your drinking habits?"

"I'm not a drunkard, either," he said, with a smile. "I went on the occasional spree when I was younger, but now?" He shook his head. "Are you worried that I'm frivolous and dissipated and shallow? Because I'm not. At least, I don't think that I am."

Pip didn't think he was, either. But he was privileged and he didn't have a vocation, and while that shouldn't be an issue, for some reason it was.

Lord Octavius must have seen something on her face—doubt? hesitation?—for he said, "What is it?"

"I always imagined myself marrying a man with a vocation," Pip admitted. "Someone who wanted to help people and who made it his life's work. A clergyman most likely, or perhaps an apothecary or a doctor."

"Ah," he said, a little sadly. "My circumstances offend you."

"They don't *offend* me," Pip said. "It's just . . . I wasn't looking to marry a nobleman."

"Because to you I *am* frivolous and shallow."

"No," she said. "Of course you're not."

"Compared to a clergyman or a doctor or an apothecary I am." His lips twisted briefly, and she couldn't quite identify the emotion that went with that little grimace. Wryness? Regret? "I used to think life was a game, but this past week . . . being here, trying to teach Rumpole his lesson, it hasn't been a game at all. It's been frustrating and difficult, but it's also been . . ." He paused, clearly searching for a word, but he just as clearly didn't find it for he said, "Yesterday, when I was in London, I suggested to my brother and cousins that we use our magic to help people."

Pip felt her eyebrows rise in astonishment. "What did they say?"

"They thought I was joking."

"But you weren't?"

He shook his head.

"Is that what you'd like to do? Use your magic to help people?"

"I don't know. I'm glad we stopped Rumpole, but . . ." He sighed, and rubbed his forehead in a gesture that she recognized as purely Lord Octavius. "I don't want to do what I did to Rumpole, ever again, but I have to because Donald hasn't been stopped yet, and—" He frowned suddenly. "Damn it. I mean, dash it. I should have brought your dress back."

"You're not going to put the fear of God into him tonight?"

"I tried, but he's locked himself in his room and he won't open the door, no matter what I say or what voice I use." He smiled, and despite the feminine softness of his face, the smile had sharp edges. "You've given him a fear of women."

"Good," Pip said.

"Yes, but I don't think it'll last. What he did to you? He's done that before, and once he's got over his fright he'll do it again. I'm certain of it."

Pip was certain of it, too.

"Don't worry, Dex and I'll stop him," Lord Octavius said. "We'll come back next month, slip into the house once it's dark, and deal with him. I give you my word."

Pip looked at him, sitting on the floor alongside her in a female body, and came to a belated realization. This wealthy, privileged marquis's son *did* have a vocation, and not just any vocation, but a vocation that impacted profoundly on people's lives.

She'd been right this morning to think him a hero, but wrong to set him on a pedestal. He wasn't perfect. No one was. And perhaps that was what they needed to be discussing. Not values and vocations, but their unrealistic expectations of each other.

"I'm not perfect," Pip said. "And I'm afraid you think that I am."

Lord Octavius looked slightly confused by this change of subject. "Perfection is in the eye of the beholder," he said, with a lift of his lips that invited her to smile at this statement.

Pip ignored the invitation. "I have flaws," she persisted. "Lots of them. Everyone does."

He cocked his head at her. "Tell me what you think yours are."

"Well . . ." Now that she had to list them, Pip found herself floundering. "Well, my red hair and freckles, of course."

Lord Octavius shook his head. "Those aren't flaws."

It wasn't a compliment, precisely, but it felt like one. Pip's cheeks became a little warm and her thoughts a little flustered. She scrambled to think of another flaw. "I have a crooked tooth. See?" She pointed to her eyetooth.

"Yes, that's a very significant flaw," Lord Octavius said gravely.

Pip pursed her lips at him. "Be *serious*," she told him.

"Then give me a serious flaw—and not something physical."

Pip thought for a moment, and then said, "I hold grudges. I find it difficult to forgive some things."

"What sort of things?"

"Selfishness. Spite. Cruelty."

He nodded. "What other flaws do you have?"

Pip hesitated, and then confessed, "I'm not as patient as I'd like to be."

Lord Octavius shook his head. "I've watched you all week with the girls. You're extremely patient."

"With children, yes, but with adults . . ." Pip looked down at her lap again, plucked at a fold of fabric, pinched it, twisted it. "I get impatient when people complain a lot. At my last position, the children's mother . . . she saw everything that was *wrong* in her life, not everything that was right." She released the twist of fabric, smoothed it down, and met his eyes. "I know I should have been sympathetic—she can't help the way she is—but it used to annoy me so much. I wanted to shake her and say, 'Look at all the good things you have! Focus on those!'"

Lord Octavius eyed her for a long moment. "Let me see if I understand this correctly. You feel impatience towards people who complain incessantly?"

"Yes."

"That's not a flaw; that's human nature."

"A truly compassionate person—"

He shook his head. "Even a saint would find such a person annoying. Next flaw."

Pip pursed her lips at him again. She searched for another flaw. "I'm too idealistic."

He smiled. "You're certainly idealistic, but it's not necessarily a flaw. What else?"

Pip cast about for something else. "I have no musical ability. I can play the pianoforte, but it sounds terrible, and I can't sing at all."

"Ah, now *that's* a real flaw," Lord Octavius said, with a grin.

The grin was disconcerting. Somehow, despite the fact that his face was a different shape and his mouth was smaller and his lips fuller, it was still Lord Octavius's grin.

In fact, it was more than disconcerting; it was actually a little bit disturbing. Pip found herself wanting the real Lord Octavius, not this female version of him.

"Fortunately, I can sing well enough for the both of us," he said. "Can't play the pianoforte, though." He paused, and his grin widened. "My cousin Ned can burp God Save the King."

Pip couldn't prevent a laugh. She pressed her fingers to her mouth to smother it, and then said, "Can you do that?"

"Alas, no." His tone was regretful, but his eyes were smiling.

Seeing Lord Octavius's dark brown eyes smiling at her from someone else's face wasn't just a little bit disturbing, it was *very* disturbing. So disturbing, in fact, that Pip almost asked him to change into himself. Prudence stopped her from uttering the words. Having a female Lord Octavius in her bedchamber was unnerving enough. Having a *male* Lord Octavius would be even worse.

Pip looked away and struggled to find something else to say. "Good," she said. "Because I couldn't marry a man who can burp God Save the King." Too late, she realized that she'd implied that she *could* marry him and that she was in fact considering it.

Pip tensed. She didn't want him to propose again. Not yet. It was too soon.

Perhaps Lord Octavius noticed her tension, or perhaps he also thought it was too soon, for he said, "What other flaws do you have?"

Pip cast about for one. "Not precisely a flaw, but a . . . an idiosyncrasy."

He nodded encouragingly.

Pip knew she ought to tell him about her obsession with threes, but she couldn't quite bring herself to. There was honesty, and then there was *honesty*.

"I wake at dawn every day," she told him instead. "Sometimes earlier. I like mornings."

"I like mornings, too," Lord Octavius said. "But I'm not usually up at dawn." He shrugged. "I can be, though, if you'd like?"

Would she like to share dawns with him? Would she like to watch colors unfurl across the sky and the world come to life? To share that quiet sense of wonder and joy?

Yes. She would. In fact, she'd like it so much that she actually felt a pang of yearning in her chest.

Pip looked down at her lap and fiddled with the belt of her robe until the pang faded.

"Any other flaws or idiosyncrasies?" Lord Octavius asked.

Threes. Threes were definitely both a flaw and an idiosyncrasy, but Pip chose the coward's route and shook her head—and that, right there, was another flaw to add to her tally: cowardice.

"Very well," Lord Octavius said. "Let's examine my flaws, shall we?" He shifted his weight slightly and then was silent for several seconds. So many seconds, in fact, that Pip glanced at him. He was frowning at the floor. "My greatest flaw is that I'm a frippery fellow," he said finally. "I have no need to earn my living and no purpose in life other than to enjoy myself."

"I don't think you're frippery," Pip said.

"No?" He met her eyes. "I have money and time in abundance, but I've only ever used them for my own amusement, and as for my magic, I could have chosen a gift that was practical, like Grandfather's, but instead I chose one that was fun." He shook his head. "Frippery. That's definitely my greatest flaw. And my second greatest flaw is what happened this morning. I lost my temper and almost killed someone—and I don't know if you can believe it, but before today I wouldn't even have said I had a hot temper." He rubbed his forehead again.

"I don't think you have a hot temper," Pip said. "I think what you have is a very protective disposition."

His expression was doubtful. "You do?"

She nodded. "Extremely protective."

He shrugged, as if he didn't quite believe her. "And as for my other flaws . . . well, they're much the same as yours. I can't forgive malice and cruelty and I have no patience for people who complain all the time." He gave a half smile. "I can sing, though." The half smile faded. "We should have talked about this earlier, shouldn't we? I'm a frivolous lout, and not at all the sort of man you'd like to marry."

"You're not a frivolous lout," Pip said. "Unless you've been pretending to be someone other than yourself this past week?"

"Pretending?" He looked affronted. "Of course not."

"Then you're not frippery or frivolous and you *do* have a purpose. You want to protect people."

He frowned at her, and she wished he was wearing his true face.

"What about idiosyncrasies?" Pip asked. "Do you have any of those?"

He thought for a moment. "I've been told I talk in my sleep," he said, and Pip wondered who'd told him. A family member? A servant? A lover?

He thought some more, and then wrinkled his nose. "I hate gooseberries. The smell and the taste . . ." He shuddered. "Ugh."

"I rather like gooseberry custard," Pip said.

Lord Octavius pulled a face. "Then we can't possibly marry," he declared, before a smile twitched at his lips.

Pip found herself smiling back; it was impossible not to, but then his smile faded and so did hers.

His gaze was intent on her face. "What do you think, Pip?"

Pip looked away from him. She studied the cheap drugget carpet on the floor, her eyes following the lines of the weave while she thought. "I think that we share a connection and that our characters are compatible and our values sufficiently similar, but I worry that our backgrounds are too different. You're a marquis's son and I'm a clergyman's daughter. You're wealthy and I'm poor. We were raised so differently and I fear . . ." She lifted her gaze and met his eyes squarely. "I fear that the differences between us are too great. There's no commonality in our backgrounds. None at all."

He studied her face for a long moment, his expression grave, and then said, "We're human. That's the greatest commonality of all, isn't it?"

Her gaze dropped. She fiddled with her belt. "Well . . . yes."

Lord Octavius said nothing. After a moment, Pip glanced at him.

He was watching her. "What does your heart tell you?" he asked quietly.

Pip was silent for several seconds, and then she said, equally quietly, "My heart tells me to marry you."

He offered her a tiny, hopeful smile. "My heart tells me that, too."

The dark brown eyes were Lord Octavius's, but nothing else was, and suddenly it was unbearable to be having this discussion with someone who was almost, but not quite, him. Pip needed to hear his real voice, to see his real face. "Please change into yourself," she said.

He hesitated. "Are you certain?"

Pip nodded.

"Very well."

Between one blink of Pip's eyelids and the next, he became himself. There were no sparks or flashes of magic; he simply changed. One second he was a woman, the next he was a man. The air didn't shimmer, but *he* seemed to shimmer slightly, if only for the merest instant.

As a man, he took up considerably more space on the floor alongside her. The robe had been voluminous on him before. Now, it wasn't. In fact his belt was tied far too tightly, judging from his pained grimace and his haste in loosening it.

Lord Octavius was the same person regardless of what body he occupied—his character didn't change, merely his outer shell—but seeing him as himself again gave Pip a profound sense of relief. She felt the relief physically, as if she'd been wearing something prickly next to her skin and now it was gone.

On the heels of that almost visceral sense of relief came another feeling: safety. She felt safer now that Lord Octavius was a man—much safer—as if nothing could possibly harm her.

Pip waited until he'd retied his belt before asking, "What does it feel like when you change shape?"

"It itches."

"Itches?"

"The parts of me that change, itch. My skin, my bones." He shrugged.

Pip looked at him. His features were the same as they'd always been—the strong eyebrows, the strong nose, the strong jaw—but she saw him more clearly than she had before. He didn't have a murderous heart, but he was a man capable of violence. He was a hero, but an imperfect one.

They gazed at each other silently for what seemed like hours. Pip felt the sense of connection grow up between them again, that intangible bond that was so much more than friendship.

"Will you marry me?" Lord Octavius asked.

The differences between them might be vast, but the differences weren't what mattered. What mattered were the things they shared.

"Yes," Pip said.

His face lit with emotions: relief, joy, elation. His smile was as bright as the sun. He opened his mouth.

Pip held up a hand to forestall whatever he was going to say. "But there's something I must tell you first. I do have another flaw."

CHAPTER 36

"This is going to sound very foolish, but..." Pip discovered that she couldn't look at Lord Octavius's face while she told him about her greatest flaw. She looked down at her lap and twisted the end of her belt. "My father had an obsession with threes. He did everything in threes. He tapped three times on every door he went through. He wiped each foot three times on the mat. He snuffed candles three times and checked the locks three times and kissed me good-night three times. He made sure to have three things on his fork when he ate. He chewed in multiples of three and he walked in multiples of three and every time he turned to a new page in a book he would stroke it three times. Everything was threes."

She risked a glance at Lord Octavius. That bright-as-sunshine smile had faded. He looked faintly perplexed.

"Threes ruled my father's life, and they ruled my life, too, but I didn't mind. It felt like a game, *our* game, but it also felt good—safe—as if everything in the world would be all right if only we did things in threes."

Lord Octavius's brow creased. He looked even more perplexed.

"It was an obsession," Pip said. "An affliction, but it was also an enormous comfort to my father. I don't expect you to understand, but threes made him happy, and they made me happy, too."

Lord Octavius nodded. It wasn't a nod to show that he understood—because how could he?—but a nod to encourage her to continue.

Pip looked back down at her lap. She twisted the end of her belt backwards and forwards between her fingers. "When my father died, I went to live with my aunt. She wouldn't let me do threes. She said it was unhealthy and unnatural and that she'd whip it out of me if she had to."

"Did she whip you?"

"Twice," Pip said. She risked a glance at Lord Octavius. He was frowning.

"How old were you?" he asked.

"Twelve."

His frown deepened.

"My aunt suffered more than I did," Pip told him.

"She cried the second time she whipped me and that was when I realized that she wasn't breaking me of threes to be cruel; she was doing it for *me*."

"So . . . you stopped?"

"I stopped fighting her," Pip said. "But it took the better part of a year before I was able to stop doing everything in threes. It was difficult."

"Difficult" was a profoundly inadequate word to describe the pain of that year. She'd lost her father, and she'd lost threes, and she'd been more unhappy than she'd thought humanly possible. Her father had given her love and stability, and threes had given her a way to make sense of the world. Without those things she'd felt helpless and alone, adrift in a chaotic sea with nothing to cling onto.

Pip shivered. Not a shiver of cold, but a shiver of remembered misery. "In the end, my aunt let me keep one three. And that's my flaw."

Lord Octavius, when she ventured a glance at him, didn't look disapproving. He had a surprisingly sympathetic expression on his face. "Which three did you keep?"

"I tap for good luck," Pip said, and tapped her thumb and forefinger together three times to show him. Embarrassment heated her cheeks as she did so, or perhaps it was shame, but even though tapping in front of him made her feel bad, the taps themselves made her feel good. In that brief instant of time she felt calmer and safer and luckier. But afterwards . . . afterwards she felt foolish, because even if those taps gave her a sense of control over her destiny, she knew that they didn't.

Pip balled her hand up on her knee. She couldn't quite bring herself to meet Lord Octavius's eyes. She was afraid she'd see derision there, or perhaps pity.

"People do lots of things for good luck," he said, and his tone was so easy, so affable, so uncritical, that she couldn't help but look at him. His expression matched his tone. He didn't look derisive or pitying. He smiled at her. "Knock on wood," he said, and rapped his knuckles twice on the wooden skirting.

Something in Pip's stomach tied itself in a tiny knot. "Three times," she said.

His smile didn't fade. It did change, though. Not derision, but warmth and affection. He knocked again. *Tap-tap-tap.*

The knot in Pip's stomach untied itself, while at the same time she felt her cheeks burn with mortification. She looked away from him. "So that's my greatest flaw," she said, balling her hand more tightly on her knee.

"It's not a flaw."

"It *is*," Pip said, looking back at him. "I do it *every day*. Several times!"

"It's not a flaw," he repeated. "It's a quirk. An idiosyncrasy." He reached out and took her balled-up hand and carried it to his lips and then, slowly and deliberately, pressed a kiss to her knuckles, and then a second kiss, and a third.

Pip's heart almost stopped beating in astonishment.

He did it again—once, twice, thrice—laying soft kisses on her knuckles, and Pip loved him *so much* that she almost burst into tears.

Her gaze was caught in his. She couldn't look away, could in fact barely breathe in sheer wonder that this man—this exceptional man—was *kissing her in threes*.

He hadn't laughed at her. He hadn't mocked her. He'd accepted her uneasy relationship with threes and was using it to show her that he loved her.

The feeling that she might burst into tears grew stronger.

Lord Octavius laid three more kisses on her knuckles, then lowered her hand. "We don't have to marry right now," he told her seriously. "We can wait. Three months, six months. However long you want."

Pip shook her head. There was no need to wait, no need to get to know him better, because she could never love anyone as much as she loved him. "No waiting."

"Are you certain?"

"Yes." She was more certain of it than she'd ever been of anything in her life.

Lord Octavius gave her another of those joyful, bright-as-sunshine smiles. "Next week at Linwood Castle?"

"Next week at Linwood Castle," Pip agreed, and she thought that her smile might be sunshine-bright, too.

Lord Octavius raised her hand to his mouth and kissed it again—once, twice, thrice. Pip felt his lips, soft and warm, and then she felt his tongue as he briefly tasted her skin.

A tingle of shock went through her. She shivered, but not with cold. Her cheeks flushed with sudden heat.

He did it again, the tip of his tongue sliding teasingly over her skin. The tingle ran through her a second time, a delicious hot-cold sensation. Her heart began to beat with great rapidity. Pip was suddenly intensely aware of the bed looming not three feet away, aware of the possibilities, aware of a fragile, nervous desire.

Lord Octavius laid another salutation on her skin, then frowned sharply and pushed up the cuff of her nightgown. "Did Donald do that?"

Pip followed his gaze and saw the ring of dark bruises where Mr. Donald had grabbed her. She shivered—a shiver that had nothing to do with desire—and nodded.

Lord Octavius's frown deepened into a scowl. He seemed to bristle with anger, to almost grow in size like a cat puffing up its fur.

It should have repelled her—that sign that violence lay just beneath his surface—but it didn't. The bristling and rage were instinct—*his* instinct. He needed to protect those he loved, to defend them, to fight for them.

"Did he hurt you anywhere else?" he demanded.

"A bump on the back of my head, that's all."

His scowl deepened. "The back of your head?"

"He threw me to the floor."

Lord Octavius's outrage magnified. He seemed to grow even larger. His rage vibrated in the air between them, but Pip wasn't afraid. This was a man who protected those he loved, not hurt them. He'd keep her safe—with his fists if he had to, with his life if it came to that—and she would do the same for him, because that was what it meant to be human and to love someone.

Lord Octavius released her hand and reached for her head, as if to examine the bump for himself.

"It's only a tiny bump," Pip said, catching his hand and entwining their fingers.

He subjected her to a long, frowning look.

"I'm fine. Honestly."

The frown became doubtful, and then after a moment the doubtful frown became a doubtful smile.

Pip smiled back at him hopefully.

The dangerous vibration in the air faded. Lord Octavius's shoulders relaxed and his metaphorical hackles lowered. He stroked the bruises on her wrist. His touch was gentle, his expression introspective rather than outraged.

"You saved me," Pip told him. "You and your cousin and Lord Newingham."

His fingers paused on her skin. He looked at her, a questioning lift to his eyebrows.

"I wouldn't have got away from him, if not for your lessons." Remembered terror prickled its way up her spine. "I almost didn't. He was so fast and so strong and so . . . so *gleeful.* He liked that he was going to hurt me. It excited him."

She couldn't repress a shiver at the memory of Mr. Donald's terrible glee.

Lord Octavius must have felt it, for he released her hand and moved closer, putting an arm around her shoulders. Pip leaned gratefully into his solid warmth. "I didn't understand until this morning what it meant to be petrified with terror," she told him. "But I do now. I was so scared. I couldn't breathe and I couldn't scream and I had no strength in my arms and legs. If I hadn't had your lessons I wouldn't have got away. He came very close to overpowering me." She shivered again, a comprehensive convulsion involving her whole body.

Lord Octavius tucked her more tightly against him and wrapped both arms around her. "I would have stopped him before he did anything," he said. "I was less than a minute from your room. I would have stopped him."

Pip imagined it: Lord Octavius knocking on the door, calling out her name. Surely she'd have found the breath to scream? One scream, even a tiny one, and he would have heard it and burst through the door and confronted Mr. Donald.

She had no doubt what would have happened then.

"You would have killed him," she whispered. "And I probably wouldn't have stopped you." And perhaps Mr. Donald would even have deserved it.

There was a long moment of silence while they both digested this statement. "It's better that it happened the way it did," Lord Octavius said at last.

"Much better."

Pip closed her eyes and let herself relax into his

warmth and his strength. Her tension drained away, the remembered terror and panic fading like wisps of mist slowly evaporating in sunlight. She felt safe. She *was* safe. It was impossible to be safer than she was at this moment. Nothing could harm her when Lord Octavius held her like this.

She'd been lucky today. Incredibly lucky. Lucky to have had those lessons. Lucky to have landed that kick. Lucky to have Lord Octavius to hold her now.

None of the other women Mr. Donald had attacked had been that lucky.

Pip's warm contentment didn't dissipate like mist in sunlight; it vanished with the abruptness of a door being slammed.

Mr. Donald had attacked other women. Perhaps other governesses. Perhaps in this very room.

It was a horrifying thought. Had she been sleeping in a bedroom where other women had been attacked? Had she been sleeping in the very *bed* they'd been attacked in?

Pip couldn't repress another shudder. Lord Octavius rubbed her back soothingly.

"He's done it before, hasn't he?" Pip whispered, her voice muffled against his shoulder. "In this room."

She was hoping he'd say *No*, but he said, "Most likely."

A sickening knot tied itself in her stomach. For a moment, Pip thought she might vomit. She concentrated on breathing, and when the nausea faded and she opened her eyes and saw the bed, she knew she couldn't sleep in it tonight. She'd take the blanket and the pillows and sleep right here, on the floor beneath the window where, God willing, nothing terrible had ever happened to anyone.

Another shiver went through her. "If we hadn't met that day in London . . ."

"Don't think about it." Lord Octavius rubbed another soothing circle on her back, and he was right, she shouldn't think about it, it was a pointless exercise, one that would only distress her.

But it was impossible *not* to imagine it.

If Lord Octavius hadn't met her. If he'd not followed her here. If he'd not offered her lessons in defensive techniques . . .

She'd be fleeing Rumpole Hall at this very moment. Fleeing, because she didn't dare spend another day in the same house as Mr. Donald. Fleeing, because she didn't have the patronage and the money to see him brought to justice. Fleeing, because it was the only thing she could do.

An idea crystallized in Pip's head. An idea that she didn't entirely want to acknowledge but that she couldn't ignore.

"There is another way of stopping Mr. Donald," she said.

She couldn't see Lord Octavius's face, but she felt his surprise. His hand stopped making soothing circles on her back. "There is?"

"Yes." She inhaled a shallow breath, released it, and said, "I can bring a case against him in the courts."

Lord Octavius was silent for several seconds, then he said, "Do you want to?"

"It would be expensive," Pip said. She'd have to hire the lawyers and pay for all the expenses, an expenditure far beyond the ability of a governess to meet—but not beyond the ability of a marquis's son.

"Forget the cost," Lord Octavius said. "Do you want to take him to court? Because if you do, I'll pay for it." He loosened his hold on her and sat back enough to see her face.

Pip looked at him, trying to read his expression. He was frowning again, but it wasn't an angry frown; it was a thoughtful frown. His gaze was steady, serious, and he appeared to be trying to read her expression, too. Pip wondered what he saw there.

"It would be a scandal," she said.

"Yes."

"My name would be in all the newspapers. And yours, too, as my husband."

He shrugged and took her hand, lacing their fingers together. "If you want to do it, we'll do it, but Pip . . . do you *want* to?"

Pip looked down at her knees. She didn't want to go to court. She didn't want people knowing that Mr. Donald had tried to rape her. She didn't want her name in the newspapers. She didn't want people imagining what it had been like, wondering which parts of her he'd touched. She didn't want them pointing her out and whispering about her. *That's Lord Octavius's wife over there, the one with the red hair. Did you know that someone tried to rape her once?*

"No," she admitted. "I don't want to, but if it will stop him from ever attacking someone else, then I'll do it." She bit her lip, and then said, "They might hang him." A shudder ran through her. Not a shudder of remembered fear, but a shudder at the thought of a man hanging by the neck until he died.

Lord Octavius must have felt it, for his grip on her hand tightened. "We'll try my way first," he said.

Pip remembered what he'd said that morning, how difficult he'd found his encounter with Baron Rumpole. "Justice is best served by the courts, don't you think?"

"Well, yes, but . . ."

"You don't like terrorizing people. It's not in your nature. Think how you felt after Rumpole."

He shook his head. "This is personal. Donald attacked *you,* and if anyone punishes him it will be *me.*"

Pip looked at the stubborn set of his jaw and the fierce determination in his eyes and decided not to argue further. "Promise me you won't kill him."

"I promise."

"And promise me that if your way doesn't work—"

"If it doesn't work, I'll finance a case against him. I give you my word."

Pip looked down at their linked fingers, and then back at him. "I thought you'd argue against going to court," she confessed. "Because of the scandal. The newspapers, your family . . . I thought you'd want to keep it all hidden."

"Stopping a rapist is more important than keeping my family's name out of the newspapers."

"I doubt the rest of your family would agree. The duke—"

"Grandfather would support you in this, most definitely."

"He would?" she said doubtfully.

Lord Octavius gave an emphatic nod. "Very strong on justice, he is. I won't deny he's a little intimidating, but he's a great gun. You'll see when you meet him—and speaking of meeting him, I'd better go. We've got a long journey tomorrow." He released her hand and climbed to his feet. The hem of his robe fell around his calves. Between slippers and hem were several inches of naked ankle. Pip averted her gaze from that glimpse of skin and stood, too.

Lord Octavius made no attempt to embrace her, merely turned towards the dresser and picked up his chamberstick. Pip was relieved. A few minutes ago there'd been a heated, tingling moment when she'd thought they might possibly make love, but that moment had well and truly passed. She couldn't make love with him tonight, not in this room where Mr. Donald had attacked her, not in that bed.

Lord Octavius paused on his way to the door and looked down at the floor. The drugget carpet was damp where she'd tried to scrub out Mr. Donald's blood. He considered the stain for a long moment, his lips pressed tightly together, then looked at her. "We'll stop him. One way or the other. I promise you."

CHAPTER 37

$\mathcal{P}$ip was halfway through breakfast with two very excited little girls when a knock sounded on the nursery door. Lord Octavius entered. Pip had a strong moment of déjà vu. Lord Newingham had looked exactly like this yesterday morning, out of breath and clutching a piece of paper.

"This just came by express," he told her, thrusting the paper at her. "From my brother. Read it."

Pip put down her butter knife and took the letter.

"Is Uncle Robert with you?" Edie asked, craning to look past Lord Octavius.

"He's downstairs eating his breakfast," Lord Octavius told her.

"Are you going to have breakfast with us?" Fanny asked.

"No. My breakfast is downstairs, too, but I had to show Miss Toogood this letter."

Pip unfolded the missive. It was written in a masculine hand.

Otto,

I found two of the governesses and you were correct— they left Rumpole's employ because they were attacked, but it wasn't Rumpole who was the culprit, it was his valet.

The word "valet" had been underlined three times.

One of the governesses, a Miss Belton, is pregnant because of the attack. She has no family and her circumstances are quite dire. I found her in a poorhouse in Islington.

I've taken her to Linwood House and put her into the housekeeper's care. It should be the baron and his wretch of a valet who provide for her, but she's approached Rumpole twice in the past three months and both times was turned away at the door.

Miss Belton is angry at the world, as you can well imagine, and wants nothing more than to see her attacker burn in Hell. When I offered to finance a court case against him, she jumped at the chance.

Pip's heart skipped a beat. She reread that last, astonishing sentence, but it still said the same thing. A court case.

Mother and Father are as outraged as I am. Father spoke with his lawyers this morning and has set everything in motion. It may take a day or two, but rest assured that someone will be along to arrest the man shortly.

Pip closed her eyes for a moment, then opened them and reread that miraculous paragraph. It still said the same thing.

Mr. Donald was going to be arrested. He'd never be able to hurt another woman again.

I wish it were possible to arrest Rumpole for his part in this, the letter writer continued, *but the lawyers advise us that it's not. At the very least, his name will be mentioned in the courts and some of the vileness of his character exposed.*

Mother and Father leave for Gloucestershire tomorrow. The rest of us are traveling a day later. We look forward to meeting your Miss Toogood.

Q.

Pip read the letter again, from start to finish, then looked at Lord Octavius. He was watching her.

"You'll not need to put your plan into action," she said.

"No." He had wanted to be the one to punish Mr. Donald, but he didn't seem upset to have lost that opportunity.

"You don't mind?"

Lord Octavius shook his head. He was clearly aware that the girls would recognize the name Belton, for he said, "The lady in question has greater need for redress than either of us. This is her fight, and I intend to help her win it."

"We both can help," Pip said.

"Yes."

Pip folded the letter and handed it to him. "Thank you for bringing this up."

"I knew you'd want to see it." He batted Edie lightly on the head with the letter, and then Fanny. "You'll be ready to leave in an hour?"

"Yes!" the girls chorused.

CHAPTER 38

$\mathcal{I}$t was while he was eating his last bites of breakfast that Octavius realized he had one more task to perform before he left Rumpole Hall. Accordingly, he didn't linger at the table with Dex and Newingham, but went searching for a footman. He found a housemaid instead. When he described the man he was looking for, the maid said, "You mean Malcolm, sir?"

"Is he tall and thin?"

"Yes, sir."

"That's him. Can you tell him I want to see him? I'll be in the library."

The library smelled faintly of urine. Someone had scrubbed the carpet where the port had spilled, but a mark remained if one knew where to look for it, hidden among the acanthus leaves.

Octavius stared at that dark blotch and

remembered Rumpole's terror, remembered him begging and weeping and pissing himself.

Rumpole had deserved to be punished for what he'd done, and Mr. Donald did, too, but Miss Toogood was correct: justice was best served by the courts.

"You wished to see me, sir?"

He turned and saw the footman who'd defended him on the staircase. "Yes. Close the door, will you?"

Malcolm closed the door and advanced into the room. "Sir?" He looked attentive but expressionless, as all good footmen did.

"It's come to my attention that Baron Rumpole has been practicing master's rights," Octavius said.

Malcolm lost his impassive expression. Shock flickered across his face.

The shock surprised Octavius. "Did you not know?" he asked.

"Yes, sir, but . . . but how did you know?"

Octavius hadn't anticipated that question. He hadn't anticipated any questions. In his experience, servants didn't interrogate their social superiors. His first instinct was not to answer—but Malcolm had come to his rescue six nights ago. He deserved an answer. Or as much of one as Octavius could give him.

"I, uh, I suspected it, so I brought a female here,

a . . . a . . . an actress, and she confirmed it for me."

More astonishment bloomed on Malcolm's face, and with it, dawning realization. "The housemaids! The ones Mrs. Clark never hired. That was your doing, sir?"

Octavius nodded.

"But there was more than one housemaid," Malcolm said. "There were at least three!"

"Wigs," Octavius offered hastily.

This explanation didn't appease the footman. He directed a frown at Octavius. "Mrs. Clark almost lost her position over that. The baron thought *she* were to blame for it all."

This was another first in Octavius's experience—earning a footman's disapproval—but unfortunately, he deserved it. He hadn't given any thought to the consequences of his ruse upon the servants. "I apologize. It wasn't my intention to cause trouble for anyone, least of all your housekeeper." Especially if the woman had been trying to protect her maids from the baron.

Malcolm looked unimpressed by his apology.

The interview wasn't going at all how Octavius had envisaged. He tried to bring it back on track. "You'll be pleased to hear that Rumpole has had a change of heart regarding his housemaids. He won't be practicing master's rights again."

If he'd been hoping for an outpouring of gratitude, he would have been disappointed. Malcolm didn't look overwhelmed with joy; he looked skeptical.

"I have every reason to believe that Rumpole's change of heart will be permanent, but on the off-chance it isn't . . ." Octavius fished out his card case and handed the man a card. "Contact me."

The footman accepted the card dubiously. "You, sir?"

"Yes," Octavius said. "I'll see to it that something's done about it."

Malcolm obediently tucked the card into his pocket, but he still looked skeptical.

"Promise me," Octavius said, a note of command entering his voice. "Promise me you'll contact me if the baron reverts to his old ways."

Malcolm's face became expressionless. "I promise, sir."

"I'm aware that the baron isn't the only problem in this household. Rest assured that Mr. Donald's time here will be short-lived. Someone will be along to arrest him within the next few days."

Malcolm may not have believed him about Lord Rumpole, but he believed him about this. His entire face brightened. "Mr. Donald? Arrested?"

"Yes."

"*Thank* you, sir."

This was the shiny-eyed gratitude Octavius had been expecting, but now that he had it he found himself embarrassed by it. He wasn't sure he deserved it, especially from this man. "You saved the actress I employed from Mr. Donald, I understand?"

"Yes, sir."

"Thank you. I'm extremely grateful to you, both on her behalf and my own." Octavius restored his card case to his pocket and took out his pocketbook instead. He thumbed through the banknotes, extracted the largest one—fifty pounds—and gave it to the footman.

Malcolm blanched when he realized how much he'd been given. He tried to give the banknote back. "Sir . . . I think you've made a mistake."

"No mistake."

Fifty pounds was probably five times what Malcolm earned in a year, but in those few minutes on the staircase he'd more than earned it.

"If you should ever have reason to leave Rumpole's employ, come to me. You're assured of a place in my household."

"Thank you, sir," Malcolm said, folding the banknote very carefully and tucking it away.

The library door opened. Dex poked his head in. "Otto? You ready to go? They're bringing the carriages around."

"I'll be there in a minute," Octavius said. He waited until Dex had closed the door, then held out his hand to the footman. After a moment's hesitation, Malcolm took it. "Thank you," Octavius said again. "And remember: contact me if the baron reverts to his old ways or if you find yourself in need of employment."

"Yes, sir," the footman said. He didn't look skeptical or reproving or dubious anymore, he looked a little dazed.

Octavius shook the man's hand and left the library, heading for the entrance hall and the sound of voices and jingling harnesses. Quite a cavalcade was drawn up on the carriage sweep. Newingham was negotiating with his nieces over who would drive with him in his curricle first. Both girls looked as if they were bursting with excitement. Octavius wasn't excited by the thought of the sixty miles that lay between Rumpole Hall and Newingham's estate in Wiltshire, but he felt an almost impatient eagerness when he thought of tomorrow and the twenty miles that would take them on to Linwood Castle.

He went to stand beside Miss Toogood. "Ready?" he asked.

She looked at him and smiled, and for a moment he was transported back to London. It had been like this the very first time he'd seen her—the feeling that the world stood still for a moment, the realization that golden eyebrows and gray-blue eyes and auburn hair were what he'd been looking for his whole life.

"Ready," she replied.

Octavius wanted to touch the scattering of freckles on her nose, to skim his fingertips over her skin, but now was neither the time nor the place. He contented himself with letting his hand briefly brush hers, then he strode forward and said, "Right, you slugabeds, let's get moving!" Because the sooner they left Rumpole Hall, the sooner they'd reach Linwood Castle.

CHAPTER 39

A day and a half later

Pip hadn't been at all sure what to expect in a castle. "Castle" was a word that brought to mind images of great dark-stoned edifices with towering ramparts perched atop grim cliffs. Linwood Castle *was* large, but it wasn't dark-stoned and there were no grim cliffs anywhere. It did have ramparts, and also turrets and crenellations and stone mullioned windows and archways and a grand marble staircase and a fireplace in the great hall that was so large that she could stand up in it, but it also had quaint little spiral oak staircases and round rooms in the turrets and a round fernery, too.

The ramparts encircled the gardens, and beyond the ramparts were parkland and woodland and rolling hills, and everything was so picturesque and so beautiful that Pip felt a little discombobulated. Was this *real*? It felt as if it might not be. It wasn't a dream, because she was most definitely awake, but she had the oddest sensation that she'd stepped out of the everyday world and entered a different reality.

Ordinary England lay behind her; she had crossed the threshold into an enchanted England, complete with a golden castle.

Linwood Castle wasn't made of gold, of course, but it was built of honey-colored limestone that glowed with mellow warmth in the sunshine. The castle wasn't enchanted, either, but it was charming—and that was puzzling in itself. How could a structure so enormous be charming? It shouldn't be possible, and yet Linwood Castle *was* charming, with its fanciful crenellations and its softly golden limestone, its spiral staircases and its whimsical arches.

Pip hadn't known what to expect in a duke, either. "Duke" was a word that conjured up images of someone coldly formal and forbiddingly stern. Maximus Pryor, Duke of Linwood, was neither of those things. He did have gravitas though, more gravitas than anyone Pip had ever met. He also had what she'd come to recognize as the Pryor nose and the Pryor eyes.

One glance at him told her what Octavius would

look like in fifty years' time: silver-haired and a little stooped, but still striking. A man with presence. A man who drew the eye.

She met the Duke of Linwood over afternoon tea on the day of their arrival. It was a private audience, just herself and Octavius. Pip felt ridiculously nervous when she entered Linwood's personal sitting room. Her legs shook while she made her curtsy, her heart beat far too fast, and she was afraid she might be perspiring.

The sitting room wasn't as ostentatious as she'd expected. In fact, it wasn't ostentatious at all. It was comfortable, if such a plebeian word could be applied to a duke's sitting room, cozy even, with its polished wood and its dark brown leather and red damask.

The duchess wasn't present. She was visiting friends in Naunton, the duke informed them, and then he politely asked Pip to pour the tea.

Pip's heart beat even faster, but she managed to pour three cups without spilling anything, which was a feat, given that her fingers were trembling ever so slightly.

"Thank you," the duke said, with a courteous smile. If he was appalled that Octavius had brought a mere governess into his castle, he hid it well. He sipped his tea and asked about their journey. There was no condescension in his manner, just polite curiosity. He was assessing her, though—Pip knew he was—watching her with those keen, dark eyes, listening with those terrifyingly acute ears, taking her measure, deciding whether she was worthy of his grandson.

Pip had never thought of herself as a liar, but she found herself scrutinizing every word she said. It was a relief to let Octavius do most of the talking. Pip listened as he told the duke about Baron Rumpole, and as she listened she found herself forgetting to be nervous, because Octavius was telling his grandfather more than just the bare bones of the story.

He started by describing what had happened at Vauxhall Gardens in such detail that Pip shivered in vicarious fear, then he told the duke about meeting Pip in London and everything that had happened after that. The duke looked amused, not scandalized, when Octavius mentioned the lessons in defensive techniques. He winced when Octavius confessed that he'd accidentally revealed his magic to Pip, and he frowned quite alarmingly when Octavius recounted how he'd terrified Baron Rumpole in the library.

"He cried, and he was so frightened he wet himself. It was awful, Grandfather. I thought it was the right thing to do, but I know now that it wasn't."

The duke's frown eased. Pip wasn't completely certain, but she thought he looked relieved.

Octavius then went on to describe Mr. Donald's attack on her. "I almost killed him afterwards," he admitted. "I might have, if Miss Toogood hadn't stopped me."

The duke regarded his grandson gravely, then turned those unnervingly keen eyes to her. "And how are you, Miss Toogood, after such a shocking experience?"

"I'm perfectly fine," Pip said, and then wondered if that sounded like a lie to him. "A few bruises," she hastened to add. "That's all."

Linwood inclined his head, accepting this answer, but still he didn't look away from her. "And in yourself?" he asked, touching two fingertips to his chest.

Pip had no difficulty interpreting that gesture. He was asking if she was emotionally well. She took a moment to find the most truthful answer.

"The day that it happened, I wasn't, not at all, but now . . ." She struggled to explain something that didn't quite make sense, even to herself. "It feels so far away, as if it happened to someone else in another lifetime—and I know that's absurd, because it's only eighty miles and two days ago, but that's what it feels like." It felt, in fact, as if leaving Rumpole Hall had been not just the end of a chapter in her life, but the end of a whole book, and that Mr. Donald and his attack were packed away between tightly closed pages in a distant library and that not even the merest memory of him remained to hurt her. Which was nonsensical. Too nonsensical to say aloud to a duke, so instead Pip said, "I don't think I'll have nightmares over Mr. Donald."

It must have sounded like the truth, for the duke nodded. "I'm pleased to hear it. And I'm grateful you were able to prevent my grandson from killing him. Extremely grateful. Thank you."

"He didn't *want* to kill Mr. Donald," Pip informed Linwood hastily, in case he had any doubts. "It wasn't a deliberate intention."

"No, of course not, but in the heat of the moment one can do things one deeply regrets later."

"Yes." Pip was relieved he understood—and relieved that *she* understood, too, because she very nearly hadn't.

Linwood turned his attention back to his grandson. "Please continue."

Octavius did, but there wasn't much left to tell. He concluded by reading his brother's letter aloud. When he'd finished, the duke nodded his approval. "I have no doubt the jury will find your Mr. Donald guilty."

Pip had no doubt either.

Octavius refolded the letter and laid it on his knee. "You know how Uncle Deuce always says there's more than one way to peel an egg? Well, Quintus's way of peeling this egg was better than mine."

The duke laughed at that, and Pip did, too, because really, peeling eggs? But then Linwood's expression sobered. "The dispensing of justice is best left to the courts, Octavius."

"Miss Toogood said the exact same thing," Octavius said, catching her eye and smiling. "I've learned that lesson. We'll do it Quintus's way next time."

The duke's grizzled eyebrows went up slightly. "Next time?"

Pip's nervousness came avalanching back. Perhaps Octavius sensed it, because he reached across to take her hand. "Mr. Donald isn't the only man who's attacked women and got away with it. There are others like him in England. Too many of them. It's impossible for one person to stop them all, but *some* people can stop *some* of them—and that's what Miss Toogood and I are going to do."

Linwood's eyebrows rose a little higher. "You are?"

Octavius gave a decisive nod. "We talked it over in the carriage. Made a lot of plans."

The duke's eyebrows were still raised. He looked rather bemused. "What exactly are the pair of you proposing?"

Octavius released Pip's hand and tapped his brother's letter. "Quintus's way of peeling eggs, for one. We're going to start a charitable fund for women who've been assaulted, so they can seek justice."

Pip held her breath and waited for Linwood's reaction. What would it be? Censure? Disapproval? Grudging consent?

Octavius didn't hold his breath; he kept speaking: "Miss Belton was wronged, but she couldn't do anything about it because she hadn't enough money—and that's not right. Everyone should have access to justice, even if they're female and even if they're poor. *Especially* if they're female and poor."

The duke regarded his grandson for several long seconds, and then smiled. It took Pip a moment to identify all the emotions in that smile. Affection. Approval. Pride.

Her nervousness evaporated.

The duke leaned back in his armchair and looked at them both, his gaze moving from Octavius to Pip and back again. "Your charitable fund will allow these women to seek justice?"

"Those who wish to, yes," Octavius said. "We'll pay for the lawyers and meet all the costs. Court cases aren't actually all that expensive, except that for maids and cooks and governesses, they *are*."

"Do you have a name for your charitable fund?"

"Not yet, sir," Octavius said.

"I hope you'll allow me to contribute?"

"Of course, sir. But the fund's not the only thing we're going to do. We've made a lot of plans."

Linwood laughed. "Eighty miles' worth of them?"

"More like seventy," Octavius said ruefully. "I fell asleep between Basingstoke and Newbury."

The duke laughed again and settled back more comfortably in his chair. Pip could see just how much he loved his grandson. It wasn't merely in his smile, it was in every line of his face.

"Tell me," the duke said.

"First, I'm going to check every one of our households, the same way I checked Rumpole's— as a housemaid. I know none of *us* are molesting the maids, but I want to make certain none of the menservants are, either."

Linwood frowned, as if this possibility had never occurred to him. He nodded. "Good, yes."

"I'll speak with the housekeepers and butlers, too. The housekeeper at Rumpole Hall, and the butler and all the footmen, were doing their utmost to protect the maids. I want to make certain that happens in our households, too."

The duke nodded again. "Of course. What else?"

Octavius glanced at Pip. *You tell him,* his expression urged her.

Pip hesitated, and hoped that the duke truly was as broad-minded as he appeared to be. "Octavius will continue to teach me defensive techniques," she told him.

Linwood didn't tell her that it was unbecoming of a woman to learn defensive techniques, and in particular, unbecoming of a nobleman's wife; he merely gave another nod.

"I'll teach Phoebe, too," Octavius put in. "If she wants to learn. Just to be on the safe side."

Pip couldn't imagine a circumstance in which a duke's granddaughter would need defensive techniques, and she doubted Linwood could imagine one either, but he nodded again. "To be on the safe side," he agreed.

Pip was relieved that hurdle had been cleared so easily . . . but it brought them to the next one. *Please be open-minded about this, too*, she prayed—and then she took a deep breath and said, "We're going to start a school that teaches defensive techniques to women of the lower classes. Servants and the like."

Linwood hadn't expected that. He blinked, looking quite taken aback.

"It will be free," Pip said, persisting in the face of that blank-faced surprise. "We'll advertise—posters and flyers—but we're not expecting many students. Servants only get one half day off a month, after all. But even if we only have a handful of women in each class—even if there's only *one*—it will be worth it, because it's important that they know how to defend themselves."

Linwood didn't cringe at the word "advertise," or at "posters and flyers," nor did he try to interrupt her. He listened until she'd finished, and then he inclined his head in one of those courteous nods and said, "Yes, it is important."

Pip studied his face. He appeared to be sincere.

"There might be negative attention," she told him. "Criticism. People who think it's improper and unseemly, or even scandalous."

"I have no doubt you'll ruffle a few feathers," the duke said. "But I hope you won't let that stop you."

"We won't," Pip assured him.

Linwood smiled. "An unusual venture, but as you say, an important one. If you'll allow it, I'd like to contribute. Perhaps I could pay for the advertising?"

Pip was so astonished that she said, "What?" On the heels of that injudicious utterance came a hot rush of blood to her cheeks, because saying *What?* to a duke wasn't just gauche, it was rude. "I beg your pardon, Your Grace."

Fortunately, Linwood didn't appear to be offended. "My grandsons' lessons saved you from a grievous assault, Miss Toogood. If similar lessons can save even one other person from something similar, your school will be worth it."

Pip might not be able to hear lies, but she could hear that the duke was telling the truth. Her hot blush faded. "It will be worth it," she said. "Thank you."

Linwood smiled at her and offered his teacup to be refilled.

Pip poured. This time her fingers didn't tremble.

They talked of other things for the next half hour. When at last she and Octavius rose to leave, the duke stood, too, and clasped his grandson's hand and said, "You've matured a lot in the last few months, my boy."

"Only since meeting Miss Toogood," Octavius said. He met her eyes and smiled.

The duke smiled, too. "Then it's a happy circumstance that you met."

I'm only a governess, Pip wanted to say. But Linwood knew that, and he truly didn't seem to care.

The duke released his grandson's hand. "It's been a pleasure making your acquaintance, Miss Toogood. I'm delighted you're going to marry my grandson."

Pip made him a deeply respectful curtsy. "Thank you, Your Grace."

The duke shook his head. "You're part of the family, now. Call me Linwood if you must, but . . ."

His smile became a little wistful. "I should prefer it if you called me Grandfather."

"Thank you," Pip said, and then she added, a little shyly, "I would very much like it if you called me Pippa."

Not Philippa, not Pip, but the name her father had called her: Pippa.

"It will be my pleasure," Linwood said. His smile wasn't wistful anymore; it was warm and friendly. The sort of smile you gave someone you liked.

"Dinner will be served at six," he told them. "Go for a walk the pair of you, get some fresh air."

"Yes, sir." Octavius captured Pip's hand and led her from the sitting room.

Pip snatched one last glimpse of the duke before the door swung shut. What an astonishing old man. He wasn't at all what she'd thought a duke would be like. She understood why Octavius loved him so much. After an hour in his company, she loved him, too.

Octavius tugged her hand eagerly. "Come on," he said. "I can't wait to show you the gardens. There's a maze, you know, and two follies."

They clattered down a spiral staircase and spilled out into a long corridor. Octavius picked up his pace, half running, pulling her along with him. Pip caught up her skirts in her free hand. Relief bubbled up inside her. She hadn't realized until now just how anxious she'd been about meeting the duke, how afraid she'd been that he wouldn't approve of her. There was still the duchess to meet, and Octavius's parents and his brother, his uncles and aunts, his other cousins, but the most daunting introduction was over.

Linwood didn't see her as an unwanted interloper. He liked her. He wanted her to call him Grandfather.

Octavius flung open a side door and suddenly they were outside on a sunny terrace. "What would you like to see?"

"Everything!" Pip said.

CHAPTER 40

*L*ord Octavius showed her the rose garden and the water garden, the maze, the Chinese Folly with its tiers of funny peaked roofs, and then he took her to the bluebell dell. The feeling that she'd stepped into an enchanted England grew stronger. "My goodness," Pip said, with a laugh. "I feel as if I'm inside a picture book. It's too idyllic to be true!"

She wondered what words the Reverend Gilbert White would have used to describe this woodland dell—the slender birches with their upraised branches, the trembling green canopy of leaves, the dappled light and shade, the drifts of blue flowers.

They wandered hand in hand through the trees, climbed a gentle rise, and came upon another folly, one Octavius called the Bird's Nest. It wasn't as fanciful as the Chinese Folly, just a tall stone tower with a winding staircase inside.

The room at the top was circular and had windows all the way around. Pip lost what little breath she had. Her *Oh* was silent. She forgot that she was an adult and ran from window to window, gazing out in wonder.

"What do you think?" Octavius asked, after she'd made two complete circuits.

"I love it!" The folly had been aptly named. It felt as if they were perched in a bird's nest, high among the treetops.

Pip made another circuit and halted where she could see Linwood Castle in all its whimsical, welcoming glory.

Octavius stepped close behind her. His hands came to rest lightly at her waist. Pip tipped her head back against his shoulder. How could this possibly be her life? The bluebell dell and this folly, the castle, the duke, and most of all, Octavius.

Two weeks ago she'd been a governess. A very ordinary governess with little money and no family.

Now her life wasn't at all ordinary. She was about to be married. She had a family.

And *what* a husband. *What* a family.

Pip wanted to laugh and cry at the same time. She chose to laugh, and to turn around and put her arms around Octavius's neck and kiss him exuberantly.

He kissed her exuberantly back. His hands settled at her waist again, drawing her closer.

They kissed and laughed and kissed again, and when they were breathless they sank down on a daybed piled high with plush cushions and the kissing became slower and more exploratory. Octavius kissed her fingertips; Pip kissed his jaw. Octavius kissed his way up her wrist; Pip kissed his ear—and then she hesitated. "Octavius? Am I meant to bite your ears?"

Octavius stopped exploring her wrist. "I beg your pardon?"

"Your cousin said that women bite his ears. Is that what you want me to do?"

Octavius laughed. She felt his body shake with amusement. "I beg your pardon," he managed to choke out. "I'm not laughing *at* you. It's just . . ." He laughed again, and then sobered and said, "You're not meant to do anything you don't want to, Pip. Only what feels good."

"Biting?" Pip said, with a dubious frown. She didn't think she wanted to bite anyone, or be bitten.

"It can feel good. It depends how it's done." He lifted her hand to his mouth and nipped one of her fingertips very lightly. It sparked a delicious little shiver, a tingling scintilla of sensation. He nipped a second fingertip and then a third, sparking more scintillas of delight—and then he leaned up and bit her earlobe. The sensation that elicited was more starburst than spark. Pip heard herself gasp. Heat flushed her skin.

"Well?" Octavius asked.

"It does feel good," Pip admitted, a little breathlessly.

He grinned. His eyes were alight with amusement—and something else that she recognized as passion.

She sank back into his embrace, into his kisses and caresses, and yes, his bites. He kissed her throat, then gently nipped where he'd kissed, soothed the faint sting away with his tongue, kissed again. Pip tried to reciprocate, but men's clothing was much more obstructive than women's. His neckcloth was in the way.

"May I take this off?" she asked, touching those crumpled folds of muslin.

"What?" he said, and captured her mouth again.

Pip forgot her question. Quite a few minutes passed. She was hot and disheveled and short of breath by the time Octavius released her.

"We have to stop," he said. "Or we're going to end up having our wedding night right here."

"I wouldn't mind that," she confessed.

They stared at each other for a long and breathless moment. Octavius reached for her and kissed her again, then drew back. "Much as I'd like to have our wedding night now—much as I *want* to—we'd be late for dinner."

The devil fly away with dinner, Pip wanted to say. Common sense and desire wrestled with one another for several seconds, before common sense won. She knew as well as he did that they couldn't be late for dinner. It would be shockingly disrespectful to his grandparents.

Pip sighed, and sat back.

Octavius sighed, too, and smiled at her ruefully. His face was flushed, his hair mussed, his lips rosy and swollen, his neckcloth in disarray. He looked quite debauched.

No doubt she looked equally debauched.

Pip reluctantly climbed off the daybed. She twitched at her neckline, smoothing the fabric. Were all those little nibbles he'd taken up and down her throat visible? She crossed to the nearest window and examined her reflection. She couldn't see any marks at her throat, but she could see that her hair needed rescuing.

Pip plucked out her hairpins and redid her chignon.

She thought her reflection looked a little neater, but it was difficult to tell; her eyes kept focusing on the view—the treetops, the parkland, the hills and valleys beyond.

Twenty miles to the south lay Wootton Bassett, where Newingham had his estate and where they'd stayed last night—and that was something she must do: find Fanny and Edie a new governess.

She'd make a start on that tomorrow.

Pip wandered a few windows further, until she was looking east. She imagined watching the sun rise over that horizon.

Octavius came up beside her. He bumped their shoulders together companionably. "What are you thinking?"

"I'm wishing I could see the dawn from these windows."

"You'd like to watch from here?"

"I'd love to," Pip said. At that moment, movement caught her eye. A carriage was wending its way across the parkland. "Is that your grandmother?"

Octavius narrowed his eyes in a squint. "I think it's my parents' carriage." He caught her hand and pulled her towards the stairs. "I can't wait for you to meet them."

CHAPTER 41

*P*ip met a marquis and a marchioness later that afternoon and a duchess that evening, and the next day she met an earl, two lords and their wives, a Miss Pryor, two Mr. Pryors, and a duke's illegitimate son. All the men had the Pryor eyes and nose, which made it extremely confusing. Pip drew a family tree and jotted down notes to help her distinguish one man from another.

Nonus, the youngest son of Lord Tertius Pryor, was the most conspicuous of the Pryor cousins. He reminded her of nothing so much as a great overgrown puppy. Or perhaps an elephant.

He wasn't a bully, but he *was* a prankster. A prankster who could become invisible. Fortunately, he was so loud that all his attempts to creep up on his family failed.

"We can hear you," his father said, not even

looking up from his newspaper as Nonus crept loudly into the library.

"We can hear you," his aunts chorused as he crept equally loudly into the fernery.

"We can hear you," three of his cousins informed him as he crept even more loudly into the drawing room before dinner.

He looked so crestfallen each time that Pip was hard pressed not to laugh. On the morning of her wedding, when Nonus had tried unsuccessfully to creep into the breakfast parlor yet again, Pip took pity on him. "You need to study the art of moving," she told him over her plate of eggs. "A year's worth of fencing lessons ought to do the trick."

"Don't help him!" Decimus Pryor said, aghast, while his sister, Phoebe, giggled into her teacup.

"Wouldn't do any good," Lord Secundus Pryor said, buttering his toast. "All the fencing lessons in the world couldn't stop my nephew being a noisy clodhopper." And then he winked at Pip.

"They might," Nonus said a little defensively, piling his own plate high with food.

Octavius shook his head. So did most of his cousins.

"They might," Nonus said again, even more defensively. He put his plate down on the table with a thump, pulled out his chair with a thump, sat down with a thump.

"Not possible," his brother, the exceedingly beautiful Sextus Pryor, said, refilling his cup of tea.

"It might be!"

Even the ever-courteous marquis and his equally courteous eldest son, Quintus, were laughing at Nonus now. There was no cruelty in that laughter, it was friendly and familial, but even so, Pip felt a little sorry for him. She'd always favored the underdog, and in this moment Nonus Pryor was an underdog. A very large, very loud underdog.

After breakfast, before they headed their various ways, she plucked at his sleeve, drawing his attention. "Fencing lessons would help. You need to learn to *think* when you move."

"I've already had lessons. I know how to fence."

"But can you do it well?"

He pulled a rather gruesome face. Pip took that to be a no. "You need lessons in the art of moving," she told him firmly. "Fencing and dancing and deportment. You need to learn to be aware of what your body's doing."

"Dancing and deportment?" Nonus said, in a horrified voice.

"Yes," Pip said. "Fencing, dancing, and deportment. And by the end of twelve months you'll be able to walk quietly."

"You think so?" he said, dubiously.

"I *know* so," Pip said, and then, as Nonus still looked unconvinced, she said coaxingly, "Go on, give it a try. One year of lessons. What harm can it do? I'm sure you'll be able to creep up on them by the end of it."

Mischief suddenly lit his face. "I wish I could!"

"Shall we make it a wager?" Pip said, holding out her hand for him to shake. "One year of lessons— fencing, dancing, and deportment—and by the end of it I bet you'll be able to creep up on anyone."

"What's the forfeit?" Nonus said. "I know! Whoever loses has to walk backwards for an entire day."

"Whoever loses has to walk backwards for *one* hour," Pip said.

"That's no fun!" Nonus protested.

"Take it or leave it," she said, still holding out her hand.

Nonus thought about it for several seconds, and then said, "All right." He clasped her hand in his giant paw and gave it a hearty shake. "One year of lessons. I'll show 'em!"

He released her hand, nodded to her, and strode off down the corridor with a thunderous *clomp, clomp, clomp* of his very large feet.

Pip watched him go . . . and felt a faint qualm of misgiving. If Nonus Pryor *did* learn how to move silently, what mayhem would he cause? But then a certain someone slipped an arm around her waist and pressed a kiss to her temple.

Pip stopped thinking about invisible pranksters and started thinking about her upcoming nuptials instead.

Three hours later, in the rose garden, Pip and Lord Octavius were married by special license. The ceremony was small and informal, family members only, but it didn't matter that Pip had no family of her own because these people already felt like family.

Following the wedding came a champagne luncheon, after which the younger members of the party headed outside for a merry game of blind man's bluff and an even merrier game of hide-and-seek.

Pip discovered that the kitchen garden was an excellent place in which to hide, and that the water garden was not. She discovered how impossible it was to be quiet when one was overcome with the giggles. And she discovered how much she liked being kissed by her husband in the Chinese Folly and in the maze and under various wisteria-covered bowers.

Later that evening, after a long and convivial dinner with her new family, Pip learned a great many more things.

The first thing she learned was that naked men looked *very* naked. More naked than naked women looked. Octavius was slightly dumbfounded when she uttered this observation aloud. "No, we don't."

"Men wear so many clothes," Pip said. "One never gets to see their throats or arms or ankles." Unless the man in question was one's husband and he was standing in one's bedroom looking exceptionally naked.

Octavius's throat and arms and ankles, now that they were revealed, were very fine. He had the sort of body that sculptors and painters prized. Pip couldn't decide which part of him she liked looking at the most. His shoulders? Those muscular thighs?

She knew which part disconcerted her the most: his groin, where that strange, fascinating, and slightly alarming appendage was located.

In that moment, Pip learned that one could simultaneously be eager and afraid, and that one's heart could beat fast in anticipation while at the same time beating fast with nervousness.

The next thing she learned was that when Octavius took her face in his hands and kissed her, tenderly and reverently, her fear faded and the nervousness melted away.

After that, she learned that kissing a man while both of you were naked was more enjoyable than kissing the same man when you were both clothed. Not twice as enjoyable, not three times, but exponentially more enjoyable. When *her* naked skin brushed *his* naked skin it set off scintillas the size of sunbursts.

Next, Pip learned that she could be kissed in places where she'd never thought she could be kissed, which produced even more sunbursts of pleasure. And then she learned that men could be kissed in places she'd never thought they could be kissed, either.

She learned how hot Octavius's skin was and how sleek his muscles were, and that some of his hair was soft and some coarse and springy. She learned that she loved the scent of his skin and the taste of it on her tongue.

She learned that she particularly liked it when Octavius kissed her in threes, but that there came a point when threes were irrelevant, when it no longer mattered whether he kissed her once or twice or twenty times, because she'd become a carnal creature, not a thinking creature, and threes meant nothing at all.

She learned what it felt like to have a man's appendage inside her for the very first time, that it stung as if it had bitten her. And after the sting had faded she learned how powerful instincts were, because she'd never had sexual congress before and yet her body knew exactly what to do.

As the clock was striking midnight, Pip learned what physical ecstasy was—not just one sunburst, but a whole host of them exploding one after another inside her.

"Was it all right?" Octavius asked afterwards. Pip couldn't see his face, because the candle had long since burned down, but she thought he sounded a little worried.

"Yes," she said. "It was good."

"A little bit good or—"

"*Very* good," Pip said.

"Truly?"

"Truly."

She felt him relax alongside her in the bed. "I'm glad," he said. "I was afraid it wouldn't be, because I think . . . it might be better for men than for women."

"Impossible," Pip said.

Octavius uttered a soft laugh. He gathered her in his arms and pulled the covers up around their shoulders. "Comfortable?"

"Yes." She was comfortable and content and tired in a way she'd never been before. And safe. So safe in his arms.

The last thing Pip learned that night, as she lay in

the warm, quiet darkness, was just how wonderful it was to fall asleep while being held by the man she loved, what an incredibly intimate experience it was to hear his breathing slow and to feel his body relax fully.

Even though he was asleep, she still felt safe in his arms. And oddly, she also felt stronger, as if Octavius had given her some of his own strength.

I hope I do the same for him, she thought. *I hope I make him feel stronger, too.*

CHAPTER 42

*O*ctavius woke before his wife. What a wonderful word that was: wife. *His* wife.

The bedchamber was still dark, but his inner clock had always been fairly accurate. When he crept out of bed and lit a candle, he saw that he'd woken almost exactly when he'd wanted to.

He tiptoed into the dressing room and did his ablutions, then donned his clothes hastily, not bothering with such things as waistcoat and neckcloth. His wife stirred while he was laying out clothes for her on the bed. "Octavius?" She sat up and rubbed her face. "What are you doing?"

"You're awake. Excellent. Come on, there's not much time."

"Not much time for what?"

"I have a surprise. Go wash your face. I'll help you to dress."

Pip disappeared into the dressing room. A few minutes later, she emerged, face scrubbed, hair pinned up.

Octavius handed her the chemise, and after that, a gown.

"My stays—"

"No need for stays," he said. "Or petticoats. Not where we're going."

Stockings came next, and then shoes. Octavius wrapped a shawl around Pip's shoulders, captured her hand, and drew her towards the door.

"Where are we going?"

"You'll see."

They tiptoed hastily along the quiet corridors, hand in hand, and exited through a side door. They crossed the dewy lawn. Octavius lengthened his stride until they were almost running.

It was no longer fully night. Predawn was lightening the sky. There was no color in the world yet, though. The bluebell dell was a place of dark shadows. The Bird's Nest folly loomed tall on the rising ground.

They climbed the stairs, puffing and panting, and burst breathlessly into the round room at the top. One of the daybeds faced east. "Just in time," Octavius said, flinging himself down on the cushions and pulling his wife onto his lap.

By the time he'd caught his breath, colors had started to tint the sky.

First came the palest of lemon yellows creeping up from the horizon, then streaks of orange on the lowest scattering of clouds, then pink on the clouds above those. The colors grew richer, stronger, more vivid, the orange like flame, the pink a brilliant magenta.

Octavius felt something akin to awe as he watched the colors change. He might be able to do magic, but this was magic, too, this sky with its glorious cascade of colors.

What was it Pip had said, back in Hampshire? That women saw more beauty in the world than men did?

She'd been correct. He'd seen dozens of dawns in his life, scores of them, but he'd never once noticed how beautiful they were.

The pink faded away, the orange grew fainter and fainter, the yellow dissolved into nothing.

"You were right," Octavius told his wife, once the final colors had disappeared. "Women see more beauty in the world."

And women not only saw beauty, they shared it. Pip had shared dawns with him, a gift that he'd have with him for the rest of his life—and that was something else that women did better than men: they enriched the lives of those around them.

Octavius struggled to find the words to express this sudden epiphany. "Pip? Do you think . . ."

Pip shifted in his embrace, until she could see his face. "Do I think what?"

"Men thrive because of women," Octavius said slowly, fumbling his way through his epiphany. "The whole *world* thrives because of women. You make everything better."

His face heated once he'd said it out loud because it sounded so ridiculous, the philosophical waffling of a fool, but Pip didn't laugh. She smiled at him with such brightness and such warmth that his heart lurched in his chest. "You think we make the world a better place?"

"Yes."

Her smile became even brighter and more joyful. "I'm glad."

Octavius tightened his arms around her, while he had yet another epiphany. It was easier to bare one's soul to a woman than to a man, easier to be vulnerable, and that ease was both freeing and empowering.

Women truly *did* make the world a better place.

He hugged his wife tightly and rested his chin on her soft hair and knew that this was the best morning of his life.

He hoped it was the best morning of Pip's life, too. This sunrise. This start to their marriage.

The sky was blue now and the scattered clouds were white and all around them was green. Green treetops, green hills, green hedgerows, green pastures. A hundred different shades of green—and that was another beauty he'd never noticed before, that there were so many greens in the world.

Octavius's stomach gave a rumble that he felt rather than heard, reminding him that he hadn't eaten anything since last night. "There's a breakfast," he said. "On that table over there. I had the servants lay it out for us last night. Pastries and fruit. Something to drink." He stroked her waist while he spoke, and as he stroked he remembered that Pip was wearing no stays. He could feel her natural curves.

He stroked again, from hip to waist to breast, a gentle caress.

Pip hummed beneath her breath.

"You like that?"

"Mmm," she murmured.

Octavius forgot all about breakfast. Instead, he bent his attention to making this best morning even better.

$\mathcal{A}$FTERWARDS

$\mathcal{P}$ip spent the first week of her married life interviewing governesses. She interviewed tall governesses and short ones, young governesses and old ones, blonde governesses and brunettes, a redhead, and two governesses with gray hair. She asked them all the same two questions. "Which of these qualities is, in your opinion, the single most important one for girls to acquire?"

The latest candidate, a Miss Bollingbroke, was short, young, plump, and brown-haired. She had a lot of freckles and a pair of spectacles. She pushed the spectacles up her nose while she looked at the list Pip had given her.

Docility
Obedience
Confidence
Modesty

Deference
Humility

Miss Bollingbroke frowned as she read her way down the list, and then glanced at Pip. "The most important quality?"

"Yes."

"Confidence," Miss Bollingbroke said, and gave the list back to Pip.

Pip pursed her lips and made a mark on her paper, then she passed another list to Miss Bollingbroke. "Of these subjects, which would you teach girls and which would you not?"

Spelling
Arithmetic
French
Geography
Climbing trees
Pianoforte
Painting
Botany
Paddling in creeks
Deportment
Elocution
Embroidery
Flying kites

Miss Bollingbroke read her way down the list. "All of them," she said, and gave the list back.

"All of them?" Pip said, dubiously. "Even climbing trees?"

"Of course. They're children, are they not?"

Pip made another mark on her paper, and then sat back and studied Miss Bollingbroke. Unless she was mistaken, she'd just found the perfect governess. "You're hired, Miss Bollingbroke."

They talked about the girls for the next hour, about how confidence was the most important thing they needed to learn and that climbing trees, flying kites, and paddling in creeks were essential parts of their curriculum. Then Miss Bollingbroke departed, to be driven the twenty miles to Newingham's estate in one of the duke's liveried coaches.

Pip tidied up her notes—the list of qualities, the list of subjects, the list of candidates' names with fourteen names crossed out and one, Miss Bollingbroke's, with two stars alongside it.

A knock came on the parlor door. A maid peeked in. "Are you finished?"

Pip put her lists to one side. "Are you?"

The maid nodded. She was a very pretty maid, with curling blonde hair, large blue eyes, and a buxom figure.

Pip pushed back her chair and left the parlor. Together she and the maid climbed the stairs to the bedchamber she shared with Octavius. Once inside, Pip locked the door. "No pinches?"

"Not a single one," the maid said, turning her back so that Pip could unfasten her dress. "No kisses either, or lewd comments. Nothing."

"That's good," Pip said. "We can cross Linwood Castle off the list."

The maid shucked her gown and petticoat and stood still while Pip undid the laces on her stays. "Thank heavens," she said, once she was liberated from that garment. "I hate stays. Dashed uncomfortable."

"Neckcloths look uncomfortable," Pip said.

The maid removed her chemise. "They are, but not as uncomfortable as stays."

Pip, who'd never worn a neckcloth, couldn't argue this point.

The maid transformed into Octavius. "Ah," he said on a sigh and closed his eyes. "So much better."

Pip held out his drawers. "Where to next?"

Octavius opened his eyes. "Gloucestershire, then down to Somerset," he said, not taking the drawers. "Then Dorset, then Surrey, then Kent." He huffed out a breath that was half laugh, half sigh. "My family owns too many estates."

Pip didn't disagree. She'd been rather daunted by the list of properties when she'd first seen it. Not daunted by the work that lay ahead of them, but daunted by the Pryor family's wealth.

"What would you like to do now?" she asked, still holding out the drawers. "Shall we go for a walk?"

"We could," Octavius said, making no move to take the drawers. "Or . . ." He caught her other hand and pressed three kisses to her palm. "We could do something else."

"But it's the middle of the afternoon," Pip protested.

"So?"

There was no rule that said they couldn't make love in the afternoon, was there? "Or perhaps we could do both?" Pip suggested, rather breathlessly.

"We could do both," Octavius agreed.

Pip dropped his drawers on the floor and let him lead her to the bed, where he kissed her a great deal more than three times.

$\mathscr{A}$UTHOR'S $\mathscr{N}$OTE

The Tichborne Dole really did exist. In the 12th century, an ailing Lady Tichborne crawled around 23 acres so that the produce from that land would be given to the poor. To ensure that her miserly husband kept his word, she also laid the following curse: if the dole were ever to be stopped, the Tichborne family would bear seven sons and those sons would bear seven daughters, resulting in the family's name dying out. The dole *was* stopped during the Georgian era and seven sons were born, the eldest of whom had seven daughters. At that point, the dole was resumed for fear that the curse was coming to fruition.

Alas, *droit de seigneur* was alive and well in England for many centuries. (The diaries of Samuel Pepys make for horrifying reading. Pepys was a member of parliament and Chief Secretary to the Admiralty—and a man who routinely forced himself on his maidservants.)

In Regency times, the Crown covered the cost of trials for treason, murder, counterfeiting, and malfeasance of public office. For everything else, the victim was required to foot the bill. Costs included hiring the investigators, paying the lawyers, and covering the expenses of any witnesses. This meant that justice through the courts was well beyond the reach of most people. However, poor women occasionally were able to obtain justice. (See the case of Harriet Halliday in 1811, if you're interested. A local surgeon came to her rescue and successfully financed the prosecution against her attacker.)

And to end on a literary note, *The Natural History and Antiquities of Selborne,* by the Reverend Gilbert White, was published in 1789 and has been in print ever since. In the words of one Regency reviewer, "a more delightful or more original work than Mr. White's *History of Selborne* has seldom been published."

Reverend White preferred to observe live creatures in their natural habitat, rather than to study dead specimens. Many people consider him to be England's first ecologist.

I'll leave you with a quote from him:

"I was much entertained last summer with a tame bat, which would take flies out of a person's hand ... insects seemed to be most acceptable, though it did not refuse raw flesh when offered; so the notion that bats go down chimneys and gnaw on men's bacon seems no improbable story."

$\mathcal{T}$HANK $\mathcal{Y}$OU

Thanks for reading *Octavius and the Perfect Governess*. I hope you enjoyed it! If you'd like to read a couple of short stories featuring Octavius's great-grandmother, you can find them on my website. Here's the link: www.emilylarkin.com/pryor-prequels.

I welcome all honest reviews. Reviews and word of mouth help other readers to find books, so please consider taking a few moments to leave a review on Goodreads or elsewhere.

If you would like to be notified whenever I release a new book, please join my Readers' Group, which you can find at www.emilylarkin.com/newsletter.

Octavius and the Perfect Governess is part of the Baleful Godmother series. I'm currently giving free digital copies of the series prequel, *The Fey Quartet*, and the first novel in the original series, *Unmasking Miss Appleby*, to anyone who joins my Readers' Group. Here's the link: www.emilylarkin.com/starter-library.

The Pryor Cousins series runs concurrently with the Garland Cousins series. The first Garland novel, *Primrose and the Dreadful Duke*, tells the story of a duke with a dreadful sense of humor, a bookish spinster, and a murderer.

If you'd like to read the first two chapters of *Primrose and the Dreadful Duke*, please turn the page.

Primrose
and the
DREADFUL DUKE

CHAPTER ONE

*P*rimrose Garland liked books. All kinds of books, but especially books written many centuries ago, and most especially books that were the *real* thoughts of *real* people. Pliny's letters, for example. Catullus's love-sick poems. Marcus Aurelius's philosophical musings.

That morning, she was reading Aurelius again, experiencing the same delight and wonder that she always felt. Aurelius had been an emperor in Rome, she was a spinster in London—and yet here she was, reading his private notes to himself, his musings on life. It was extremely intimate, this insight into a man's thoughts. Sometimes it felt as if he were talking directly to her, that if she turned her head, there he would be: Marcus Aurelius, Emperor of

Rome, seated at the writing table, and he'd look up from his notes and say to her, "Dwell on the beauty of life. Watch the stars, and see yourself running with them."

That was one of her favorite quotes. It had made her cry the first time she'd read it. Two sentences that a stranger had written more than sixteen hundred years ago, and they'd made her cry.

Which was why she loved Aurelius so much.

So when she looked for the second volume of his *Meditations* and realized that she'd left it in Staffordshire, Primrose was a little annoyed. But only a little, because it wouldn't take more than a few minutes to fetch it.

She went upstairs to her bedchamber and locked the door, so that no servant could walk in and discover the Garland family secret, then she clasped her hands together, took a deep breath, and pictured the library at Manifold Park, and in particular, the shadows behind the black-and-gold lacquered screen in the corner.

Primrose wished herself there.

In the next instant, she was.

There was a familiar moment of vertigo—the library seemed to spin around her—and then everything steadied into place.

Primrose held her breath and listened intently. The library *sounded* empty.

She peeked around the edge of the black-and-gold screen. The library *was* empty. As it should be when the Garland family was in London.

Primrose crossed quickly to where Aurelius was shelved, selected the volume she wanted, and wished herself back in her bedchamber in London.

In the blink of an eye, she was.

The vertigo hit again, as if she'd spun around a thousand times. Primrose waited until it passed, then glanced at herself in the mirror. She always expected her hair to be disheveled and her clothes to be a windswept tangle after translocating, but they never were. She looked as neat and well-groomed as one would expect of a duke's daughter.

Primrose unlocked her bedroom door and went down to the morning room. A housemaid was clearing away the tea tray. "Would you like another pot of tea, Lady Primrose?"

"Yes, thank you, Elsie."

Primrose crossed to the sofa, thinking how shocked the maid would be if she told her she'd just traveled to Staffordshire and back.

But of course she didn't tell the housemaid. She couldn't tell a soul. It was far too great a secret. And even if she *did* tell Elsie, the girl wouldn't believe it.

No one would.

Primrose curled up on the sofa and returned to her reading.

CHAPTER TWO

An evening in early June, London

Oliver had enjoyed being a soldier. Not the killing, of course, but the camaraderie, the sense of purpose, the challenges, the fun. When the letter had arrived informing him that he'd inherited his Uncle Reginald's dukedom his first emotion had been astonishment. His second had been chagrin. He'd planned to be a colonel by the time he was forty; instead, at twenty-nine, he was a duke. Not that being a duke wasn't without its challenges or its sense of purpose. Or its fun, for that matter.

Oliver glanced around the ballroom. His gaze passed over shimmering silks and spangled gauzes, glossy hair and rosy lips—and the bright eyes of young ladies searching for husbands.

He'd enjoyed balls when he'd been a cavalry

captain in India. They'd been rare events, something to look forward to—the dancing, the flirting, the snatched kisses in shadowy corners.

Balls as a duke in London were quite a different matter. In fact, when a duke had so many caps set at him as Oliver did, he had to exercise caution else he'd get caught in the parson's mousetrap. A prudent duke didn't snatch kisses from respectable young ladies—not unless he wanted to end up with a wife. A prudent duke didn't even flirt while he danced.

A prudent duke could get mightily bored if he wasn't careful . . . but Oliver had a strategy for that.

He made his way across the ballroom, replying to the murmured greetings of *Your Grace,* and *Duke,* and *Westfell,* before coming to a halt in front of Miss Elliott and her mother.

"Lady Elliott." He inclined his head in a coolly ducal nod. "Miss Elliott."

"Your Grace." Miss Elliott curtsied and glanced up at him through her eyelashes. She was only nineteen, but she had mastered the trick of tucking her shoulders back slightly to bring her bosom into more prominence. Lush breasts tilted up at him, snug in a nest of ribbons and silk.

Miss Elliott—like most unmarried young ladies—was on the hunt for a husband, but even if Oliver had to be prudent, it didn't mean that he couldn't enjoy her efforts to snare him. He awarded Miss Elliott one point for the upwards glance and two points for that enticingly displayed bosom, then he gave her his most charming smile and led her onto the dance floor.

Miss Elliott started the cotillion with three points. She increased this to six points rather rapidly—by sending him three more of those glances—and then she exercised a masterful ploy: she bit her lower lip briefly and moistened it, a move that looked bashful but most definitely wasn't, not with the glimpse of her tongue she'd given him.

That was five points, right there, and they'd been dancing less than a minute.

Oliver gave her his most charming smile again. "Do you like horses, Miss Elliott? I must tell you about my mount, Verdun."

He described Verdun in detail, from his ears to his hooves, while Miss Elliott tilted her enticing bosom at him. "I'm certain you're a magnificent horseman, Your Grace," she said, when he'd finished describing the precise length and color of Verdun's tail.

The compliment sounded genuine. Oliver added another two points to her tally and launched into a description of the horses of every officer he'd ever served with in India. He was rather enjoying himself. This was a game: Miss Elliott's bosom versus his ridiculous monologue.

The cotillion lasted twenty minutes, and Miss Elliott made very good use of them. When Oliver returned her to her mother, she had accrued one hundred and forty-three points.

⁓

His next partner was Lady Primrose Garland, the sister of his oldest friend, Rhodes Garland—and the only unmarried young lady in the room whom he knew *didn't* want to marry him.

"Lady Prim," he said, bowing over her hand with a flourish. "You're a jewel that outshines all others."

Primrose was too well-bred to roll her eyes in public, but her eyelids twitched ever so slightly, which told him she wanted to. "Still afflicted by hyperbole, I see."

"You use such long words, Prim," he said admiringly.

"And you use such foolish ones."

Oliver tutted at her. "That's not very polite, Prim."

Primrose ignored this comment. She placed her hand on his sleeve. Together they walked onto the dance floor and took their places.

"Did I ever tell you about my uniform, Prim? The coat was dark blue, and the facing—"

"I don't wish to hear about your uniform."

"Manners, Prim. Manners."

Primrose came very close to smiling. She caught herself just in time. "Shall we discuss books while we dance? Have you read Wolf's *Prolegomena ad Homerum?*"

"Of course I haven't," Oliver said. "Dash it, Prim, I'm not an intellectual."

The musicians played the opening bars. Primrose curtsied, Oliver bowed. "I really *must* tell you about my uniform. The coat was dark blue—"

Primrose ignored him. "Wolf proposes that *The Iliad*—"

"With a red sash at the waist—"

"And *The Odyssey* were in fact—"

"And silver lace at the cuffs—"

"The work of more than one poet."

"And a crested Tarleton helmet," Oliver finished triumphantly.

They eyed each other as they went through the steps of the dance. Oliver could tell from the glint in her eyes and the way her lips were tucked in at the corners that Primrose was trying not to laugh. He was trying not to laugh, too.

"You're a fiddle-faddle fellow," Primrose told him severely.

"Alliteration," Oliver said. "Well done, Prim."

Primrose's lips tucked in even more tightly at the corners. If they'd been anywhere but a ballroom he was certain she'd have stamped her foot, something she'd done frequently when they were children.

"Heaven only knows why I agreed to dance with you," she told him tartly.

"Because it increases your consequence to be seen with me. I *am* a duke, you know." He puffed out his chest and danced the next few steps with a strut.

"Stop that," she hissed under her breath.

"Stop what?" Oliver said innocently, still strutting his steps.

"Honestly, Daisy, you're impossible."

Oliver stopped strutting. "No one's called me that in years."

"Impossible? I find that hard to believe." Her voice was dry.

"Daisy." It had been Primrose's childhood nickname for him, in retaliation for him calling her Lady Prim-and-Proper.

Oliver had been back in England for nearly a month now, and that month had been filled with moments of recognition, some tiny flickers—his brain acknowledging something as familiar and then moving on—others strong visceral reactions. He experienced one of those latter moments now. It took him by the throat and wouldn't let him speak for several seconds.

Because Primrose had called him Daisy.

Oliver cleared his throat. "Tell me about that book, Prim. What's it called? *Prolapse ad nauseam?*"

"*Prolegomena ad Homerum.*"

Oliver pulled a face. "Sounds very dull. Me, I much prefer a good novel. Especially if there's a ghost in it, or a headless horseman."

And they were off again, arguing amiably about books, the moment of emotion safely in the past. Primrose knew a lot about books. In fact, Oliver suspected that she preferred books to people—which would be why she was still unmarried at twenty-seven. Primrose was a duke's daughter *and* she was pretty—that ash-blonde hair, those cool blue eyes. If she wanted to be married, she would be.

Therefore, he deduced that she didn't want to marry. Which made her unique in a ballroom filled with young ladies on the hunt for husbands.

"Do you know Miss Ogilvie?" he asked her.

"Vaguely. She seems quite nice."

"Nice? She's a dashed harpy, is what she is."

"You can't call her a harpy," Primrose objected. "A siren, perhaps, but harpies have claws and—"

"Miss Ogilvie is a harpy," Oliver said firmly. "Beneath the evening gloves, she has claws."

"Now *that* is hyperbole."

"It's metaphor," Oliver corrected her. "She's a *metaphorical* harpy. She wants to feast on my carcass." And *carcass* was a metaphor, too; it wasn't his body Miss Ogilvie wanted to devour, it was the title and fortune that he'd so unexpectedly inherited.

Primrose uttered a small sound that his ears barely caught.

"Did you just snort, Prim? That's not very ladylike."

"You're the most idiotic person I've ever met," she told him severely.

Oliver opened his eyes wide. "Ever? In your whole life?"

"Ever."

"High praise, Prim. Very high praise. You quite unman me."

This time Primrose *did* roll her eyes, even though they were in the middle of a ballroom.

Oliver grinned at her. He could tell she was struggling not to grin back.

At that moment, the dance ended. Oliver escorted Primrose from the dance floor. He could see Miss Ogilvie out of the corner of his eye: the glossy ringlets, the ripe bosom, the dainty evening gloves that hid her metaphorical claws.

"Marry me, Prim," he joked. "Save me from Miss Ogilvie."

"I'd sooner marry a crossing-sweeper. You're even more of a fribble than that cousin of yours."

"I'm wounded." Oliver placed his hand over his heart, tottered a few steps, and sank down on a gilded chair. "*Mortally* wounded. I may expire here, right in front of your eyes."

"You can't expire now," Primrose told him. "Miss Ogilvie is waiting to dance with you."

Oliver pulled a face. "Maybe I *should* become a crossing-sweeper."

"Addle-pate," Primrose said.

Oliver laughed, and climbed to his feet. "Thank you for the dance, Prim."

Primrose demurely curtsied, as all his other partners tonight had done. "It was a pleasure, Your Grace."

"Don't, Prim," Oliver said, and this time his tone was serious.

Primrose's glance at him was swift and shrewd. She didn't ask what he meant; instead, she said, "Away with you, Daisy," and made a brisk shooing gesture. "Miss Ogilvie fancies herself as a duchess."

"Not *my* duchess," Oliver muttered. "Not if I have any say in the matter."

Miss Ogilvie had alabaster skin, a delightfully full lower lip, and a bosom to rival Miss Elliott's. Like Miss Elliott, she had mastered the trick of displaying her bosom to full advantage.

Oliver didn't like her at all.

His antipathy had been instantaneous and instinctive. Miss Ogilvie was pretty, charming, vivacious—and ruthless. Oliver wasn't certain exactly how he knew she was ruthless. Something in her eyes? In that light, musical laugh? All he knew was that he had seen people like Miss Ogilvie before, not in ballrooms but in the aftermath of battle, looting the wounded of their belongings.

But the fact that he disliked Miss Ogilvie didn't mean that he disliked dancing with her. On the contrary, dancing with her was often the highlight of his evening. He had a special voice for her—a monotonous drone—and a special topic—Trésaguet's method for paving roads—and he always managed to stand on her toes and fall out of time with the music.

Primrose Garland would have given him the sharp edge of her tongue if he'd tried such tactics with her; Miss Ogilvie gave him smiling glances and flaunted her breasts and at the end of the dance she said in a soft, sweet, admiring voice, "You're so knowledgeable, Westfell."

Oliver could imagine the expression on Primrose's face if she'd been close enough to hear those words. He puffed out his chest and said, "I fancy I know a lot about a lot of things." Then he escorted Miss Ogilvie back to her aunt.

Her score: one hundred and sixty-one.

The ballroom had become rather warm. Faces were shiny and shirt-points wilting. Oliver found himself craving fresh, cool air. He was bespoken for two more dances, but after that he'd slip away, and that was something he'd never done as a soldier: leave a ball early. Lord, he'd danced until dawn more than once—

"Oliver," a cheerful voice said at his elbow.

Oliver turned. "Uncle Algy." He shook his uncle's hand heartily. "How are you, sir?"

"Very well, my boy. Very well indeed."

Lord Algernon Dasenby was one of Oliver's two surviving relatives. He was a burly fellow with graying hair and merry eyes and a booming laugh. It was Uncle Algy who'd dealt with the paperwork while Oliver had undertaken the six-month-long journey back from India, Uncle Algy who'd gathered the documents required by the House of Lords—proof of his parents' marriage, proof of his birth—so that by the time Oliver had finally set foot on English soil there were only a few legal hoops to jump through and it was done: he was the ninth Duke of Westfell.

Ironic, that. He trod in the footsteps of the seventh and eighth dukes every day, drank from the same glasses they'd drunk from, slept in the same great four-poster bed, even pissed in the same chamber pot, and yet he'd never met them when they'd been alive.

Not that he repined.

Oliver didn't need to have met his grandfather to know he'd been a coldhearted bastard—how else could you describe a man who cut off a son for daring to refuse an arranged marriage? And Uncle Reginald had been a coldhearted bastard, too, for obeying the parental injunction to sever ties with his brother.

Uncle Algy hadn't obeyed the parental injunction. Oliver had childhood memories of his uncle's brief, secretive visits—the rumble of voices in the parlor, the laughter, the pipe smoke, his uncle winking at him when he arrived and slipping him a guinea when he left.

Strange to think that Uncle Algy was now Oliver's heir.

He would have stayed talking to his uncle if he could, but the musicians were picking up their instruments again and the next aspiring duchess awaited him. Regretfully, Oliver bade his uncle goodbye. A dozen more steps and he hove to in front of Miss Buxton.

Miss Buxton's main ploy for hunting dukes was a simper. Oliver didn't like simpers. Every time Miss Buxton simpered, he deducted one point. Her score rapidly sank below zero. By the time the musicians played the final notes, she had reached minus eighty. Tonight's lowest score.

One more dance to go and he could call it a night.

It was while he was heading towards his final partner that Oliver encountered the second of his two surviving relatives: Uncle Algernon's son.

"Ninian." Oliver looked his cousin up and down. "You look very, uh . . ." *Pretty* was the word that sprang to mind.

Their Uncle Reginald, the eighth duke, had been in his grave for more than a year. The time for mourning was long past, but Ninian was lingering in shades of lilac and lavender.

Lilac and lavender were colors Oliver would never willingly wear, but there was no denying that they suited Ninian's golden hair and blue eyes. He looked beautiful. But Ninian always looked beautiful.

"Do you like it?" Ninian said. His gaze was bright and hopeful, and he might be a fribble and a fop, but he was also Uncle Algy's son and Oliver's only cousin.

484

Oliver strove for a compliment. "Very pretty coat. What color do you call it?"

"Periwinkle," Ninian said, beaming.

"Suits you," Oliver said, and then, "Excuse me, Ninian; I'm claimed for the next dance."

His last partner for the night achieved a respectable one hundred and twenty-eight points, not because of her bosom, but because she had a very pretty pair of dimples. Oliver liked dimples, and in another time and place he might have tried to coax a kiss from Miss Norton. But he was no longer a devil-may-care dragoon captain, he was a prudent duke, and so he escorted Miss Norton back to her mother, unkissed.

Oliver was aware of young ladies hopefully eyeing him. He made for the door, not pausing long enough for anyone to catch him.

A flight of stairs beckoned him downwards. He breathed a sigh of relief and descended to the vestibule. A footman fetched his hat for him. Oliver stepped outside. It wasn't completely dark under the portico—flambeaux burned, keeping the night at bay—but it was blessedly cool and quiet after the ballroom.

A dozen marble steps led down to the street, gleaming in the light from the flaming torches. Oliver stood for a moment on the topmost step. Funny that one could feel lonely in a city as large as London, but he did feel lonely at this moment, had in fact felt lonely rather often in the month he'd been back on English soil.

If this were India, he'd have Ned Lovelock at one shoulder and Tubby Hedgecomb at the other, and they'd be laughing together, enjoying being young and alive.

But this wasn't India.

Oliver put his hat on, tilted the brim until it sat just right, and promised himself that he'd call on Rhodes Garland tomorrow. A few hours in Rhodes's company would make him feel less alone.

His ears caught the faint scuff of a shoe behind him—and then someone shoved him violently between the shoulder blades.

Like to read the rest?
Primrose and the Dreadful Duke is available now.

ACKNOWLEDGMENTS

A number of people helped to make this book what it is. Foremost among them is my developmental editor, Laura Cifelli Stibich, but I also owe many thanks to my copyeditor, Maria Fairchild, and proofreader, Martin O'Hearn.

The series logo was designed by Kim Killion, of the Killion Group. The cover and the print formatting are the work of Jane D. Smith. Thank you, Jane!

Emily Larkin grew up in a house full of books. Her mother was a librarian and her father a novelist, so perhaps it's not surprising that she became a writer.

Emily has studied a number of subjects, including geology and geophysics, canine behavior, and ancient Greek. Her varied career includes stints as a field assistant in Antarctica and a waitress on the Isle of Skye, as well as five vintages in New Zealand's wine industry.

She loves to travel and has lived in Sweden, backpacked in Europe and North America, and traveled overland in the Middle East, China, and North Africa.

She enjoys climbing hills, reading, and watching reruns of *Buffy the Vampire Slayer* and *Firefly*.

Emily writes historical romances as Emily Larkin and fantasy novels as Emily Gee. Her websites are www.emilylarkin.com and www.emilygee.com.

Never miss a new Emily Larkin book. Join her Readers' Group at www.emilylarkin.com/newsletter and receive free digital copies of *The Fey Quartet* and *Unmasking Miss Appleby.*

OTHER WORKS

THE BALEFUL GODMOTHER SERIES

Prequel
The Fey Quartet novella collection:
Maythorn's Wish
Hazel's Promise
Ivy's Choice
Larkspur's Quest

Original Series
Unmasking Miss Appleby
Resisting Miss Merryweather
Trusting Miss Trentham
Claiming Mister Kemp
Ruining Miss Wrotham
Discovering Miss Dalrymple

Garland Cousins
Primrose and the Dreadful Duke
Violet and the Bow Street Runner

Pryor Cousins
Octavius and the Perfect Governess

OTHER HISTORICAL ROMANCES

The Earl's Dilemma
My Lady Thief
Lady Isabella's Ogre
Lieutenant Mayhew's Catastrophes

The Midnight Quill Trio
The Countess's Groom
The Spinster's Secret
The Baronet's Bride

FANTASY NOVELS
(Written as Emily Gee)

Thief With No Shadow
The Laurentine Spy

The Cursed Kingdoms Trilogy
The Sentinel Mage
The Fire Prince
The Blood Curse

Made in the USA
Las Vegas, NV
15 August 2022